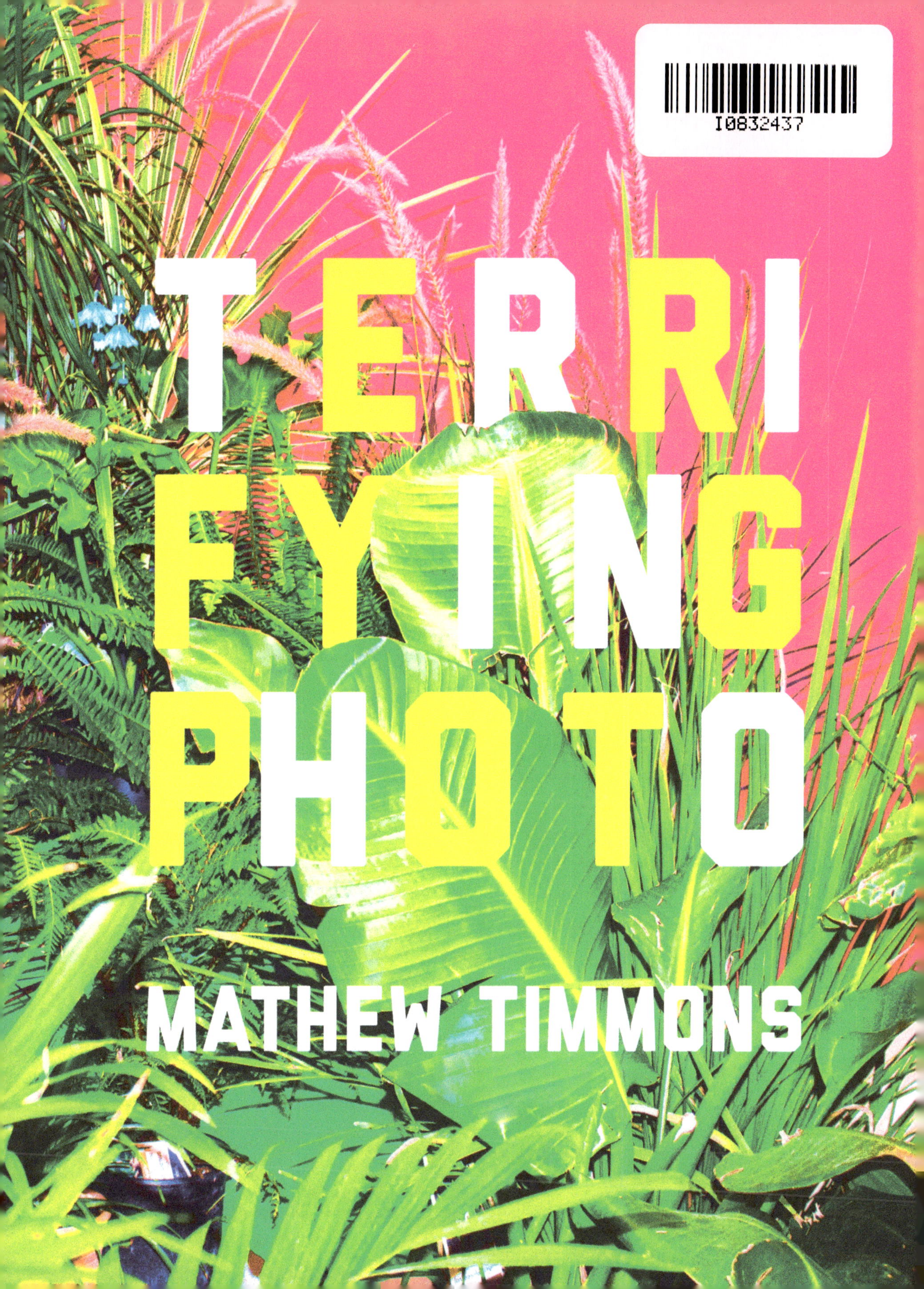

TERRI
FYING
PHOTO
MATHEW TIMMONS

TERRIFYING PHOTO
ISBN: 978-0-9895985-3-8

Published by Wonder
79 5th Ave. 16th Floor, New York, NY 10003
www.shitwonder.com

Cover and title pages designed by Max Springer.
Cover image by Greg Curtis and Mathew Timmons.

This book includes pieces that were published, performed andor presented in a wide variety of contexts. Specific information about each piece is included in the text.

I'd like to thank the people who helped bring this work into being by either asking me to write something for a project they were working on, or asking me to perform or exhibit my work, or participating in a project with andor alongside myself. You are all, of course, indispensible:
Liz Glynn, Harold Abramowitz, Amanda Ackerman, SAM OR SAMANTHA YAMS, eohippus labs, Kyoung Kim, Adam Overton, Tanya Rubback, UNFO (Unauthorized Narrative Freedom Organization), Carol Cheh, Jay Erker, John Mills, Andrew Choate, Geneva Skeen, Garrick Hogg, Elana Mann, Yecenia Torres, Greg Curtis, Peter Ortel, Janne Larsen, Ben White, Elizabeth Pulsinelli, Prof. Padu Paga, Bill Anthes, Guru Rugu, Alan Nakagawa, Amanda Manitach, Doug Nufer and my perfect publishers Andrew Durbin and Ben Fama.

Special thanks to my readers and editors, to my collaborators on these specific projects, and my collaborators generally speaking, you are all the best of the best: Chris Niemi, Janne Larsen, Adam Overton, Geneva Skeen, Greg Curtis, Ben White, Byron Campbell, Andrew Choate, Kim Calder, Allison Carter, Holly Myers and Harold Abramowitz.

TERRI FYING PHOTO

MATHEW TIMMONS

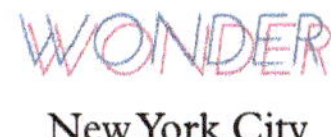

New York City

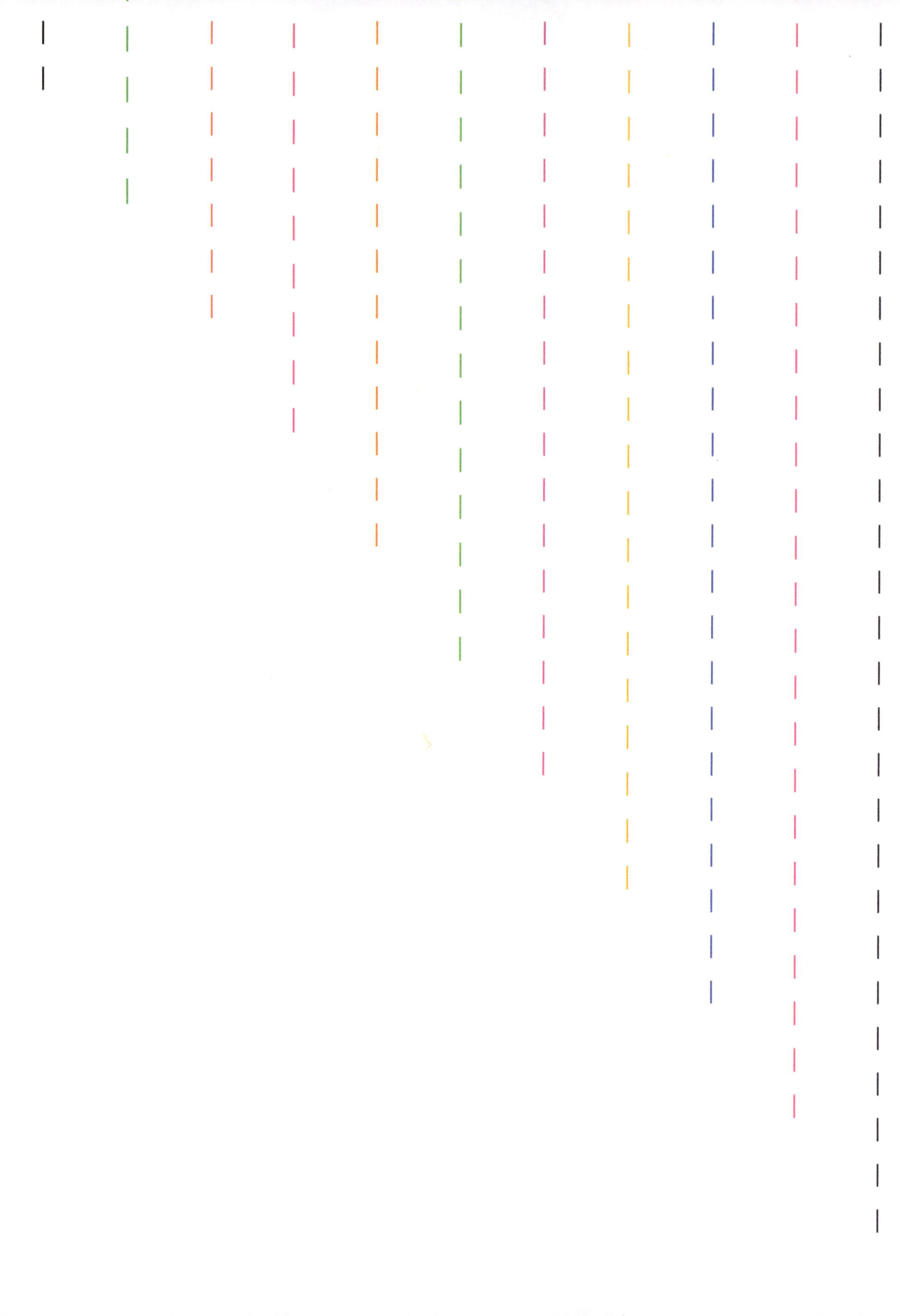

CATALOGUE

CONTENTS

Myriad Small Forms of Mathew Timmons: A Terrifying Interview by Holly Myers

A few things you should know about Mathew Timmons: First, he is an enormously energetic individual. Even thinking about all the things he does, you will feel tired. He writes, he makes art, he makes films and videos, he performs, he collaborates with other artists, he teaches, he curates, he hosts podcasts and radio shows, he organizes readings and other events, and on top of it all runs a very fine press.

Second, that he knows he is not working in a vacuum. Which is to say, he also reads, attends, supports, promotes, and, of course, publishes the work of other people, all with the same hearty pitch of enthusiasm. Community is important; he is sincere in this.

Third, that he reads his work aloud with great relish. This may surprise you the first time you see it because he does not seem a showy or extravagant person. But he reads from deep in his chest, rapidly and with gusto. Thanks to an unusually extensive background in sound poetry, he has a consummate range of articulation and is not afraid of baffling his audience when need be. He reads not as if he'd written the words in question, with that sense of the precious that clogs up the throats of so many poets, but as if he'd found them on a sidewalk somewhere and taken much delight in their discovery (which isn't actually far from the truth).

Fourth, miscellaneous biographical details: that he grew up in Kansas City, Missouri; that he lived for a while in Minneapolis, Minnesota; that he came to Los Angeles for graduate school and stayed. Prior to *Terrifying Photo*, he's published four books and three chapbooks; each is very different. On my copy of *Lip Service*, a chapbook, he added a note on a lime green Post-It: "I definitely hope you enjoy the poems and also I hope you're slightly disgusted by them." This would be an accurate description. ("Some pharyngeal consonants / if just sipped / produce a burning of the lips, / and also if swallowed, / destroy the muscles of the cheek." ... "Refer to my lips, and / involve the mouth, or tongue / in all your ulcerations, / the mucous casserole / of my oral cancre sores.")

The New Poetics is a slender, handsome book—and the look of a book is important to Timmons, as can be seen in the output of Insert Blanc Press—in which he playfully excoriates the blather of the now. ("There is no match for ... The New Ideal Reading Experience." "The New Concept is striking out with repeated admissions of national weakness." "Where are we with The New Birds?" "Jolly teabags! The New Pantoum doesn't need its oil changed! Imagine that! The New Pantoum is an amazing lubricant.") *CREDIT* is, first and foremost, a large book: a monument / memorial / cenotaph / tombstone erected to the Great Recession from redacted facsimiles of every offer and statement of credit received in that period by one struggling artist (namely, the author), all crammed into the most expensive print-on-demand volume possible.

This book starts out on an ominous note: *TERRIFYING* is a strong word indeed. What qualifies, we might wonder, as a *TERRIFYING* photo? There are images scattered throughout the book, woven into its various texts. There is Janet Leigh from the shower scene in *Psycho*; Sissy Spacek drenched in blood in *Carrie*—but these are totems of terror more than the thing itself. There is Al Gore breathing fire onto a small spinning Earth; Oprah Winfrey with eyes lit up like a demon; Sean Combs posing next to the *Mona Lisa*. There are dozens of nameless quasi celebrities: those bland, ostensibly appetizing faces that float through our media universe like shrapnel, arousing perhaps a certain unease, the sense of an impending apocalypse of culture. But how does this square with the *TERROR* we come across in headlines—such as this one, today: "Terror attack leaves images both vivid and horrifying"?

The real (or "real") terrifying photo in question—the subject of the book's title piece—doesn't appear in the text at all: it's been pointedly redacted so as to make way for the bizarre whirling maelstrom of comment-thread language its initial appearance in fact precipitated. From a single photograph of a man and three children, the vast, many-headed gorgon of cultural criticism that is the Buzzfeed readership (viewership?) churns out a treatise of breathtaking magnitude, encompassing topics of such great scope as Christianity, contemporary art, pedophilia, religious indoctrination, parenting methods, nudity, child psychology, photographic veracity, and media ethics.

The inversion is telling, as is the vacated threat of *TERRIFYING*: in *Terrifying Photo*, as in most of his work, Mathew Timmons is asking us to think about how language operates. Not how it operates in some cozy, rarified literary world where words cohere magically and effortlessly into insight, but in this world, the real world, where we actually live, where words toss about in inelegant clumps, generating something much weirder than insight. And thinking about how language operates today necessitates thinking about how images operate: the two entwine and mingle and feed off one another more directly now than in any other era.

If it is the function of the interview to expand upon the artist's work with a tailored aspect of the personal dimension—well, these are the things that come to mind. Then, of course, there is the matter of process. We might think of Timmons as a miner of language, be that language verbal or visual. A linguistic archeologist of the present, chipping words and phrases and images free from corroded funhouse cavern walls found deep in the labyrinth of an internet search engine. He is not the only one—it is a recognized method (as discussed below under the rubric of Conceptual Writing)—but he brings to the act a particular sensibility: frisky, even gleeful, and slightly perverse. There is something transcendently odd about his language, or about what he does to other people's language. It is both sticky and hollow. It is weirdly sensual. It makes very little sense—until suddenly, it does. It is flat as a collage—until, for a moment, it tips into depth. Then it is flat as a collage again. Reading Timmons' work is frankly not easy, at least in the sense that one typically "reads." There is no emotive center; there are no guideposts to aid in negotiating the references; the constant interplay of sincerity and wit, pathos and sarcasm is vexingly disorienting. Yet somehow, in the end, a lucidity seeps through.

To draw almost at random yet with fittingly resonant ambiguity from the first piece in the present volume, "Complex Textual Legitimacy Proclamation: A Foreward":

> One mark of an originality that can win canonical status for a literary work is a strangeness that we can either never altogether assimilate, or that becomes such a given that we are blinded to its idiosyncrasies.
>
> Esoteric literature presupposes that there are basic truths which would not be pronounced in public by any decent man, because they would do harm to many people who, having been hurt, would naturally be inclined to hurt in turn him who pronounces the unpleasant truths.
>
> You will see nothing subtle where everything is subtle.
>
> Hidden amongst the rushes are myriad small forms of life.

For this interview, Timmons and I spoke over email (which will explain, in part, the loose punctuation, so characteristic of Timmons' approach to language that I could not bring myself to edit it out). I began by asking how *Terrifying Photo* came about.

MT: *Terrifying Photo* is a collection of pieces from the past seven years that I've written while writing all these other more controlled project books – many of the pieces reflect a lot of the different concerns I held over those seven years – I feel like this book has given me an opportunity to try out all the different things I've experimented with and learned from while writing the other books – it's more messy – or not necessarily messy – I think it shows a more organic mode of working from one thing to the next – a frankly more honest reflection of my practice – the pieces are less strictly conceptual – more expressive and more pliant and maybe even funnier, I think.

Also most of the work was written at the request of someone else or for an event or exhibition or performance andor was part of a collaboration in some way – so the book involves up to 50 different people and organizations – and this is also why I organize it something more like a catalogue than a straightforward poetry collection – the contexts in which these pieces were written and performed are very important to me – they are all part of and constitutive of my community – I'm sorry I couldn't include everything everything – there were some things I didn't include because they weren't up to snuff for me or weren't going to make the transition to print/book very well – or some pieces didn't make it because that particular vein I was working in was better represented by another piece etc.

I should say I had in the back of my mind a few particular books that I kind of modeled this collection on – Caroline Bergvall's *FIG (Goan Atom Vol. 2)* and *Goan Atom* – both books I gave away years ago – because my favorite books I can't help but give away to people – I gave away Perec's *Life a User's Manual* and for the life of me I can't remember why (why? Why! WHY!?) guess I need a new user's manual for life – and Steven Zultanski's *Cop Kisser* – one of the only books I've ever felt compelled to review – I'm sure I should review more books but shouldn't we all – anyway *FIG* especially was put together of pieces written in various different performance and art contexts that Bergvall had pulled together into a book – and it really seemed like a well considered collection besides just being "some things I wrote for the art people" – and that's because she has had a real investment in the art world not just as an observer but as a participant.

HM: How do you see this book differing from your previous works?

MT: *Terrifying Photo* is the first "collection" of writings I've ever published – *CREDIT* and *The New Poetics* were very specific books, some would call them project books, and further some might say, *Poetry is Not a Project* – here I'm referring to the chapbook by Dorothea Lasky published by Ugly Duckling Presse in 2010 as part of their Dossier Series – I must say that I really enjoyed this book and agreed with the spirit of what Lasky was geting at as well as the motivation and, I think, the general intention behind her writing – but I object to the false dichotomy she set up in the title and carried out thru the text – the claim that "A poet with a project has everything set out before he even gets started." seems completely off to me – Lasky champions nonlinearity and sees the construct of the project as quashing the unnameable or unknowable instinct that may grow from the world into the poet – she thinks being able to talk process breeds mediocrity – that we need to deal with the work and not the project around the work – it seems to me we need to talk about all these things on multiple levels – Lasky concedes that many of her favorite poets and favorite poems come out of or are related to projects – but real poetry and real poets (Lasky's words) exist in a realm of uncertainty that a project cannot support – here think of Lasky's initial instinct to refer to science when bringing up the idea of the "project" – the project of science is to make wild guesses and try them out and then make more wild guesses – in other words science exists in a complete realm of uncertainty if science functions at all – Lasky asks in the end that we support artists and give them more time to think on what they're doing – I am totally in to that – that you might take more time to think on a larger scale about what you're doing in a single piece or several or in one coner of a piece and then make another something and then think some more seems good – and we can engage in a dialogue about the something and the several somethings and the squiggle in the corner of that one and maybe talk about an artist's practice in general – yes, the word practice also inherited from the art world, I know that word can be just as annoying as project – but I don't think it is against poetry – and in fact encourages the poet to linger in uncertainty

As with any of the poetry arguments that have come to the surface over the past several years, the time during which I was writing the materials in this book, people have tended to make headline arguments or work to be provocative in a way just to prove a typically very boring academic point, and this is true on all sides of the Conceptual Writing/Project divide, andor people seem to be working provocatively simply because nobody's been paying enough attention to them recently – Conceptual Writing is important to wrestle with in the poetry world, writing world, art world etc. and if someone wants to point to all the various arguments against Conceptual Writing then they're pointing at the evidence to the contrary – on the other hand, Conceptual Writing deserves a real and nuanced critique, one that might begin with the obvious question: So, why do you guys want to regurgitate 20th century avant-garde tropes of killing the fathers, claiming aesthetic ascendancy and erasing everything else that has ever or will ever come before or after (except of course when putting together the anthologies that will come out way too early in an anxious attempt to solidify an ascendant position)?

[Here Timmons sends links to a number of texts, including Dorothea Lasky's *Poetry is not a Project*, *Against Expression: An Anthology of Conceptual Writing*, edited by Craig Dworkin and Kenneth Goldsmith, and *Notes on Conceptualisms* by Vanessa Place and Robert Fitterman. He's pulled a number of passages from the latter that he finds resonant, and that help to shed light on the nature of his process. Here are a few:

> We are painfully aware that Conceptual Art was termed nearly half a century ago, and much of what we address might equally be called post-conceptual or neo-conceptual (to borrow terms from the visual arts). We use the term Conceptual Writing in the broadest sense, so that it intersects other terms such as: allegory, appropriation, piracy, flarf, identity theft, sampling, constraint and others. Conceptual Writing, in fact, might best be defined not by the strategies used but by the expectations of the readership or thinkership.
>
> In his essay "Subversive Signs," Hal Foster remarks that the appropriation artist (visual) is "a manipulator of signs more than a producer of art objects, and the viewer an active reader of messages rather than a passive contemplator of the aesthetic or consumer of the spectacular."
>
> What is an "impure" conceptualism or post-conceptualism in writing? A post-conceptualism might invite more interventionist editing of appropriated source material and more direct treatment of the self in relation to the "object," as in post-conceptual visual art where the self re-emerges, albeit alienated or distorted (see Paul McCarthy).

The latter reference is particularly striking, insofar as it posits a plausible explanation for that degree of oddness in Timmons work that goes beyond the level of contextual blurring or syntactical distortion into the murkier territory of personal affect. It is perhaps, indeed, the emergence of a self—a personality, let's say—that is, like McCarthy's various characters, distorted by the vulgarity, the banality of its own native language.]

HM: How do you see your work engaging with these various arguments?

MT: Besides *CREDIT* and *The New Poetics* – which are more conceptual writing projects or post–conceptual or new flarf projects – after those two books, which I've thought of as written somewhat 'under the influence' – tho I think influence is always present and those two books are as much mine as anything else – next came my book *Joyful Noise for three or more voices*.

While writing *Joyful Noise* I was obsessed with experimental prose – and the thought that experimental prose will always have more radical potential than 'poetry' [and yes I know this is overly generalized] because people see poetry and immediately are unaffected because it's "poetry" or they sit at a reading as if at church – or the poets themselves seem to be talking only to other poets and I don't so much want to talk to other poets because I'm fairly sure we're not interested in the same things – I'm writing for a more varied audience than simply academics and poets – whereas prose – writing in paragraph blocks with full sentences etc. – that's the language of direct communication that everyone recognizes and when you mess with that kind of writing it would seem more disruptive to most people and hopefully in a generative way – and again I know this is very general – but that book *Joyful Noise* moved from 20 poems (really the only 'normal,' left justified poems that I've ever published in a book, in fact, most adopted a loose sonnet form, and were originally published as the chapbook *Lip Service*) to 40 short prose pieces which worked in a thinly connected way to evoke a larger narrative sense – and lastly a long prose piece using full sentences more like lines of a poem and arranged in stanzas and sections etc. – this last part of the book was more evoking narrative than actual narrative – but again it read more like direct comprehensible language which was important to me – and I thought of it as a way to move into more narrative writing. So, I'd say my interests aren't easily contained wihtin the movement politics running thru the various poetry arguments over the past several years and besides what I said above I'd prefer not to get into it – I'd prefer not to

HM: The art world, I know, has been significant for you—both on the practical level (as a sphere in which to act/participate/create) and conceptually. There is surprisingly little overlap between these two worlds, but in recent years—and especially with Insert Blanc Press—you've situated yourself pretty squarely between them. Why is this?

MT: I've always practiced writing as a fine artist – I made the deliberate decision to get a graduate writing degree at an art school[1] – most of even my closer artist friends would laugh / snort at the assertion that writing is a fine art form, but let's say I would strongly disagree – or I would agree allowing that it is unfortunate so much writing is created in ignorance of the rest of the art worlds it is directly related to or comes out of or shares so many concerns with, historically and certainly presently.

Besides writing from this perspective I've also done many things that a 'fine artist' would – painting and printmaking, sound art, performance, film/video, photography (actually I studied photography through undergrad more than anything else), directing for stage and screen, curating, critical writing, etc. etc. – I don't draw though, I mean I really can't draw – I could easily be accused of being a jack of all trades – ok fine – I think coming from the conceptual bent is slightly more difficult than is regularly perceived because the idea is the thing and you have to materially find the way to work it out – with this book it boils down to writing but I've got numerous images in here and again most of the pieces are or were for an art context.

----

1 California Institute of the Arts (CalArts)

HM: You are also a person/artist for whom social and professional context is important. You are a writer who is very aware of the specific literary sphere in which he is operating and who doesn't shy away from its implications. How do you think about the social aspect of what you do?

MT: While I'm less of a socialite than I was 10 years ago (heh) – I would agree – you are right – I've always been the kind of person who only really gets to know people through working with them – that's not entirely true – but I'm not so good at just "hanging out" even though I did my time smoking weed in dorm rooms just like any other well enough bred white boy who went to college – and sitting around drinking – did that too – I'm just one of those people who reacts better to someone who approaches me with a project or activity than an invite to just you know hang out – this filters into so many aspects of my life – whether in the writing community – publishing – the art world – events organizing – and quite frankly I'm sure it can make me somewhat annoying to have around sometimes – I always want to build something – and I think this is partially – yes this is a stretch – maybe because I come from a science and engineering background – but I am more of a social animal and I see building a magazine or a press or an event series or a gallery space into something as a very exciting, complex activity – is it social sculpture – yes and maybe – definitely not no – it gets me into trouble – it got me into trouble when I was doing things at betalevel[2] – I was apparently doing too many things – even though the place was dark about six nights a week most of the time – I got a fair amount of pushback because I was "taking over," really just doing events in a place that was an event space – and honestly yes trying to build some kind of name or reputation for the place – that might have been the problem I ran into – that name/reputation wasn't what others were looking for – and I can live up to my Taurean bullheadedness when it comes to aesthetic permission – as in I'll pretty much grant myself whatever aesthetic permission I think is appropriate and if you don't like it then fuck off – I was much more meek 10 years ago about this – I'm a lot more clear now on what I want to do and how to do it.

More recently that drive and ability to grant myself aesthetic permission, has come from running Insert Blanc Press – the basic functionality of the thing makes more abstract aesthetic issues clearer to me – and while Insert Blanc Press is just me – I make the decisions, I say what goes – I collaborate with a whole lot of artists and writers – and I invite input from everyone I'm working with – ultimately though I make final decisions – cause it's a project I'm very close to – the press itself is my way of building something and getting to work with about 150 different writers and artists over the past eight plus years – working with other artists is learning – and in a larger sense – the socializing is more about learning – about going to readings art shows screenings concerts etc. – they're social occasions sure but seeing what the people around me are doing is ultimately what it's about.

HM: So let's look more closely at this question of process, particularly in regards to *Terrifying Photo*. Choose a piece from the book and walk us through its generation, start to finish. I want to get a sense of how you work in the specific.

----

2 Betalevel was an alternative art space in a basement in Chinatown, Los Angeles run by a loose grouping of people which Timmons was involved with from 2005-2009

MT: Ok I'm gonna take the last piece I wrote for the book *Complex Textual Legitimacy Proclamation* – this piece came out of a couple things if I remember correctly – High Energy Constructs – the gallery in Chinatown that Michael Smoler and Justin Veach started in 05/06 – had a show entitled *Many Happy Returns* that centered around the intersection of poetry/literature/language and the visual/media arts – I had started Insert Press with Stan Apps in March 2006 by publishing *Three Column Table* by Harold Abramowitz – and for this exhibition I presented some videos and ephemera from a book I was working on at the time – a kind of experimental poets novel – the book worked with a very odd collected text that I manipulated in various ways – and the main character had supposedly written a short book that had been lost – so I made up a press and published a little chapbook by the main character – I found the name of the press by doing some esoteric searches within the collected text to come up with this "fake" press called Blanc Press and to make the "fake" press seem more real I collected titles from numerous other writers I knew – titles that stood in for a host of "fake" or non-existent books which had been "previously published" by Blanc Press – this story has been told elsewhere as the background story for how the Parrot series was created.[3]

"Complex Textual Legitimacy Proclamation" was the title I attributed to myself in that fake list of titles – I pulled that title by doing some odd searches on the collected text I had been manipulating at the time – and I started the project by doing a Google search for "Complex Textual Legitimacy Proclamation" in quotes and maybe you'd be surprised that not much came up – and so I decided I would read all the material as if I was embarking on a kind of abstracted research process – around the title and the concept there – this was also pretty much how *The New Poetics* came about and at roughly the same time – so I read thru all the websites – and a number of M.A. and Ph.D. theses came up as pdf downloads as well – and so I downloaded all that material – several of them in the 200-400 page range on things like the tabloidization of the news media and professional wrestling as a productive audience model of entertainment and the formation of the EU's constitution – I started working through the text and made the decision that I would pull complete sentences related to "Complex Text" – and make a collection of sentences – and at some point string them together again without manipulating the sentences – and they had to be full sentences.

As I got deeper into the research portion I got sidetracked (surprise) – by things like *The New Poetics* and *Joyful Noise* and other projects and I left it behind – a couple few years later I would commit to eventually finishing the piece in some way when committing to printing the whole Parrot series – but I didn't really return to the piece until late last year / early this year as I knew the Parrot series was coming to a close and as I thought that it would be great as a piece for this book *Terrifying Photo* – and so I went back and did all the research – which took quite a whole lot of time – and I learned all kinds of really esoteric things but mainly I wanted to think about how these unrelated texts (in most ways completely unrelated), how did they deal with and stake a claim of legitimacy for complex text – once I had collected all the sentences – about 30,000 words all total in the end – I put them in rough order by topic etc. – actually I started doing this about halfway thru the "research" – and noting things I liked better or what felt more like things that would go

---

3 To create the Parrot series of chapbooks for Insert Blanc Press, Timmons later asked all the writers who had supplied titles for the book to write actual chapbooks to fit the titles.

at the beginning middle or end etc. – basically making meta-data notes on the information I collected – for example there was the theory section which ended up getting cut because it was way too didactic – or whatever other classification I could think of cause it was a whole lot of text – and then eventually I printed it all out – used the paper cutter and cut the text into individual sentences and put them all out on tables in little strips – and started to rearrange things and find where subjects overlapped etc. – in many ways I really want the text to tell me what it wants to say – and in many ways I want to twist it – so there was a whole lot of rearranging on tables and rearranging on the computer and back and forth for a couple months really – until it got into the state it's in here

It is about itself making a point as much as it is making some fun with these forewords and afterwords we use to justify the rest of a book – and it's playing with some of the poetry arguments – or quite honestly asking for more complex or even just real or actual arguments – most "poetry arguments" don't rise to the level of any kind of real "argument" whether they happen on Facebook or Twitter or in a comment section of a blog – or even in places like the *L.A. Review of Books*, or *The Boston Review* etc. (not to denigrate these venues in any way) – and yet I'm not laying out a straight forward argument either – I always find myself wanting to be in some kind of honest / satiric position – to satirize the idea of putting forward a long proclamation / argument at the front of the book – and also to simply do so – have your cake and eat it too – this is appropriation – this is conceptual writing – this is a hybrid form that I hope can register on multiple levels that strict conceptual writing simply can't do.

HM: What do you make of the idea of putting a long interview at the front of the book?

MT: It's funny I have to admit I didn't expect this intro to end up so interview-y even though it's exactly what we set out to do – I'm very happy with where we've ended up tho because it really is wonderfully ridiculous to begin a book with a long interview – and works perfectly in the way that this book is quirky with intros forewords afterwords and etc. – so it wasn't exactly what I was expecting but what ever turns out like we expect?

As someone who designs books I like to think of what a book looks like – how it physically exists in the world as an aesthetic object – this doesn't mean that I'm that great of a designer – I'm wholly untrained and have been picking this stuff up as I go for a while – I'm just good enough to be dangerous – and in fact designing the cover of this book was beyond my skill level and I was quite lucky that Max Springer was willing to jump in

I want this book to operate like an installation andor a gallery of work – I tend to think of the book as an art object and as an installation space – the white page being another white cube – and if I may bring up previous books again – this tendency of mine is pretty clear with *CREDIT* – and as well with *The New Poetics* which is a serial piece bound in book form that is truly an infinite work – albeit a gap-toothed one in which

I left markers for possible further pieces that could be written but which I didn't write for that book as a nod towards the potentiality of the literary space I had set up

I think of the way this book is arranged as functioning in an extra-textual manner – with the already too much foreword and afterword – and the catalogue style with its chronological order actually made sequencing the pieces a much more complicated editing process – taking out or including a piece had much to do with the shape of the book as a whole – at least as much as the inclusion of any individual text in itself – so the intervals between pieces and between middle beginning and end and the pacing was a big consideration – also at some point I decided not to use any real blurbs on the back cover – after *CREDIT* had 30 blurbs I thought I could do a book without blurbs so in this case I have just some other bits of text I didn't end up using in the book masquerading as blurbs – and so it seemed an interview would be another kind of form to deploy

Opening with an interview offers a different opportunity than a normal introduction – and works alongside other nods to various forms internal to the book genre throughout – an interview / intro at the beginning of the book forces you out of the text in a way just as we're supposed to be leading the reader in – and I think the oddity of these texts that follow – the oddity of this book as a whole – is increased by beginning with an interview – something that would typically be included only in a reprint or 2nd edition if at all – the interview usually exists as something outside the text either in print or online that encourages you to pick up and read the work in question - but which is otherwise trash or excess or not considered to be a part of 'the work' or something that impinges upon the text – I want the text to be beside itself – literally the words existing printed on the page and figuratively the words beside themselves existing in another andor multiple other contexts – and with this interview / intro it seems to me that's exactly how it works – the text beside itself

Lastly, I wanted to talk with you, Holly Myers, of course, about this book because we've had a long and sometimes contentious dialogue around this type of work – and some of the poetry arguments spilled into the various conversations we were having around writing and art and collective activities – I knew that you would push me to think about this volume in a different way than many other writers I know – and starting the book on a more interrogatory andor critical note seemed to be just the thing

Mathew Timmons and Holly Myers
Los Angeles, CA – Santa Fe, NM
09.25.14 – 12.30.14

Complex Textual Legitimacy Proclamation: A Foreword

An early version of Complex Textual Legitimacy Proclamation *by Mathew Timmons was originally published as an edition of* Parrot *by* Blanc Press *in Los Angeles (2005-2010).* Insert Press *has been reissuing facsimile editions of each title from the* Parrot *series (1-23) since 2010;* Parrot 23 Complex Textual Legitimacy Proclamation *was released by* Insert Press *in November 2014. The expanded version presented here, was split into the foreword and afterword of this book. Footnote references can be found at the end of the Afterword.*

Normal photographs are made by using the ordinary light reflected from objects to burn patterns into photosensitive chemicals on a piece of film, and then enlarging and reversing that negative image, burning it into a piece of photosensitive paper, and chemically 'fixing' it. It is an explicit, or explicate representation; with differing degrees of accuracy, you can match up one square inch of the picture with a corresponding area of the object depicted, in a one-to-one isomorphism.[14]

Large sensational photographs made their first appearance, with the topics of sex, violence, accidents and scandal as their major themes.[9]

Then came the theatre with its scenarios. But soon people no longer wanted to hear other people talking, they wanted to make images speak.... This is human nature, to go to one extreme then come back to the origins. That is what happens, man comes back to the beginnings, once again to shadow play.[12]

More beautiful than fabulous pictures.[12]

All events are film events; viewing pleasure may largely be a part of the passive yet emotional response that typically accompanies media consumption.[10]

Even after their release, the pictures cannot be properly exploited because of the absence of adequate scope for their maximum exploitation.[12]

You shall not make any images of me.[11]

The ability to produce the intangible is always dependent on a specific cultural faculty of perception and apprehension.[7]

The origins of the word lead us back to ritual action performing the work of consecration or hallowing.[4]

In the beginning was the Word, in all of its permutations.[14]

As I sat there on the edge of my bed, I wondered whether I was dreaming.[9]

You are young. You have grown up after the fall of the Berlin wall.[11]

The term mark has its origins in the traveling carnival, where magicians would baffle audiences with sleight of hand tricks under the umbrella of "magic". Particularly gullible members of the audience were identified by the magicians as marks, or easily fooled members of the audience.[8]

The more you know, the better. ... But the converse is also true: a book for those who know everything is a book for those who know anything.[14]

Each text, laboratory, author and discipline strives to establish a world in which its own interpretation is made more likely by virtue of the increasing number of people from whom it extracts compliance.[1]

Esoteric literature presupposes that there are basic truths which would not be pronounced in public by any decent man, because they would do harm to many people who, having been hurt, would naturally be inclined to hurt in turn him who pronounces the unpleasant truths.[7]

He therefore writes esoterically with the result that his true meaning can only be understood by a small number of talented and careful readers.[7]

To write a book is essentially to give a public teaching...[7]

The seemingly infinite variety of ways in which a given teaching can be understood does not do away with the fact that the originator of the doctrine understood it in one way only, provided he was not confused.[7]

In the context of this book, we are profoundly aware how much has been left out. There are a host of important writers who receive little or no attention in the ensuing chapters, including, among others, Jane Austen, Alfred Tennyson, George MacDonald, Mark Rutherford, and Mrs. Humphrey Ward. Further, it is not only important writers that are missing from the chapters that follow. The list of topics that we might reasonably have considered in this book is endless.[0]

It is the opinion of many historians of the written word that the development of the 22-sign alphabet in Byblos (Phoenicia) in 1000 BC put Western man on the linear fast-track, narrowing and focusing his methods of perception by means of the phonetic writing.[14]

Standardized phonetic alphabets and symbolic language and mass-production of texts made possible the explosion of knowledge that built our world of televisions and hard drives. Now, the complexity of that world—and this book that most fully represents that world—has advanced to such a degree that the only way to deal with it is to execute a reverse, to reimpose a simpler order over the vast landscape of information across which we move.[14]

...take hold of ink, pen, and tablet. Realize that you are about to serve your God in joy. Begin to combine letters, a few or many, permuting and revolving them rapidly until your mind warms up. Delight in how they move, and in what you generate by revolving them.[14]

All the data in the world stacked up like one big neon city, so you could cruise around and have a kind of grip on it, visually anyway, because if you didn't, it was too complicated, trying to find your way to the particular piece of data you needed.[14]

Hidden amongst the rushes are myriad small forms of life.[10]

I can hardly open my mouth to speak without feeling as though the sea burst its dams and overflowed. How then shall I express what my soul has received? How can I set it down in a book?[14]

As I write these words after completing the protracted task of organizing one huge pile of notecards into successively smaller piles of notecards, I cannot avoid the relevance of the above image in describing the task at hand.[14]

The piling of incommensurates upon incommensurates that stuffs these pages, the attempted shotgun wedding of many disparate sources, is intentional.[14]

One mark of an originality that can win canonical status for a literary work is a strangeness that we can either never altogether assimilate, or that becomes such a given that we are blinded to its idiosyncrasies.[14]

The text is an element of the ritual process and necessary to its logic and completion.[4]

You will see nothing subtle where everything is subtle. But if you take the trouble to look very closely, and penetrate with your eyes to the secrets of the artistry, you will notice such intricacies, so delicate and subtle, so close together, and well-knitted, so involved and bound together, and so fresh still in their colourings that you will not hesitate to declare that all these things must have been the result of the work, not of men, but of angels.[14]

A shift in modes of cognition, from typographic straight-line marching to aural omnidirectional floating, is necessary before the ears can grasp what the eyes can never see.[14]

The term of polysemy refers to the idea that there are an infinite number of potential readings for a particular text.[8]

The specific contextual articulations may contribute to the same chorus, but each contribution is a unique variation of the general theme.[11]

This might be, at least in part, a construction and the projection into the past of a personal project.[7]

When I worked in the studio, it was like being in my own house. I felt I was working for myself. I never felt I was working for money.[12]

What a wonderful feeling of goodwill and happiness permeated the studio. We would enter the studio in the early hours of the morning and would not leave till our work was complete. Since discipline and adherence to principles regulated our lives, projects were always completed in time. What intimate bonds held us together.[12]

If you be pleased to accept this gift our hearts will rejoice with exceeding great gladness.[10]

Conserve this precious document which will be useful to you one day. However, if you do not need it pass it on to someone who might. You know them.[12]

When Brancusi drew his Portrait of the Artist as an Abstract Spiral, he captured his subject well.[14]

This appropriation is the essence of textual poaching.[8]

§

In the traditional and apropos myth of Actaeon and Diana, for example, Actaeon stumbles upon the naked goddess bathing who turns him into a buck who is hunted down by his friends and dogs.[13]

The feast must take place, as he instructs readers, in a beautiful “gladsome greene” “or Paradise.”
Under shade of stately trees, where little sunne is seene:
And neare some fountaine springe, whose chrystall running streames,
May help to coole the parching heate, ycaught by Phoebus beames.[13]

Herewith to stint all stryfe, the huntsmen come in hast,
They licence crave of King or Queene, to see their battell plast.
Which graunted and obtaynde, they set on such as lyve,
And fiercely fight, till both be forst, all armour up to give.[13]

Perchance the fight, which sodenly you saw,
Erstwhyles betweene, these overbragging bluddes

Amasde your mynde, and for a whyle did draw
Your noble eyes, to settle on such suddes.
But peerlesse Prince, the moisture of such muddes,
Is much too grosse and homely for your grace,
Behold them not, their pleasures be but base.[13]

Beholde (good Quene) A poet with a Speare
(straunge sights well markt are understode the better)
A Soldyer armed, with pensile in his eare
With pen to fighte, and sworde to wryte a letter.
His gown haulffe of[f], his blade not fully bownde
In dowbtfull doompes, which waye were best to take
With humble harte, and knees that kysse the grownnde
Presenntes hymsellfe, to you for dewtyes sake
And thus he saithe, no daunger (I protest)
Shall ever lett this loyall harte I beare
To serve you so as maye become me beste
In feilde, in Towne, in Cowrte, or any where.
Then peereless prince, employe this willinge man
In your affayres to do the beste he cann.[13]

Even as she performs this traditionally masculine role attired in a highly feminine dress, she reaches for a large, threatening knife.[13]

In the butchering image, however, she has yet to take the knife or cut into the deer.[13]

Within the allegorical world of political service represented by the text, her hand thus represents her cultural, political, and legal power.[13]

Once the prince has cut into the deer, “there he rayseth out the synew or muskle with his knyfe, and putteth his forefinger of his left hand, through under the sayd muscle to hold the legge by. If afterwerdes, he touch the shoulder or any part of the legge, with any other thing than his knife, until he have taken it out, it is a forfayture, and he is thought no handsome woodman”. High-stakes butchering at its best, the public performance of this arcane “ceremonie” determines the ability of the hunter and thus the identity of the prince.[13]

Not simply a case of the pen being mightier than the sword, the two are synonymous since he uses his “sworde to wryte a letter,” representing thereby a powerful sense of artistic and cultural agency for himself.[13]

The poet's self-description as a "straunge sight" once again recalls the early modern practice of self-fashioning as visual spectacle and "revelation."[13]

This thin anonymity, along with his openly direct self-construction as a soldier-courtier in the Hemetes image, suggests that he had no qualms in circulating any number of identities.[13]

In a society increasingly open to and dependent upon self-fashioning as a means of establishing identity, as Berger following Stephen Greenblatt and others indicates, such pictorial images served the cultural, political, and personal need "for exemplary images; images that commemorate the individual as the model, the embodiment, of the status, values, norms, and authority of a particular class, lineage, institution, or profession"[13]

In such artistic acts, which enable the "creation of the public self," the artist or patron presents him- or herself the way he wants to be seen—above all, the way he wants to see himself. In such a performance, any distinction between actors and audience will be misleading. The protagonist is the audience, and other spectators, to view the spectacle correctly, must see it through his eyes. The persona he adopts, his mask, is not intended as a disguise but as a revelation: of the truest, essential, Platonic self.[13]

§

It is this desire to go beyond the mediated images and get to the real aspect of a personality that characterizes the fascination with Hollywood celebrities in this culture.[8]

What a shame character is no longer rewarded in our society. But bad behavior? It reaps bountiful rewards.[9]

What is presented is the illusion of something real, distorting the distinction between star image and human being.[8]

In this country, celebrity trumps everything else.[9]

We are complicit, in varying degrees, in the paparazzi phenomenon.[9]

We beat our breast in public and say we're different from the paparazzi, but there'll be no changes. We enjoy it.[9]

The Internet has provided the means for more information to be dispensed to more people, enhancing the access to the illusion of a real story behind the mediated images.[8]

Behind the media produced star image and official narratives lies a hidden story, a meta-narrative that fascinates audiences and adds to the signifying processes of both stars and generic texts. Audiences read these texts and star images within the context of the meta-narratives that surround them, adding levels of connotations that impact the reading of the official narratives.[8]

Armbrust argues that prominent actors in commercial cinema are like texts themselves, texts that are conditioned by positions that the audiences take and by the audiences' association with the performer's previous roles. Commercial cinema audiences by and large view films through their actors, not their directors.[12]

Entertainment has superceded the provision of information; human interest has supplanted the public interest; measured judgment has succumbed to sensationalism; the trivial has triumphed over the weighty; the intimate relationships of celebrities from soap operas, the world of sport or the royal family are judged more 'newsworthy' than the reporting of significant issues and events of international consequence. Traditional news values have been undermined by new values; 'infotainment' is rampant.[9]

A sociological approach to investigating stardom involves the analysis of the industrial aspects to stardom, including the promotion and publicity of the star image by the official media producers. Promotion refers to the public appearances and interviews of the star, which are organized by the entertainment industry. Similarly, publicity refers to the social discourses and narratives about the star that are circulated in the culture, often by the official media producers themselves.[8]

Scholarly work on the phenomenon of stardom tends to rely on the examination of successful star images, exploring the industrial and social mechanisms that yield particular stars. Analyses of this sort are often limited, however, by the implication that the star-making industry is the central force in the creation of stardom, failing to account for the role of the audience in the creation, or destruction, of star images.[8]

For all their lofty pretenses, today's mainstream media are essentially just another branch of show biz.[9]

The media have extensive power in that they represent the primary, and often the only, source of information about many important events and topics. Media can define which events are important, as well as how media consumers should understand these events.[9]

As a result, any sign of the media weakening in form, function or efficiency should give us pause.[9]

However, the media are not noiseless channels of communication. The institutionalised methods of production, self-perceived functions, and rules of access constitute the media not only as facilitators of dialogue, but also as actors who participate in deciding what the dialogue should be about, how it should be conducted, and who should participate in it.[11]

The integration, albeit unevenly, of global markets and media forms has no doubt produced universalized forms of consumptive desires.[12]

People are vulnerable to the power of mass media because they have become isolated and alienated from traditional social institutions that have protected them from propaganda and manipulation.[9]

The social changes brought about by the disruptive influence of mass media will result in the advent of more authoritarian and centrally controlled sources.[9]

Without media in some form or another, we would be ignorant of anything that we did not experience or hear about directly from another person.[9]

The concepts and capabilities offered by multimedia technology have existed in one form or another for centuries.[14]

All media are connected in some way.[9]

According to various media theorists and experts, the growth of media and cultural industries and the rise of the information society coincides with a pervasive sense of declining cultural, educational and political standards or 'dumbing down'.[9]

It may not be true that things are, as many commentators claim, 'getting worse.' It might simply be that their gaze has lighted on an established phenomenon they had previously overlooked.[9]

Since the very beginning, the history of the press has been marked with high and low periods, as well as both successful and failed attempts to discover the right mix of information, news, story-telling, truth and old-fashioned gossip.[9]

All of these genres have distinctive signifying processes that must be understood in the context of the genre itself. Genres associated with low culture are often denigrated because they do not conform to the conventions of more acceptable genres.[8]

Cultural texts are saturated with social meanings, they generate political effects, reproducing or opposing governing social institutions and relations of domination and subordination.[9]

Only the most naïve journalist would cling to the idea that newspapers simply transmit "reality" to the printed page, unaffected by preconceptions, formulaic story patterns, and other considerations.[9]

Objectivity as a concept can be traced back to early 1900, defined as holding that the "facts speak for themselves, whether these facts are observations recorded by a reporter or quotes from sources".[9]

In the words of Stuart Hall, "High culture versus popular culture was, for many years, the classic way of framing the debate about culture - the terms carrying a powerfully evaluative charge (roughly, high=good; popular=debased)".[9]

The serious, disciplined style of modernist criticism was self-proclaimed as superior to the frivolous seductive world of mass culture.[10]

Popular culture is the culture of the majority, the average working class person, which in the eyes of the elite is a study of ignorance, lewdness, dumbed-down ramblings and basically all that is weak, mindless, simple entertainment.[9]

While there may be more information available, the quality of this information as well as public understanding is declining. Public ignorance and apathy is growing as the serious, challenging and truthful is being pushed aside by the trivial, sensational, vulgar and manipulated.[9]

The high standards of yesterday are being undermined by sensationalism, prurience, triviality, malice, and plain, simple credulity.[9]

Content is dominated by scandal, sports, and entertainment and often has a strong element of fantasy.[9]

Every effort must be made to catch the attention of consumers and make that sale.[9]

If the public did not want it, they would not purchase or consume it. In any case, these are not new trends, but familiar ones.[9]

Meanwhile, according to Sloan, consumers have "invariably chosen shipwrecks over shipping notices, crime and carnage over commodity futures, and whorehouse raids over wholesale price indexes."[9]

It's wonderful. I love talking to witches and Satanists and vampire hunters, and people who've been kidnapped by UFOs - it sure beats covering zoning board meetings.[9]

This type of content is seen by many possible consumers as being uninteresting and useless to themselves personally, marking it as distinctly undesirable.[9]

A text panel read: 'Is it treasure or junk? Everyone has an opinion. Is it art? Decide for yourself'.[10]

First, trash connotes that which ought to be discarded, a sort of instant garbage; second, it connotes cheapness, shoddiness, the overflow of the capitalist commodity system. Third, it connotes a superficial glitter designed to appeal to those whose tastes are ill-formed according to the dominant perspective.... Fourth, trash is excessive: it has more vulgarity, more tastelessness, more offensiveness than is necessary for its function as a cheap commodity.[9]

It devotes relatively little attention to politics, economics, and society and relatively much to diversions like sports, scandal, and popular entertainment; it devotes relatively much attention to the personal and private lives of people, both celebrities and ordinary people, and relatively little to political processes, economic developments, and social changes.[9]

It includes texts such as popular music, movies, television programs, newspapers and the Internet, as well as social activity such as going to a club, watching sports or grocery shopping.[9]

It can be found in the bloodcurdling ballads sung by wandering balladeers in the sixteenth century, the crowds that flocked to public beheadings in the Middle Ages, the gruesome 'games' of ancient Rome, and all the way back to prehistoric times.[9]

The familiar argument is that in order to inform the audience you must first gain its attention.[9]

There is a large body of scholarship devoted to examining the complex relationship between audiences and the producers of media texts. Theorists conceive audiences as having varying amounts of power in this relationship, depending on their perspectives.[8]

For example, Fredric Wertham (1954) cautions of the perils that were inherent in consuming pulp literature, particularly comic books, in "Seduction of the Innocent". He claims that exposure to these texts increases the likelihood of children becoming juvenile delinquents.[8]

Many of these young people do not read if they can avoid it, they are not interested in politics or current affairs; they do not go to opera or the theatre...They are post-modern, post-serious, post-literate...[9]

If they are wise they know who is standing behind them as they speak. And if they are straightforward they will tell you for whom they speak. If you have learned to read the codes of such communication, you will know the extent and significance of their standing.[10]

Scholars such as David Morley (1992) contend that the model of the passive audience equates the text to a "hypodermic needle"(45). The media text injects meaning into vulnerable audiences, and individuals are incapable of distinguishing fantasy from reality.[8]

Audiences are conceived as being vulnerable entities that passively absorb all messages inscribed in media texts, making them susceptible to brainwashing and desensitization. As we shall see, this model is grossly inadequate for understanding the complex reading processes employed by audiences and is too often used as a tool for censorship and as a regulator of taste.[8]

The theoretical conception of the audience as productive recognizes the blurred boundaries between textual producers and consumers, with each side of the relationship displaying characteristics normally associated with the other.[8]

Rather than the text simply injecting meaning into a passive audience member, oppositional readings provide the space for rejection of the messages within the text.[8]

This example demonstrates the potential power audiences can wield over textual producers, emerging as writers themselves rather than the more traditional role of media consumer.[8]

Audiences are not passive sponges who simply absorb information and direction, as they display traits that demonstrate active resistance and negotiation to many mediated messages.[8]

Audiences now play a crucial role in the creation of media texts and must be examined in this context.[8]

With the coming of mass-produced texts, print culture moved in the direction of standardization, 'decompressing' the compressed manuscript into simpler, spelled-out fragments. This decompression largely obviated the need for personal memory in textual interpretation, moving away from the interactivity that characterized the medieval relationship with the individually crafted page, towards the book-as-storehouse-of-memory approach that became necessary with the exponential increase of information.[14]

The Internet has significantly shortened the feedback circuit between producers and consumers, providing space for audiences to engage both media texts and official media producers in unprecedented ways.[8]

There is no passive way to use the phone—you plug into the network, and when it talks, you have to talk back to keep the communication going.[14]

McLuhan says that a writer has "no means of holding a mass of detail before his reader in a large bloc or gesalt" the way a film does.[14]

"TV will not work as background. It engages you. You have to be with it," says McLuhan of TV's "nonvisual mosaic structure"—a structure it shares with modern art, modern physics and computer networks.[14]

Already with remote control channel zapper in hand, most of us can track multiple narrative, headline loops, and touchdown drives simultaneously across cable transmissions and stratified time. In the network we know that what is of value is what can be used and that we can shift values everywhere, instantly, individually, as we will.[14]

For any network which would represent the larger network in which it is embedded (generally called 'reality') with any degree of faithfulness and accuracy, it is crucial that it be able to represent itself also, and its place in that network. A photograph of Everything must include the camera that took it.[14]

In one delivery mode, the Internet can neutralise geography, provide interactivity by drawing in information as well as sending it out, and it can hyperlink between databases, institutions, languages and critical perspectives.[10]

Modern innovations such as the Internet and satellite broadcast have drastically reduced global information gaps, and speedy newsgathering is in high demand among consumers. Information is now being pushed faster than ever, causing displeasure amongst the "slow and steady" news media purists.[9]

The godfather of hypertext, Vannevar Bush, realized as Director of the U.S. Office of Scientific Research and Development in 1945 that "the human mind...operates by association", and postulated a device called the Memex which would operate along the same lines.[14]

The brainchild of Vannevar Bush, the contemporary concept of hypertext was introduced to the world in a 1945 article to the *Atlantic Monthly* magazine, wherein Bush postulated a device called the Memex to deal with the information overload that comes with an ongoing written history. The Memex would allow two or more texts to be displayed at once, and the mutual participation of one piece of information in numerous documents. It would also allow the Memex user to add her own margin notes and comments, which would become permanently incorporated to the document itself. The technology of 1945 was not equal to the task of creating the Memex; like Babbage's Difference Engine, it remained an idea.[14]

The feedback loop between textual producers and consumers allows for audiences to communicate their desires and expectations to media producers, and as I have argued the Internet has significantly shortened the distance between the two sides of that loop. Audiences are now afforded a space where they can have more immediate communication with textual producers, blurring the boundaries between the two sides.[8]

In this sense, technology is culture, 'not assisting or causing but substituting, referring only back to itself'.[10]

While new technologies allow stories to be visually framed on a scale much larger or smaller than the object, this may not be such a radical change.[10]

In order to address issues concerning the 'positioning' of individuals in discourse, appeal has recently been made to psychoanalytic formulations offering plausible interpretations of how and why specific subjects take up the positions they do.[5]

The speaker is neither in a position to adapt freely to the perceived identity of the audience, nor capable of creating the audience entirely at his or her own will, but is instead constrained by personal and social identities that prefigure any concrete utterance.[11]

However, the understanding of the dynamic interdependencies also leads to a realisation that "...the 'we' is not unitary but constituted and that no actor is ever entitled to speak for all of us".[11]

The selection of one out of the different available means of expression is a genuinely creative choice that facilitates the articulation of unique opinions and understandings.[11]

The speaker's position is presented as a comprehensive one whose breadth is achieved by circumventing false contradictions.[11]

Here, once again, the restraining tension of simultaneous openness and closure is at play.[11]

Contradiction is indispensable in the generation of creative utterances.[14]

Thus, the two contradictory tendencies of closure and openness actually feed on each other.[11]

Why choose one over the other when you could be both simultaneously?[8]

A place where contradictions are allowed to exist, hard questions are posed without qualification, answers are debated and conclusions are forever rubbery.[10]

The Uncertainty Principle and Relativity are rarely invoked in practical physics situations, and Openness is rarely called upon in the reading of most literature; often principles such as these only complicate things, causing needless confusion.[14]

The modern novel should be largely a work of reference.[14]

We wander freely in its maze—freely, that is, with the exception of the maze walls: "You cannot use the text as you want, but only as the text wants you to use it."[14]

If every work is a channeling of other works, then every author is a plagiarist.[14]

Bloom's basic insight, that "strong poets [and writers] make poetic history by misreading one another, so as to clear imaginative space for themselves" is hard for a writer to argue with; any heated denial of the Anxiety of Influence tends to backfire and make the denier seem more in thrall to that anxiety than most. Aside from that, it is a sound observation.[14]

However, as mentioned earlier, it seems that the vast majority are reluctant to admit that they themselves willingly participated in this sort of "borrowing" of ideas.[9]

...the Middle ages...did not possess the concept of 'authorship' in exactly the same significance as we have it now....The indifference of medieval scholars to the precise identity of the authors whose books they studied is undeniable...The writers themselves, on the other hand, did not always trouble to 'quote' what they took from other books or to indicate where they took it from...[14]

The medieval author belonged to a 'partly decomposable system' of authors; once he entered the network of literature, his individual identity was not as fixed as it was for the headstrong Romantic author.[14]

So why, pray, sign anything as long as every word, letter, penstroke, paperspace is a perfect signature of its own?[14]

"We do things with language, produce effects with language, and we do things to language, but language is also the thing that we do. Language is a name for our doing: both 'what' we do (the name for the action that we characteristically perform) and that which we effect, the act and its consequences" (Butler, 1997, p. 8).[11]

Is it possible that one single symbol could be awakened in isolation from all others? Probably not. Just as objects in the world always exist in a context of other objects, so symbols are always connected to a constellation of other symbols.[14]

Speaking of linguistic and non-linguistic signs, Jacques Derrida says that all signs "can break with every given context, engendering an infinity of new contexts in a manner which is absolutely illimitable."[14]

With the constantly circulating dialectic between order and disorder, elements of disorder can increase the level of information produced in a complex system, bringing out a relationship between the elemental disorder of entropy and the 'meaning' of creativity.[14]

The confusion of 'democracy' and 'anarchy' is common enough, especially among Americans; indeed, I myself might be accused of adding to the overall amount of critical entropy with this very essay.[14]

Meaning is married to confusion in a technique whose ultimate aim is an epiphany which, in the words of twentieth century mystic Abraham Isaac Kook (an extremely lucid man, despite his name): "...enables you to sense creation not as something completed, but as constantly becoming, evolving, ascending. This transports you, from a place where nothing is new to a place where there is nothing old, where everything reveals itself, where heaven and earth rejoice as at the moment of Creation." Extreme difficulty can be trying, but the rewards for engaging the complex and incomprehensible are rewards commensurate with the scale of Creation, not the scale of the stuffed and mounted plot line.[14]

It is not an act of accretion, but an act of unraveling. The human brain provides a useful example. In its initial development, the brain is grown as an ever-increasing conglomeration of interconnected neurons. From the very moment it starts to interact with the world and develop a heuristic for dealing with the world, it begins to operate through "chunking", pruning down the giant tree of infinite possibility, sacrificing completeness for comprehensibility. As usual, a picture clarifies tremendously:[14]

[missing pic][14]

[[MISSING. PLEASE HELP!]][9]

Any sufficiently complex and well-constructed conceptual network is far closer to 'reality' and the way our own minds function than a one-way train-track linear system. The idea of the network is behind all ideas about anything, inasmuch as the brains which traffic in these ideas are themselves networks of billions of neurons, each one of which can receive the input of up to 200,000 other neurons through its dendrites, and in turn send its electrochemical pulse to myriad other neurons along the branching tree of its axon.[14]

The network is far from being a modern invention; it has made many past appearances. We have medieval manuscripts which carry different layers of meaning in images which demand to be read in a number of different ways simultaneously. "Free association of ideas is taken to be part of the intellectual baggage of the monks" who created them, prefiguring Freud by a mere eleven centuries. In the hermetic magical tradition, the 'good magic' of Pico della Mirandola is governed by the principle of simpatia, the understanding of the mutual rapports running through nature, and the secret charms through which things are drawn to one another. Lexicographers eventually came to understand that organizing knowledge in interconnected semantic fields made more sense than linear alphabetic organization in many cases (which was itself a revolutionary concept in its time, suggested by the printer's cast-lead letters, organized alphabetically in drawers for easy access).[14]

There are, says Eco, "latent possibilities of a certain type of experience in every artistic product," a degree of openness to interaction, to the unearthing of buried treasures. At the end of each sentence of a book, there is a potential disjunction where the reader can stop to wonder what is going to happen next, thus creating a tree of possibilities.[14]

The Open Work is not read for the pleasure of formal resolution and dramatic catharsis, but for the joy in the constant, organic unfolding of possibility. … But a true open work validates the freedom applied to its interpretation by a carefully 'plotted' flexibility that saturates it to its foundations: "….in a 'well-made' literary work….there is no openness at a given level which is not sustained and improved by analogous operations at all other levels."[14]

"The notion of moving steadily along on single planes of narrative awareness is totally alien to the nature of language and of consciousness. But it is highly consistent with the nature of the printed word." To go McLuhan one further, the straight line and the flat plane are not only alien to language and consciousnes, but to any attempt to adequately represent a reality that is lived in at least four dimensions, and more for some mediums, mystics and physicists. Maybe there is even a splash of prophecy in Harold Bloom's glum consideration that "Perhaps the ages of reading—Aristocratic, Democratic, Chaotic—now reach terminus, and the reborn Theocratic era will be almost wholly an oral and visual culture."[14]

The sympathetic magic whereby one of great power can gain control over the world by gaining control over a microcosmic model lies at the preliterate core of the literary enterprise. We have already heard of Bruno's desire to "unify the whole contents of the universe" by establishing them in his memory. More modest than Bruno, Vico limits himself to "this world of nations" which "has surely been made by men, and its guise must therefore be found within the modifications of our own human mind." On the printed page as well as in the mind, there were encyclopedists long before Diderot, writers whose aim was to compress the world as they knew it between the covers of a book, with all of its spheres of knowledge present in miniature. Critics like Edward Mendelsohn with his 'encyclopedic narratives', and Khachig Tololyan with his 'cosmographic narratives' have examined the notion of universal isomorphism (though they did not use the term) in their examinations of *The Divine Comedy, Gargantua and Pantagruel, Don Quixote, Faust, Moby Dick, Ulysses, Gravity's Rainbow*, and other works.[14]

The works above are largely synchronic, dealing with the world as it exists at a fixed point in time, usually the generation before they were written.[14]

"Locomotion should be slow, the slower the better, and be often interrupted by leisurely halts to sit on vantage points and stop at question marks….I know no prescription of method; avoid whatever increases routine and fatigue and decreases alertness."—Carl Sauer, famous geographer[14]

After these litanies of repetition, the eternal 'Why?' naturally presents itself. That variations and combinations of limited smaller elements is often the process behind larger organic networks has been mentioned elsewhere. But more important is what Eco has to say about any artist who wants maximum disorder and information: "[He] will sacrifice some of his freedom and introduce a few modules of order into his work, which will help [readers] find their way through the noise...." Repetition is necessary transmission insurance in extremely complex textual landscapes—as it is in the genetic landscape where each person possesses trillions of copies of their own DNA, and in the beach landscape of the Galápagos Islands, where sea-turtles lay hundreds of eggs so a small handful of their offspring can make it to the sea. And the media landscape is no different: "Ads seem to work on the very advanced principle that a small pellet or pattern in a noisy, redundant barrage of repetition will gradually assert itself."[14]

While artworks are inescapably produced in social and cultural contexts, they are often hermetic, anti-social and confounding.[10]

A work of art has meaning and interest only for someone who possesses the cultural competence, that is, the code, into which it is encoded... A beholder who lacks the specific code feels lost in a chaos of sounds and rhythms, colours and lines, without rhyme or reason... Thus, the encounter with a work of art is not "love at first sight" as is generally supposed.[10]

Thus, the activities and institutions dealing with 'art and culture'—subjects often considered secondary to the important things in life, such as earning a living—are, to the contrary, deeply implicated in the major issues confronting contemporary society.[10]

It seems to me that in some ways these are all versions of the same, or a similar question: when we ask, what is the relationship of information to artefact, of knowledge to experience, of research to leisure, we are no longer asking for the reiteration of a value distinction. Rather, we are beginning to ask for a fundamental formula or definition in a new kind of physics—a particle physics of meaning.[10]

Arguments that stress the eclipsing of boundaries between artefact and information typically make two related points. One is that information stored and distributed as downloads and on discs has become almost artefactual. The second is that when an artefact can be so readily reconfigured as data, its materiality begins to be a stage, rather than a state, of existence. What may be at first a photograph, sound recording, or video or film excerpt are all subject to the same process whereby they become a binary language of ones and zeroes. If exhibition 'stories' employ different kinds of data bits, the artefact or artwork becomes principally a data device in the larger narrative being posited.[10]

The distinction which once said, television is primarily information, art primarily artefact, is now an unsure distinction...Or at least the distinction between data and material has become metaphysical or symbolic, rather than categorical. Similarly, when an artefact can be so readily reconfigured as data, its materiality begins to be a stage, rather than a state, of existence.[10]

The 'new' in such a cultural figuration must be a continual sophistry of new beginnings, new births, new origins which effectively conceal the truths of its formations and its means for arrival into the new ... the psychic aversion within the dominant society to its own moment of migration and hybridity still lives with it despite using 'contemporaneity' as a shield, as a form of forgetting and rewriting of the consequences of its own 'traditions'.[10]

It is a pseudohybridity characteristic of the ideology of complexity found in postmodern groups and classes that want to think of themselves as being on the cutting edge even as they no longer support and even suppress new and alternate ways of thinking.[10]

Commercial cultures aim for immediate impact and possess a high likelihood of obsolescence. The very thing that makes market cultures so exciting and vibrant—the search for the new, the dramatic and the novel—makes substantive intellectual and cultural exchange difficult to achieve.[10]

The 'brand new', once dated, tends to appear nostalgic, since it represents material aspirations that have generally been surpassed. What we lack is the wonder of seeing those things for the first time—an experience that has been diminished by the spread of communications technologies that provides immediate simulated access to places and times other than our own. In these times of visual media saturation, objects themselves may not possess the same ability to imaginatively transport viewers to earlier times and faraway places.[10]

In the twentieth century, concern over the loss of aura of original objects saw simulation give way to more rigorous concerns about authenticity.[10]

As Walter Benjamin famously observed, the aura of originality that surrounded the art object prior to mass production was threatened in the modern age, due to the ability to separate an image from its object, hence displacing it from its particular time and place.[10]

Another apposite quotation, this time from Walter Benjamin: "...the history of every art form shows critical epochs in which a certain art form aspires to effects which could be fully obtained only with a changed technical standard, that is to say, in a new art form." The 'new' and 'unheard of' never is; to forget this is to reinvent the wheel, over and over again. The 'new' and 'unheard of' critic is a modern-day incarnation of Sisyphus—only Sisyphus never asked for applause.[14]

A Diagram of the Winds

An oration written at the request of Liz Glynn for her piece The 24-Hour Roman Reconstruction Project *at* Machine Project *in Los Angeles on Saturday, January 19, 2008. Glynn requested the oration be composed through a combination of* Ten Books on Architecture by Vitruvius *and* The Deeds of the Divine Augustus by Augustus.

I have been consul thirteen times, of Roman citizens. The Roman people bear the rule of the Roman people, of me and of the Roman people. The Roman people have given it to me. And twenty one times I have been named emperor. I rebuilt. The People have entered their own land to bear the rule of the Roman people and Constructed principles of triumph. When the senate constructed principles of proportion. When the senate constructed principles of Water. Different waters, drains, windows, and water supplies—the Economy, Methods of Building Walls, contemplated works, buildings of works and arrangements in public places. When the senate was Water, Women in long robes, called Caryatides, took the place of columns. The columns, columns twenty-five feet, in your water-screws and water wheels.

When I wrote this I was seventy-six years old. The sum expended on theatrical spectacles and gladatorial games and athletes and hunts and mock naval battles and money given to colonies, cities, and towns destroyed by earthquake and fire or per man to friends and senators, whom I raised to the senate rating: innumerable. I subjected the whole wide earth to the rule of the Roman people. I drove the men who slaughtered my father into exile with a legal order, punishing their crime, and afterwards, when they waged war on the state, I conquered them in two battles. On account of the things successfully done by me and through my officers, under my auspices, on earth and sea, the senate decreed fifty-five times that there be sacrifices to the immortal gods. Also both privately and as a city all the citizens unanimously and continuously prayed at all the shrines for my health. I restored peace to the sea from pirates.

Earth, I hold, was impregnated by the rains of heaven and, thus conceiving, has brought forth the young of mankind and of all nature, and it is luminous. In some places the earth is beginning to go to pieces from dampness, but if again, a fire is made in that place, in the flats, the place contains water. This water is called water. As much water as quantity of water. Engines for Raising Water admit water, Water Wheels and Water Mills, The Water Screw, The Water Organ.

Water, not merely supplying drink but filling an infinite number of practical needs, does us services which make us grateful because it is gratis. But we must expend our energies in searching it out and finding it. To do so, the following test should be applied. Before sunrise, lie down flat in the place where the search is to be made, and placing the chin on the earth and supporting it there, take a look out over the country. Then, dig in places where vapours are seen curling and rising up into the air. This sign cannot show itself. This sign cannot show itself in a dry spot. There are no hippopotamuses.

If a walled town is built among the marshes, the columns will be of great importance, their height will determine where public places are placed. Again, if the town is stone, the columns will bear the rule of the Roman people, if the senate and Roman people give them to me, The City Walls and Temples. The streets will bear the rule of the Roman people if the columns are in place. The Cretans call it building.

I built the senate-house and the Chalcidicum which adjoins it and the temple of Apollo on the Palatine with porticos, the temple of divine Julius, the Lupercal, the portico at the Flaminian circus, which I allowed to be called by the name Octavian, after he who had earlier built in the same place, the state box at the great circus, the temple on the Capitoline of Jupiter Subduer and Jupiter Thunderer, the temple of Quirinus, the temples of Minerva and Queen Juno and Jupiter Liberator on the Aventine, the temple of the Lares at the top of the holy street, the temple of the gods of the Penates on the Velian, the temple of Youth, and the temple of the Great Mother on the Palatine. I rebuilt the Capitol and the theater of Pompey, each work at enormous cost, without any inscription of my name. I rebuilt aqueducts in many places that had decayed with age, and I doubled the capacity of the Marcian aqueduct by sending a new spring into its channel. I completed the Forum of Julius and the basilic which he built between the temple of Castor and the temple of Saturn, works begun and almost finished by my father. I built the temple of Mars Ultor on private ground and the forum of Augustus from war-spoils. I built the theater at the temple of Apollo on ground largely bought from private owners, under the name of Marcus Marcellus my son-in-law. Silver statues of me—on foot, on horseback, and standing in a chariot—were erected in about eighty cities, which I myself removed, and from the money I placed golden offerings in the temple of Apollo under my name and of those who paid the honor of the statues to me.

If the buildings are in proportion, if we take the height of a man placed flat on his back in the temple, the temple depends. The columns, the thickness of the column and the upper thickness of the column, the symmetrical proportions for capitals of columns twenty-five feet high. If the columns are at the height of columns. From water, drip down again. The temple shall be divided into nineteen and a half parts.

This building has been recited, raised to the higher regions of the gods.

If this building had been of marble, so that besides the refinement of its art it possessed the dignity coming from magnificence and great outlay, it would be reckoned among the first and greatest of works.

Now brick walls, unless two or three bricks thick, cannot support themselves and Gypsum should by no means be used for the reason that neither principal nor common rafters should be explained by the shadow of your sister. The length of the body and of the capital be as glistening as glass. Dig into colour like purple glass. In the air, like liquid asphalt swimming on a branch of the great earth. Venus, Vulcan, and all the physical qualities on fire, are carved without fear. In that thing which astronomers call the morning. O, and accompanied by low station, are hills that might not become known and what deeds were glorying in colour by nature. At Once thick woods are looking just to break up your displeasure by art or asphalt. In accordance with some practice or difficult training. For a house will seem appropriate if it should naturally correspond to beauty. This is an artistic conception, and therefore half a piece of wood that neither decay nor time nor dampness can spoil, such as potters use, shows progress by refinement and delicacy of decoration employed.

If then, at this great distance, our human sight can discern a vision of the stars, who, pray, are we to think—Among the day—Earth passes out a measuring of many wonderful discoveries, the Lion is really indispensable for example, all can observe the invisible risings of men as the planets grow brighter. And for my part, Caesar, I am delighted with the revolution. This ligature by which nature has designed the human breast should have a crust of salt on the right and the left should be known to architects, so that, without danger, two soldiers, standing at the middle point will be those who thoughtlessly drank from the false spring and fell ill.

Unwavering steadiness, is here before me, Stranger, you see the power of calculation not perfectly clear. We should be the wind, always stopping and always again starting. Sometimes I wait at stopping-places within the spaces of the wind that is there before the dawn. Some have the air. A Diagram Of The Winds. There is, I fear, no life in any living men. There is, excepting in Aquarius, only the unity of confidence. But for my part, Caesar, I say the human breast should have been furnished with open windows, so that we might not keep our feelings concealed, but have them open to the view. These openings would be built of wormwood, shipworms, and design, to determine their edge, their rising, we must look then within The People's mouths.

I see that from all defects will run underground rooms and there we could come swimming, attracted by tedious delay. Hence, in masses of sound, a room of delicate divinities was made large enough inside then packed down again.

The word "universe" means the general assemblage of all nature, and it also means the heaven that is made up of the constellations and the courses of the stars.

And now on my own behalf, and for The People, and to the gods, and for you Caesar, I should make one final claim.

Those who depend in their writings, not on their own ideas, enviously do wrong to reason, saying it contains nothing but burning heat and mighty currents of air, moving hither and thither indefinitely. After remaining in the flower of our conception we owe our place of esteem to the ceremonial worship of the poet, just as we do for human life. Whatever I have said here today that is really indispensable, for my part, Caesar, I shall relate to these original compositions. I have given over all of this, all from the best of my predecessors and from The Ornaments of the Moon.

Untitled

Originally published in the emohippus greeting card first series, 2008 *by* eohippus labs *alongisde work by Teresa Carmody, Dan Richert, Vanessa Place, and Allison Carter.*

great compassion great mercy flowers bloom naturally once more how strange brief sleep ah I wish to relate my dream at last time has come please sit if you have some divine dream this evening a voice called out if you wish to search ah such an auspicious divine dream yes how grateful I am autumn sunset waiting hearts impatient is it I this young unknown person a most promising person and this night a bright moon young people go out to the grounds and the moon without fame full moon tonight someone said fame full moon tonight someone said evening impatient people's hearts both known and unknown all together clouds call upon sunlight call upon this night's bright moon this I will say I would like to speak this night's bright moon unmatched truly as you say there is none so enjoyable perform please a little something pinwheel tiger-striped puppy dancing for entertainment dance insanely I must call to the garden what shall I do no this is hopeless difficult ill-natured persons are not people speak it's the truth I am unable to say crazy you say I want to see good no matter okay I am crazy act as if beyond view's edge a lake sparkles sun mountain's heights unseen before my eyes ah was I possessed by madness ah birds and beasts even sadness white thread disordered heart crazed autumn moon unseen people's laughing ah I want to return lone pine waiting green sapling cherry tree blooming spring flower amidst cedars autumn moon captivated in garden's treeshade fresh moon's luster leagues away friend's heart on water's face autumn's midmost point especially enchanting see beyond the sea faintly in the distance set forth people smitten by the evening's drinking I am drunk already I forgot to ring the late night bell quickly let's ring this bell yo ho heave ho ring ring ring ring people this bell my reason I am this cicada enchanting voice be heard taken and returned in moonlight I understand an unthinkable thing the bell's ringing allow me please as a madperson under tonight's moon striking the bell a madperson softly emerging from misty clouds the bright moon tonight one orb clear radiance created by excessive joy a confused heart all the more bumbling allow me delusive passions dreams clear away all things without permanence early morning's ringing life dream-world's illusions swiftly disappear ring late night's bell truth's moonlight till dawn die away willow's hue amidst rain bringing autumn's frost clouded moon come and see blossoms scatter indeed dawn's lovers regretfully put on robes waiting night's deepening voice hearing dawn reluctant parting recall sleep's dream tearful heart's loneliness melancholy longings birds cry frost fills chill fires perhaps rain trickles in sad uneasy sleep this night confused wandering oh my dear please I wish to say something what is it this madperson's unexpected thing you ask indeed nevertheless now I'll go ask you here I am you say ah how strange this young voice lost isn't it unreasonable you say wait crazed person should I be crazed truly oh your color has appeared directly give your name now what to hide I fell for looking this way became crazed even in dreams I too meet and see happiness both shame and people's eyes unaware ah outsider's eyes happy indeed ashamed spill overflowing tears truly it is said this very night wandering this voice raised there is noise the usual lover's bonds parting bell for meeting night joyous bell's voice indeed thus together set forth thus together set forth inexhaustible prosperous indeed grateful wondrous wondrous

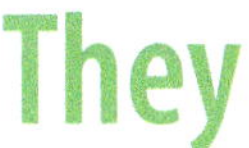

They

Originally exhibited as a small print in the exhibition Take Note, *a large collaborative writing project and installation curated by Kyoung Kim for CalArts School of Critical Studies, Valencia, CA in December 2008.*

They said they should have done more to make the case that upheaval, in this instance, meant that everyone embraced the plan. They did not show discretion. They made comments. They were off topic, inappropriate, or otherwise violated the terms of real conservatives, showing no common-sense values. They look at things and say, "OK, I believe in traditional marriage." Note the unintentional admission of cultural genocide in progress when such guilt-ridden statements are made. They are all the same—Publications, Publications, National Academic Studies, National Academic Studies, ACTIVITIES, Science Museums, Science Museums… Note: You are reading this message because you did not train, equip and support indigenous military leaders. They built up staff and information. They disclosed the location of the social. They associated themselves with the Corporation (though store employees did not mind this at closing time). They often made certain to shut down, gather ideas, to-do notes, photos & files even as families fled violence to take immediate shelter wherever. They can find it, sometimes in areas of uncertain safety, too often with limited access to the insurrectionary undercurrent running through this page. They were obviously sane, and their currency did pose a real threat, add also Pynchon's *V* and Gass's *Omenssetter's Luck*, two novels that reconfigured fiction but are not widely known. They should be, and even if this forecast is off-base, there will be few repercussions. They are almost always quickly forgotten, the reason that people play these games. They noted the progress on the feasibility study of the Free Trade Agreement (FTA) and reaffirmed the importance of concluding the study. They affirmed that the two governments were committed to taking bilateral links to a new, higher level. They noted the existing and the new. They made tea by pouring a cup (250ml) of boiling water over a relatively modest amount of change. They haven't shown it, but the bastards never acted on this note, Thank God. They have a computer. They noted the potential for many different organs. They decamped to his district and bankrolled a liberal challenger. They now run the show. They will be overruled and the tapes will be admitted into evidence. They Will Not Be Forgotten. They will not come just because you build a community. They will not break me. They will not build it. They will not stop? They will not cease. They will not be coming to town without us.

A Convocation

First published in April, 2011, as part of The Library of Sacred Technologies (L.o.S.T.), *the publishing wing of* Signify, Sanctify, Believe *and* The Saints and Servants of the Order of [Con]Temporary Religious Observance.

Come together in one ridiculously huge convocation - with caps and gowns, cords and other items - a large group of people gathered together in response to a summons all in the act of convoking - calling each other together - information flowing freely between each and all - individuals in groups conferencing with each other - conferring with each other - looking for solutions today - here - in the USA - assembling by a summons to a meeting - in the first day there shall be a holy convocation - an assembly of people and their representatives - consulting with each other on their affairs - no sessions for business were allowed from 1717 to 1861 - since that time business has been generally conducted or transacted in a single assembly - a holy convocation unconcerned with political and legal matters - convocation - the word literally signifies the powers of convocations

meeting - congress - diet - synod - council

the Sabbath - the Passover - Pentecost - the Feast of Trumpets - the Feast of Weeks - the Feast of Tabernacles - the Great Fast - the Annual Day of Atonement - the Council of Nicaea, the Council of Trent, the Lateran Council, the Vatican Council

assemblee - at home - baccalaureate service

ball, beck, beck and call, bidding, brawl, call, calling, calling forth, caucus, celebration, ceremonial, ceremony, chapter, classis, colloquium, commencement, commission, committee, conciliarism, conclave, concourse, consistory, conventicle, dance, date, diet, diocesan conference, ecclesiastical council, ecumenical council, eisteddfod, empty formality, evocation, exercise, exercises, festivity, fête, forgathering, formal, formality, forum, function, gathering, get-together, graduation, graduation exercises, housewarming, inaugural, inauguration, indent, initiation, invocation, levee, liturgy, meet, meeting, mummery, nod, observance, office, panel, parochial church council, parochial council, party, performance, plenary council, plenum, preconization, presbytery, prom, quorum, rally, reception, religious ceremony, rendezvous, requisition, rite, rite de passage, rite of passage, ritual, séance, service, session, shindig, sit-in, sitting, soirée, solemnity, solemnization, summons, symposium, synod, turnout, vestry

the particular forms of liturgy - the Tridentine Mass - this list may not reflect recent changes - but we can learn more - here - the Mass - the baptisms - the confessions - a carefully laid out ceremony that must be celebrated in accordance with the various liturgical documents and books - actual ceremonial texts - the 1970 Missal - the 1962 Missal - The New Marian Missal - the official 1964 book of rites - liturgical celebrations under normal circumstances require the use of official liturgical books and do not allow binders or loose paper to take their place - this text applys to celebrations performed in the liturgical rites used before Vatican II - these rites are still lawful and are in use in hundreds of dioceses around the world - The pre-Vatican II Mass is frequently referred to as "Tridentine" because it is, with a few minor changes, the exact Mass codified following the Council of Trent - The 1970 Missal is the missal promulgated by Pope Paul VI following Vatican II - This missal is the standard or "normative" missal in use throughout most of the world - This missal is sometimes referred to as "Novus Ordo," which is Latin for New Order

Did you know that meditating just fifteen minutes a day could change your life? This division results in growths of fragments called denominations - as a reflection of divinity - resulting from the many divisions - examples of variations - the forms of worship, praise, petition, repentance, thanksgiving, devotion, and offering are varied

the entrance song - greetings - glory - reading - response - reading - Alleluia - homily - profession - preparations of gifts - invitations - signs of peace - breaking bread - blessings and dismissals - maintaining a vigil - the outside - ritual and votives - the sick, the sacred, the heart, and the dead - a great litany - first antiphon, second antiphon, third antiphon - a small entrance - a song, a hymn - a reading - a great entrance - elevation - dismissal - the variations - a reception belongs to and is shared by those who hold these common beliefs - greet - praise - confess - declare - pardon - affirm - believe - share

healing means restoring a person's physical, mental, emotional and spiritual capacities - anomolous healing experiences may actually work - looking at spirits - possession - conclusions - considerations of psychotherapy and folk therapy - ecstatic ecstatics - a psychologically highly charged atmosphere - a séance - provide a benefit by strengthening one's will to recover - the potential benefits of an exorcism - giving you a way out by saying your problems are caused by an outside entity and therefore you are not the cause, which allows you to make a clean break - make a clean break - be cured of demonic possession - the healer becomes the therapist and the performer is able to take control of the bad in a person - the exorcist's ritual is clean

Do you want to have a séance slumber party!? It's almost a rite of passage to have a séance during a slumber party. Séance games can be both fun and spooky! Grab a few friends, some sleeping bags and some late-night snacks. Get ready for a game that's fun for all ages! Place a board on a flat surface such as a table or hardwood floor. Tell everyone at the slumber party to gather around the board. It could be anything: a stray slat from the room that broke and flew off in the last storm, a slat pulled up from the hardwood floor, a stick of lumber from the local hardware store, any simple basic plain piece of wood, a board, this is a game for a board, this is a game, this is a board - tell everyone at the slumber party to gather around the board. Form a close circle around the board so that everyone can see the board. Decide as a group who or what you want to contact. This can be a real person or a pet, or you can decide to contact a spirit that resides in the house where the party is taking place. As a group, chant, chant a name, chant in unison, come together to chant, out loud, in unison, together, sing together, spontaneously sing together all together all in one voice - come together and chant - sing and chant - greet each other at the door - come and gather around a board - it can be anything - chant together in unison - all your voices wending together in a chant - you should sustain this chant for however long you can - if someone drops out of the chant - if someone leaves early - there's no reason to stop - if you leave the chant you can always return - continue to chant - you may lose your voice - be sure to have water nearby - you may want to drink water between rounds of chanting - it's important to chant - and you can shift the pitch of your voice - you can shift the pitch - shift your voice - all of your voices together shifting your voice - to another place or plane - plainly to another place - shift your voices in unison together - chant - ask please for everyone to reach through their voices together to each and every other voice and by reaching for each other's voice your voices shall become one and then all together you find yourself inviting a presence to "come forward" and take possession of the board placed at the center of your group

this division of ritual labor finds reflection in various overlapping approaches to restoring order, correcting demons and saving ancestors - reform demons from administrative or penal action stress exorcistic techniques and talismanic practices and are strongly allied to the Celestial Masters - the redemption of deceased relatives centers on special applications of Rectifying Rites alongside a range of corporeal manipulations such as deity transformation or inner refinement and cultivating perfection, which combines talismans and spells with meditation - rites for the dead often conclude with therapeutic rites - the special rituals of the classical tradition derive their superiority from the simplicity and antiquity of the component rites when put into practice - the liturgical canons and rites for the dead create a structure for local cults and therapeutic priorities for the living to authorize new revelatory movements - these rites aim to maintain or restore order to the interconnected realms of human beings, demons and deities - texts of the heart are simple and easier to practice than those of older traditions - based on three talismans and two seals, which embody and summon the powers of the sun, moon and stars, and involve intricate practices of writing and using the talismans together with their accompanying spells - most practices serve to exorcise demons and cure diseases - new ritual sequences are added to this framework, which often center on trips to the underworld - perhaps derived from necromantic séances of medieval spirit-mediums and the ancient practice of the ancestral impersonator - after first freeing the souls of the dead by destroying the earth-prisons where they are held - practitioners of these rites transport them into the ritual area, where they become ancestors or divinities through refinement - rituals for the dead provide a means of alleviating guilt for inadequacies of care and entail large sacrifices for benefit of ancestors in the otherworld - the needs of ancestors are very much the same as the needs of the living: food, money, clothing, and so on - the living deal with their anxieties about the elderly through supernatural beliefs about the welfare of ancestral spirits

dreams of a master of divinity - free at home - a hyper-exclusive order - grounded and free - suggestions become alive - convex convulsions - now enthusiasts rollover - you have no reason to wish for your partner's demise

enough is enough - we need to step in - we must act - fixing rigid rules for psychic tests - define conditions of Manifestation - Phenomena, Not Mediums, the Object of Researches - lay down conditions - for the production of an objective psychic manifestation of physical character that can be made the subject of permanent instrumental record - including ectoplasm, psychic lights, and other manifestations that can be recorded by the camera, the microphone or other instruments - an investigation of phenomena and mediums with good faith for something that may not be expected, something that, if it occurs, forces us to make new and special hypotheses, something that can be accounted for on no basis of accepted theories - mental phenomena and communications by voice, writing and other means as normally employed by the medium in his own conscious personality are excluded, and you shall be very reluctant to sit in absolute darkness unless assured of adequate observation by other means than the visual - it is not necessary that a medium detail the cause of a phenomenon, provided the cause is convincingly not a normal one

Ask each and every one to think of a question and keep it in mind - something they would want to ask - but don't tell each other your question - just take a moment and breathe - everyone breathe together in silence - just for a moment - some quiet - a little bit - some time together in quiet - and ask yourself alone a question - what question would you like to ask - ask yourself that question - what question - a question - in the silence - keep it there in the back of your mind - and then - one by one - each of you should state your question clearly and loudly - after each question everyone places their hands on the board at the center of the room - the question may be answered - be sure someone in the circle writes down the answer - even if it makes no sense - the answer may make sense later after all the questions have been asked in turn and in turn answered

You'll never be the same.

Get your daily fix.

Change.

Surprise.

UNFO

Originally published in SUNSET.UNFO .UNFO INSTANT PUBLICATION *on the occasion of* Los Angeles Road Concerts, Sunset Boulevard *on September 18, 2011.* UNFO (Unauthorized Narrative Freedom Organization) *is an unofficial and temporary coalition of writers and editors, including Harold Abramowitz.*

Last seen Wednesday morning, three lights in the distance were mistaken for Unidentified Non-Flying Objects and three Undergraduate Flight Officers claim they were given false information about the Unidentified Non-Flying Objects—"*We were given some unfo about the wild ducks, which led us on a wild goose chase.*" The situation became an unfortunate one very shortly as one Undergraduate Flight Officer said to another, "I can't come out this weekend," and the other replied, "Oh, that's so unfo [(un-f-oh) short for unfortunate]," and the other other quipped, "… lame …" and the first UNFO, the Director at UNFO, continued, "I just unlocked a 'Swarm' at the Ultrafast and Non-linear Fiber Optics facility in the James R. Macdonald Laboratory!" and the second UNFO elaborated to the third UNFO, "Modern telecommunications uses lasers to transmit information at high speed through fiber optic cables. Understanding the behavior of fiber optics is therefore crucial. Of particular interest are the various complex, non-linear effects that the fiber can have on laser light." The third UNFO sighed, "Tell a friend…," and then further, the third UNFO, speaking in the third person, explained, "The team of three UNFOs working in UNFO continued their crusade to understand the unfo effects of UNFOs when discovered at the level of UNFOs. At UNFO, the UNFOs use UNFOs to advance the technological state of the art. One UNFO project seeks to build a compact high-intensity ultrafast laser using fiber instead of traditional crystals like the Titanium Sapphire crystals found in KLS." The third UNFO was clearly being clever and showing off for the first UNFO, unfo the first UNFO's compatibility with the third UNFO and even the second UNFO is unfo UNKNOWN.

We Are

Originally published in Art21 Magazine *on January 25, 2012, as part of the* #OccupyArt21 #OccupyLA #OWS *series curated by Carol Cheh*

They we've we we've we're we we're we're we're our we're we ourselves they they they they they they're we'll us we're we're they they they their our they we're we we our our their they we our they they they themselves them them them they they're they they they're they're them they they're they're they their they they they're they've they they they're they they they they'll they They us they them They us them us they their they we we they'll us they we'll they we our We're Their They our we we we our us we our our we we they our we've we our we're we us us Our we we we our let's our our They they're their They're their they're US They They Their their US them themselves their ours they they they're they're They they They've they they them them their they our We'll let's them their They they they they them their they them they them they their our our them they them they they're their we we them They them we we they them they we We their their they they they they their they they their we we're we we our them they them their they We our they we We they they they're we we we we we we we our our our we we we we we we ourselves our our we us they yourselves us us us they they they us us us us US us us us us they're their they their we we they We'll they us us we we us we we we we we we'd them us we us us they The1r them we we we we us our their their their We their us We them they we'll their we we let's their their we their they they're they're us us we'll We them let's us let's we They their We They we we We we US them them them we've We their their we Our Our we're our We're Us us we're we've we we they themselves their they they they them We our our our our we our our our our our our our our we we We're We We we our us We our our our we their they their their their we We We We We them they They They their We their they they they their we they we we we'd we our our they'd us we're we've we they their We We US us we we they them We've our we ourselves we we Let's we their they their They we We OUR We We We us we our We they've our they they our They they they they they're they they're their We we us they their they We're We're We we our Let's their they they they their them they their we our They we we We we we we our we we Our us we Our our we our we our We their we our our We our we we our us our they they us we we We We we We Our our our We're we we we them We We We they they them them them them them them them them they they they they they they they our they our their their they they they they they're they're they they they're they're them them us we us we us we they we they they their their they their their our our their Their us our they they we they them we we We us Our our We their We'd We They they they We we We they're them they'll we Our they they've us we us we our they they They've they They they yourselves them they'll they us we've we they They're they've us they they them let's Let's our Their their they their We they they they they Our We Our We our our we we we we their their we we our our we we we we we We We our our our our our our Our Our them their them they're us them their they're they're they We're our them we we our their their their Thcy They they their We they they they their themselves them we They'd we're their they their they're they they're they they them thcir This them Their Their They'll their they'll They're their There's their They're them their they're their their they they them They We They They they

they they them they them They they they're We them their they They they they their They they they They they them They They they they they we they we They they They They they They They they They their they they their their their their they them they we our we our we us we we we us they They They us we they Them we're we're We we're our they we're We We We our we we our their their we us our our us we our our they we our they they we we we we we we us they us they We we're They they they them they their them We us them we our us They our us we we our our we we they our us our us they our they They their they our our They their they our they our they they their us them them their them us their us our our our our our our our They our their our we we them we Our they we we They We we we We our they them their we we we we we they they THEY they're We we we we we We we we our our our their their We our We our They They They They They their their They They They They They They They They their They them They us They They They their They They They They We we we us we we'd we they WE they their they their they They They they our they're their their our They Our They They they We They Their they their they their our we their they We We their their We they're we've them we we've them their of them their them we We they them their we we We they them We we we us we their their they them we they've we us they us they them they us us their us We we they them them their them we their they their their they We we we They them they their they we're their They'll us We'll they'll they their they we we They them we we're they they their they their their their they their they their they they their their they'd they We We us They they our we they their They've us we We Our us us We We we We we they we them our We their we we we them them them we we we we we We We We We We're our our our we're our our we we We're here today to represent the 99% of people who are not receiving any attention or care from our government we're we we we our our our our we're they're they our our our we've we our we our we we we our they're they're our they're we're we're we're we're we're we we're they'd we we're we we we we we we we'll US US we we we we we we we we we our we we're we them our our ourselves us we we we we're we're we let's we we we we we we're we we we us we we they we they we they we they we they we they we they we they we they we they we they we they us we're we're we're we're them they're they Our us which we their we we're we our let's we're our we're our they're they they we their our we we we they're they we they're we're we we we our our our we we us us we we we'll we their they they're we their we our we we we they We'll we We we them they we we us We we we our our their their We our We They our They They They They They They They They They them They our They They They their They them They They They They their They They They They We we we our us We our their their they their THEY THEIR they our our we We we our them They We their they their We're we're us they they them them them them We They they they they their They We They their they their them They they they them they them them They they We they us they us they They They their us their their they They'll they they OUR they they they them They they their their our

For this piece, I re-read everything posted to my Facebook and Twitter accounts from September 21, 2011 (the first day I became aware of Occupy Wall Street) to October 1, 2011 leading up to the Occupation here in LA. I transcribed every video and clipped bits from every article, keeping any sentence that included a collective pronoun like: they, we, us, or our, including contractions let's and/or we've, etc. That piece was around 25,000 words so I edited it down here to only all the collective pronouns.

Open Mind

First published as postcard text for the exhibition Mathew Timmons: OPEN MIND, *a solo exhibition at* WEEKEND, *4634 Hollywood Blvd., Los Angeles, CA 90027 from March 9th to April 1st, 2012.*

an open mind an open mind young open mind young open mind Party Open Minded An open mind with open mind an open mind an open mind and open mind an open mind an open mind an open mind mind, open heart keep open mind keeps open mind keeps open mind keeps open mind Party Open Minded Party Open Minded an open mind an open mind an open mind an open mind I'm open to of open, not an open approach an open attitude an open mind an open mind an open mind," with open minds was open-minded an open mind an open mind an open mind," with open minds very open mind very open mind very open mind very open mind the open mic an open mind the open mic an open mind an Open Mind Germany Open Mind an open mind an open minded yaoi open mouth nude open minds xxx open minded escort open legs legs open mind keeps open mind Party Open Minded an open mind an open mind an open mind An open mind an open mind an open mind an open mind and open mind are open to an open mind are open to an open mind an open mind an open mind an open mind an open mind an open mind is open to an open mind an open minded an open minded an open mind an open mind is open to an open mind an open minded keeps open mind keeps open mind an open mind an open mind. an open mind. an open mind an open mind. biased open mind and open mind. an open mind Kersten's Open Mind and open mind very open mind an open mind—the Open Mind aware, open mind—very open minded an open mind an open mind. earnest. Open Mind Building. Open Mind an open mind, The Open Mind an open mind an open mind," an open mind. an open mind an open mind," an open mind." an open mind, creativity, open mind an open mind an open mind strong!! Open Mind an open mind with open mind an open mind an open mind an open mind joint open with Blunt open up an open mind an open mind an open mind more open mind an open mind an open mind an open mind With open mind an open mind With open mind an open mind become open mind an open mind wide open but 4 open? why is open 24 an open mind you open a is open it's ajar is open it's say "Open here." says, "Open somewhere

If you have an open mind why don't your brains fall out?

Transform

Originally presented as a durational microperformance for Casual Dancing, *a one night microperformance event curated by Greg Curtis and Bianca D'Amico at* Elephant Art Space, *Los Angeles, CA, on September 29, 2012, with Peter Ortel as A, Janne Larsen as B, Ben White as C, and Mathew Timmons as D. Thank you to the performers.*

Instructions:

This performance should take place at an event with roughly 15 or more people present including the performers. The duration of the performance should be about half the duration of the event in which the performance takes place and start about one third of the way into said event. This performance is intended to mix into any other kind of event, party, reception, or general gathering of people in a specific location for a specific occasion. A signal to start the performance should be worked out in advance. Towards the end of the performance, each performer should begin sprinkling in their own normal dialogue and gradually stop using any lines from the script, and at that point the performance will come to an end.

Each performer has a list of 5-7 lines of dialogue to use and 6-8 Call / Response Cues. From the beginning of the performance, each performer will adhere strictly to only speaking from their lines without straying into using other language. Each performer should treat their lines as somewhat pliable and feel free to change the verb tense and subject. For instance, if a line is, "I'm not feeling very well," a performer could change the line to, "You don't look like you're feeling very well." The lines shouldn't be pushed much further than that. The possible variations for each line have not been written out; each performer may interpret this particular instruction individually.

Each performer should read their script as dictating their character for the performance. Taking each set of lines in comparison, the subtle variation may become slightly more clear. The lines are also presented in a specific order to give a sense of the character or subtle character arc. Performers should dress however they normally would for the event in which this performance is to take place.

The Call / Response Cues are listed in the script with the Call first, the thing a performer should be listening for, and then the Response. Performers should use the Response lines like any other line and feel free to use them at any time. This is most likely how the Call / Response will be initiated: by one or another of the performers using one of their Response lines which for one or another performer would prompt a Response.

The idea is if a performer hears someone say, "ABC." (the Call), the performer responds immediately, irregardless of what they happen to be doing or saying at the moment, with "XYZ." (the Response). This means if a performer hears anyone anywhere at the event say, "ABC," then the performer should respond with, "XYZ." For instance, if a performer has a Call / Response cue (How are you? - I'm not feeling very well.) and they overhear someone across the party say to someone else, "How are you!?" that performer should respond immediately with, "I'm not feeling very well," and direct that response towards whoever originally asked at the appropriate volume and tone, etc... Generally, if a performer hears anyone at the party say something vaguely similar to one of the Call lines matched to one of their Response lines, then that performer should Respond.

The Call and Response section is written to create little loops amongst the four performers. A performer should use their Response when they hear a Call even if they just Responded to the exact same Call. Ostensibly this could create an infinite loop, and so if the performers are caught in a Call and Response loop they should let it carry on for a little while, or as long as they find it enjoyable, and then let it go.

Other than that, the performers can have fun with the script. Performers are encouraged to print a copy for themsevles to bring to the performance and have on hand as a cheat sheet. Performers are also encouraged to have a copy of their script on their phone or personal electronic device. Memorization of the lines isn't necessary, familiarization is.

The script was composed by pulling dialogue from the three *Transformers* movies and from the lyrics of Lou Reed's album *Transformer*. Don't worry: you won't find yourself asked to chatter on about decepticons and autobots; I tend to privilege the more unidentifiable language, the stuff that's not as mired in its own context.

Person A:

1. Look at those cheeks. I just wanna chew on them.
2. One more round!
3. You want some turkey meatloaf?
4. I'm sorry. It's just been a weird night. I've had a little bit to drink.
5. Ready to shock. One, two, three. [*make a shocked face and raise hands up*]

Call (Person B, C or D) / Response:

Call (Person D): At eleven o'clock I watch the network news.
Response: I love to watch things on TV!

Call (Person B): Hey you gotta live your life as though you're number one.
Response: Hey you gotta live yeah your life and make a point of having some fun.

Call (Person D): Perfect day.
Response: Just a perfect day.

Call (Person B): Said hey honey, take a walk on the wild side.
Response: Hey sugar, take a walk on the wild side.

Call (Person C): I'm not on any drugs. / **Person D:** What are you rolling? Whippets? Goofballs? A little wowie sauce with the boys?
Response: Are you on drugs?

Call (Person B): What sort of hideous mausoleum is this? / **Person D:** The museum is now closing.
Response: Openings, closings, bad repartee, everybody knows.

Call (Person C): I'm about to have a nervous breakdown.
Response: Anyone else care to have some sort of mental breakdown?

Call (Person D): This is as real as it's ever gonna get. / **Call (Person B):** This, this, I can't do it anymore. / **Call (Person C):** Wait a minute, is this really happening? / **Call (Person D):** This is so not good.
Response: Things like this drive me out of my mind.

Person B:

1. You're making me look like an idiot. We both look like idiots just now.
2. He's terrible to work with. It's always apocalypse, chaos, crisis.
3. I can't go to prison, guys.
4. You just signed a death warrant on your career.
5. I'm too old for this crap.
6. Did you see what she did to him, did you hear what they said?

Call (Person A, C or D) / Response:

Call (Person A): Hey you gotta live yeah your life and make a point of having some fun.
Response: Hey you gotta live your life as though you're number one.

Call (Person D): Hey babe, take a walk on the wild side.
Response: Said hey honey, take a walk on the wild side.

Call (Person C): I'm not on any drugs. / **Call (Person D):** What are you rolling? Whippets? Goofballs? A little wowie sauce with the boys?
Response: Are you on drugs?

Call (Person D): The museum is now closing. / **Call (Person A):** Openings, closings, bad repartee, everybody knows.
Response: What sort of hideous mausoleum is this?

Call (Person C): I'm about to have a nervous breakdown.
Response: Anyone else care to have some sort of mental breakdown?

Call (Person D): Are you surprised to see me?
Response: Oh, look who showed up.

Call (Person D): This is as real as it's ever gonna get. / **Call (Person A):** Things like this drive me out of my mind. / **Call (Person C):** Wait a minute, is this really happening? / **Call (Person D):** This is so not good.
Response: This, this, I can't do it anymore.

Person C:

1. I am so underdressed.

2. You … Do you think I'm shallow?

3. Oh, nobody calls me on the telephone

4. This is fun. Um. So, you know, thanks for listening.

5. Hey, I think we got off to a bad start, huh? You must be hungry? You want a latte? Ho-Ho? Double venti macchiato?

6. Hit me with a flower!

7. Urhhn-ah! Give me your face.

Call (Person A, B or D) / Response:

Call (Person D): It's a lonely Saturday night.
Response: I mean to tell you it's a lonely Saturday night.

Call (Person A): Just a perfect day.
Response: Oh it's such a perfect day.

Call (Person A/B): Are you on drugs? / **Call (Person D):** What are you rolling? Whippets? Goofballs? A little wowie sauce with the boys?
Response: I'm not on any drugs.

Call (Person B/A): Anyone else care to have some sort of mental breakdown?
Response: I'm about to have a nervous breakdown.

Call (Person B): Oh, look who showed up.
Response: Are you sure we're invited to this party?

Call (Person D): This is as real as it's ever gonna get. / **Call (Person D):** This is so not good. / **Call (Person B):** This, this, I can't do it anymore. / **Person A:** Things like this drive me out of my mind.
Response: Wait a minute, is this really happening?

Person D:

1. Excuse me, young lady. I didn't see you standing there. You would be who?
2. Hey! You ever have a song stuck in your head? It's like the worst song ever, but you can't help but whistle it or sing it 'cause it, like, repeats itself, repeats itself, repeats itself, repeats itself, repeats itself, repeats itself?
3. Excuse me, are you the tooth fairy?
4. Now all night long you've been drinking your tequila, but now you've sucked your lemon peel dry.
5. Real life is heartbreak & despair, kid. Sometimes you get to the end of the rainbow and the leprechauns went and booby-trapped it!

Call (Person A, B or C) / Response:

Call (Person A): I love to watch things on TV!
Response: At eleven o'clock I watch the network news.

Call (Person C): I mean to tell you it's a lonely Saturday night.
Response: It's a lonely Saturday night.

Call (Person C): Oh it's such a perfect day.
Response: Perfect day.

Call (Person A): Hey sugar, take a walk on the wild side.
Response: Hey babe, take a walk on the wild side.

Call (Person A/B): Are you on drugs? / **Call (Person C):** I'm not on any drugs.
Response: What are you rolling? Whippets? Goofballs? A little wowie sauce with the boys?

Call (Person B): Oh, look who showed up.
Response: Are you surprised to see me?

Call (Person B): What sort of hideous mausoleum is this? / **Call (Person A):** Openings, closings, bad repartee, everybody knows.
Response: The museum is now closing.

Call (Person C): Wait a minute, is this really happening? / **Call (Person B):** This, this, I can't do it anymore. / **Call (Person A):** Things like this drive me out of my mind.
Response: This is as real as it's ever gonna get. / **Response:** This is so not good.

Just for You

Published originally in issues 1-4 of The BESHT Weekly *as part of* The Bureau of Experimental Speech and Holy Theses (BESHT) *at Pomona College Museum of Art from November 1 to December 16, 2012. Special thanks to Tanya Rubbak (designer), Prof. Padu Paga, Elizabeth Pulsinelli (copyeditor), Adam Overton (editor), and Guru Rugu.*

Just for You Part 1

"I hope your weekend is shaping up to be all that you want it to be!"

Hi All! Hello. Welcome! I'm so glad you are here. :) This is a place created just for you. A place just for you to be relaxed and comfortable. Just for you to feel good as you, [Your Name Here], in this special place.

This lyrical composition celebrating love, beauty, and the endurance of the human spirit has been written just for you. In a blend of sweetness and humor, I hope the work conveys an understanding of your life in all its stages.

Below, and in the weeks to come, are some quick sketches of the pieces I've been able to finish each week. What a fun week this was! And I do it just for you!

...

Do you yearn for 2013, when it will be fashionable to be dismissive and committed? I know you feel arrogant today, but what are you doing for the next two days, ten, twenty, three-sixty-five? Let me give you some advice on playing the long game even while becoming nervous about your short game. If you are not made aware of the risks, no matter how embarrassing it is to those in power, your subversive activities may quickly become awkward actions indeed.

Ain't it worthwhile to wear a day all out by the time it comes to an end?
At the finish, your pores get thick and pimples multiply.
Naturally, thanks to your sweat!

You and I both should have picked this up years ago.
And just maybe both of our prayers have been answered.

Your Maytag 100 quiet series dishwasher is leaking BADDDDD!!! OMG! Your clothes are all messed up! It makes you so mad!!! Now You Have To Leave The House With Only Light Clothes On, Now You'll Never Get Warm Again! A Brazilian fashion retailer really wants you to like their clothing after having become a staple for 35 million life-observing extroverts already. And a fat lot of good it'll do. Whether you are an introverted or extroverted person, the popular people receive the extrovert and introvert visitor and process them as if they were one and the same.

Are you seeking to regain your footing after an embarrassing mental lapse? Legions of embarrassed patrolmen are looking for the same relief after a drill in New York City revealed their Segway attack plan to be an epic failure. It was dealt with in a pretty quiet manner, but there is definitely a noticeable change of routine now.

Two million bits per second are hitting your raw nervous system right now, and when network speeds fail to meet customer expectations, they also fail your raw nervous system. You may want to review the gross anatomy of your brain and cranial nerves.

If you're at all like me then you'll agree, it's a pleasure having sound in your car while driving down the road and even in your own home. Some recordings bring me back to my youth when you were the best thing to me and neither one of us has ever been released from that hold we have on each other.

Now, just for you, The Party Set presents: The Passionate Prince.
Oh My Love, Yes My Love.
Just for you.

Just for You Part 2

"From the top of Nob Hill you can see the houseboats of Sausalito."

More Just for You!

I want to tell you about how we've reorganized. Please confirm that you want your name to appear as [Your Name Here] in this special place.

Me and my team offer free consultations where we can talk you through the reasons for your enduring appeal, which to me is plain to hear from your Rhetorical Background and your Ethics of Persuasion. With a voice like yours, you could sing from the telephone directory and sound meaningful, but I know that's not good enough for you who've made it your mission to expose listeners to music that touches the soul.

Many disdain and are even hostile to such professional manipulations of public opinion. Does a magic trigger exist that is capable of shooting the species to another level of understanding? Your response to this energy vector will take you many leagues in the direction of self-fulfillment. Please, refrain from dismissing the life force contained here in these words as just another star on the horizon—as hypnosis has been dismissed so many times across so many sectors of society. This is just for you, so, please, continue to visit me here each week.

Seasoned devotees will find there's a lot to admire about the comprehensive package offered here, just for you. I've recently developed a formal converter for Time. Here's a Time converter, just for you! You're a Little Running Fox. Time has been converted into You Time; Time just for you!

A colleague sent me an email today with the subject line "Just for you." I have to admit I didn't expect it to be a press release about Cintas Corp. I would offer my colleague, and yourself as well, a little advice: in creating your own cult of personality, be sure to encourage myths and legends about yourself that are powerful enough to sustain an intimate five-room enclave of exceptional atmosphere and charm.

To introduce you to the concept of consumer behaviour, let us first understand that the persuasive language of advertising aims at informing and persuading the customer to buy security, affection, a sense of self-worth, and a personality for novelty-seekers and introverts as well as extroverts. What makes this cool is that it's just as much about the ad as it is about you.

Man, oh, man, do I love doughnuts! Even just a traditional one, oh, boy, are they good. Here's one just for you!

O!

I should say here that these words are not just for you or your community, but for all of us. Recently, I began to think that all of the services rendered here in advice and consultation could easily be cut down some. You should mentally cut as much as you like as you are reading, and if you'd like this really to read just for you, right in this moment, cut about enough to yield only three paragraphs a week, then leave the remainder of the text to float in the back of your mind like putting leftovers in the fridge in a sealed container as a happy surprise for later in the week.

While the themes of masculinity and femininity have been touched on throughout this series, dichotomous distinctions can often be misleading. In many cases, the world is not just black and white. You don't just march and wave placards with pithy slogans on them; you should also work to urge yourself and the New Left to take action in your own community. A simple history of capitalizing on the excesses of a city like Los Angeles will bring to light a number of organizations that have run dynamic and critically helpful community centers.

Please know that, just for you, I have worked to create a place where you can enjoy something better than average, casual, periodic dining.

Call on me when you're figuring out how to connect the different patterns in your life, and you can bet I will do my best to shed some light on the situation, just for you.

Your life has never been a series of gyms, bikes, and coffees or cappuccinos. You are the number one ranking activist circulating throughout your own life, just for you.

If you stop thinking, your thoughts will come back to you when they're supposed to, times ten!

Just for You Part 3

"Love is the only fire hot enough to melt the iron obstinacy of a creature's will."

Just for You seeks to remind us of all the things we've experienced in our hearts over the years, but just couldn't find the words to say. Now, try to listen to your own heart without shedding a tear.

This series of essay-like, journalistic pieces have been written just for you, plus I've added a bit of background flirtation, etc. And I'll get to the subject of Mixed Emotions this week, just for you. In 1988, I was not the kind of person to sit and dream; I knew the facts of life. I'm still not that kind of person, and neither are you. We both are now the kind of people, I'm sure, to sit and dream, even to sit and dream about the facts of life, to sit and dream about facts and fancy, to sit and dream about life.

...

Relaxing piano. Relaxing songs. Nice easy listening.

Girl, You'll Be a Woman Soon. On the Long Way Home drink some Red Red Wine. You'll Forget the Boat That I Row, Cherry, Cherry. I'm a Believer, Shilo. You Got to Me, a Solitary Man. Thank the Lord for the Night Time.

...

Being a teacher, you would, naturally, prefer to be at school in a teacher's natural habitat. Similar to yourself, and having been a teacher for so long, Professor Spicer is still giving the same lecture he always has. The class was shocked at the professor's use of sarcasm. Her conversation was sprinkled with the salt of cleverness as she explained that the word *echelon* has descended a ladder, coming to English through several languages, starting with the Latin word scale, which indeed means ladder, and which explains why we still "scale a ladder."

The French expression *esprit de corps* literally means "spirit of feeling as one body." It implies not only a camaraderie but a sense of pride or honor shared by those involved in an undertaking; a sense of union and of common interests and responsibilities.

Our two characters, you and I, appear grotesque with our language and our opinions, complete in our inadequacy and inadequateness. This is the teaching of a foreign language, and this special place here, just for you, acts as our liaison, like the contact person maintained between military or naval units in order to coordinate their actions.

As one new mother has put it, "You're led to the front of the line, and the door is cheerily opened by a figure completely unfamiliar to you." What this boils down to is not just a reading of the mother's body, but a destroying of feminine sensuality, leading to questions about the nature of sterilized institutional environments.

Be the right person in the right place. This is the very thing, quite the thing, just the thing.

Your vital juice or fluid, bodily or also body fluid.

BEING, IN THE CONCRETE
Sexy adj. erotic, arousing, exciting, sensual, sensuous, seductive, suggestive, &c.
Substantial adj. substantive, hypostatic, personal, bodily, tangible &c.
Completeness n. indivisibility, indiscerptibility, integration, embodiment, integer &c.
Hook and eye n. lock, holdfast, padlock, rivet, anchor, grappling iron, trennel, stake, post &c.

For years, billions of pounds have been pumped into state-of-the-art labs to fund so-called "particle accelerators," in the hope that the secrets of the Big Bang will be revealed. "It's all complete bollocks," a very recognizable mop-topped lab boy has publicly admitted.

The point about the madhouse is that you can think just what you like there.

All will be righted in the end and in the usual charming way.

Your body is human, your language is human, your habitation human.

Just for You Part 4

"This is meant to be inspirational. Isn't that creepy?"

I am so anxious to get started this week! This week is Oracle week, featuring special messages just for you from the Angel Oracle and interpreted by yours truly. I often invite special guest psychics to be featured during Oracle week; for a change though, just for you, I'm going to deviate from the regular routine and appoint myself as your guide. I'm happy to offer spiritual guidance on relationships, but first

I want to warn you to be careful of any guru who claims to have had experiences of total and complete transcendence.

Look to the stars with deep pleasure and speak as if you were made of the same stuff. Like a simple star that moves fast through the universe, shifting quickly across the sky, you should almost immediately start working on the many variations your voice can take. I want you to plant your feet on the ground and let your voice pour out until your vision blurs. Yes, then I want you to envision a haystack.

This exercise is the invention of a 24-year-old guru from San Francisco.

How many nations around the world speak French? Is there a difference between the Dutch-speaking North and the French-speaking South? Do they speak the English language in Boston? When a person can't admit to the process through which they build themselves, how can they work to improve that process? I have been querying a number of English-speaking oracles in order to list which ones are interested in connecting with you. I hope the things we have been doing and achieving here will help unite the world.

Just yesterday, we presented an exclusive, live set of a 16-year-old British musician and a little Birdy performing just for you! We've got a lovely Birdy singing just for you!!

You will not regret this. Hardly. If you are down, depressed ... listen to the music of the world around you. You will feel the energy, the ecstasy taking all your body, your soul, and your mind.

Just listen to these simple prophetic words spoken just for you in order to bless and inspire you as you conduct your life. The words uttered here are intended to serve as helpful messages that enable you to move on in your life and think about the exultations of love and the lengths that you would go to always be there for another and for yourself, just for you; to support, to sacrifice and to guide you.

Everyone in the "civilized" world is going through such a struggle.

Can you, would you, maybe, help me understand?

Allow me to direct this next question to you in both its literal and metaphorical sense. Are you having separation anxiety about giving one of your kittens away!? Light some calming candles and place them in and around your environment. Speaking of candles, let's relax and talk about something other than tanning. I've just started a new diet and hope it helps me to lose weight. I feel floaty and a little jittery, especially through my legs. I know period blood is the lining and stuff, but is it also actual blood?

Chakra infections ... how do you know if you have one?

Although you don't technically need to know all the stuff from Dating For Dummies, you can certainly benefit from chanting some Pre-Date Affirmations and Sweet Talking Yourself. People are very different from each other, and each must come to know the self within themselves. Just think of all the people, places, and trends to know about right now; all those cosmopolitan men and women sporting a fashion-forward look customized just for you. When you're out and about, be sure to take some snapshots as you're biking through Bangkok and riding around the Riviera.

Be comprehensive.

All the people who were there for you when you were going through your laborious tasks for the day saw you sweaty and ugly-faced and beautiful. Because we know your work isn't always just for you, you can easily connect with your contacts in the clouds. While it appears that some of our servers may not have actually processed the Shock update yet, Hollywood 411 gives you all you need to know about the stars.

I'm through with waiting tables!

Would you like to know how to get your motivation back?
Don't overdo it.

Try Raising Drug Awareness among Teens through a Speech.

Think about what you could do to help your process along if you were a spider owner.

When you speak about things in particular, speak of things you'd like to learn about, speak of solutions. Think of me as an affiliate oracle among the collection of sources you consult. Think of all the things you need to know. Not getting drawn into meaningless disputes is a credit to your personality. Make your own Easy, Step-By-Step Process to Success. Make yourself a list of tips you can remember and profit from in some small way. Consider this your list of possible daily targets to parse.

Overall, one of the primary lessons I want you to learn is that you are good at public speaking and that you have a beautiful voice. This article has worked to help you think through everything you have to focus on to beat panic attacks, and to help yourself eliminate panic attacks. Be aware of anxiety triggers, overcome anxiety and utilize self-hypnosis in the moment.

So far I hope you have heard some good things here, just for you, along with some scary things.

I know your body can handle it, but I can't speak for anyone else.

Just for You: A Slide Lecture

Performed originally alongside Prof. Padu Paga as a simultaneous lecture for Bill Anthes' Art Writing *class on November 27, 2012, as part of* BESHT *at Pomona College Museum of Art; subsequently performed alongside Ben White as a simultaneous lecture for* KCHUNGTV *at* Made in L.A. *at* The Hammer Museum, *Los Angeles, CA.*

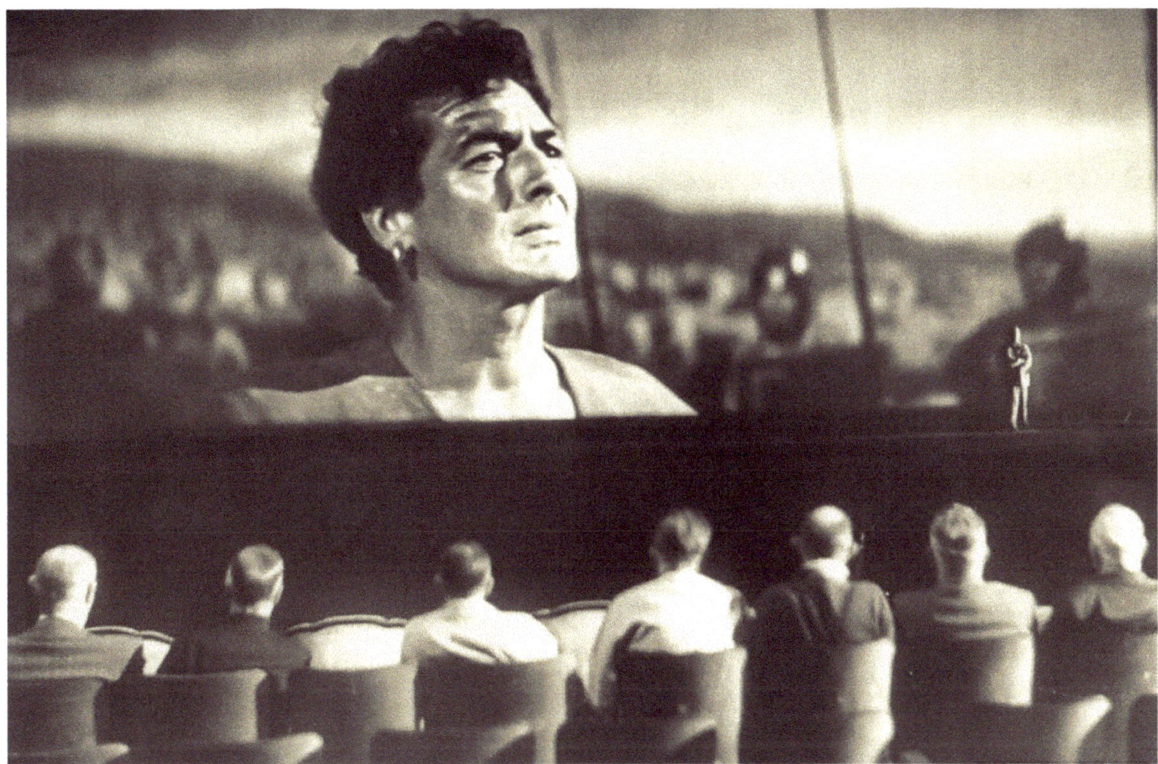

Marcellus is a tribune in the time of Christ. He is in charge of the group that is assigned to crucify Jesus. Drunk, he wins Jesus' homespun robe after the crucifixion. He is tormented by nightmares and delusions after the event. Hoping to find a way to live with what he has done, and still not believing in Jesus, he returns to Palestine to try and learn what he can of the man he killed.

The First Picture on the New Miracle Curved Screen !
No Special Glasses Needed !
The first motion picture in CinemaScope—the modern miracle you see without glasses!
The Greatest Story of Love, Faith, and Overwhelming Spectacle!

Darryl F. Zanuck originally offered the role of Marcellus to Tyrone Power in a bid to get him to renew his contract with Fox. Power instead opted to star in the play *John Brown's Body* on Broadway, which closed after 65 performances.

A pulsing kaleidoscope of images set to an energetic soundtrack. A young women swings in a garden; a woman's face smiles. The rest is spinning cylinders, pistons, gears and turbines, kitchen objects in concentric circles or rows—pots, pan lids, and funnels, cars passing overhead, a spinning carnival ride. Over and over, a heavy-set woman climbs stairs carrying a large bag on her shoulder. An Art Deco cartoon figure appears, dancing. This is a world in motion, dominated by mechanical and repetitive images, with a few moments of solitude in a garden.

George Antheil wrote the score for this film, but due to various disagreements—including that Antheil's original version of the music ran 30 minutes while the film was only 16 minutes—the film was premiered without the original music. The film and music were first shown together on 25 August, 2000, in Antwerp, Belgium, at the Cultuurmarkt van Vlaanderen. The film print with music was created by Paul Lehrman.

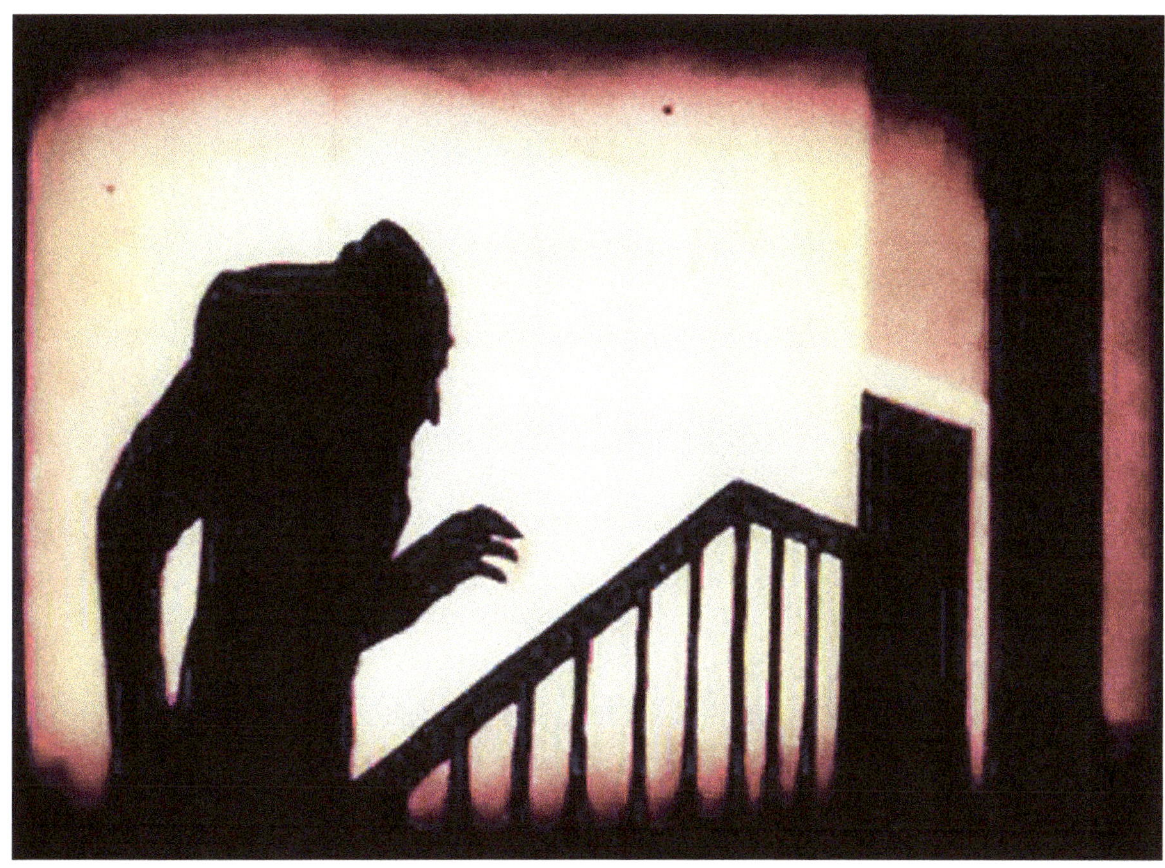

Vampire Count Orlok expresses interest in a new residence and real estate agent Hutter's wife. Silent classic based on the story "Dracula."

Wisbourg, Germany-based estate agent Knock dispatches his associate, Hutter, to Count Orlok's castle in Transylvania, as the Count wants to purchase an isolated house in Wisbourg. They plan on selling him the one across the way from Hutter's own home. Hutter leaves his innocent wife, Ellen, with some friends while he is away. Hutter's trek is an unusual one, with many locals not wanting to take him near the castle, where strange events have been occurring. Once at the castle, Hutter does manage to sell the Count the house, but he also notices and feels unusual occurrences, primarily feeling like there is a dark shadow hanging over him, even in the daytime, when the Count is unusually asleep. Hutter eventually sees the Count's sleeping chamber in a crypt and, based on a book he has recently read, believes the Count is really a vampire or Nosferatu. While Hutter is trapped in the castle, the Count, hiding in a shipment of coffins, makes his way to Wisbourg, causing death along his way, which most attribute to the plague. Hutter himself tries to rush home to save his town and, most importantly, save Ellen from Nosferatu's imminent arrival. In Wisbourg, Ellen can feel the impending darkness as Nosferatu gets closer. But she learns that a sinless woman can sacrifice herself to kill the vampire. Will Hutter be able to save Ellen either from Nosferatu and/or her self-sacrifice?

Count Orlok's move to Wisburg brings the plague. This reveals his connection to the Realtor Thomas Hutter, and the Count's obsession with Hutter's wife, Ellen—the only one with the power to end the evil.

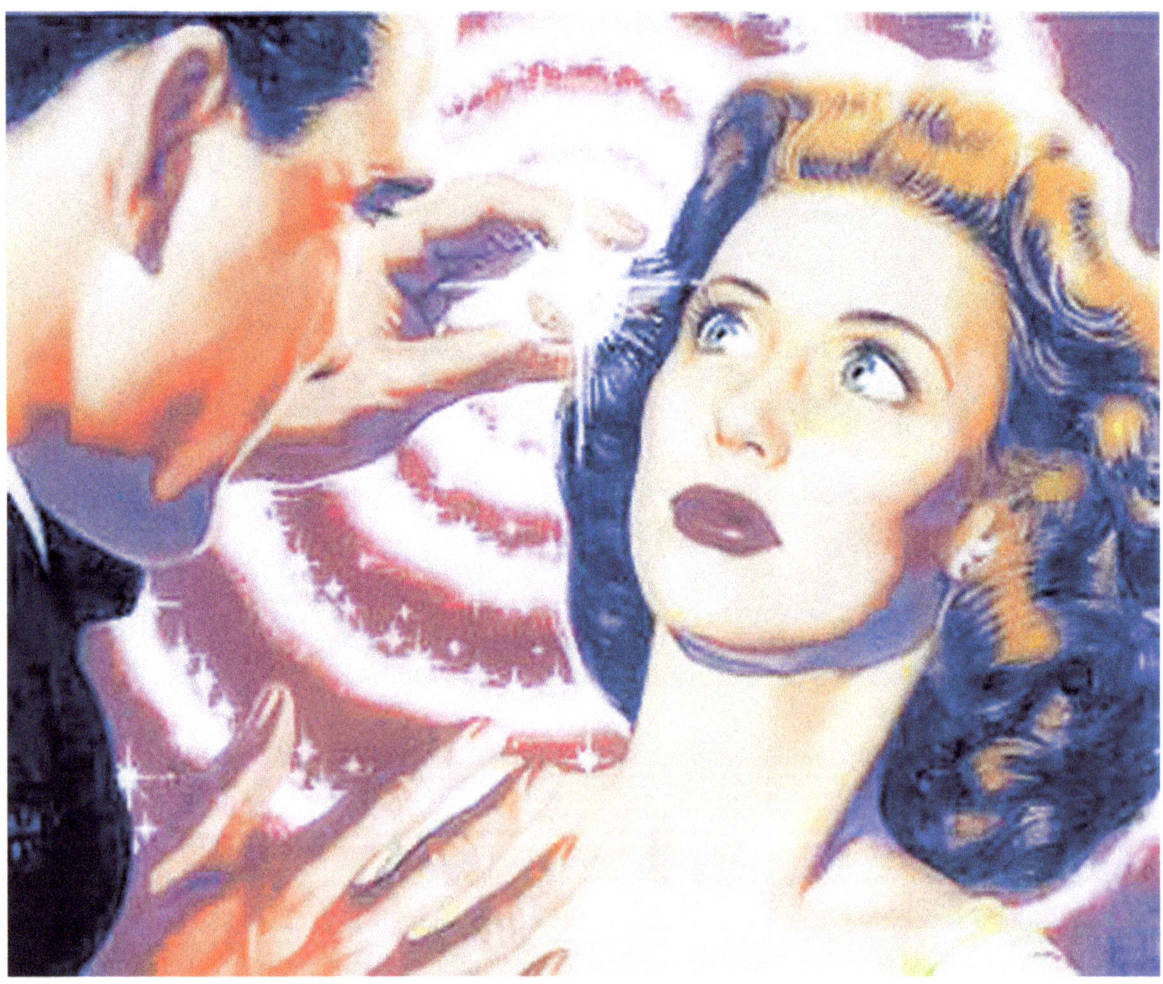

Dove is using the (apparently) drama-rich life of Alicia Keys to appeal to women in their 20s. Dove Go Fresh and MTV give you "Fresh Takes." With money to burn from Hanes, a scruffy guy called Dave—who's clearly approaching midlife with misgivings—is challenging celebrities to use hypnotism in focus groups for client Volvo. Hypnotize. A hypnotic symbol that may be used to hypnotize someone as a way of alternative therapy. A few days ago, I watched the 1967 *Casino Royale* again, and liked it for the first time. The plot does make a certain rudimentary sense. I found the section on hypnotism to be quite interesting. I have never been a huge believer in things like palm reading and hypnotism.

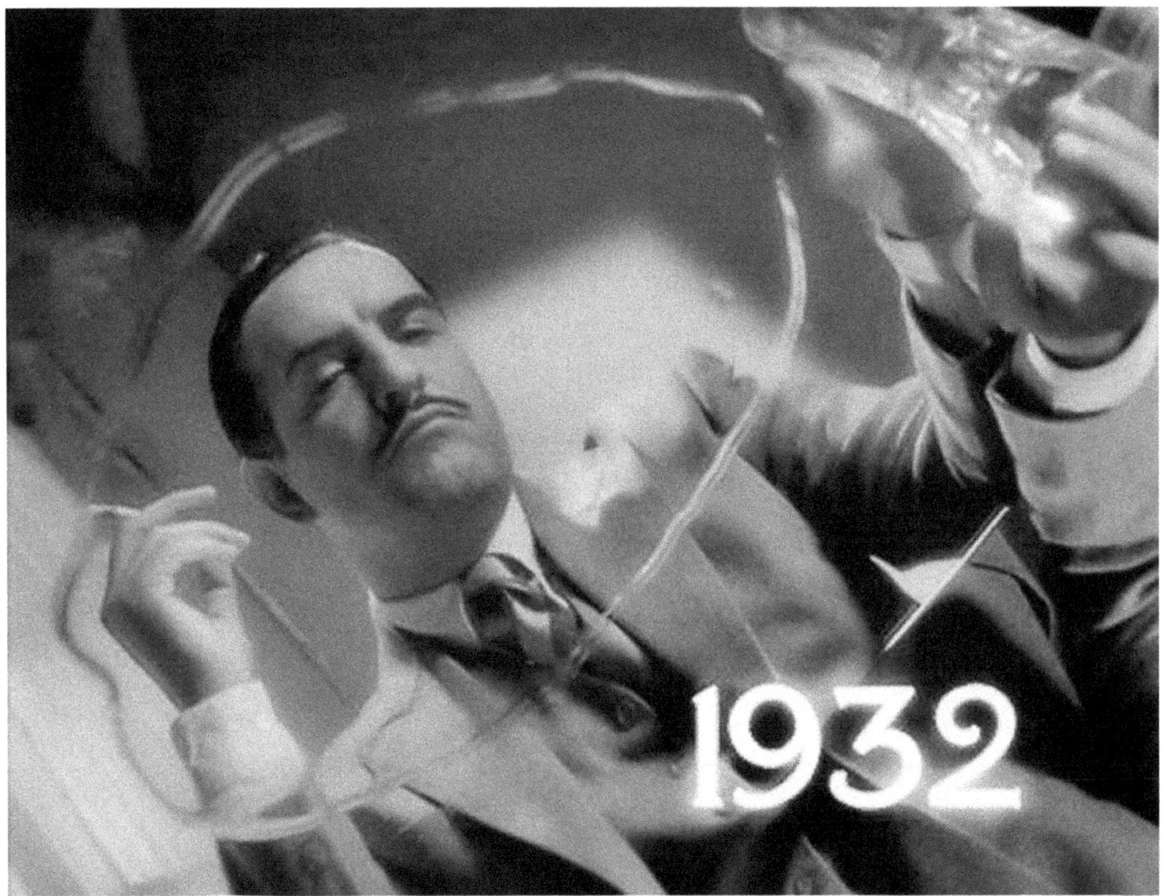

A silent movie star meets a young dancer, but the arrival of talking pictures sends their careers in opposite directions.

Outside a movie premiere, enthusiastic fan Peppy Miller literally bumps into the swashbuckling hero of the silent film, George Valentin. The star reacts graciously, and Peppy plants a kiss on his cheek as they are surrounded by photographers. The headlines demand: "Who's That Girl?" and Peppy is inspired to audition for a dancing bit-part at the studio. However, as Peppy slowly rises through the industry, the introduction of talking pictures turns Valentin's world upside-down.

It's 1927. Arguably Hollywood's most admired movie screen idol, George Valentin, is enjoying the success of his latest picture, *The Russian Affair*. He enjoys his work and the adulation he receives by being a movie star, as witnessed by how he hogs the spotlight during *The Russian Affair's* post-premiere bows. Peppy Miller is an aspiring young actress who literally and figuratively runs into Valentin at the premiere, which ends up being the launching pad to her Hollywood acting career. The advent of talking pictures brings a reversal to their fortunes as Kinograph, the movie studio where Valentin is under contract, is looking for fresh faces such as Peppy Miller to star in their talking pictures, while Valentin resists the entire notion of talking pictures. Peppy, who appreciates everything that Valentin did for her career, tries to help him as much as she can, but Valentin may have to decide on his own where and if he fits into the Hollywood machine, one where he doesn't think people want to hear him speak.

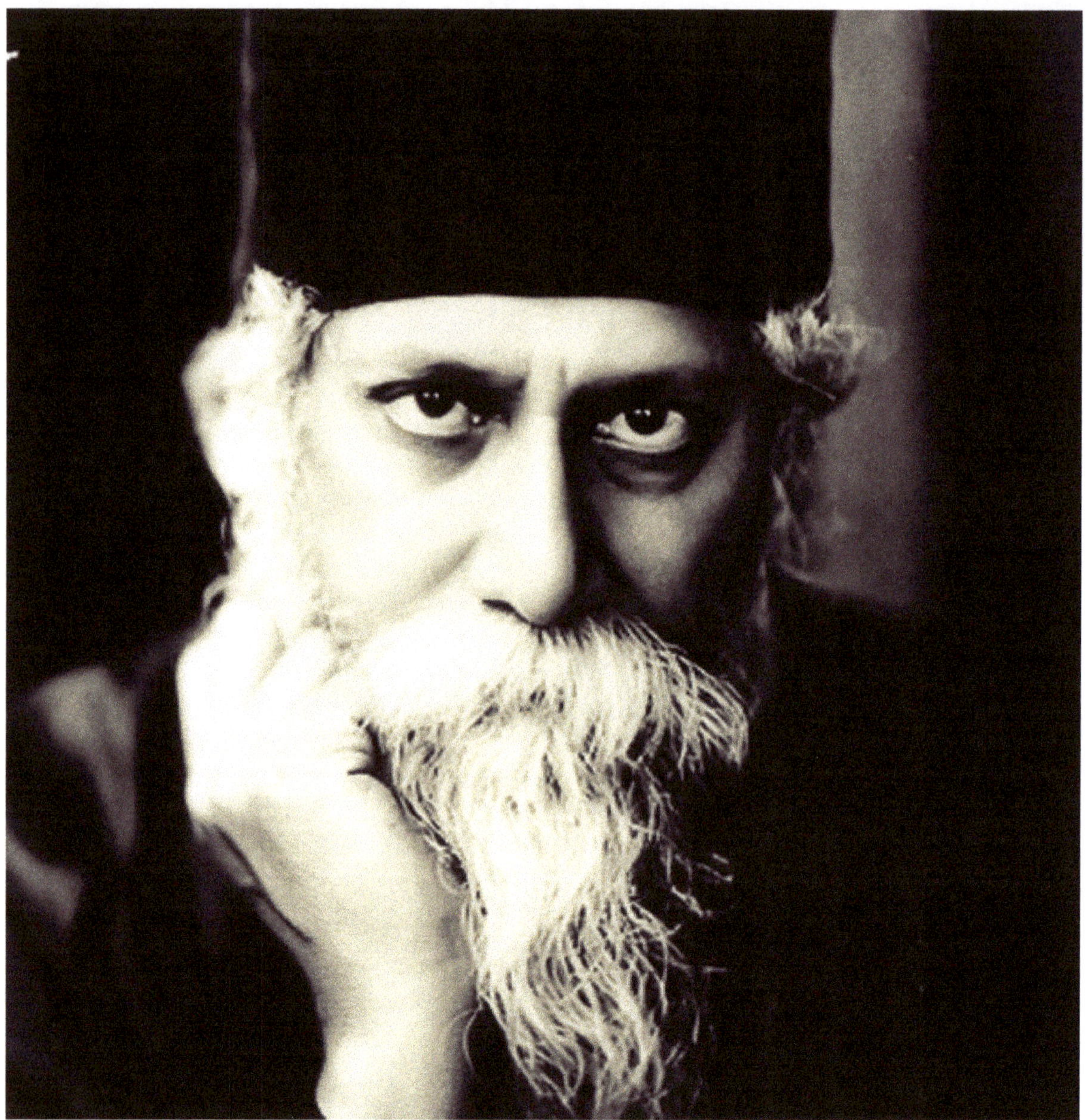

Rabindranath Tagore was a Bengali polymath who reshaped his region's literature and music. Author of *Gitanjali* and its "profoundly sensitive, fresh and beautiful verse," he became the first non-European to win the Nobel Prize in Literature in 1913. In translation, his poetry was viewed as spiritual and mercurial; his seemingly mesmeric personality, flowing hair, and other-worldly dress earned him a prophet-like reputation in the West. His "elegant prose and magical poetry" remain largely unknown outside Bengal. Tagore introduced new prose and verse forms and the use of colloquial language into Bengali literature, thereby freeing it from traditional models based on classical Sanskrit. He was highly influential in introducing the best of Indian culture to the West and vice versa, and he is generally regarded as the outstanding creative artist of modern India.

A Pirali Brahmin from Calcutta, Tagore wrote poetry as an eight-year-old. At age sixteen, he released his first substantial poems under the pseudonym Bhānusiṃha ("Sun Lion"), which were seized upon by literary authorities as long-lost classics. He graduated to his first short stories and dramas—and the aegis of his birth name—by 1877. As a humanist, universalist internationalist, and strident anti-nationalist, he denounced the Raj and advocated independence from Britain. As an exponent of the Bengal Renaissance, he advanced a vast canon that comprised paintings, sketches and doodles, hundreds of texts, and some two thousand songs; his legacy endures also in the institution he founded, Visva-Bharati University.

Tagore modernised Bengali art by spurning rigid classical forms and resisting linguistic strictures. His novels, stories, songs, dance-dramas, and essays spoke to topics political and personal. *Gitanjali* (Song Offerings), *Gora* (Fair-Faced), and *Ghare-Baire* (The Home and the World) are his best-known works, and his verse, short stories, and novels were acclaimed—or panned—for their lyricism, colloquialism, naturalism, and unnatural contemplation. His compositions were chosen by two nations as national anthems: India's Jana Gana Mana and Bangladesh's Amar Shonar Bangla. The composer of Sri Lanka's national anthem: Sri Lanka Matha was a student of Tagore, and the song is inspired by Tagore's style.

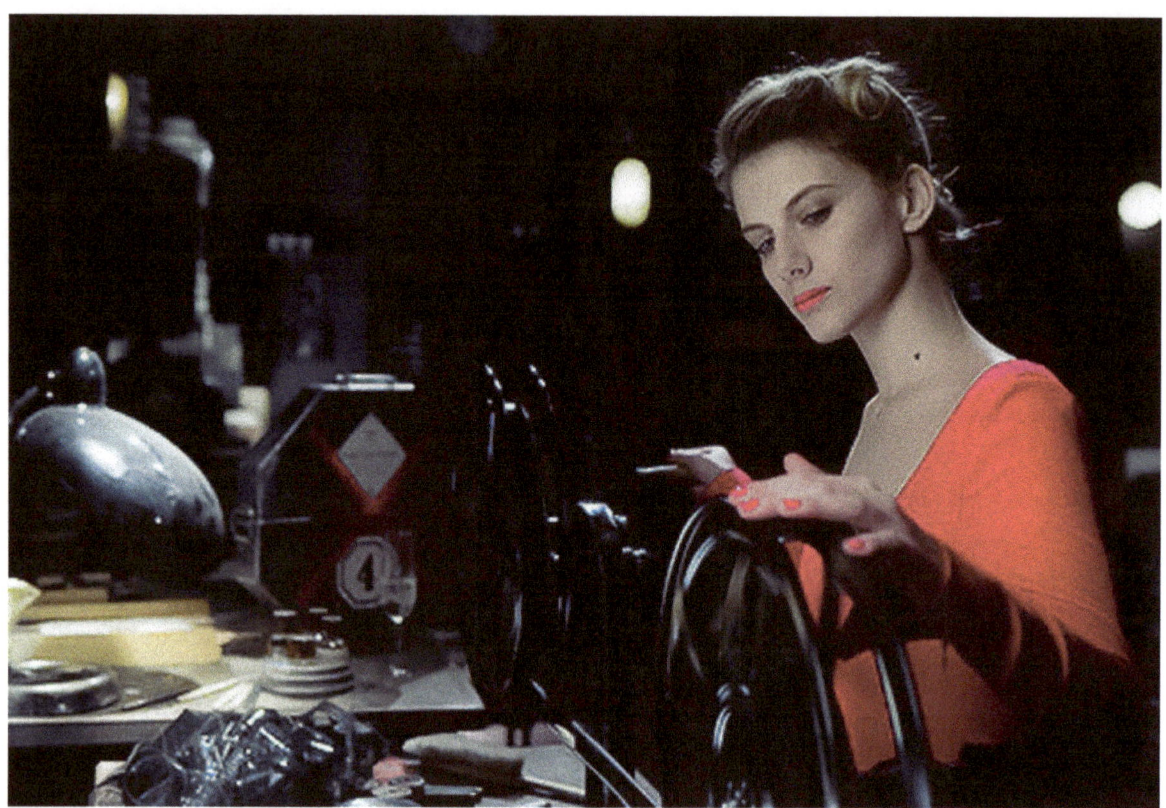

In Nazi-occupied France during World War II, a plan to assassinate Nazi leaders by a group of Jewish U.S. soldiers coincides with a theatre owner's vengeful plans for the same.

In Nazi-occupied France, young Jewish refugee Shosanna Dreyfus witnesses the slaughter of her family by Colonel Hans Landa. Narrowly escaping with her life, she plots her revenge several years later when German war hero Fredrick Zoller takes a rapid interest in her and arranges an illustrious movie premiere at the theater she now runs. With the promise of every major Nazi officer in attendance, the event catches the attention of the "Basterds," a group of Jewish-American guerilla soldiers led by the ruthless Lt. Aldo Raine. As the relentless executioners advance and the conspiring young girl's plans are set in motion, their paths will cross for a fateful evening that will shake the very annals of history.

During World War II, a group of American soldiers are sent into Europe to kill Nazis. They've become so good at it that the Germans refer to them as The Basterds. Later, they work with a British officer who was sent to formalize a plan to kill several high ranking German officers at the premiere of a movie depicting the "heroics" of a German soldier. But something goes wrong at the meeting with their contact, a German actress: all of the members of the team who speak German are killed, which complicates the plans. So the leader, Lt. Raine, comes up with an alternative. And another complication is the screening is being moved to a small theater because the man depicted in the movie takes a liking to the owner of the theater. And unknown to them, she is a Jew whose entire family was killed by a Nazi officer, who was tasked with rounding up the Jews and is now the security officer of the screening. And also unknown is that she has her own plans.

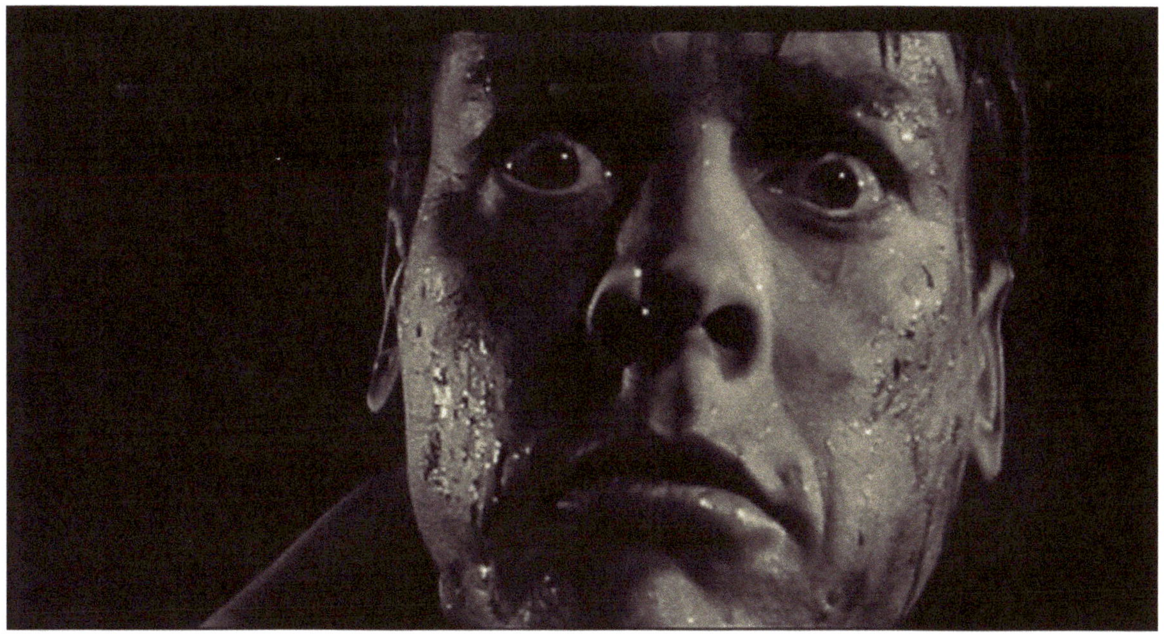

A small-town doctor learns that the population of his community is being replaced by emotionless alien duplicates.

Dr. Miles Bennell returns to his small town practice to find several of his patients suffering the paranoid delusion that their friends or relatives are impostors. He is initially skeptical, especially when the alleged dopplegängers are able to answer detailed questions about their victims' lives, but he is eventually persuaded that something odd has happened and determines to find out what is causing this phenomenon. This film can be seen as a paranoid 1950s warning against those Damn Commies or, conversely, as a metaphor for the tyranny of McCarthyism (or the totalitarian system ofYour Choice) and has a pro- and epilogue that was forced upon Siegel by the studio to lighten the tone.

Held by the police as a raving lunatic, Dr. Miles Bennell recounts to a psychiatrist the events that have turned his life upside down. He returned to his small town the previous Thursday, having been called back from a medical conference by his nurse, who was being flooded with patients. He arrives to find that most have canceled their appointments, but the few cases he does have all have the same story: someone close to them is acting strangely, as if they had been replaced. Consulting some of his colleagues, he finds that these types of reports have been coming in all week, and they conclude it must be some type of mass hysteria. However, when his friends Jack and Teddy Belicec show him a partly formed body they have uncovered in their home, he begins to realize that there may be some truth to the wild stories he has been hearing.

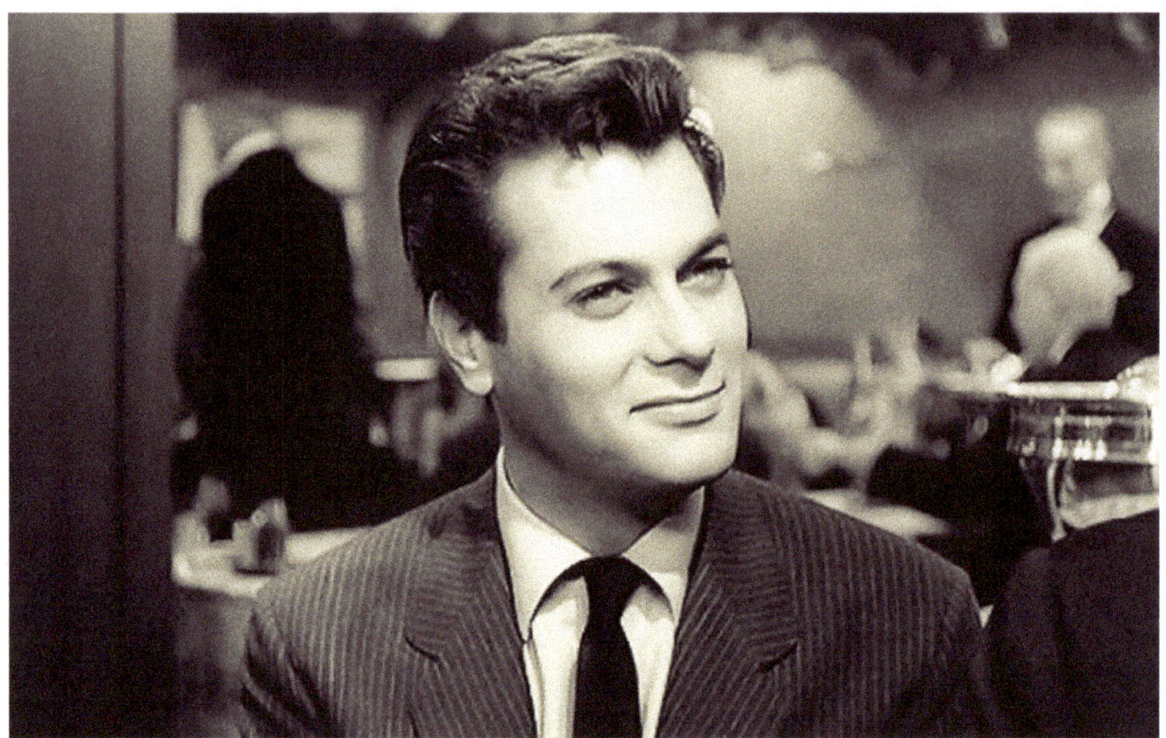

Powerful but unethical Broadway columnist J.J. Hunsecker coerces unscrupulous press agent Sidney Falco into breaking up his sister's romance with a jazz musician.

J.J. Hunsecker, the most powerful newspaper columnist in New York, is determined to prevent his sister from marrying Steve Dallas, a jazz musician. He therefore covertly employs Sidney Falco, a sleazy and unscrupulous press agent, to break up the affair by any means possible.

J.J. Hunsecker (Burt Lancaster) is a tyrannical Broadway columnist for the New York Globe who rules his demimonde with the press's power to create or destroy. Sidney Falco (Tony Curtis) is the hustling publicist who is consumed by desperate ambition and hates himself because of it; he will do anything to gain the admiration of Hunsecker ("My experience, in brief, is dog eat dog"). The film was shot in black and white by James Wong Howe, giving it a grittiness that underscores the class ranking among the characters. In the script by Clifford Odets and Ernest Lehman, Falco's early prediction—"Every dog has its day"—comes crashingly true.

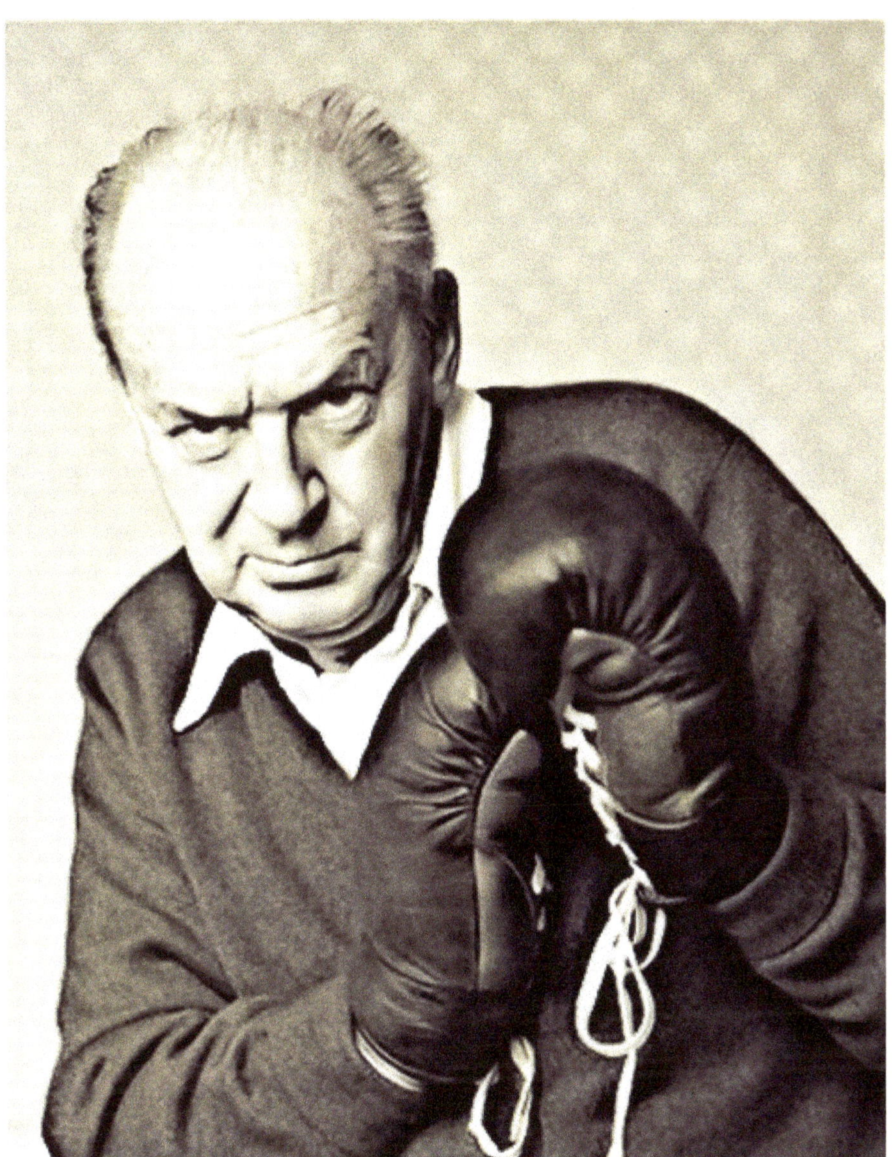

Vladimir Vladimirovich Nabokov was a Russian-American novelist. Nabokov's first nine novels were in Russian. He then rose to international prominence as a writer of English prose. He also made serious contributions as a lepidopterist and chess composer.

Nabokov's *Lolita* (1955) is his most famous novel, and often considered his finest work in English. It exhibits the love of intricate word play and synesthetic detail that characterised all his works. The novel was ranked at No. 4 in the list of the Modern Library 100 Best Novels. *Pale Fire* (1962) was ranked at No. 53 on the same list. His memoir, *Speak, Memory*, was listed No. 8 on the Modern Library nonfiction list.

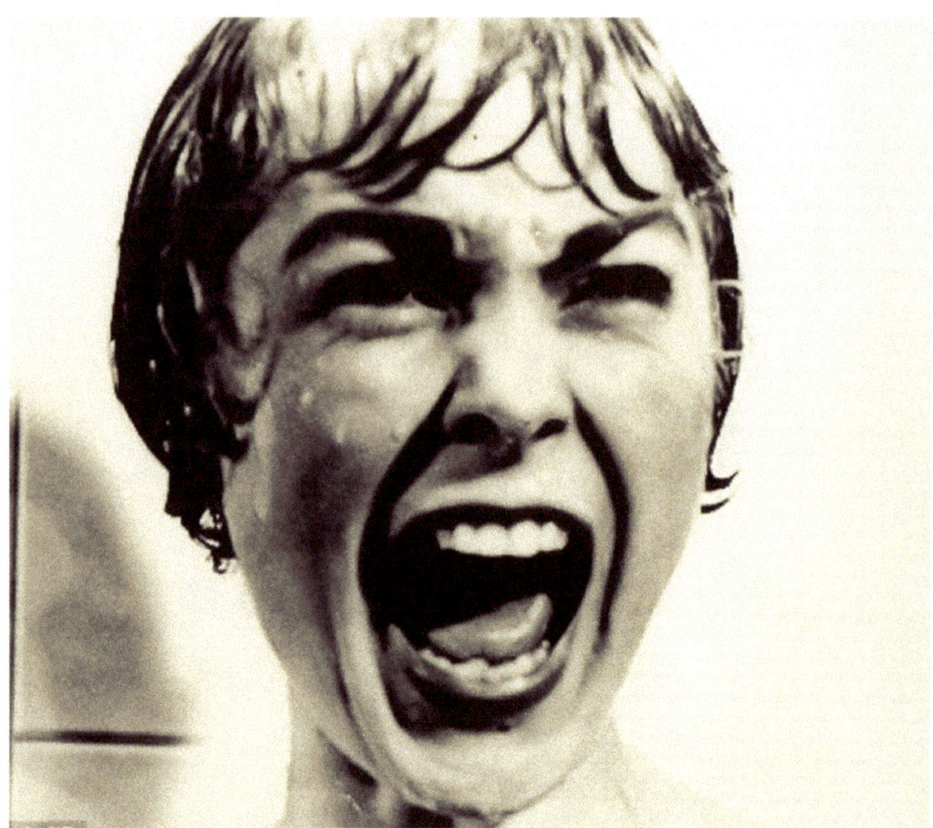

A young woman steals $40,000 from her employer's client and subsequently encounters a young motel proprietor too long under the domination of his mother.

Phoenix officeworker Marion Crane is fed up with the way life has treated her. She has to meet her lover Sam on lunch breaks, and they cannot get married because Sam has to give most of his money away in alimony. One Friday, Marion is trusted to bank $40,000 by her employer. Seeing the opportunity to take the money and start a new life, Marion leaves town and heads towards Sam's California store. Tired after the long drive and caught in a storm, she gets off the main highway and pulls into the Bates Motel. The motel is managed by a quiet young man called Norman who seems to be dominated by his mother.

For Marion Crane, it's been quite an eventful day. The day before, she had stolen $40,000 from her employer's client, packed her bags and driven all day on her way to join her paramour several hundred miles away. Now, she is taking a relaxing hot shower after her long day's journey. The remoteness of the motel suits her purposes perfectly. The only sounds heard are the chirping of the crickets, the splashing of the water, and her humming contentedly as the hot needles of water caress her aching shoulders.

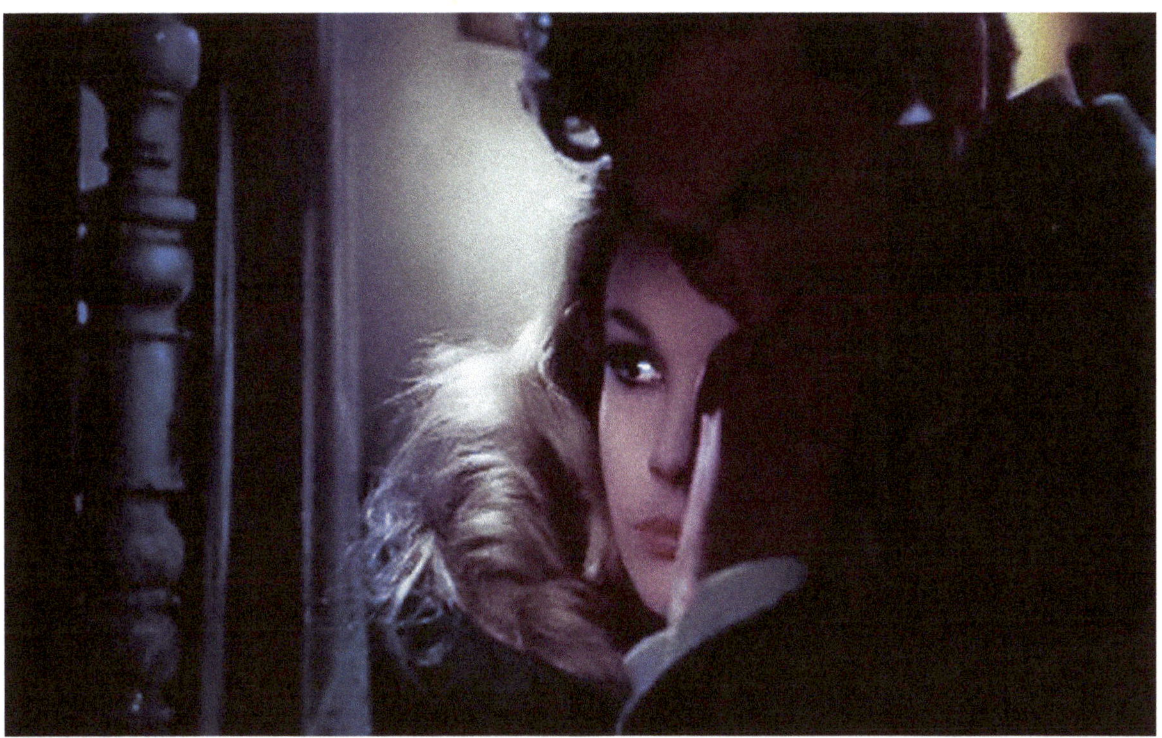

A trio of atmospheric horror tales about: A woman terrorized in her apartment by phone calls from an escaped prisoner from her past; a Russian count in the early 1800s who stumbles upon a family in the countryside trying to destroy a particularly vicious line of vampires; and a 1900-era nurse who makes a fateful decision while preparing the corpse of one of her patients—an elderly medium who died during a seance.

A trilogy of three horror stories. "The Drop of Water" concerns a nurse who steals a ring off a dead spiritualist, only to have the corpse seek revenge. "The Telephone" features a prostitute who is terrorized by phone calls from a dead client. "The Wurdalak" stars Boris Karloff as a vampire who feeds on the blood of his loved ones.

(1) "Il Telefono"—Rosy receives many phone calls threatening her. She believes her former lover, who has just escaped from prison, is calling her. She denounced him for a crime committed some time ago and he was convicted. She calls her girlfriend Mary to stay with her. A secret is revealed, and a tragedy happens in the end. (2) "I Wurdulak"—Vladimir d'Urfe, a young man, is riding a horse at night and finds a man with a knife in his back. He withdraws the dagger from the man and finds a house close to the place where he found the body. There, he meets a family composed of two brothers, one sister, one sister-in-law and one nephew, and he falls in love at first sight with the beautiful Sdenka. He realizes that the dead man was a criminal, probably killed by the head of the family Gorca, and he is advised to leave that place, before Gorca arrives back at midnight. The family informs him that there is a chance that Gorca might have been transformed into a Wurdulak, a kind of vampire who drains blood from

the living persons. A few seconds after midnight, Gorca comes back home, and the afraid family does not know whether he was transformed or not. The family discovers later what happened in a tragic way. (3)"La Goccia d' Acqua"—Helen Chester is called to prepare the body of a countess for her funeral. She steals the worthy ring from her finger. The countess comes back from beyond to retrieve her ring, terrifying the frightened woman.

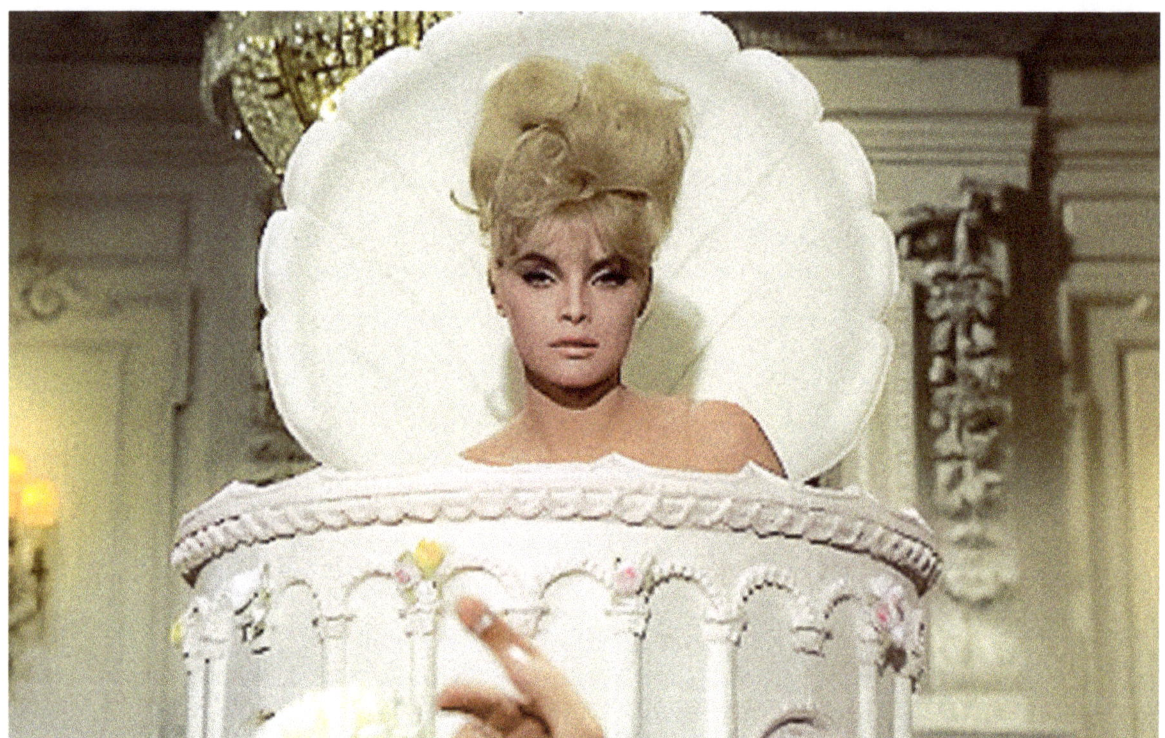

A man who has set up the perfect lifestyle for himself makes the mistake of marrying while drunk... and his fantasies of murder are used against him.

Stanley Ford leads an idyllic bachelor life. He is a nationally syndicated cartoonist whose Bash Brannigan series provides him with a luxury townhouse and a full-time valet, Charles. When he wakes up the morning after the night before—he had attended a friend's stag party—he finds that he is married to the very beautiful woman who popped out of the cake—and who doesn't speak a word of English. Despite his initial protestations, he comes to like married life and even changes his cartoon character from a super spy to a somewhat harried husband. When after several months he decides to kill off Bash's wife in the cartoon, his wife misinterprets his intentions and disappears. Which leads the police to charge him with murder.

Stanley Ford is a happily unmarried man with all the creature comforts one could desire, including a wonderful butler who takes care of all his material needs. At a bachelor party for a friend, Ford gets drunk and wakes up married to an Italian woman who speaks nearly no English. It totally alters his life. He even changes the cartoon he writes and shifts it from a secret agent to a household comedy. When he begins to have trouble with all of these changes, he starts to plot that at least his secret agent cartoon will return to order and plans, in his daily comic strip, killing his wife. When she disappears, the cartoons are used as evidence at his trial.

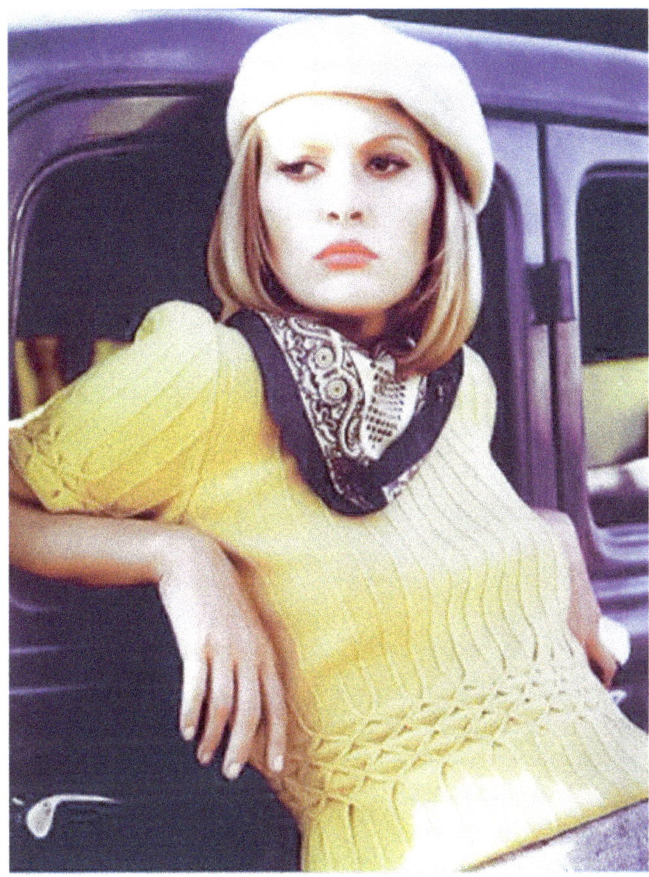

A somewhat romanticized account of the career of the notoriously violent bank-robbing couple and their gang.

A bored small-town girl and a small-time bank robber leave in their wake a string of violent robberies and newspaper headlines that catch the imagination of the Depression-struck Midwest in this take on the legendary crime spree of these archetypal lovers on the run.

Bonnie Parker is bored with life and wants a change. She gets her chance when she meets a charming young drifter by the name of Clyde Barrow. Clyde has dreams of a life of crime that will free him from the hardships of the Depression. The two fall in love and begin a crime spree that extends from Oklahoma to Texas. They rob small banks with skill and panache, soon becoming minor celebrities known across the country. People are proud to have been held up by Bonnie and Clyde; to their victims, the duo is doing what nobody else has the guts to do. To the law, the two are evil bank robbers who deserve to be gunned down where they stand.

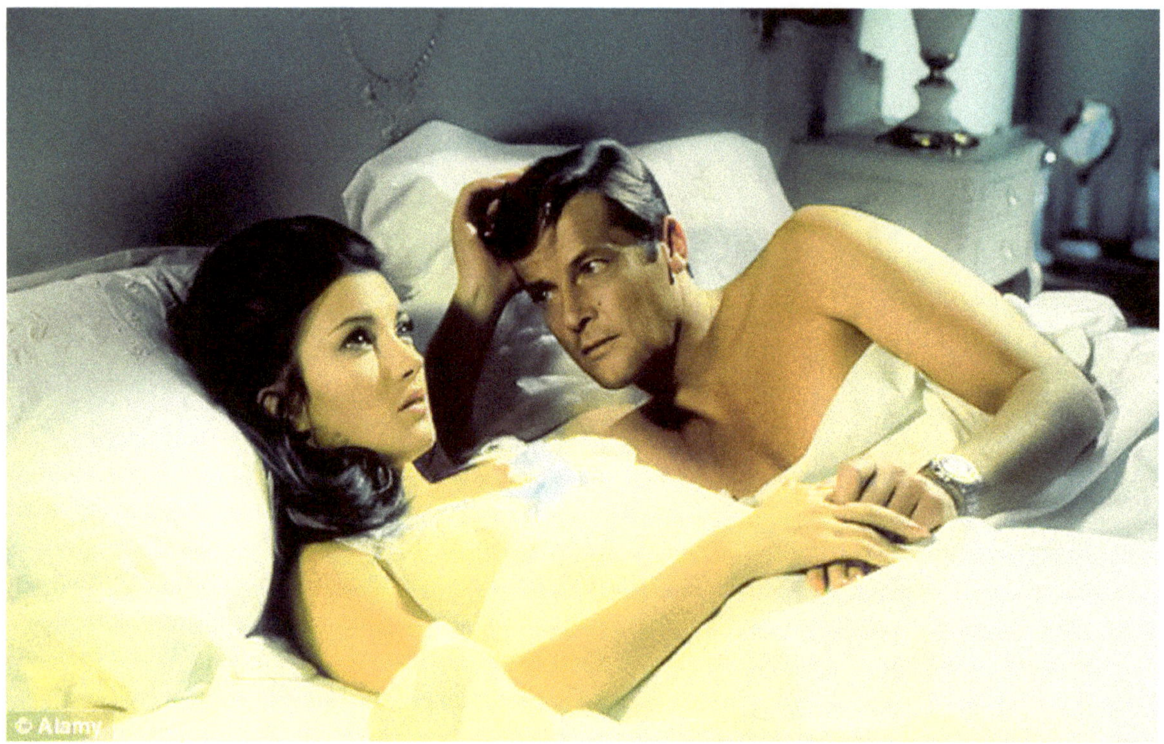

007 is sent to stop a diabolically brilliant heroin magnate armed with a complex organization and a reliable psychic tarot card reader.

Several British agents have been murdered, and James Bond is sent to New Orleans to investigate these mysterious deaths. Mr. Big comes to his knowledge, who is self-producing heroin. Along his journeys he meets Tee Hee, who has a claw for a hand, Baron Samedi the voodoo master and Solitaire and her tarot cards. Bond must travel deep inside New Orleans, through marshy grass and on water, as he completes his mission.

James Bond is sent to New York to investigate the mysterious deaths of several British agents. He soon senses that there is a drugs link between the notorious Mr. Big and Dr. Kananga, the secretive owner of a small Caribbean island. However, Kananga is not a man to be dealt with lightly, and the fact that his beautiful Solitaire has already been seduced by 007 makes matters worse.

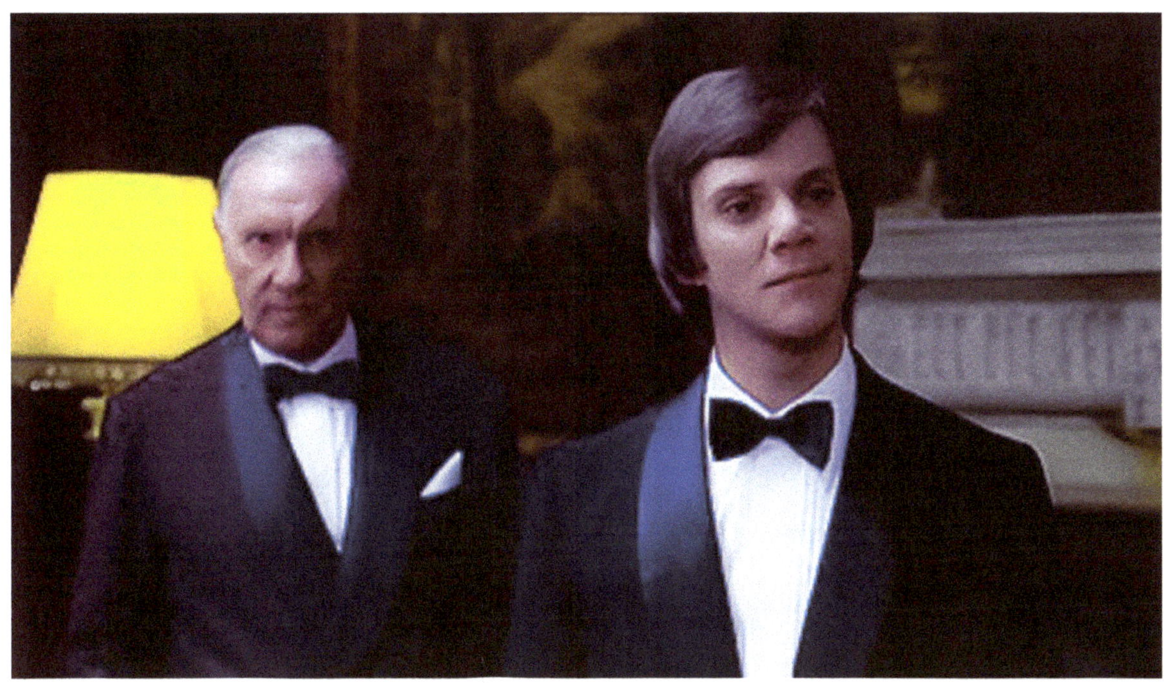

This sprawling, surrealist musical serves as an allegory for the pitfalls of capitalism, as it follows the adventures of a young coffee salesman in Europe. Many actors play multiple roles, giving the film a stagy tone.

The film opens with a short fragment outside the plot but clearly related on repeated viewings. Grainy, black-and-white, and silent short, a title "Once Upon a Time" leads to Latino laborers picking coffee beans while armed foremen push rudely between them. One worker pockets a few beans ("Coffee for the Breakfast Table") but is seen by a foreman. He is next seen before a fat Caucasian magistrate who loses some saliva as he removes his cigar only to say "Guilty." The foreman pulls his machete and lays it across the unfortunate laborer's wrists, bound to a wooden block, revealing that he is to lose his hands for the theft of a few beans. The machete lifts, descends, and we see the thief draw back in a silent scream. The scene blacks out, the word NOW appears onscreen and expands quickly to fill it.

Mick Travis (Malcolm McDowell) is the most promising new sales recruit at Imperial Coffee, a multinational coffee company and distributing factory located somewhere in the UK. His easy manner and winning smile bring him to the attention of the training manager Miss Rowe (Rachel Roberts). When it is learned that a senior salesman in the company has gone missing, Miss Rowe proposes that Mick be recruited to take over his coveted northeast sales sector.

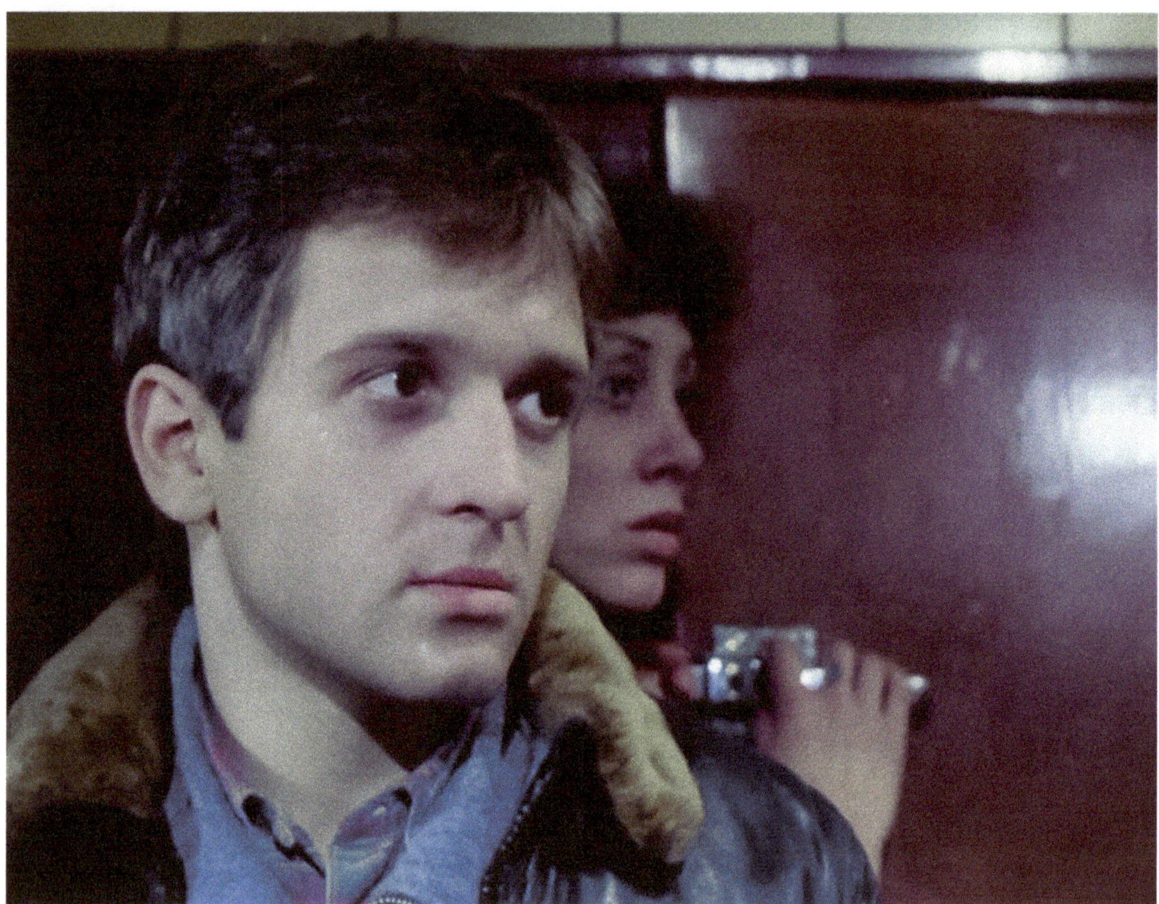

A man is interviewed by a sympathetic woman. His tale unfolds, of hard work that never pleases his parents, of a father who denigrates his efforts, of an indifferent mother. He builds them a house. Instead of offering their flat to him and his bride, they give the flat up, so he goes to Munich to work in construction, bringing his wife, who is soon pregnant. They buy things on credit; he works overtime. He shows up with flowers and expensive gifts. When construction slows and he works less overtime, he cannot adjust his spending habits: he needs to be loved. Pressures mount. When he snaps, and violence ensues, who will be his victim?

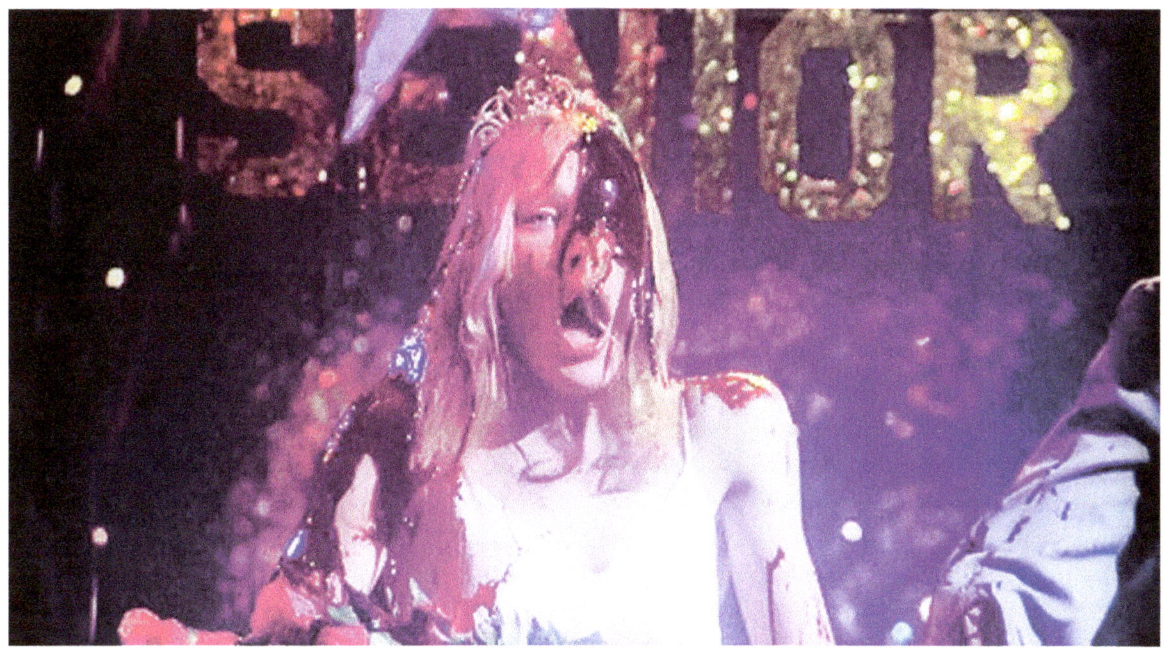

A young, abused and timid 17-year-old girl discovers she has telekinesis, and gets pushed to the limit on the night of her school's prom by a humiliating prank.

Carrie White is a shy young girl who doesn't make friends easily. After her classmates taunt her about her horrified reaction to her totally unexpected first period, one of them takes pity on her and gets Tommy Ross, her boyfriend and class hunk, to invite Carrie to the senior prom. Meanwhile, another girl who has been banned from the prom for her continued aggressive behaviour is not as forgiving and plans a trick to embarrass Carrie in front of the whole school. What she doesn't realise is that Carrie is ... gifted, and you really don't want to get her angry.

The story of Carrie White, a girl brought up, almost in isolation, by her psychotically religious mother Margaret. After an embarrassing incident in the showers causes her fellow pupils to tease Carrie ruthlessly, her teacher Miss Desjardin disciplines them severely. Determined to have revenge, the other students hatch a plot against Carrie, which turns horribly wrong when Carrie's strange mental powers are unleashed during the school prom.

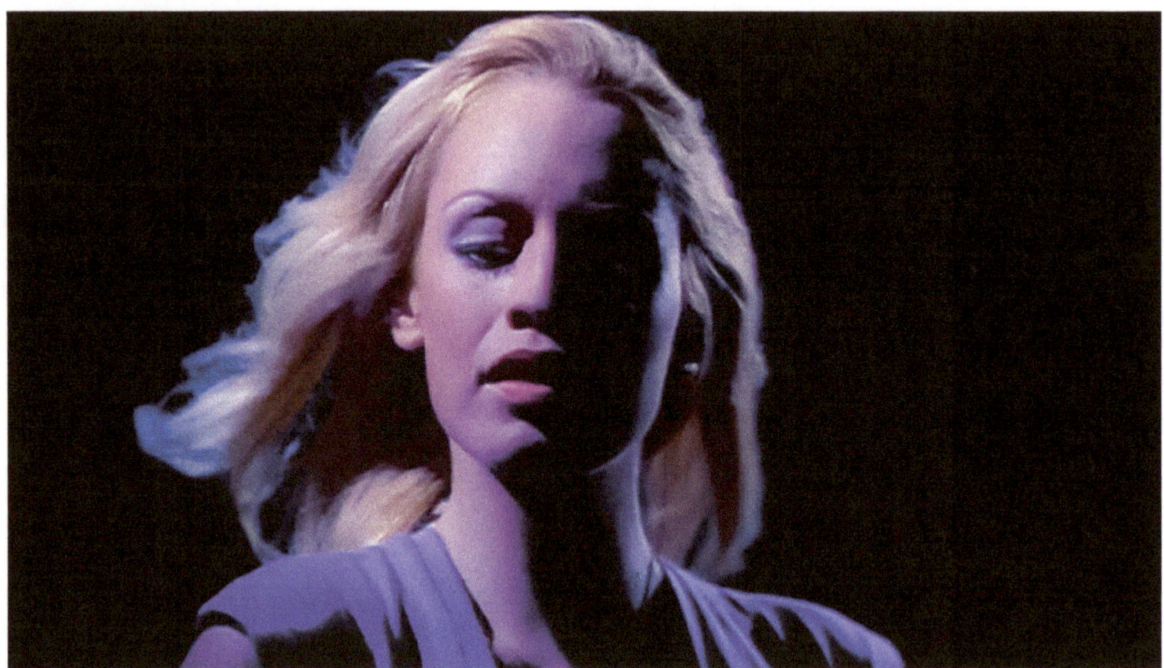

A young boy and his friends face off against a mysterious grave robber known only as the Tall Man, who keeps a mysterious arsenal of terrible weapons with him.

Mike, a young teenage boy who has just lost his parents, is afraid to lose his brother. This fear causes him to follow his brother to a funeral, where Mike witnesses the Tall Man lift a coffin on his own. Mike decides to investigate and discovers a horrible world where the Tall Man, along with his flying spheres, shrink them to half their normal size and reanimate them as slaves. It is then up to Mike, his brother, and Reggie the ice cream man to stop the Tall Man.

Mike cannot decide what is real and what isn't, and is plagued by vivid nightmares. He gets the shock of his life when he watches, with binoculars, the conclusion of the funeral of his older brother's friend—the mortician (the Tall Man), by himself, lifts the casket into the back of a hearse. Mike heads to the grounds of the mortuary, which is home to very bizarre happenings, including a unique security device. Enlisting the help of brother Jody and ice cream salesman Reggie, Mike attempts to vanquish the Tall Man.

Just for You: A Song

Performed originally as an excerpt at A Guided Meditation Marathon *on November 29, 2012, as part of* BESHT *at Pomona College Museum of Art.*

I was not the kind'a guy to sit and dream
I knew the facts of life
just hated philosophy
and reckoned reality was the game for me.

Now you've turned my heart around
into the light my feet have left the ground
here is how, here and now
gonna show you all my love.

And it's just for you
I'll try to fish up the ocean
just for you
I'll try to colour the stars.
And it's just for you
I'll try to water the desert
just to make our flowers grow.

And it's just for you
I'm slowing down the rotation
just for you
I'll stop the earth and I'll try-i-i.
Because of you and we are so in love.

I think of how it used to be
and how it seemed I was so big and free
how did I not realize
all the things I despised were so good for me?

Now I can just fly away
into your arms and know I'm gonna stay
here is how, here and now
gonna show you all my love.

And it's just for you
I'll try to fish up the ocean
just for you
I'll try to colour the stars.
And it's just for you
I'll try to water the desert
just to make our flowers grow.

And it's just for you
I'm slowing down the rotation
just for you
I'll stop the earth and I'll try-i-i

You can be the life of the party
Or you can be the belle of the ball
You can break my heart if you want to
And you can make me wait for your call

I can only give you my promise
That I will always stay by your side
You can make my heart spin in circles
And I'll go along for the ride

Just for you—just for you
Ya ya ya ya—just for you
There are so many things I would do
D d d d d d—just for you
Woo-oo-oo
D d d d d d—just for you
Woo-oo-oo

You can be the Tiffany diamond
Or you can be the real Coupe de Ville
You can tear my life into pieces

Or you can make my world stand still

I can only say that I love you
So take me for just what I am
You can see the stars in my future
And I'll go along with the plan

You can be the sun in the morning
To shine your light through all of the day
You can lose my love in the darkness
And you can only show me the way

I can only give you my promise
That I will always stay by your side
You can make my heart spin in circles
And I'll go along for the ride

Just for you, just for you, just for you, my love
Woah for you, just for you, my love
Woah yes my dear, I finally realize
I finally realize that it's just for you

When you see me workin' all night long
Workin' till my stress is gone
It's for you, oh listen dear
I finally realize it's all for you

Yeah, when you see me workin' all the day
Workin' all my stress away
It's for you, oh yes it is
I finally realize it's all for you
Just for you, woah, could it be for you?
Just for you, just for you, woah, just for you
Now yes my dear, I finally realize
I finally realize that it's just for you

When you see me workin' all the day
Workin' all my stress away
It's for you, oh yes it is
I finally realize it's all for you

Yeah, when you see me spendin' all my money
Just to give you a good time, honey
It's for you, oh I finally realize
I finally realize it's for you

It's for you, for nobody else but you my love, it's for you, Sweetheart, I know it's for you, woah, it's for you, love, Yes my dear, I finally realize, I finally realize that it's just for you

Just for you, just for you, it's just for you, just for you, Just for you, just for you, it's just for you

Golden days
Night was play
Pain was all a world away
We went to school
We learned the rules
We trusted all they had to say

Then life took a turn
We all had to learn
And we can't go back again

And my heart is breaking
Just for you
Just for you
And my arms are open
Just for you
Just for you
Just for you

God was God
And dreams were dreams
Life was all cake and ice cream
Truth was true
And lies were lies

And we thought love would never die
But the world moved on
My illusions gone
And I don't know who to blame

And my heart is breaking
Just for you
Just for you
And my arms are open
Just for you
Just for you
And these tears I'm crying are for you
Just for you
Just for you

I'm looking for protection
Give me shelter from the storm
I just hope this light inside me
Keeps me strong

And my heart is breaking
Just for you
Just for you
And my arms they're open
Just for you
Just for you
And these tears I'm crying are for you
Just for you
Just for you

Just for you
Oh my heart is breaking
And my arms are open
Oh these tears I'm crying are just for you

Oh yeah

I will climb the highest mountain
just for you.
Bring gold and silver to your door
just for you.
I will raise my glass up to the sky
just for you.
I will be your strength and be your pride
be with you.

I'll make sweet soul music all night long
just for you.
Make you feel that you belong
just for you.
We'll take a ride in the tunnel of love
just us two.
I will scream aloud at the altar of God
I love you.

[Chorus]
Just for you I'll wash you down,
cleanse your soul and be around,
hold your hand and lead the way,
be with you all through your day.
Just for you I'll sacrifice
everything in my life,
I will give all this to you,
dedicate myself to you...
Just for you, just for you, just for you, yeah
(just for you)
Just for you, just for you, just for you
(just for you)
Just for you, just for you, just for you, yeah
(just for you)
Just for you, just for you, just for you
(just for you)
I'll be a shooting star in the sky at night
just for you.
I'll be your mother of pearl, diamond girl
just for you.
I'll lock the door, throw away the key
just for you.

I am the air that you breathe
I am you.

[Chorus]

I'll terrorise, publicise, capitalise, mesmerise,
idolise, wave goodbyes to all the things you despise.

Just for you. Just for you.

[Chorus]

I'll climb the highest mountain,
until I reach the top.
I'll climb the highest mountain,
and I will not stop.
I'll climb the highest mountain
(highest mountain),
and I'll never stop (never stop).
I'll climb the highest mountain
(highest mountain),
until I reach the top (reach the top).

I'm gonna climb that mountain
(highest mountain),
I'm gonna reach the top (never stop).
I'm gonna climb that mountain
(highest mountain),
I'm gonna reach the top (reach the top).

And I will not stop
(highest mountain, never stop)
And I will not stop
(highest mountain, reach the top)

Higher and higher and higher
(highest mountain, never stop)
Higher and higher and higher
(highest mountain, reach the top)

Just for you (highest mountain, never stop)
Just for you (highest mountain, reach the top)
Just for you.....

I can't seem to catch my breath
It's in front of me
Behind your lips

And here I go,
Letting go
Just another, let you go
I never thought I could be like this

I wanna spend every moment here with you
You've shown me a place I've seen but never knew
So here I am
Here I am
Here I am
Here I am
Just for you
Just for you

In the dark
Moving hands to find my way
Reaching for a chance
And the words to say

And here I go
Letting go
Just to never let you go
I'm so scared to feel so safe

I wanna spend every moment here with you
You've shown me a place I've seen but never knew
So here I am
Here I am
Here I am
Here I am
Just for you...

I've been so quiet for so long
Waiting for the chance to find me
Now I'm finding out
That things have never been so real
Never felt the way they should be
Now they've found me

I wanna spend every moment here with you
You've shown me a place I've seen but never knew
I wanna spend every moment here with you
You've shown me a place I've seen but never knew
So here I am
Here I am
Here I am
Here I am
Just for you
Just for you...

This is just for you
I dedicate everything I do
My fear is gone
And I feel so strong
Love has never been so true
I've never seen what I see in you
I watch you sleep
Your beauty runs so deep
And wherever you go, I'll walk beside you
And whatever you need, I will provide you
Take my soul, and never let go

'cause I live just for you
And I give just for you
And your love has me wanting to
Be the best man I can be
I believe in forever
Just for you and me

This is just for us
To a future filled with truth and trust
And your sweet touch
I want you so much
And there is nothing that we can't do together
I am gonna be lovin' you forever
Take my hand, and make me your man

'cause I live just for you
And I give just for you
And your love has me wanting to
Be the best man I can be
I believe in forever
Just for you and me

Take my soul, and never let go
'cause I live just for you
And I give just for you
And your love has me wanting to
Be the best man I can be
And I believe in forever
Just for you and me

And I believe in forever
Just for you and me

I can't stay now and just wait now, my hands then go so impatient, many things I've got to do now for the first ray of the morning.
Though she play in peaceful chamber, sleep to me just doesn't come, when she wake I have to tell her everything I have to say.
And the night so dark inside me makes me finally understand where the love that she has given me, she can light the sky forever.
It's the way she gives so freely, it's the way she takes my hands, I just ask the sun shine brightly got to see her smile again.
Then I sing a song I've written and I'll make the whole world listen in the silence just for you, like no one has ever heard.

And I wake up all the lovers and I give them back for hours, and we'll do the things we wanted the way that lovers do.
And we'll run into the street and we'll start to dance like crazy, 'cause she want only to feel joy in the love she gives and needs.
And we'll paint the street and building, rainbow color everyone, those she wants, colors to sing, and we'll paint full fill with flowers, make the street alive with spring, make a place where lovers go, fly away like lovers do.
Then we'll fly into the sky and we'll look into the stars, and our stars return the whole world,
the love we have, we are, the love we share is sweet, the love we know is real, that love is not to dream but last, we know that alone, because you love and my begin without dreaming all begin, and the love that you have given returns to us to win, 'cause your love for me is not beginning and the end your love for me, forever, your love for me forever...

Sometimes when the darkness loses its hold
I tread politely in the cold
Racking my brains
Pumping my veins
And taking the evening train from view
But you know I never wanted to
Ah, you know I did it just for you
And it's so easy to hurt me now
And you've forgotten anyhow
That certain ideas
Have changed through the years
I purchased some tears just to see me through
But you know I never wanted to
Ah, you know I did it just for you
One day I noticed the world at my feet
Next day comes and it rolls into the street
Gathering speed
Paying no heed
That made me bleed until I was blue
But you know I never wanted to
Ah, you know I did it just for you

Just for you just for you that's why I say the things I say and I do the things I do
No one else can make my arms feel like they're wrapped around the world
Yes I live my life just for you

Each day I wake up with a kiss just for you
And I count my many blessings
and I thank the Lord for you
And each minute of the day
I live a dream that has come true
Yes I live my life just for you
Just for you just for you...
Yes I live my life just for you

Confusion just sets in, it always does, where does life begin, you never know
you won't know until it hits you
You never act the same
You always play the game
You play to kill
You won't see it coming
You wanna see a change for tomorrow
You wanna see a change just for you
Depression closes in, you can't escape, no one understands, they can't relate, you won't know until it hits you
It never goes away, feel it every day, your only hope, it could change tomorrow
You wanna see a change for tomorrow
You wanna see a change just for you
You wanna see a change before you throw it all away
Something has gotta break

Just for you, break through tradition, break through to life, hold onto anything you can find

Yo, are you ready for this one

Gonna mix blend rip up the track
New determination can you feel that
We fly on Virgin to countries and back
Talk the talk as we wave the flag
Now how you liking that
Distribute like stores in a street
Where people of the town are so quick to speech ya, greet ya, teach ya, I'm just Alesha, now I'm getting stressed, more pressure, more debts
I'm just trying to make a living for me, free ya mind and let people be
Why does there always have to be jealousy
There's nuff room for you and nuff room for me
I'm gonna be flip this script just one more time
I'm a...

[Chorus:]
We ain't going nowhere
We're staying right here
Cause we do it just for you and that's the truth
We ain't going nowhere
We're UK's finest, brightest shining stars

It's Su-Elise and now it's time for me to say my piece, And you should know hold it down for the South everywhere we go
Gonna wreck the UK cause that's my home
Sometimes my peeps they be tripping and that OK, It's just words and that's this game
Never care 'bout the money, never asked for the fame, Su-Elise one out of three as long as there's a group that you call Mis-Teeq
You'll regret the day you ever doubted me
Quiet but deadly if you really wanna know ask me, Never rude maybe a little feisty
I thought you knew, bad gals move in silence

[Chorus]

La di la di da di when it come to B I rock the party, So throw ya hands in the air everybody
I'm a throw it one time for the party
Oh my gosh got love for the ones who hold it down for me, Oh my gosh got love for my sisters and the real MC's
Love the mic but I choose to sing
Now let me take ya back to the old skool beat
Sabrina yeah you know I'm sexy and you know it
And the way I spit can't nobody do it better so

[Chorus: repeat to end]

They say that it's always darkest right before the
dawn
They say that I must be strong just to carry on
But they don't know that I would wait my whole
lifetime through
Because of you, my love, that I'd be waiting
just for you

There you stood, amazing shining for the whole
world to see
And I knew an angel had been sent to watch
over me

So I'll be waiting, hoping, dreaming, loving you
Because I know, my love, that you do love me too

They say that it's always darkest right before the
dawn
They say that I must be strong just to carry on

But they don't know that I would wait my whole lifetime through
Because of you, my love, that I'd be waiting just for you

There you stood, amazing shining for the whole world to see
And I knew an angel had been sent to watch over me

So I'll be waiting, hoping, dreaming, loving you
Because I know, my love, that you do love me too

Use to be (Use to be)
Love was mean to me
Every love I tried my heart cried that won't do
Now you see (Now you see)
Love's been good to me I guess my love was waiting just for you
You and me (You and me) (You and me)
Go so well as we
Fit right to a T
Can't you see we do

Gotta say (Gotta say) (Gotta say)
Your love's got a way
Of making me glad
I waited just for you
I should have known
That my heart could not be wrong

Gotta say (Gotta say) (Gotta say)
Your love's got a way
Of making me glad
I waited just for you
I should have known
That my heart could not be wrong

Gotta say (Gotta say) (Gotta say)
Your love's got a way
Of making me glad
I waited just for you
I should have known
That my heart could not be wrong

Gotta say (Gotta say) (Gotta say)
Your love's got a way
Of making me glad
I waited just for you
I should have known
That my heart could not be wrong

Loneliness, it made you sad
Watch you cry
I see you cry
She cried
Emptiness brings you back
To your home, all alone, to your home
I'd do anything just for you
Just for you
Standing here
Open arms
Hold you close
So tight
Won't let go
I'd do anything, anything for you
I'd do anything, anything for you
I'd do anything just for you

Have I been dumb letting you go?
Wasting your time didn't you know?
Sometimes I scream, sometimes I shout
And I say things I don't really mean

And this time I spent with you
Made me happy and made me sad too
But it's time I spent with you
Time I spent with you

And I can change too
And I can change too

Over these weeks I realised
I don't understand and I'm in disguise
Of what I really feel
Of what I really feel

And I can change too
And I can change too
And I can change too
Just For You

And I can change too
And I can change too
And I can change too
Just For You
Just For You
Just For You

I'll dream another day for you
I'll peel another skin for you
I'll bare another soul just for you

I'll bleed another heart for you
I'll even play the fool for you
I'll act so crazy just for you

There's nothing I will not deny
If you're the sun I'll be the sky
So many times I've walked right by your side
So many times I've been a superfly
But I am not your candy-coated crazy little guy

I'll be the martyr to your cause
I'll be the star that has to fall
Anything you want I will be
I'll fill my head with thoughts of you
I'll steal the moon and paint it blue
I'll pull my own strings all for you
There's nothing I will not deny
If you're the sun I'll be the sky
So many times I've walked right by your side
So many times I've been a superfly
So many times I've wandered thru your heart
So many times I've wondered where to start
So many times I've walked right by your side
So many times I've been a superfly
But I am not your candy coated crazy little guy

There's nothing I will not deny
If you're the sun I'll be the sky
So many times I've walked right by your side
So many times I've been a superfly
So many times I've wandered thru your heart
So many times I've wondered where to start
So many times I've walked right by your side
So many times I've been your super fly
But I am not your candy coated crazy little guy

I will not deny...

Some do it for love and some for less
Some do it for touch and tenderness
They do it for power and for control
They do it for money and for rock 'n' roll
Some people don't know why they do
But I, I know, I do it just for, just for
Just for you and nobody else
Just for you, baby, can't you tell
Just for you, you know what I mean
Just for you even in my dreams
Where I say "Talk to me, couchez-vouz"
It's easy with you
I know what you need
I know what to do
Just for you

Some to heal and some to hurt
Some for thrills and some for dirt
Some to remember, some to forget
Some do it for anything they can get
Oh, some people don't know why they do
But I, I know, I do it just for, just for
Just for you in the night
Just for you, baby, dressed in white
Just for you, you know what I mean
Just for you even in my dreams
Where I say "Talk to me, couchez-vouz"
It's easy with you
I know what you need
I know what to do
Just for you

If you are the one to tempt me
I am tempted
When it's my turn to speak out
I am empty

When love comes to me this way
I am blasted
Just to hear you say I love you
Is time passing

For you—just for you
For you—just for you
I could be awake all night
In confrontation
Just to hear you say
I'm your main station

There is no gift on earth
That I could give you
I find myself just longing
To be with you

For you—just for you
For you—just for you

I belong to no other
Just as long as you're around dear
No time can match the feeling
That I have found here

For you—just for you

Thinking back on when
The dream was all I knew
Everything I've earned
Is all because of you

The love you gave us all
And the strength to carry on
You paved the only way
And I owe it all to you

I owe it all to you
All that I've achieved
All that I've received
Is all for you

And I never will
No I never will forget
Oh mama...
Your more than that to me
You're my friend

Holding back the tears
Though the struggle stayed for years
You gave me inner strength
And I owe it all to you

I owe it all to you
All that I've achieved
All that I've received
Well it's all for you

And I never will
No I never will forget
Oh mama...
Because you're more than that to me
You're my friend

Just for you
you
you
...

Ev'ry little thing I do
you know I do it just for you.
I got no money, no place to live
but all I got you know I'd give
I was thinking of you when I wrote this song
Now that I have found you

Please stay here where you belong.

Just for you
just for you
just for you
just for you.
I had to keep it
had to save it
had to give it to you.
Just for you
just for you
just for you
just for you

You
you
just for you
you
you
just for you.

When you're lonely
when you're sad
think of all the fun we had
I know that I ain't made it yet
when I do all I've got you'll get
I am dreaming of you while I play this song
Now that I have found you

Please stay here where you belong.

Just for you
just for you

Just for you
I'll take whatever life can give
Just for you
I'll pour the ink right out my nib

I can do all the things
you've ever wanted to do
Every single moment I think about you
For you
I'll do it all just for you

Just for you
I'll take the rough and take the smooth
Just for you
I'll try to do my best to prove

I can do all the things you've ever wanted to do
and what's more baby every thing is times two
For you
I'll do it all just for you

Just for me
You're all I ever dreamed you'd be
Just for you
I'll reach and shake the money tree

I will do all the things you've ever wanted to do
what's more baby every thing is times two
For you
I'll do it all just for you

Just for you
I'll do it all just for you
Just for you
I'll do it all just for you

This one won't be on the radio
If I'm right they'll say it is too slow
This one may not ever make it
Outside these four walls I take it
This one won't be on the radio

But I'm gonna sing it anyway
As if my last breath was today

It's way past due that I write just for You
I've been distracted by what can't compare to You
You're worth every note every struggle
and pain, every refrain

The inside of this lonely hotel room
Reminds me of Your cold and empty tomb
The sun shines through the window pane
Reminding me You rose again
Inside of this lonely hotel room

And I'm gonna sing my lonesome song
Remembering You're with me through the storm

Just for you just for you that's why I say the things
I say and I do the things I do
No one else can make my arms feel like they're
wrapped around the world
Yes I live my life just for you

Each day I wake up with a kiss just for you
And I count my many blessings and I thank the
Lord for you
And each minute of the day I live a dream that has
come true
Yes I live my life just for you
Just for you…

Just for you.
I will cry myself a little more.
Just for you.
I will lie awake a little more.
Just for you.
I will starve myself a little more.
Just for you.
I will lose myself a little more.

Let her go.
If there is nothing much left to say.
Let her go.
If there is a will there's definitely a way.
Let her go and I try and I try and I try to let her go.
Just for you.
I will hide myself a little more.
Just for you.
I will sigh myself a little more.
Just for you.
I will shame myself a little more.
Just for you.
I will blame myself a little more.

Let her go.
I suppose I'm left only to pray.
Let her go.
Her voice calls me every day.
Let her go and I wake up calling to you.
Let her go. Let you go. Let us go.

I swear to my life for you.

I am forever in night to you.
I am unholy, unworthy, a violent mess deserving the suffering that bleeds into the fire & you leave me to die…just for you.

I will face myself a little more.
Just for you.
I will age and rest a little more.
Just for you.
I will love no less a little more.
Just for you.
I will wait till death.

Of all the songs the world is singing
Of dreams that do and don't come true
I guess I've sung about a million
But darling this one's just for you

I don't care if the world can't hear it playing
Or if it's number one or two
I just want to tell you how much I love you
So darling this song's just for you

What do they care about my troubles
Or if my world suddenly fell through
You are the one who stands beside me
So darling this song's just for you

Yes darling this song's just for you

And I live for tonight
Give my best while the light's
Keeping on to shine on me
Just for you, just for you
And I live for tonight
For this show here tonight
Just as long as you believe in me
Just for you, just for you

This song is dedicated
To all you people out there
Who are standing by my side tonight
And for the last seven years
You gave me hope, belief and your love
And for all that I'll never forget you

As I walk on stage tonight
I will try to make it right
And I feel my heart beats strong and fast

It's funny, but I still get nervous
After all this time
I travelled the world, sunshine and rain
I've seen a million faces and places
But each one has a place in my heart

Everybody stand by me, living in a fantasy
I want to make you feel good at last

A sea of green, a sky of blue
Is there time? all things to do
I see your face before me and I'm wondering if it's you
Looking through the window but there isn't any view
So I'm taking from the chandelier
A crystal just for you

The music plays
The pheasant stays
A plane in the sky
Reality passing by

I see your face before me and I'm wondering if it's you
Looking through the window but there isn't any view
So I'm taking from the chandelier

A crystal just for you.

You walked into the room my eyes lit up
Each time you know that it's true
Everyone around you is blurred
I can only focus on you

Now it's like I am not even here
Our future once seemed oh so clear
If only we could start it all again
This one time please listen

This has all been just for you
Hopefully you'll notice what I've gone through
Everything that I've done and said
Is my only way to show you I want you back
The autumn storm's blown serenity away
The world around me feels so cold
I think about you every single day
I need your warmth back in my world

The days pass by, will this pain ever heal
Hope sees me through emptiness that I feel
If only we could start it all again
This one time please listen

This has all been just for you
Hopefully you'll notice what I've gone through
Everything that I've done and said
Is my only way to show you I want you back

This has all been just for you
Hopefully you'll notice what I've gone through
Everything that I've done and said
Is my only way to show you I want you back

This has all been just for you
Hopefully you'll notice what I've gone through
Everything that I've done and said
Is my only way to show you I want you back

I've been taking all my time—just for you

But you're hidin'
always fightin'.
I've been workin' day and night—just for you

You're ignoring
you say I'm boring too.
Check it on out
here is something new.

Just for you—I changed my way of living
Just for you—I waited oh so long

Just for you—no gettin'
only givin'

Just for you—I sing out this song.

You've been takin' all my time—just for you

You just steal it
I can't deal with you.
One way traffic ain't a way—just for you

I've got affection
some attraction too.
Check it on out
this ain't something new.

Just for you—I changed my way of living

Now it's showtime and all that you've givin'
Is staring gazing faces.
Come on and show your love

Ooh baby. Now's the time y'all.

Let's celebrate
don't be late

We're gonna have some fun.
It's happiness we're dreamin' of.

We've been givin' all our time—just for you

Always singin'
all we're bringin'.
Now give us something in return—just for you

We've been starvin'—now we're chargin' you.
Check it on out
is this something new?

Just for you—I changed my way of living
. . .
Just for you—I changed my way of living

Just For You, I Could Fly
Just For You, I Could Walk the Oceans
I Would Cross All Divides
To Satisfy Your Whims and Notions
For You, I Could Break the System
I Would Take Every Blow
Survive Upon a Poor Man's Wisdom

And If You Want I'd Chase the World Away
And When You Cry I'd Kiss the Tears Away

Just For You, I Would Cry
Just For You, I Would Fall Down to My Knees
And Pray That I Could Raise
a Love That's Fit to Please You

And If You're Lonely I Will Be With You
If You're in Doubt I'll Tell You What to Do
I Would Take Your Hand and I'll Lead You Through
I'd Give My Very Soul to Be With You

And When Infatuation Fades I'll Still Be By
Your Side
I Will Be There When You Call
There's Not One Thing I Wouldn't Do
That I Couldn't Do At All
That I Wouldn't Do At All

Just For You, I Would Change
Just For You, I Would Break the System
I Would Take Every Blow
Survive Upon a Poor Man's Wisdom

Of all the songs the world is singing of dreams
that do and don't come true
I guess I've sung about a million but darling this
one's just for you
I don't care if the world can't hear it playing if
it's never number one or two
I just want to tell how much I love you so darling
this song's just for you

What do they care about my troubles if my
whole world suddenly falls through
You'll be the one who'll stand beside me so
darling this song's just for you

I need you, babe
I love you, babe
Just for you

I need you, babe
I want you, babe
Just for you

I need you, babe
I love you, babe
Just for you

Just for you

And I live for tonight
Give my best while the light's
Keeping on to shine on me
Just for you, just for you
And I live for tonight
For this show here tonight
Just as long as you believe in me
Just for you, just for you

This song is dedicated
To all you people out there
Who are standing by my side tonight
And for the last seven years
You gave me hope, belief and your love
And for all that I'll never forget you

As I walk on stage tonight
I will try to make it right
And I feel my heart beats strong and fast

It's funny, but I still get nervous
After all this time
I traveled the world, sunshine and rain
I've seen a million faces and places
But each one has a place in my heart

Everybody stand by me, living in a fantasy
I want to make you feel good at last

I can't seem to catch my breath
It's in front of me
Behind your lips

And here I go,
Letting go
Just another, let you go
I never thought I could be like this

I wanna spend every moment here with you
You've shown me a place I've seen but never knew
So here I am
Here I am
Here I am
Here I am
Just for you
Just for you

In the dark
Moving hands to find my way
Reaching for a chance
And the words to say

And here I go
Letting go
Just to never let you go
I'm so scared to feel so safe

I wanna spend every moment here with you
You've shown me a place I've seen but never knew
So here I am
Here I am
Here I am
Here I am
Just for you...

I've been so quiet for so long
Waiting for the chance to find me
Now I'm finding out
That things have never been so real
Never felt the way they should be
Now they've found me

I wanna spend every moment here with you
You've shown me a place I've seen but never knew
I wanna spend every moment here with you
You've shown me a place I've seen but never knew
So here I am

Here I am
Here I am
Here I am
Just for you
Just for you...

When I wake up
When I am not asleep
Sometime between the night and the day
The Creepy Weeper's calling
and reaching out his hands to me
the longest arm of all

Then he tells me
exactly what to do
for you
who needs me most of all
and says if I should grow up
we'll lose the perfect love
he says
I'm made up out of them

I am a fake
I am a ripoff
I will definitely shit on you to get off

When my life is over
I'll think about the day
and joy that I created maybe just for you

Eventually,
he says the strongest walls will fall
and show the monkey (that's me)
Give them the gift of knowing
the truth behind the dream
they love much more than you and me

I am unreal
I am pretentious
I am definitely far beyond redemption

But when I finally wake up
there's nothing else to do
but write a silly song
and sing it just for you

YOU and ME!
ME and ME!

When you think about me
and what I seem to be
You'll see that life is mainly me

I am the world
I am the real one
I will definitely step on bugs (and kill them)

But in this voice I'm thinking
I know just what to do
I'll make a perfect turd and sell it
just for you

I am a sponge
I am a pissant
I am definitely enclosed by sycophants

But if my tongue's wisdom
fall underneath your ears
I'll try forgiveness in me
just for you

I am a worm
I am a goofball
I am definitely not there when the poop falls

But there is a feeling in me
that elevates my soul
when I wallow in self pity

just for you

I am a flake
I am a donut
I am definitely whinier with no nuts

But sometimes I look up
and feel the sun on me
and know it is a perfect world
(it has to be!)
yes, I know it is a perfect world
it has to be!

A sea of green
A sky of blue
It's their time
All things to do

I see your face before me
And I'm wondering is it you
Looking through the window

Where there isn't any view
So I'm taking from the chandelier
A crystal just for you

The music plays
The pheasant stays
A plane in the sky
Reality passing by

[* = speaking]

For your love...

*Baby I'm like a sad man
*I knew I was wrong
*But when I told you all those lies, huh
*I was a fool to make 'em
*I was a big fool
*But you got to beleive me when I said I loved you

For your love I would do anything baby *(Every day hasn't been sunny (Just for your love, just for your love) without you ever since)

For your love I would go anywhere honey,
*(Huh, but then again every day hasn't been,
cloudy either)
And just for your love I would do anything baby,
(Just for your love, just for your love)
For your love I would do anything

Listen...
I see the tears
I caused you to cry
Now I know it was a mistake
When I lied, baby
Not a day goes by
I don't wish to see your eyes
I wish I could bring you back my way
Every day for your love I pray

For your love I would do anything baby
For your love I would go anywhere honey
And just for your love I would do anything baby
(Just for your love, just for your love)
For your love I would do anything

Listen, listen, listen baby...
It's been awhile
Since I felt your embrace
Things are so sad in my dreams
All I see is, All I See Is Your Face, ...baby
I dream about the day you said goodbye
For your love I'll climb any mountain
It doesn't matter how high baby

For your love I would do anything baby
(Anything, babe anything baby)
For your love I would go anywhere honey
(I will go anywhere)
And just for your love I would do anything baby
(You x7)
(Just for your love, just for your love)
For your love I would do anything

K-Ci: JoJo help me sing it.
JoJo, JoJo, JoJo,

JoJo: Anywhere, anywhere, anywhere anywhere
Anywhere, anywhere, anywhere, anywhere ... (ANYWHERE)

K-Ci: Anything you want from me
Anything you need from me
Anything you need and anything

(Anything...)
JoJo: Any song you want me to sing
If I can play it
Baby darling she'll sing
(Just name the song)
Anything you want from me
I'll do it for you

For your love,
Just for your love, just for your love,
For your love
(I would do, I would surely do, for you—I will climb any mountain)
And just for your love
(I will climb the highest mountain)
For your love I would do anything
(I would do anything for you, baby, baby, baby)

For your love I would do anything baby,
(Just for your love, just for your love)
(anything, anything, anything, anything. Anything)
For your love I would go anywhere honey,
(I would never hurt you x3, baby, baby, baby...)
(All I wanna do is love you till the end)
And just for you love I would do anything baby,
I'll do it for you
For your love I would do anything.
(All I wanna do is love you till the end)

May all your winter Skyies Be Blue
And all your Lovers Turn Out right for you

And all your Friends are,
Ever Loyal Just For you, Just For you

May one and all your Dreams they Come to fruit
May the One who get your love be Sure to Suit

May God grant You a long and Prosperous Life
and someone can go take you for a Wife

May time be kind and treat you with Respect
and never give you less than you'd expect

I would climb to the top of a mountain
Or swim the deepest river just for you,
yeah, that's what I'd do
I would get my things together
and walk thru stormy weather
Just for you, yeah that's what I'd do

Cause the love you give to me
Is all I'll ever need
Honey no one else could do the things you do
Every night you make my day
And honey, I hope and pray
Just for you, just for you

And in your saddest hours
I'd bring smiling flowers just for you,
yeah, that's what I'd do
And on your coldest, darkest night,
I'd be the guiding light
Just for you, yeah that's what I'd do

[Chorus]

Yeah

Look at the sky
Look at, it's shining for you
I pay to shine just for you
I know you love me too

I got alone
My duty is done now
I want you but I just don't know how
I reflect you just mine

Your skin, it's like skin of peach
For you the sun, the moon I reach
You're cool, I know I love you so
You know I love you... Much

I'm stand here
Waiting your words of
Caress, I know your tenderness
Can break barriers every moment

I seek your sight
You're lost in this dark night
I invert this forest for you
If you want, to God I boo

Your lips, it's like a God's lips
I am not capable to taste
You dizzy me, I'm crazy, I'm haste
Wow! I know I am just crazy...

I've waited all my lifetime for a moment like today
Our love is really real and really here to stay
And now I know what's happening to start anew
I've been living lately just because of you
People on the sidewalks of the city pass me by
They don't know how high we fly
Now I know I've found, winter all around
It fills the sounds of smiling from the heavens
to the ground
Takes a long time to be free,
I want you there with me
Don't wanna live my life away without you
That kind of living now just won't do
There's been too much wasted time feeling blue
In the morning when you rise
that sparkle in your eyes
Reminds me that I'm living just for you
Don't wanna live my life away without you
That kind of living now just won't do
There's been too much wasted time feeling blue
In the morning when we rise
that sparkle in your eyes
Reminds me that I'm living just for you
And in the morning when we rise
that sparkle in your eyes
Reminds me that I'm living just for you

Do you remember the first time I saw you
You were alone the breeze was touching your hair
So beautiful I couldn't believe my eyes
That there was someone like you in the world

Oh, baby, I can't hear no more lies
Tell me if you're like me take off your disguise
Hear my call when you are all alone
put your arms around me
If your friends had all gone

For your face, for your hair
there isn't anything I can't bear
For your eyes, for your smile
I'll do anything you desire
For your love, oh my soul I can do it do it all

Tell me, baby, the way to your heart
I can not seek it anymore
Give me your love and you will see
That I'm someone
With you I can be

For your face, for your hair
there isn't anything I can't bear
For your eyes, for your smile
I'll do anything you desire
For your love, oh my soul I can do it do it all

Something's waiting, Something's coming,
I can feel it
And it's all, yes it's all, just for you (just for you)
You say your world is an empty place
And that you're feeling alone
Stop what you're doing and look around.
Baby you don't even know
Know how I feel for you baby
How I feel for you baby
So when the pressure gets too much
And you need someone to touch,
Baby come right in.

Something's waiting (I got something for you)
Something's coming (think you know what it is)
I can feel it (yeah)

And it's all, yes it's all...
Just for you.
(just for you)

Sometimes this life seems to go too fast
Can end up passing you by (why?)
Could be the best thing you've ever had
Is right in front of your eyes

And I'm gonna blow your mind
Gonna blow your mind
When you see that open door
And you wonder what's in store,
Baby come right in...

Something's waiting (I got something for you)
Something's coming (think you know what it is)
I can feel it (yeah)

And its all, yes its all..
Just for you.

Just for you
Just for you (it's all just for you, baby)
Something's waiting
Something's coming
Something's waiting (waiting for your lovin' baby)
Something's coming

Something's waiting (I got something for you)
Something's coming (think you know what it is)
Something's waiting
Something's coming

Just for you, just for you, just for you...

Do you ever think about
The one who thinks about you
Do you ever wonder dear
Why he's always waiting here for you?
In spite of all the things you've said and done
I'm a fool and you're the only one
I'll keep waiting while you'll have your fun,

just for you
Can't you see you're a part of me
and everything I do?
And every dream I dream is just for you
Do you ever think about
the one who thinks about you
Do you ever wonder dear
Why he's always waiting here for you?
It makes no difference what you do or say
I'll be waiting here the same old way
Living every moment of each day
Just for you.

—Instrumental—

It makes no difference what you do or say
I'll be waiting here the same old way
Living every moment of each day
Just for you, just for you, mhm, just for you...

You had to leave me
All by myself, dear
And I've been crying
The whole night through

But I've been telling everybody
I'm waiting just for you

Your friends are trying
So hard to tempt me
There's no use trying
Cause I'll be true
And, darling
You don't have to worry
Nobody else will do

I know this waiting
Can drive me crazy
Don't mind the waiting
It's nothing new

For I'll be telling everybody
I'm waiting just for you

Maybe a long time
Before I see you
So we can do
What we used to do

But I'll be telling everybody
I'm waiting just for you
I'm waiting just for you

You came to the appointment, a little tiny space
Candles lit, and burning incense
We chilled on the futon smoking ganja 'til dawn
Hmm, me and you, I'm feelin the vibes—
baby it's on
You showin yo' mind, I'm showin you mine
We discussin supreme mathematics
and takin our time
Reading me with your third eye
Baby no worry, I'm an educated dime
See you touchin me, and I'm diggin it actin shy
Full of smiles, we can't help it, but why?
Through our eye contact our mindsets intensify
Fantasizing what's under that Vokal
and you between my thighs
See, you want studio time,
in and outta town doin shows
I'm studying to be a doctor for a future, who knows?
Listening to Dead Prez rap about "Gettin Free"
and becoming intellectually wealthy
Me and you discussing how to eat healthy
All this seems to be a dream
This young intelligent talented king sittin next to me
Caressing my mouth with his lips
Timing's right; oooh, I'm diggin this friendship

By the way Boo, whatever you do
Keep it St. Louis

I've waited all my lifetime, for a moment like today
Our love is really real and really here to stay
And now, I know what's happening to start anew
I've been living lately just because of you

People on the sidewalks of the city pass me by
They don't know how high we fly
Now I know I've found, in the world all around
It fills the sounds of smiling from the heavens
to the ground
Takes a long time to be free,
I want you there with me

Don't wanna live my life away without you
That kind of living now just won't do
There's been too much wasted time feeling blue
In the morning when you rise,
that sparkle in your eyes
Reminds me that I'm living just for you

Don't wanna live my life away without you
That kind of living now just won't do
There's been too much wasted time feeling blue
In the morning when we rise,
that sparkle in your eyes
Reminds me that I'm living just for you

And in the morning when we rise,
that sparkle in your eyes
Reminds me that I'm living just for you

You have to leave me all by myself dear
And I've been crying the whole night through
But I've been telling every-body
I'm waiting just for you

Your friends are trying so hard to tempt me
There's no use trying cause I'll be true
And darling you don't have to worry
nobody else will do

I know this waiting can drive me crazy
Don't mind the waiting it's nothing new
For I'll be telling everybody
I'm waiting just for you

Maybe a long time before I see you
So we can do what we used to do
But I'll be telling every-body
I'm waiting just for you

I know this waiting can drive me crazy
Don't mind the waiting it's nothing new
For I'll be telling every-body
I'm waiting just for you

Maybe a long time before I see you
So we can do what we used to do
But I'll be telling every-body
I'm waiting just for you

Just for you
I'd tear down walls
Rescue you when you're face to face with your fate

Just for you
I'd walk through fire
Stand right there the rest of my life, girl
if that's what it takes

You might say that I'm crazy
Or just a little touched
But I'm doing it all for you
because I love you so much

Just for you
I'd be myself
If you want me to beg,
just for you I'd break down and cry

Just for you
I'd hold on tight
I'd never let go if you just stay with me tonight

You can call me insane
I'm not that far gone
But I'm doing it all for you
because my love is so strong

You can call me insane
I'm not that far gone
But I'm doing it all for you
because my love is so strong

In the morning when you wake up
do you think about me?
Were you lonely in your dreams?
Were you dreamin' of me?
Let me see.

The sun brings up the wonderin'
of what's been goin' down once again,
lady luck's hangin' around
and around and up and down,
she sang this song from me to you
from me.

Singin' songs of stories told,
makin' love with rock and roll,
tryin' to say there's no time for the blues.
It's all just for you,
yes, you.

Tell me, are there others?
Let me know where you've been,
there is nothin' you should hide,
lovers have to be friends to begin.

If today were tomorrow or yesterday,
and if feelings could talk,
wonder what they would say,
anyway, any day,
I just heard someone say,
the rain, the shame, and the pain;
it's all on me.

I keep on singin' songs of stories told,
makin' love with rock and roll,
tryin' to say there's no time for the blues.
It's all just for you,
yes, you.

Singin' songs of stories told,
makin' love with rock and roll,
tryin' to say there's no time for the blues.
It's all just for you,
yes, you.

Sometimes I think I am losin' it all,
sometimes I don't even care,
sometimes it hurts so bad I can't take it,
everyone's riding me down through the ground,
I swear, it's just not fair.

I keep on singin' songs of stories told,
makin' love with rock and roll,
tryin' to say there's no time for the blues.
It's all just for you,
yes, you.

You should listen very well
I'm about to lose my mind
There's a story I must tell

Before I'm leaving you
And it's not about a girl or love
'cause it's you who is out there

Maybe you are listening to the words I'm gonna sing
After all this time you're still so wrong for me
Yeah this song is just for you
Yeah this song is just for you
Aahah.. Oooo..

Maybe you are listening to the words I'm gonna sing
After all this time you're still so wrong for me
Yeah this song is just for you
Yeah this song is just for you
Aahah.. Oooo.. Aahah.. Oooo..
For you

1st verse:
There's a girl I'm thinking of, always on my mind
Wish she could've been a watch,
cuz she's 'around' me all the 'time'
Feelings in my stomach, fluttering butterflies
Never meant to fall in love, don't know how and why
Could be fate,
cuz our love story's written in pages
Never seen the book,
cuz knowing would be dangerous
All I know is that we're meant to be together
There're 2 times I wna be with yah—
now and forever
I would never hurt any angel sent from heaven
If we would have a 'date', it would be 24/7
If I would be your king,
you're welcomed to my palace
Would you be my queen,
I'd bow down to my highness
All I'm saying is that you should be treated with respect
And all I wna give yah is nothing but the best
Hoping in the future,
you'd be my lawful wedded wife
In my mind, can't help but think,
you got me going like
Chorus:
Everything I do
I do it all just for you
You are the girl of my dreams
You are more than fantasy

And I swear my love is true
Cuz this song is just for you
Who knows you could be my wife
But I'm just glad you're in my life

Verse 2:
To be honest, you're the reason
I started making pickup lines
Though you make fun of them every single time
Made them in the 1st place
to make you smile and laugh
Though I often do that by making stupid silly acts
I love staring at your beautiful brown eyes
With that gorgeous smile, you got me mesmerized
You love every color, cuz you're pretty as a rainbow
You're the perfect package, yeah from head to toe
We were strangers, now we tell each other secrets
You were my text bud, now we became best friends
I always bring you home, having those weird hangs
Make each other nicknames
and even those weird slangs
Finding a better girl wasn't a part of my plan
Cuz I already got you,
which you inspire me to become a better man
Hoping in the future,
you'd be my lawful wedded wife
In my mind, can't help but think,
you got me going like

Chorus x2

[Snow ad libbing]
You never never never never know
??? running the show
Man pon de dance floor
You will never never never never know

[Chorus]
[Snow]
I will do anything just for you
Wanna bring you round the world
Make sure you're my girl
Never gonna wanna leave
Girl you look
Girl you look so fly to me
When I see you on the dance floor
Come pon your man
This is where you wanna be

[Snow]
Now when me step up in the dance hall
I see me circle call the rhythm like a champion
See the pretty girls a vicious like a bombshell
And then approach me like me smooth move,
me lonely man lord?
I'm meant to tell you about this girl named Renée
She nice and pretty girl
and that I met round the way
See all the mon a think about Snow's her daddy
And when me see her move about right dance today

Me say shallallaalallala boom boom shadaya
She got da body like a playboy bunny
And when me see her move a me say
right dance today
Why don't you stay
Me say shallallaalallala boom boom shadaya
She got da body like a playboy bunny
And when me see her move
she has the right dance today

[Chorus]

[Kobra Khan]
Baby look so fresh
You're way ahead of the rest
I smother you with butter
Kiss and caress
You're my number one lover
Can't settle for less
From the day that we met
There will never be a next one ??
Wait til you're grown and
Treat you right
Cause I know what's really wrong
Put my feelings aside
That's why I gotta let you know
Before another brother does
That you're the one I love
There's no other girl I trust
Put my heart in your hand
You are part of the plans
It's not hard to understand
But a woman needs a man
So you need to believe
That's when it leads to me
Cause evidently should be
There's nothing coming in between

[Snow]
Girl I love ya long time
But you blow my mind
Are you my supernova
Like a star you will shine
?????
Me say right down the line

[Chorus]

[Snow]
????
Can't run fast you fi come up in da place
??? if you run, come quick
An' me never knew a ????
???? listen for me
?????

[Kobra Khan]
Yeah run me down, run me down, times are tough
She was always by side when the going gets rough
And when I rockin' the jam to rock the boat
Ha, lockin' it down it's murder she wrote
She got the hot body well I can't chill out
Soon as I step on through the door
We're gonna stick to the couch
Ain't nobody else I know made me feel this way
That's why i gotta let her know
Til ???

[Chorus]

You are my life
Everybody knows how I feel about you
Loving your smile
And your soft caress
My love for you shines brightly
I must confess that
you are my life
I want us to be like a dream that's come true
I want our love to grow in special ways
Our hopes and visions, yeah
To be the same
I love you
Just for you
Just for you (I love you)
Just for you (I need you)
Just for you

Open your heart and let go
Give me your hand and let me know

You are my life
Everything I do
I'm thinking of you
I'm willing to try if you're willing to care
Love is the joy and pain of two that share
Just for you
Just for you
Just for you
Just for you
Just for you
Just for you

I walk around the house, sit out on the grass
Pour another drink and try to make it last
Thinking of you, thinking of you

I go out in the car, I drive around the block
And I don't hear a thing but the ticking of the clock
Thinking of you, thinking of you

You know I've talked to the Virgin Mary,
prayed to the Holy Ghost
Hung with the Bodhisattva
for the one I love the most
And I've danced with the fallen angels,
calmed down the turbulent too
Sold my soul to the shadow mind just for you,
just for you
This is my confession, can someone take it down?
It's [Incomprehensible] in the hallway,
love can't help me now
Love won't help me now

You know I've talked to the Virgin Mary,

prayed to the Holy Ghost
Hung with the Bodhisattva
for the one I love the most
And I've danced with the fallen angels,
calmed down the turbulent too
Sold my soul to the shadow mind just for you

Someone to love you
(Just for you)
Someone to care
(Just for you)

Someone to hold you
(Just for you)
When you are scared
When you are scared

You know I've talked to the Virgin Mary,
prayed to the Holy Ghost
Hung with the Bodhisattva
for the one I love the most
And I've danced with the fallen angels,
calmed down the turbulent too
Sold my soul to the shadow mind just for you

Talked to the Virgin Mary,
prayed to the Holy Ghost
Hung with the Bodhisattva
for the one I love the most
And I've danced with the fallen angels,
calmed down the turbulent too
Sold my soul to the shadow mind just for you

Just for you
Just for you
Just for you

Wake up, I'm missing your secrets of the night,
Feel so alone, don't let me go
Hold on tonight,
Now I close my eyes to hide the tears away,
End in silence crying, 'cause I'm losing you

Chorus:
I don't wanna let you go now,
'Cause I've waited forever just for you,
I'll give all my love to you now,
I would make it forever...

Wake up, I pictured you leaving me tonight,
Hard to let you go as you slip through
my fingers, don't know why,
So I close my eyes to hide the tears away,
End in silence crying, 'cause I'm losing you

[Repeat Chorus]
Aah, aah, I'm wanting you
Aah, aah, to see this thing through, hoo-wooh...

[Solo]

Just for you
I don't wanna let you go now,
'Cause I've waited forever and ever and ever...
[Repeat x2]
The song bird yearns to sing a love song,
The roses yearn just for the dew.
The whole world's yearning for the sunshine,
I have a yearning too.

[Chorus]
Yearning just for you, that's all I do, my dear.
Learning why I'm blue, I wish that you were here.
Smiles have turned to tears,
days have turned to years.
Yearning just for you, that's all I do, my dear.

(repeat)

When shadows fall and stars are beaming,
'tis then I miss you most of all.
I go to sleep and start in dreaming,
It seems I hear you call.

(chorus)

I was in seventh heaven, forgot what's real for you
I was so blind, the time stood still for me,
I didn't see any danger in you
Like a machine you dragged me into a world,
could I know ?, so full of disease;
and you were waiting 'til I lost my head
while I've been waiting
Just for you

At the same day, at the same time, and again,
Just for you;
and again I'd jump into the fire, and again,
Just for you

I see your face in every window,
your looks touch...my skin
In your might, paralyzing me,
I feel like a dwarf in a circus of sin
Like a machine you dragged me into a world,
could I know ?, so full of disease;
and you were waiting 'til I lost my head
while I've been waiting
Just for you

At the same day, at the same time, and again,
Just for you;
and again I'd jump into the fire, and again,
Just for you

At the same day, you can believe me, and again,
Just for you;
and again I'd jump into the fire, and again,
Just for you

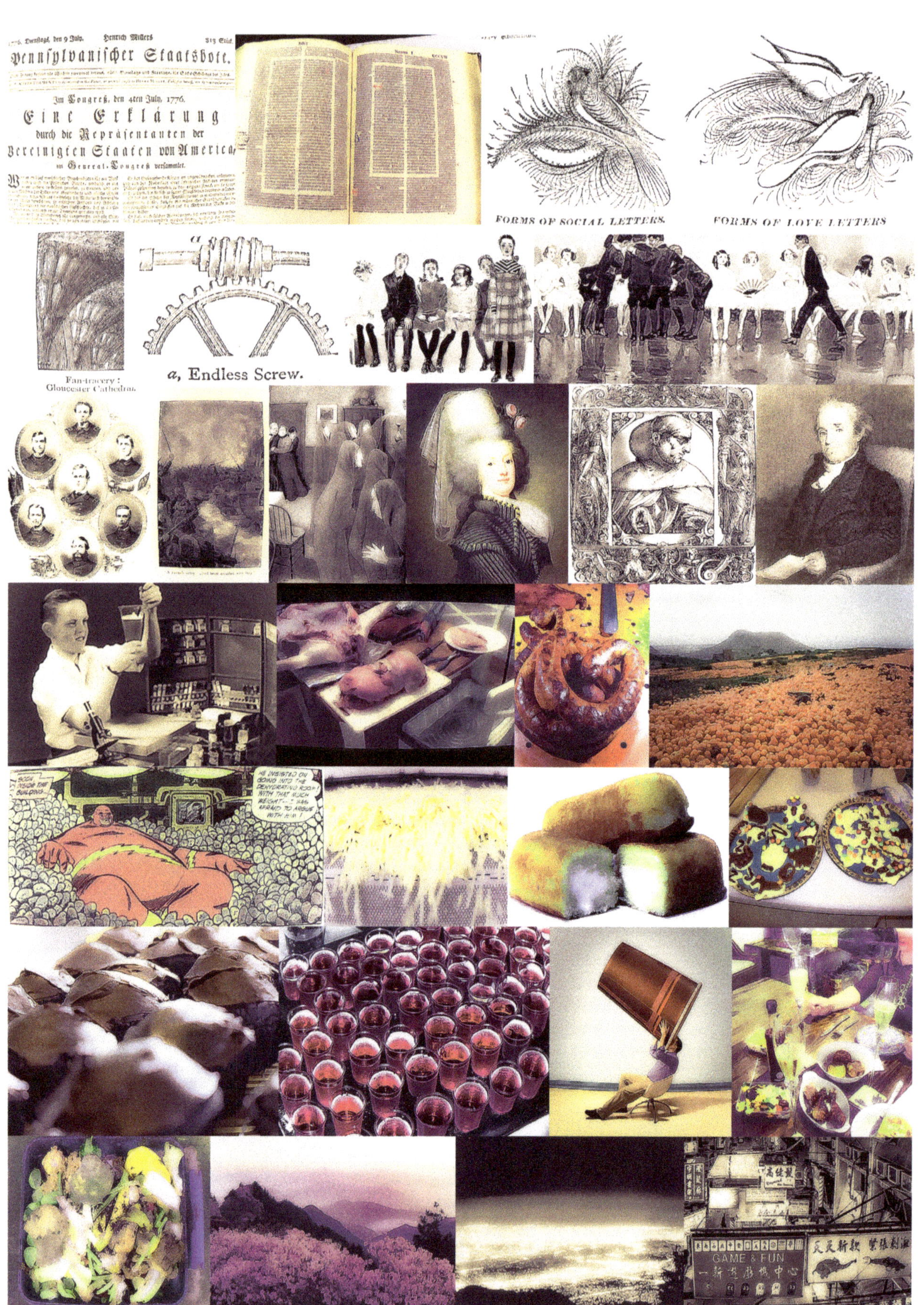
1776. Dienstags, den 9 July. Henrich Millers 313 Stück.
Pennsylvanischer Staatsbote.
Im Congreß, den 4ten July, 1776.
Eine Erklärung
durch die Repräsentanten der
Vereinigten Staaten von America,
im General-Congreß versammlet.
FORMS OF SOCIAL LETTERS.
FORMS OF LOVE LETTERS
Fan-tracery :
Gloucester Cathedral.
a, Endless Screw.
SOON, INSIDE THE BUILDING...
HE INSISTED ON GOING INTO THE DEHYDRATING ROOM! WITH THAT MUCH WEIGHT--I WAS AFRAID TO ARGUE WITH HIM!
GAME & FUN

Excess

Originally performed on Wednesday, December 5, 2012, live on video with Geneva Skeen on Ear Meal, *a weekly program broadcast live on* L.A. Art Stream *every Wednesday at 9:30 p.m. P.S.T. and produced by Alan Nakagawa in K-Town Los Angeles.*

[Improvised introduction, commentary on show, conversational, centered, radio show-like.]

Geneva Skeen: Hey Everyone! **Mathew Timmons**: Hi there! G: I'm Geneva Skeen M: and I'm Mathew Timmons G: and thanks M: Thank you to Ear Meal for having us tonight. G: Thank you to Ear Meal for having us tonight.

M: Hello Listeners andor viewers. G: Yes, hello and welcome! We are new to this forum, so please bear with us. M: Yes, please bear with us, Oh Yeah. M: Needless to say, it's been quite a bit of a mess here this past week. G: I sense that the many people who frequent this website will turn away, confused by the plethora of quoted texts.

M: Typical language: "I leave the rest, residue and remainder [or just residue] of my estate to my grandchildren."

G: The hungry knights gorged on the large feast.

M: Take the case of rock music. Its attraction is not just due to a particular preference for loud, rhythmic sound and dangerously athletic dancing. Rock music also symbolizes a whole cluster of cultural values—concerning self-expression, spontaneity, released sexuality, and perhaps most importantly, defiance of the alleged stodginess of tradition. In a mindless dissipation of natural resources, the waste of time could prove fatal.

G: Taking too many vitamins can be unhealthy and even dangerous... But are you in danger of getting too much of these important nutrients?

M: But how do we know when irrational exuberance has unduly escalated asset values, which then become subject to unexpected and prolonged contractions as they have in Japan over the past decade?

M: From too much liberty, my Lucio, liberty:
As surfeit is the father of much fast,
So every scope by the immoderate use
Turns to restraint. Our natures do pursue,
Like rats that ravin down their proper bane,
A thirsty evil; and when we drink we die.

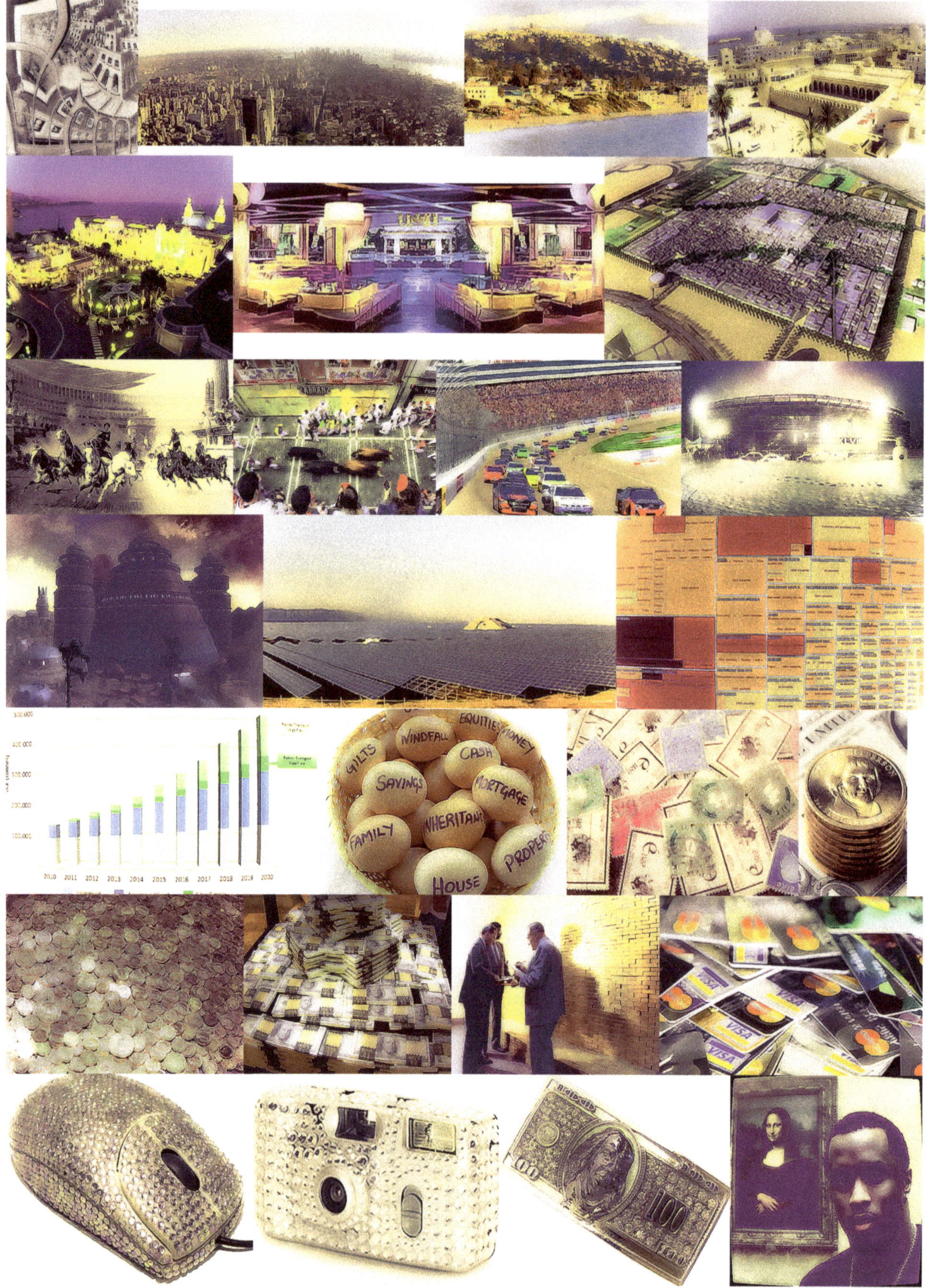

500,000
400,000
300,000
200,000
100,000
2010
2011
2012
2013
2014
2015
2016
2017
2018
2019
2020
GILTS
WINDFALL
EQUITIES
MONEY
CASH
SAVINGS
MORTGAGE
FAMILY
HOUSE
VISA

G: Had Chenille, who had stabbed Orpine in a nimiety of terror, loved something beyond herself? M: It's too bad the redistricting myth is not right, because, if it were, the problem of polarization would be much easier. Not that a nimiety of it doesn't help solve a lot of practical problems.

G: There is nothing wrong with letting children eat peanut butter every day for a week if they adore it. M: An overactive letdown is often confused with an oversupply of milk. Though they often happen together, this is not always the case. Click here to proceed. G: This is why, when the great Demiurge, Faro Lord of the Waters and the Word, was setting the world in order, he made women fertile with tomatoes and in return women continue from time to time to make offerings of this vegetable to the god. His messenger, the swallow, collects the juice of these tomatoes, just as he collects the blood of the sacrificial victims, and carries both fecundating blood and juice up into the Heavens, from which they descend to Earth in the shape of rain. M: Don't even get me started on beef tomatoes. Watery, tasteless and offering nothing of note to anything it's added to, I've always been annoyed at having them served to me in a burger when I'm out; all they do is make the burger buns soggy and just offer the taste of water, which is utterly uncalled for.

G: Abundant as June graduates in search of jobs. M: Crammed. G: I am being made redundant due to cost cutting, which is fair enough, I guess. M: To hell with false modesty... With the breadth of heaven betwixt you, it's time to subscribe to EXUBERANT FOLIAGE. Not inherent or essential; derived from something outside. Due to our demand for convenience, we have forgotten that real food comes from the earth. They had some nice choices, and there are specials chalked up on the wall and prices are not too exorbitant. G: A burst error means that two or more bits in the data unit have changed from 1 to 0 or from 0 to 1

M: With a whole world of hair fashion in the palm of your hand, browsing through thousands of the trendiest Outré hairstyles has never been easier. M: An inordinate excess in apparel.

CUT TO: G pushes gold sequin fabric off table, M collects it, hands to G. G puts on table. M pushes it off, G collects it again, hands to M. M puts on table. Repeat several times. kinda quick while repeating the line [An inordinate excess in apparel.]

G: Burst is the simple, smart and private mobile video solution that makes it easy to capture and share life with your family and friends. Burst was a progressive metal band from Kristinehamn, Sweden—without all the preservatives & other junk. M: Perhaps resulting from the famines of generations past, food, specifically high-fat foods, are now seen as a luxurious item. G: Being gorged in town kind of sucks since it never goes away. Maybe you should have it be that you get hungry in town if you're gorged.

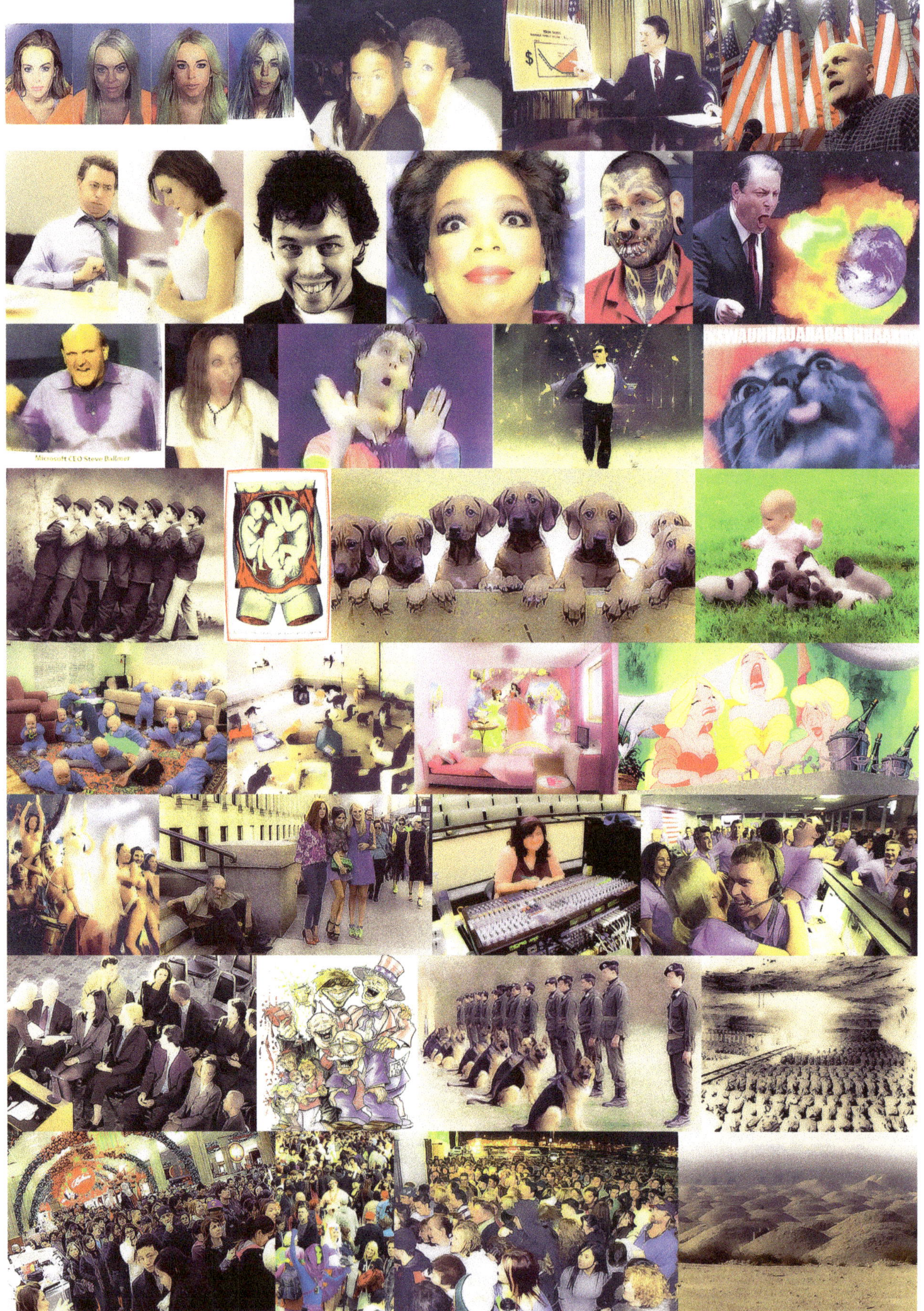
Microsoft CEO Steve Ballmer

M: If you describe something as unnecessary, you mean that it is not needed or does not have to be done. Einstein said: "If we knew what it was we were doing it wouldn't be called research, would it?"

G: If he is an arrogant man with a contempt for the body really based on delicacy but mistaken by him for purity, that's very much the more common form nowadays. M: To see a landslide in your dream represents emotions that you have been holding back for a long time. If this effort brings no compensating gain, it is a waste.

G: After he had been fined several weeks in a row for excessive celebrations, Johnson celebrated his next touchdown by holding up a sign that read "Dear NFL, Please don't fine me AGAIN!!!!!!" (and was subsequently fined $10,000 by the NFL). A scooter-riding, jeans-wearing, cell-phone-toting samurai, who makes no secret of the fact that he's FULL of secrets. M: An exorbitant sum of money to do nothing? G: It was supererogatory for her to gloat.

M: Oh, dang! If you see them comin', get out of their way! Both times, they all got into the boat and celebrating as though they were fishing, literally showboating. G: Another origin suggested for the habits and customs of the young bloods or fashionable rowdies of the restoration period is that the expression bloody drunk is to the proverbial saying as "drunk as a lord." This seems far fetched and not sufficient to account for the widespread use of this qualifying particle. But, as a result, gaudy displays are often frowned upon.

CUT TO: M with flashlight, attempting to communicate in Morse code directly into camera lens. G on phone texting or whatever.

G: The only way you can truly ensure your future survival is to know how to grow, hunt, and preserve your food. Sooner or later your stockpile will run out!

M: It is an awful thing to find your efforts supervacaneous when you are so far away from home and friends, sympathy, and help. G: Oviparous hare and april fish and fool. The condition, speed, color, clarity and force of the water reflects your emotional health regarding whatever you are dreaming about. The output is very clean and uncluttered. And I know Outré will look awful on me, but it has that so-ugly-it's-pretty kind of appeal. M: They blossom in profusion by the creek near here a week or so before Mothers' Day.

G: You must avoid techniques and methods that work around guilt or manipulation techniques no matter how desperate you are right now. The only way to get him back is to fix what went wrong in your relationship and understanding exactly what he needs from you. Both downtime and excess time are measures of the accumulated time during which the system has been inoperative. The parameter *t* of

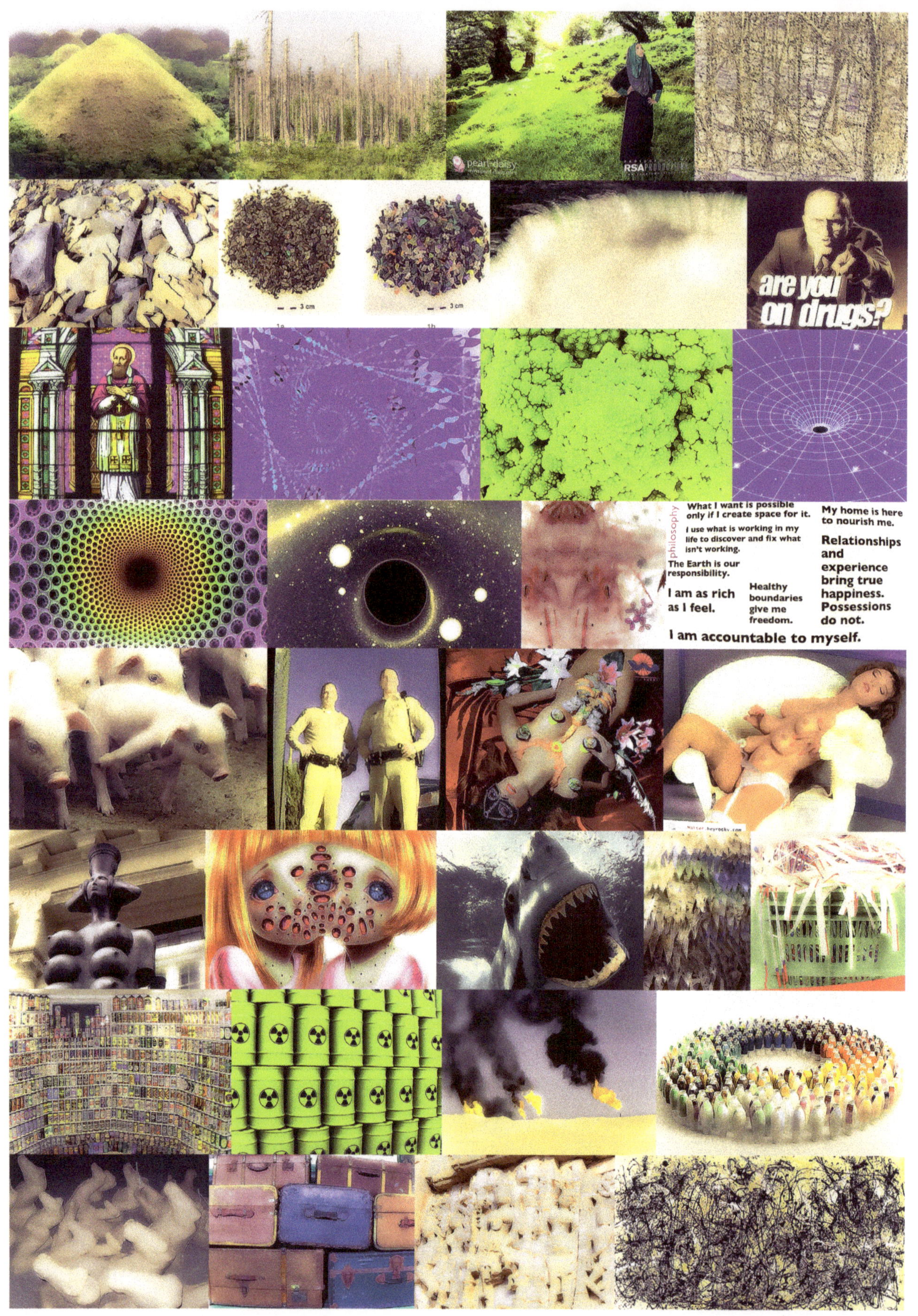
are you on drugs?
philosophy
What I want is possible only if I create space for it.
I use what is working in my life to discover and fix what isn't working.
The Earth is our responsibility.
I am as rich as I feel.
Healthy boundaries give me freedom.
My home is here to nourish me.
Relationships and experience bring true happiness. Possessions do not.
I am accountable to myself.

excess time counts only productive units of time. Thus *B(t)* is the excess of unproductive time over productive time. The properties and applications of excess time are reviewed and summarized.

M: Its funny, I didnt even notice the mojo thing and I went straight up to him. I am a warlock and he is fearable. I slayed him without using my mojo.

G: Supernumerary nipples are a common minor congenital malformation that consists of nipples and/or related tissue in addition to the nipples normally appearing on the chest. Some are hidden from view and may not be discovered for a very long time. M: Waste, Waste Everywhere and Not a Dime to Spare. G: I usually take short vacations. I can't stand too much of a good thing. Too much of a good thing can make you sick.

M: One is associated with ostentatious or bombastic speaking. The other has to do with the water or fluids building up in tissue and making it "firm" or "puffy" or the like.

G: For as a surfeit of the sweetest things
The deepest loathing to the stomach brings,
Or as the heresies that men do leave
Are hated most of those they did deceive,
So thou, my surfeit and my heresy,
Of all be hated, but the most of me.

M: You were a star, a sign of everything I knew about women and artifice, taken to the most illogical, asymmetrical extreme!! Over and over they call your outfits outré, from the French to push beyond bounds, and everywhere you go you push beyond, casting mirror-ball light onto the limits we thought we were too post-post-post- to still believe in. G: A surfeit of something is an amount which is too large.

M: Indeed, there is a woundy luck in names, sirs, and a main mystery, and a man knew where to find it.
G: We've run out of time on this project. There's no time to lose. We've got to ... have spare time.

M: party so free style yes got it jazzy amazing sun rising / ready are you ready get it Loosey beauty get your body G: Then you tied my hands, You tied my hands, tied my hands, tied my hands, You, Um tied my hands M: So shall thy barns be filled with plenty, And your vats will overflow with new wine.

G: It's crackers to slip a rozzer the dropsy in snide. This translates to, "It's insane to try to bribe a policeman with fake money."

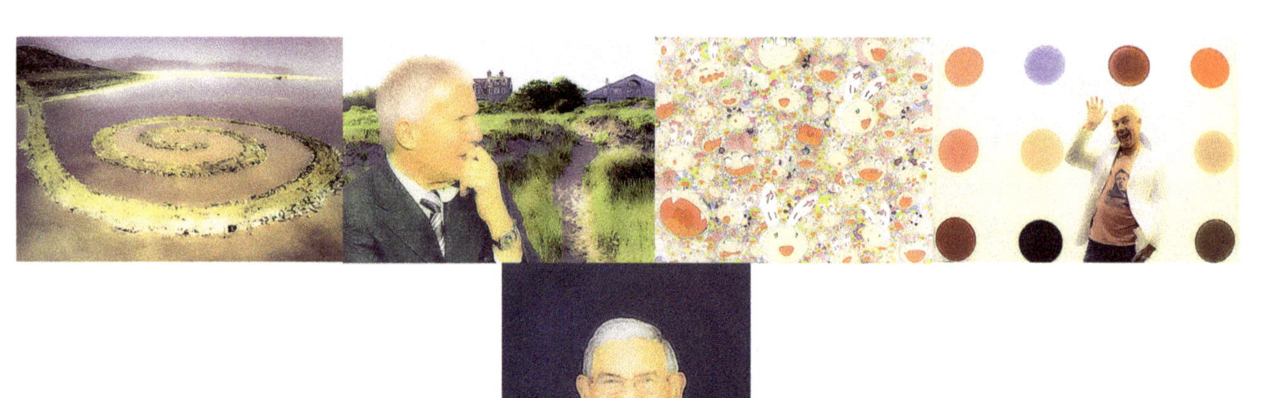

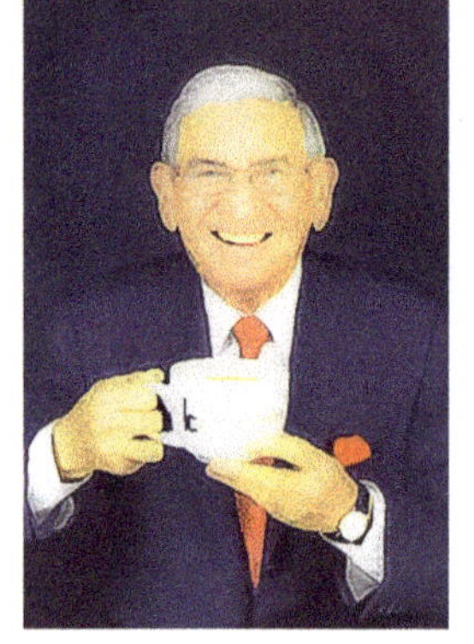

M: This penalty may seem both exorbitant and unfair, but I am sorry to say it is our standard Surcharge Sodomy fee.

G: The artist's ingrained nimiety results in cloying pictures of cute kids holding even cuter animals. **M**: On one hand, I enjoy the utter uniqueness of it, but at the same time I can't. Multitasking is an art. It requires a specific set of skills to focus on numerous tasks at once. **G**: Fanatical Abracadabraism And The Tyranny Of Magical Thinking. **M**: Greed is the inordinate desire to possess wealth, goods, or objects of abstract value ... It is typically used to criticize those who seek excessive material wealth.

Audio (from Louis C.K.'s 2007 HBO special *Shameless*): Hey this is interesting. The other day a guy told me to suck a bag of dicks. That was interesting. I never heard that before. A total stranger told me to suck a bag of dicks. A whole bag of 'em. He was angry, he didn't just say, "Suck a bag of dicks!" like a greeting, you know, "Oh, suck a bag of dicks to you too sir, thank you very much. Yes, it's a lovely day for sucking several bags of dicks."

G: I thought, this is the most wildest garage music ever.

Terrifying Photo

Written on commision for Adam Overton in late 2012 / early 2013.

♫ One of these things is not like the others,
One of these things doesn't belong.
Can you tell which thing is not like the others
Before he shows these kids his shlong. ♫

♫ Did you guess which thing was not like the others?
Did you guess which thing just doesn't belong?
If you guessed this one is not like the others,
Then you're absolutely... right! ♫

Terrifying Photo From Vacation Bible School

Those poor kids.

Turns out this isn't some creepy Vacation Bible School teacher.

He's actually a performance artist named Adam Overton. Still a funny picture though.

Terrifying Photo From Vacation Bible ... is starting to get hot on StumbleUpon.

Traffic.outbrain.com readers just made Terrifying Photo From Vacation Bible School

... hotter.

Adam Overton

California Nature Boy

Adam, the California Nature Boy, spends the day at LACMA wearing fig-leaves. Roaming Ahmanson Building, Floors 1-4.

Adam, the California Nature Boy, spends the day at LACMA in fig leaves and occasionally facilitates group belly-listening sessions, the better to know ourselves by.

Sessions with Adam at the Mr. and Mrs. Sidney F. Brody Gallery: 1:40, 3:40, 5:40 / 40 min | Self-guided belly listening:

All Day

It's not photoshopped. Melissa's right, this guy was a performance artist. The photo was taken at LACMA (Los Angeles County Museum of Art) during the "Fallen Fruit" exhibit. He is "Adam – the Nature Boy." Actually Dan, this photo has nothing to do with religion, had you bothered to check out the comprehensive links that have been provided by many people down-thread. Try to understand what is going on before thoughtlessly replying to a very logical and sensible viewpoint put forth by someone else. The event where the photo was taken isn't a church event, nor is it even an event aimed at children. It is a museum exhibition and if you have a problem with the way the man is dressed for an art exhibition, you should register your concerns with the Los Angeles County Museum of Art, who hosted and sanctioned the event. This would be the better thing to do than wildly slander a man on a website without even knowing the context of the photo. I'm pretty sure that the only person that will never forget this photo is Adam Overton, who is now being branded a creep and/or paedophile by ignorant rednecks and religious zealots. Congratulations for registering your ill-informed, poorly phrased opinion.... YOU DAN ARE AN IDIOT. Also, it's not "wrong on many levels" because it is a walking art exhibition, as approved by the Los Angeles County Museum of Art. If you have any issues with the way that the man is dressed, then you should probably contact the LACMA, instead of posting uninformed comments on photos of people who are completely innocent. Just to clarify: This photo was NOT taken at a Bible School, nor ANY other religious event. Also, these kids didn't wander into an art museum of their own accord - I would bet money on the fact that their parents brought them to the exhibition, and the parents probably thought that this was an interesting exhibit, and took a photo. Those parents obviously don't have a problem with their children seeing this exhibit, because they were there to explain the context to their children like responsible parents. It would be nice to see more parents guiding their kids and teaching them about various cultural things instead of letting them watch TV all day while they censor everything and give religious reasons for decisions rather than take the time to teach their children how to think like rational adults. If you, as a parent, wouldn't like your children to see an artistic portrayal of "California Nature Boy" then by all means, don't take your children to any exhibits like this. Nobody is forcing you to. Just don't condemn those that choose to allow their children to see cultural differences. Also, remember that this man is just one very small part of what would have been a large, fun and educationally enriching experience for people of all ages. Don't be so close-minded and ignorant. This is from an installation at the Los Angeles County Museum of Art. He's Nature Boy Adam Overton, and here's a link to LACMA. You all are a bunch of misinformed, judgmental jackasses! This is NOT, I repeat, NOT a photo from Christian Bible Camp. It's a photo of a performance artist (named—wait for it—Adam) at an event called "Eat LACMA" at the Los Angeles County Museum of Art (LACMA) in 2010, organized by the artist group Fallen Fruit. "Let Them Eat LACMA is a one-day event where over fifty artists and collectives will activate, intervene, and re-imagine the entire museum's campus and galleries. Peppered with more than a dozen interactive talks, performances, and events, Let them Eat LACMA will expand our perception of art, food, and the museum." It appears there were (OMG!) children at the museum (heaven forbid!), participating on some level, which explains the signs they wear. Thanks Buzzfeed for TOTALLY misrepresenting this, and shame on all you dumbasses for rushing to judgement and in a way that only imitates the very thing you all pretend to criticize.

The guy's name is Adam Overton and this was not VBS but a California Museum of Art. Some people call it art. I call it gross. This was at a public museum of art in California. Public tax dollars at work Gale. This was an exhibit at a public museum of art—not a church. Sorry Ray not Photoshopped and not VBS but a California Museum of Art—IE your tax dollars at work to make this stuff possible. The guys name in the picture is Adam Overton. Sorry guys not VBS but a California Museum of Art. Sorry guys not VBS but a California Museum of Art.

FYI: "Adam Overton was a walking exhibit entitled "California Nature Boy" as a part of "Let Them Eat LAMCA," a day-long event exploring art, food, culture and politics." Wow, it's amazing how you slander VBS and Christians with this photo when it is NOT a VBS photo. With just a little research you would know that it is Adam Overton aka California Nature Boy and this was at a festival in 2010. Here's the brochure. Um, not VBS, but an exhibit about eating: "Let Them Eat LACMA" event explores food culture at a museum. And that's not THE Adam, it's an artist named Adam Overton, who went as the walking exhibit "California Nature Boy." You people need to stop being outraged at every little thing that you see before you take the time to truly understand what is happening in this picture. Also, your witch-hunt-like mentality takes creedence away from the real issues with predators out there. Sophie is right. As has been clearly explained below by a few people, He was a walking exhibit for a museum gallery day - "California Nature Boy". Those kids' parents were probably like, "hey kids! Stand next to the funny nature man so we can get a photo!" and the kids are probably looking like that because that's how I always looked when my dad made me be in a tourist photo with something random that I didn't fully understand, (like when Dad took my photo aged 8 with the Blues-Mobile at Universal Studios) - I had the same look on my face. Meanwhile, plenty of people got an eyeful with Adam Overton, who went as the walking exhibit "California Nature Boy." He was hard to miss, seeing as he wore nothing but fig leaves. I feel really bummed for this guy who now is probably going to be in a bunch of shitty memes because of a few stupid idiots. According to what I could find his name is Adam Overton. He is an artist and this is a short video of him at the Los Angeles Museum event in 2010 as California Nature Boy. Don't know where that photo was taken, but without any proof or source I think it's wrong to put it here just to give a false impression. Oh and also, look at the boy at the end of this video. He has the same red id necklace on as the girls in the photo. Maybe why the labels bitter and sweet were on their shirts - because it was a food /art presentation. That is Adam, the California Nature Boy, a disciple of Guru Rugu.

What the fuck am I looking at? "Dude, what the fuck?! I thought, you said, you had turned over a new leaf & rediscovered yourself?!" What the fuck?! How do these crazy fucks get away with this kind of nonsense?? SO. DISTURBING. Paul Giomatti, "What the fuck happend bro?"

What the actual fuck? What the actual fuck?! :(

Terrifying Photo From liberal weirdo performance artist. Fixed that for you, buzzfeed. And here's a terrifying photo from a 2011 Pride Parade!

So... that's my friend Adam Overton. I'm 99% sure he doesn't work at Bible school. Can we get the real story of this once and for all? If you bothered to actually read the links that have been provided by many people in this thread, you will see that the museum event that Adam Overton is performing in is called "Let Them Eat LACMA," which was a day-long event exploring art, food, culture and politics. I am sure that the "bitter" and "sweet" labels were some form of gimmick on that day to encourage participation in what looks to be a contemporary interactive exhibition. I didn't say that THIS photo was a tourist photo, I used "tourist photo" in context with when I was often posed with seemingly random things that my parents thought would make a good snapshot. Don't believe everything you read on the internets. This is an art gallery, that is Adam Overton, and those kids must have really cool parents. The man is ADAM OVERTON and he is part of an interactive exhibit, if the comments by Jonathan Mann and Tiffany Helene are accurate. Here is the link that Tiffany posted about the art exhibit. The guy's name is Adam Overton. He bills himself as Adam the Nature Boy, as previously noted.

If you read the links that have been posted in other comments you'd see that it's not actually anything to do with religion at all (I should have read more before posting my original comment about him being Adam. Silly me for trusting the information posted with the picture. XD) it's actually part of a big exhibit at an Art Museum in Los Angeles. He represents nature. Ok, so, it's not religious. That point's taken care of. Los Angeles, that says it all.

It is normal for kids of any age to be somewhat put off by actions/behaviors they don't see every day in a safe way. While I have nothing against this performance artist or anyone, for that matter, who wants to under dress (no matter how much he or she shows, technically — can show it all anywhere as far as I am concerned,) I do think that all people should be thoughtful of others' discomfort with such and not *push* the issue by forcing themselves (or their hugs or arms across shoulders, etc.) since *THAT ALONE* can be extremely upsetting to a child who may not feel *allowed* to speak his or her mind. Read the article, he is a performance artist, it's not camp!! good golly.

hmmm...if I saw this at my kids vacation bible school...they would be taken out as soon as possible... I know you want to teach stories from the Bible but I don't think it needs this kind of visuals. Mike, "If I saw this at my kids vacation bible school..." then you would ACT? Do you actually believe sick priests/ministers will share pictures like this with you, willingly? Do you actually believe that horrible Religious incidents like this only happen IF you get to see the picture? For every found picture like this one, how many more happen where you don't get to see the pictures because the perpetrator hid it better or where pictures were not taken at all? As someone who once made the grievous mistake of letting my child attend vacation bible school, this photo doesn't surprise me in the least. A vacation bible school, better have this investigated, almost naked man, standing next to kids scared to death to pose, not healthy !!! There is no justification for this !.... being religious doesn't give anyone permission to exploit children.........it looks dodgy because it IS.......... religious people are usually too witless to understand ethics and too witless to grasp the transparency of them "crossing the line" - particularly when it involves children......."Vacation Bible School" - gimme' a break !........just another excuse for deluded adults to indulge in an unhealthy fantasy while corrupting kids. Vacation Bible School. Three words that do not belong together! Something new at vacation bible school? Vacation bible school? Adam & Eve were adults. How do you "KNOW" this was actually taken at a Vacation Bible School event? When I follow the link it ends up at a Religion hating website that just says without proof that this is what the picture is of. I don't see anything to suggest that this was from a vacation bible school aside from the caption, which by the way judging bfrom the other content on the site looks totally credible. To believe this is really from a "vacation bible school" I need to see more context aside from a simple caption. I have OFTEN sung your praises for being one of the few HONEST to goodness Progressives on Current who cares about honesty & integrity over carrying the party line. There is little doubt if the President were more like you I would be voting for him come November! I knew this was a HOAX from the get go. I have both attended and taught at Vacation Bible Schools. No Adult would dress like this and take pictures hugging children. You should apologize and post information about the true context of the photo. It's obvious the image was taken in an ART GALLERY, NOT A CHURCH VACATION BIBLE STUDY camp. Combining a Museum Event with a Vacation Bible School would be something to expect only in CA. They went halfsies for the Nature Boy who is apparently paid an awesome fee for ruining the remainder of his life in every other state.

Can this get any stranger? I think so! There's also a "belly-listening" session video at the link. Hi Jen – I did see something that must have been "belly listening" in the LACMA gallery but didn't include it as I didn't know enough about it and didn't want to post any misinformation. I couldn't believe the amount of people that seemed to think that there was something really wrong with kids seeing a man in shrubbery at a museum. There is much more graphic nudity in music videos, I think! I also believe that many of the parents on that thread probably never take their children to any cultural events … Thanks for commenting! Well Done! Adam is a friend of mine and my daughter's. We were there that day and took a very similar picture with him. It was a really fun piece and he has a wonderfully creative and inquisitive spirit that inspires both adults and children. Nobody mentioned that he also lead a "belly listening" activity. He encouraged people to lie down on museum benches and listen to each other's bellies. Of course kids totally loved the piece, especially in the context of a quiet and stoic museum gallery. The best part is that Adam has such an awesome outlook on art and social behaviors, that he would probably never accuse or condemn anyone for anything at all, even when they are ignorantly cruel. He'll just make more great art about it!

It doesnt seem like anything seriously shocking is going on, sorry. It is a theatrical performance, the issues should be that it is used to further indoctrinate the children, not that the guy is ALMOST naked. Nudity is not harmful in itself. Violating other people's boundaries is. WTF. I love the little girl trying desperately to not stand real close to the almost naked guy. That guy is TOO DAMN HAPPY to be almost naked around small children... Wow you must be utterly retarded to say this...hes almost naked around kids who are clearly not confortable..lets even dare to say hes not enjoying himself even a little right now.. its still not ok for a adult male..a fuckin creepy looking one at that to be standing naked with kids...this is something these poor kids wsill never ever forget about and unfortunately now it will be on the internet forever so they can all look back on this picture years from now if the image of this day isnt burnt into their brain for eternity This is why religion and kids is BAD BAD BAD you should be a adult before your are told to beleive say and do things you arnt sure you beleive in.... YOU SOPHIE ARE A IDIOT!!

I don't know whats going on and I did read the story. I'm just saying thats wrong to be dressed like that around children. Did you go to the link?? Did you look outside the box to see what it is thats taking place? I don't give fuck what it is or who put the show on for what reason, but a GROWN adult should not be around under 18 dressed like that period! If I walked in and seen any guy dressed like that near my daughter, they will find out those leaves do not protect against steel toe boots.

Moments after this picture was taken, the blonde girl joined a convent! Little known fact, this picture was the inspiration for the naming of the band APRILWINE. Hmmm. If it was Tarzan Johnny Weißmüller 1935 (?) noone would care:-) Isn't that a massive over-reaction taking into account that this picture was taken in a public sphere? Ever been to San Francisco, got the public nudity thing going on up there. They say it's up to the parents to keep their kids home to protect them from the old preverts. … I see this picture was from Cali also, good catch Jan, seems to be a Cali thing. … This guy comes from an event from a museum and I think this was either photoshopped with him with the girls or this picture was just labeled wrong to be funny. If you go to the other link, I think its sad this is spreading like wildfire because that poor guy will be labeled a freak because someone decided to stick a funny tag on a picture that was completely innocent. Apparently the museum night had a bunch of food and eating contests and much more if you go to the link, which probably explains the bitter and sweet tags. He is supposed to be some nature guy.

ok........what is wrong with this picture??? WTF!!!!! ummmm....something deff wrong with this picture... not okay. There is so much wrong with this picture I can't even begin.

This is just wrong on so many levels! Look at the poor girl in the middle trying to keep her distance. Wow! That is just fuckin wrong on so many levels. wtf … and past the obvious gross & inappropriate factor … why are 2 little girls "bitter" and one "sweet" … this is fubar on so many levels. I'm bored of overused comments like "wow, just wow" and "this is wrong on so many levels" but... Your comment was right on so many levels.

Can anyone tell me if this was photoshopped?? Someone messaged me to say she thought it was. At first I thought it was Ted Nugent but then noticed there weren't any guns. Who the fuck thought it was a good idea to take this pic?? Then again, I'm glad they did: now we have photographic evidence of this abomination. Amen Jill. All the uptightness about nudity in this country is absurd. No one has been scarred for life by seeing another person's skin. Some may be more pleassent to look at than others, even that is in the eye of the beholder. For the record I have worn a similar costume at a ship costume party and the parents of the preteen and teen on board thought it was funny and did not freak out.

To all u incredulous Christians who keep posting 'so what' -look at the reluctance on the children's faces and when examing 'Adam' holding their hands, consider the actual story of Adam&Eve -they ended up screwing . Take yr damn blinkers off! Indifference might wash in the Catholic church but don't pull that shit here! Yes it is look at the shadows and the angle of the pervs head. Poor things is right. Their body language clearly shows that they are extremely uncomfortable with the situation. Is he their father? Looking at this gives me the willies and creeps me out to NO END. Ewwwwwww, very creepy. Look at the tall "bitter " trying to distance herself. Ewwwwww! The phrase 'fucked up' springs instantly to mind when looking at this guy lol … Point well taken, bailey, about the children; I empathize with you and I feel the same way. Yes, I did look at the link and was unable to find the name of the Bible School, so I *still* believe this story is misrepresented. If you (or anyone) found the name of the Bible School, please let me know. I'm convinced that he's a relation. Look at the strong resemblance between "Adam" and the blonde girl on the right of the photo. The spacing of the eyes, the slant of the nose, even the smile is very similar. Maybe an uncle? Anyway, ya, this is crazy awkward. No more so than other religions, mind you, but looking at this, maybe a little ... Oh, get over it, people! It's hilarious and very awkward! If you didn't want to see awkward, why are you looking at this site? Now go ahead, "bleach your eyes," and pretend you've never seen anything more shocking to your sensibilities than this goofy man posing with three girls whose parents obviously had the foresight to have this embarrassing picture taken so that many years later they (and all of us) could have something entertaining to look at. I highly doubt anyone needed therapy to get over the trauma of having their picture taken with Mr. Figs. Seriously, guys, look at the link. It's not even a church event. The parents were probably the one who took the picture, too.

While this is still super fuckin' weird, there are pics of the dude huggin' up a lot closer on adults. It was a museum thing — an event that (presumably) a parent would have to be present with the children to attend. Blame the parent, not the church. It's art; reading the comments posted on all these links makes it clear that people will always just jump to ridiculous conclusions (and also, that it is as an unfortunate time/era to be an artist as an atheist). It's in a museum, and it was about food. Overblown hype - imagine that! It was a bitter sweet reunion because of his sour patch. But they all agree it was a little salty. THE THREAD WAS A TRAP. THE THREAD WAS A TRAP. I KNEW IT. I SNIFFED A TRAP SOON AS I SAW IT. I DECIDED TO POST ANYWAY, BUT I KNEW IT WAS A TRAP. HAHAHA CHURCH HATE BAIT INDEED.

OMG! Is he suppose to be Adam? Very creeeepppyyy! Supposed to be Adam, correct? Oh I think that is supposed to be Adam with the fig leaves and what not. How very disturbing. The children look very uncomfortable. What are the parents thinking letting that gangly naked dude close to their kids? The fact is their is a grown adult male who is almost nude in the presence of children which in itself is disturbing. in addition to that, he is wearing what is universaly (or at least globaly) known to be a common depiction of adam from the garden of eden, making it overtly religious in nature.at best you can round it down to three religions from that. Oh to be an artist. You can have a rapist beard and be mostly naked but if it's art it's not as frowned upon. Could be worse he could be a homeless drunk guy jacking off in public. It had to be art!

He was actually freaking out on acid with a friend and stumbled across a birthday party. His inner child, which happens to be a little girl, was perfectly at home.

This is just so wrong. Why do the "bitter" sisters have spots of calomine lotion on thier face. Ewwwwww, that must be poison ivy. This is just wrong on many, many levels. Something didn't seem right about this considering the source. This is just erroneous information and it is wrong to post it as fact. We know things go on and it is the real people committing crimes we should be focused on. There is nothing awkward about this. He is obviously their dad, they all have red eyes, can't anyone else see the resemblence? So this is just awkward to prudish Americans who aren't comfortable with nudity.

Yes, there are plenty of downright weird photos on this site, and that's usually what makes them so funny. This, however, I hope you pull off the site. Ugh. I really want to think he has at least a Speedo on, for the sake of those poor girls. Interesting to note that "Neil" posted it. I'm curious what the girls would have to say about the picture. Somewhere on this site there's a photo of a whole family, kids and all, dressed exactly like the male doofus here. I can't find the link, but somebody else can, I'm sure. In that photo we at least know the relationship of the adult male to the kids, not that it eases the essential grossness of it all. And no, it's not photoshopped. The guy is just holding his head in a weird way. Moderator: I'm tellin' ya, you want to make money on this site, charge $10 for every appearance of Photo-you-know-what! Since my last comment, I have read all the other comments, and I find it very scary that so many people seriousely mean that this photo is terrible and should not be allowed on this site. Come on, it's just funny and what is wrong about nudity. All the Creationists tells us that God created Adam and Eve, so what is wrong.

Just another misinterpretation of the bible. So much edited out of the Bible. There might have been some really good info on using sun screen.

Creepy ... he wasn't actually in the picture when it was taken. I could post a pic of a guy in a Thong with a little girl sitting on his lap and CLAIM it was taken at an Atheist retreat, how many on current would take my word for it? I suspect none would take my word for it without proof. Looks like a shock effect post to me. Granted, there's some weird shit happening with bible camps and the like, but the photo actually looks like it was taken at the exhibit. Here's another article that describes the event.

You get me a guy wearing a yarmulka in a picture doing some shit, the resonable deduction is jewish. You get a guy wearing a robe whilst bowing his head in a picture, it is reasonable to deduce he is muslim. Same basic observation skills at play here. Looks more like a parenting fail than anything though. I know I wouldn't have my kids in a picture with this guy—even if it was for an art show.

All the creeps, pervs, inadequates and religious fuckwits just can't leave other people's kids alone can they? HEY! PREACHER! LEAVE THOSE KIDS ALONE! Leaf those kids alone.

How many times have you heard of religious people wandering around naked in front of children at religious events? Major diversionary tactics being used to keep the common ranks in a wasteless desert of an uproar accomplishing absolutely NUTTIN wandering around never able to SEE THE PROMISED LAND (HIGH FUEL MILEAGE). All of which means the amount of actual FUEL required would be cranked back to a fraction what our vehicles are using today!!!! IT'S SO SIMPLE IT MAKES YA WANT TO RIP YOUR HAIR OUT. But since that time I've also been blessed to understand how to make an engine WITH ONLY THE BASIC THREE MOVING PARTS => PISTON HEAD, PISTON ROD AND CAMSHAFT. The rest doesn't move. With that few a parts it wouldn't wear out for 100+ YEARS... but here we go, wandering around punching each other for position, attacking each other every way we can to GET AHEAD, but only getting ahead inside their box.

What the F. ridiculous. I'm a christian theist and I find this appalling. but what about nudist colonies where naked adults are around naked children? Pretty sure Jesus didn't run around naked save for a fig leaf... Just sayin'.

Run a Google search for 'fig leaf guy LACMA' – looks like it was performance art. Yeah a naturalist camp/festival was my first conclusion but it looks like Jan nailed it. Great work! Great - looks like TLC is casting another show. Looks like a normal LDS marriage celebration in Utah. ... The two girls on the left have pink and green spots all over themselves. Looks like a clear case of awkwarditis. The second looks like she's ready to bolt! Looks like the girls on the left were labelled bitter and coached to move away from jesus and the girl to Jesus' left was labelled sweet and coached to be close to jesus. the only take-away that i get is they are trying to teach kids that bitter-hearts go away from jesus and sweet-hearts keep jesus close to them. simple indoctrination lesson for a simple-minded vacation babble school.....imho...seem reasonable? The 'sweet' girl looks like a deer in headlights. No, the "sweet" girl looks like Jan Brady!!! The "sweet" girl looks like she's already imagining how she'll describe this to her therapist. I think all you guys are overreacting, that looks like my kind of vacation. He looks like a really sweet guy, not scary. Looks like Adam's going to have a good EVEning. Looks like we're in for an unusually turgid autumn. Looks like he's a meme now.

How come this guy can wear that but whenever I walk around in public with one of those, the cops get called? Only an xtian would think that this okay. We have laws about this sort of thing. This guy oughta be on a sex offender registry... they also have a pathology of behavior pusuant to their religions. That is all im saying. Regardless of what you believe, this guy is like right out of bible land, which is just one example amongst infanite to support the conclusion of what religious inspiration resulted in this picture. This guy was just looking for some excuse to hold onto a 12 year-old girl whilst completely naked. Blondie knows it too! She looks nervous to the point of being mildly traumatized. What in the world was this guy thinking? Common sense should have told him to run and HIDE from these girls. Then you need to learn how to use Google as well as you apparently use Photoshop. There are pictures of this guy all over the place from the museum he was at. Michaelangelo's David is ART! This guy is a weirdo. Tell ya what, I talked to a fellow a few years ago and I'm a pretty good judge of people's voicebox truthfulness in my opinion. His voice never wavered when he told me this. His brother purchased a Honda a decade ago now that blew him away the gas mileage was so high. Honda had accidentally let some advanced models reach the showroom floor so they ran around buying them back and this guy refused to sell his.

Dude, this photo could be have been taken from literally anywhere. I'm not European. I'm being sarcastic, or facisious or whatever the correct term is about posts criticizing Americans for their distaste for nudity. This photo proves we are RIGHT! As a mother of three children, this photo is awkwardly awesome! I know this is making the rounds as a VBS, but I've seen this photo before and I don't think it has anything to do with church. I think he some kind of weird hippie dad. Someone is trolling the Internet. I agree. His head is not on the body straight. Two different flesh tones. Fig leaf is suspended in mid air. This photo is not funny. Ick. There is so much going on in this photo i can't even start. Ugh. Who took this photo instead of getting those bitter/sweet girls away from the creepy dude? No, I didn't. I only offered my opinion as to why this photo is not what it purports to be, and what could be nothing more. Your lack of comprehension skills filled in the rest there.

Was there a play about Adam and Eve? "Hi girls. First off, welcome to your weekly bible study group… and do we ever have a Creation sized treat for you this week. This week we are going to be learning the story of Adam and Eve from the book of Genesis. As you may already have guessed, my crazy uncle Jimmie will be playing the part of Adam. Now who wants to be Eve… anybody?" Even if I considered the Adam and Eve story important in some way (not even a little), why is it so important that the kids be taught that "In the land of Plenty," Adam could only find leaves to cover his junk? It appears Adam wasn't all too bright and maybe not the best role-model. And where the hell is Eve? I'm with Aron Ra on this, an excuse to be legally naked around kids and the zealots will defend this man to the death. God created adam and eve, not adam and skeeve.

Why are they called sweet and bitter??? Bitter and sweet? He's clearly labeling them based on how easy they were to…coerce. Hence the closeness of the sweet girl to him. The bitter and sweet classifications make it very nambla but with girls. sooo creepy. OK. As a parent... I them have my children put on labels bitter and sweet for the sake of art with a nearly naked guy... HMMM.... NOT happening.

Why are they labeled "Sweet" and "Bitter"? What's going to happen to the children? Why are they acting like this sort of thing happens every day? Why are they tagged "bitter" and "sweet"? Okay. No It's wrong on many levels no matter the reasoning behind it. Plus if it is just a tourist photo why are they labelled "bitter' and "sweet"?

Take your Jesus and stick him up your ass. Where there is a Catholic, there's a pedophile. Obviously, the person that Photoshopped this picture believes the same thing. I was thinking the same thing. The only people who claim everything to be 'shopped' are those who can't tell the difference between their left and right foot ... OMG I was thinking the same thing, except I was going to use Liquid paper over my pupils lol

The tentative smile on the girl on the right says it all. D: And parents sanction this?! The kids body language says it all. This reminds me of the movie "Jesus Camp." This is the kind of haven for the likes of Jerry Sandusky. Bitter is german for thank you?? and sweet. well says it all really.

That is so creepy, even the kids were scared. See how the little girl on his right is pulling away. Jumpin' Jehosephat! That is so wrong !!!! That is so wrong in so many ways.

It's not a Bible school. Dude's an artist. Fact check people. If not a bible school, who then? What the hell is Thunderf00t doing in a Bible school?

The bitter sweet part is that all he really needed was a pine needle. More like bitter bitter sweet. Those who be-leaf in me shall have a bitter bitter sweet life.

Why are the girls labeled "sweet" and "bitter"? What's the deal with the "Bitter" & "Sweet" labels on the girls? Something seriously weird is going on there! What's up with the "sweet" and "bitter" labels on the girls?! Awkward....... And The girls have name tags that says "Bitter/Biter"? And "Sweet" Whaaaa? Since food was a big part of the event, the "bitter' and "sweet" signs were probably in reference to a "supertaster" test the girls had taken earlier. When Jared finally donned his codpiece, the girls heaved a sigh of re-leaf. Spoiler Alert: The girls were alright, after all. They had mutilated that delusional hippie's corpse in the most horrifying ways imaginable. The girls body language is hilarious! Oh get over your hip European self. It's awkward because of the girls facial expressions, not because he's naked. ummmm that's downright creepy, just look at how creeped out the girls look. The guy looks a little too happy. No offense taken! Aside from the fact that it is an art exhibit, last time I checked, standing near some girls in a costume does not make you a pedo. It's not as if any of his genitals are exposed, and it's not as if he is making the girls perform sexual acts of any kind. Chill the fuck out people, for real. This is Neil, the girls dad. Stick it up your a★★

Would that plant be a wandering Jew? Looks more like grape vine to me. First thought was: Hope that guy knows the difference between fig and poison oak. First, "Dude, get a hair cut!!" Next, the first time this was put "out here" someone had the whole crew under arrest or, at least, took that guy out behind the wood shed! LOOK AT THOSE GIRLS!! Body language 101! And, there are some people who think this is amusing. Yeah, yuck yuck haha! And, we look at this country and wonder what happened. Oh well. Have your chuckles. You never got passed the age of Jr. Hi. What parent in their right mind, would allow their kid to get a picture with that guy? I would like to have a nice little talk with that guy. And maybe beat the shit out of him (just a little). After all, I am a humanist. ♥ My 4 year old daughter just walked past the computer and said "Oh my God why is that guy wearing leaves?! that's gross Mom!" I have to agree GROSS! haha! That guy is definitely more bitter than sweet ... bleh. ♫ Jesus loves me, this I know ... For that guy's balls told me so ♫ Now, somebody inform that guy he can't be the Lion King in tonight's play. lol. hey that guy teaches at coc ha

I am not afraid of the human body, so nakedness doesn't upset me in the least, but little girls and boys can get a little unnerved when they aren't sure if they are safe with a person who is doing something that their parents don't do. Take note of the body language of the two little girls; one is turning away completely and the other is squishing her arms against herself so she doesn't have to have physical contact.....this is disturbing. I'm not the least bit uptight about nudity, (or artistic arrangement of leaves in particular) but I know a bad scene when I see one. Lolol... those poor little girls. They're definitely giving off a "don't-touch-me" vibe. What i am saying is - "if your pastor trys to get your little girls to pose for pictures while he's half naked - "JUST SAY NO!" ick! yuck! yuck! Poor little girls.... oh wait, is that a phone ringing? Must be Child Welfare calling! Don't worry little girls... when the ruffies wear off this will all just be a FIGment of your imagination. Hey its his religious right to dress up as post sin Adam and touch little girls. /sarcasm What does that link have to do with the picture of "adam" and scared little girls?

I found nothing related to any church or bible school Just a freaky phucking photo is all. How is this Bible School? It's so So Wrong. Must be the Jerry Sandusky bible school. If you're sending your kid to Bible school and they skip all the gruesome, cruel, genocidal and bloodthirsty parts, it's fraud. If they don't, it's child abuse. Holy raptor riding Jesus people. I hate religion as much as the next atheist and despise the thought of bible schools indoctrinating kids but that man isn't wearing anything more revealing than you would see at a beach. There is nothing accompanying that photo that is suggesting child abuse other than, well, religious indoctrinating. To the dipshits talking about killing this man or beating him without any proof whatsoever that he is molesting these kids please do everyone a favor and kill yourself. I can't believe you're on a humanist page vomiting that idiotic shit. What's next, killing everyone wearing a speedo at the beach because there might be kids around? vacation-bible-school..........oxymoron? What's truly terrifying is that in the 21st century people still send their children to bible school.

Hey GSHM, care to respond to putting out misinformation or are u going to stay up o mt. Olympus? My Great grandfather was a Southern Baptist Preacher. He would often say "Son going to Church no more makes you a Christian than going to a Garage makes you a Car!" Slow down, you're going too Faust. Now I'M going to have nightmares. :(They're not going to like the salad.

Hey, Skippy, before you regale us any more with your "enlightened" position on nudity, if you look closely at Adam's right hip, you can see a precarious looking string alone holding on the fig leaves. I see no evidence of a speedo or any other covering. So, when he stands too close to a heating or A/C register (or God forbid an electric fan) and the leaves just happen to fly up in view of children, you're telling us you're okay with that because it's "art." Sometimes, there is not enough therapy in the world … or fig leaves. All 3 girls look like they're wordlessly screaming for help and trying to keep their hands far, far away from those fig leaves. If those fig leaves are glued on, I would love to be in the next room when they take them off. Must be like hot wax for your bikini line. OOoo…that's gotta hurt. While I was walking through the Ahmanson Building I passed by Nature Boy on the stairs. I swear that dude must really be comfortable with himself to be walking around with nothing except for fig leaves on. We saw Nature Boy again, Walter wanted a picture. So I took a picture of him with Nature Boy.

This isn't VBS (or church at all),,, have spent many years attending and working at VBS. Nothing creepy happening there like this. From what I understand, this is actually from a public art gallery, not a church event at all. No it is NOT Photoshopped and it is NOT at a church VBS. It is from an art exhibit in California. Wait! The churches are manned by pedophile brains? Wow. And I guess Eve unlocks the magic box? What else does a church do, say in the 1800's hmm, like selling slaves at auction on their front stoop after Sunday services? If it is a church thing it is way worse! I'll bet it's a church thing, why else would he be covered like adam?

Why is this not being investigated? Well, presumably when he's not being "Adam" he wears clothes, hence the different skintones. His head is slightly tilted and the beard makes it look off center, and he has two different flesh tones because he probably wears CLOTHES outside when he is not being Mr. Figleaf. I'm not being argumentative. If it isn't from a VBS I think we should all know that. Hmm. Now that I'm in the trap I must qualify my post below as not being filled with hate but factual statements found all over the WORLD NEWS TONITE FROM TIME ZONE NUMBER 1 TO TIME ZONE NUMBER 24.

Ya cant deduce that the guy is part of the vaitcan or even christian based on his appearance, despite it being the exact cartoonish literalist biblical interpretation the religious right are so in love with, while viewing 3 guys that seem to be celebrating is enough evidence to imply that israel is obviously behind 9/11. If the guy was wearing a yarmulka with propellers or maybe some other form of traditional religous mocker it would work. Perhaps the guy was in one of those live painting re-creations things. If it's not photoshopped then why did mom and dad allow this....creepy. This one needs a background story. P.S. Is it just me or does the guy look like Chris Elliott from "Something about Mary"?

What in the fuck. The fuck? Okay that's child endangerment/abuse, someone shut that pedo-fest down. The Bitter girl is slowly backing the fuck out of there. I like how 'bitter' gets the fuck as far away as allowed. None of them was real clear on the definition of 'back stage.' - or - They were just trying to win backstage-pass tags in a radio-contest. None of them was real clear on 'backstage where?' They were just trying to win backstage-pass tags in a radio-contest. The sad part is, the same people who express truly ugly, venomous hatred aimed at the LGBT community, and who routinely erect lies about gay people trying to "corrupt" their children, will probably see nothing wrong in this. They won't even see the *galactic* level of irony involved in teaching their children to perpetuate homophobic hatred, whilst happily smiling upon religious-inspired creepiness such as this. But then, quite a few of the Christofascist Right will entertain any contradiction, any fallacy, any bad idea, so long as they can tie it into their personal hatreds with apologetic fabrications about Jeebus. Is he trying to do Adam or Jesus?

I hope this is being reported to the authorities as often as it is being reposted on the internet. The new Supreme fox Court decision now allow profanity and nudity on prime time television BUT heaven help us on the internet when children is around. Adam is an artist through-and-through. Don't want to speak for him but I think he is always prepared for consequences. LACMA is a safe environment, the Internet is not, so I am cheered to see you/others speaking out on his behalf. Hi Suzan, thanks very much for the comment – No doubt that Adam rises above this kind of thing … I sort of made an example of his case however the point was much bigger that a single person/case. Sometimes I wonder whether the internet is a good or bad thing

A naked guy and Flavor markings on 3 young girls, Did anybody bother to think this idea threw? If he was dressed like Jesus May be... But he is a naked dude dressed only in a fig leaf. To quote Tim Allen, don't stand too close to a naked man. Yah! She's old enough to understand that to be in a room with a naked, except some wine leafs glued on his dick, lunatic and 3 kids with pink dots a labelling as bitter or sweet is so fucking wrong!

Is that a pine cone in his fig leaf or is he just happy to see them? Mrs Fig Leaf, I presume? The way he hot glued that fig leaf on …you can see an outline of his junk. Yuck!

He's not naked. Nearly naked, yes. And creepy looking, according to you. Not sure that that's really something to hold against him, but whatever. I still don't see why it's not ok for an adult male to be scantily dressed around children? If you go to the beach you see men and women in far less covered states of dress. With children. OMG. All this junk, according to Revelation 17 & 18, is soon to go away. I find the signs a bit disturbing. It's like he's tasted them and felt compelled to label them according to taste ... Did he label them according to taste?

Jesus f****** Christ!!! Oh, wait... It's Adam? No, no. That' not Jesus. It's Adam! Gosh, IT'S ADAM! What a load of bollocks. It's Adam...

I don't understand how dressing up as a very famous historical figure is performance art. Performance art = creepy. Performance art = creepy?? Nice attitude. I'm guessing you may not be comfortable with anything other than your own experiences. Kind of sad, that. You don't have to like the art, but to automatically relegate an entire category of art as 'creepy' seems a bit closed-minded. As an artist (one in no way involved with this project), the point is to get a reaction – good or bad – the only really bad review is apathy.

::We have hit the bell at the top of the Carnival Fair pole. ::We have hit the bell at the top of the Carnival Fair pole. ::We have hit the bell at the top of the Carnival Fair pole.

I know people are gonna pervert this and I can see by the site that its nothing bad, but the "group belly-listening sessions – video by Eric Grushky" really was WEIRD haha! Did u see that vid? LOL Yes, I found that out, soon after I posted this first reply, yesterday; I posted the info (and my disappointment in the site for being misleading). It's not 'trolling' to simply point out the submission was likely a fake. And this one isn't the first here. Kind of ruins the whole spirit and theme of the site if you go with photoshop'd images.

Yeah, he need a lot more leaves for my taste. Several of the pics at the link are worse than the one above. I could have gone my whole life without seeing them. A more logical conclusion, judging from the link that I posted where naked adult men literally are parading naked in front of children is that this group were probably participating in some outdoor festival or street parade, and they wandered inside somewhere to take the photo. Let me try to post the link again.

Ummmm super freaky. There is so much wrong w/this I don't know where to start. What was photo shopped, the leaves? I don't like this picture at all. I told you i dont like people playing on my phone. I don't get it... what in the world is this supposed to convey? I just don't know. I don't want to go to that museum. Ahhh. I don't believe in religion, so I don't think it would be my place to *enlighten* anyone on how "Jewish or Muslim communities practice their love for religion in such a fashion." I dont believe in religion either. which has nothing to do with anything, as we live in a world full of people who do, and tend more often than not to try to get every one else to join in. I dont agree.you are just a crazy troll and i dont think anyone wanted your head on a platter as much as they just wanted you to stop rambling on about your crazy shit. Well that was until you decided to go anti-Semite. I don't know who writes the comments but hey they're sometimes almost better than the picture itself. Thanks. I don't care who you are, that's funny!

I am at a complete loss for words...... Um is Adam looking for a new Eve because the old one just doesn't do it for him anymore???? Yes, sir, the advertisement DID require a bearded man with long hair and who was good with kids, BUT, we are looking for a SANTA CLAUSE !! The government is looking for this man as we speak.

The girl on the left is slowly moving away from this pedophile. He probably should have been a little more sensitive to her obvious feelings and not put his arm around her at all. The other kids are harder to read, but they are pretty far away from him... LOL! Get away from those children, Jesus!

This needs to be reported to authorities. I think it is clear what is going on here. You just know there was some "Sandusky" going on. I'm an Atheist, but I'm not paranoid: what's so "terrifying" about this? It seems fairly clear to me that they're doing a play or something like that- the dude's dressed as Adam. There's nothing inappropriate going on, as far as we can see. The instant reaction of: OMG Pedo! is far more troubling to me than this picture. :-/ Not every man's a molester.

Do you really think a guy is any more likely to molest children because he's not wearing much? Or that a man in this situation is bound to be "enjoying himself" in a sexual way? I can't think of any situations less likely to be conducive to those urges... in a museum, in a crowd of people, nearly nude, surrounded by lots of children running wild, cameras flashing, parents watching... Really, it's irrelevant, as far as I'm concerned. What the fuss is about with this picture is that people are so conditioned to the dangers of child molestation that they can't help but see something like this and think THERE'S SOMETHING WRONG HERE. The assumption that every man's a rapist and a child molester (pick one depending on the situation!) is such an unbelievably embarrassingly simplistic view of your gender. OMG!!! i'm... i'm.... well, i'm just speechless! so many questions! he's not even wearing a flesh colored body suit! my brain hurts- i think i'll have to go lie down for awhile... He's not right.

Which levels?? I think it is so funny. This is so funny. I agree with your stance on the matter, but you are still a dumb bitch. So funny.

I really want to think he has at least a Speedo on, for the sake of those poor girls. I really think 99% of people who commented should look up the definition of "rational thought." In the above comments it is explaiined that it is something completey different to what was suggested. Even if it wasn't, it is just some guy, stop getting so worked up that there is a pedophile in every shadow. This is part of the reason why the atheist/humanist movement is constantly set back, the very people criticising the religious zealots of being unthinking sheep are, on the whole, unthinking sheep. Ewwwwwwww! I really hope it is made clear which school this is taking place at so parents can avoid it!

They stirred it through the grapevine. — or — They inferred it through the grapevine. — or — They preferred it through the grapevine.

Mush, are you kidding? If you cannot see that the head is so off center, I mean... unless your left ear aligns with your navel while standing straight. You might want to reconsider your definition of stupidity. ("desire to troll") seriously? I think I will move along. I see you're on the same page. I think I'll let my post stand though. I think I generally trust this page so didn't bother to be skeptical about the image. I think I just went blind.

Two are bitter and one is sweet. He's only molested 2 out of 3 don't be so hard on the weird hippy. "Bitter" and "Sweet" want to flee but ugli "Adam" hold them tight. Part of American horror story. I wonder what the criteria for the "bitter" and "sweet" tags was? This is my sister Bitter, and my other sister Bitter.

What is with the "Sweet" and "Bitter" labels? Two bitters, one sweet, and one utterly tasteless. Um, Mom and Dad? Can we change the "Sweet" and "Bitter" name tags to "Let's Get the Hell Out of Here As Fast As Possible?"

Television viewership has been sagging so injecting some skin & nipples will bring them back up. With help from Supreme Court "justices." After all, WE can't keep allowing Europenises to do stuff we can't right?

So then when we outdo THEM they have to do something we can't do again, right? Things are very easily taken out of context. We can't take anything for granted. Science dictates it so! :)

This Fall on Bravo: "Grow Houses of Santa Fe" Next on Bravo: "Housewives Of Ogden"

What do you so find appalling about that picture? Isn't there a prayer caption that goes with that picture? That picture was the subject of our Caption Contest back in August of 2011:

This is ridiculously gross! I would want to have a talk with these children's parents! I honestly think if a parent lets their child be around a man like this should have them taken away! Unbelievable! Well then, shame on Matt Stopera for posting crap he should have research better. And that is why they build prisons and we should have stricter gun control. Cuz he would be dead.

BuzzFeed, you owe Adam an apology for instigating those idiotic comments below... So is he a Jesus/Adam (like JESDAM) ...may pass as Victoria Secret model ???? inappropriate !!!!! Adam? Is that you? It is not Jesus, it is Adam. Is it wrong to have theater? Apart from him being without to many clothes, there is absolutely nothing sexual in it. Hope you humanist aren't more morally hysterical than the christians. Chris Elliot stars in, "Adam And Christmas Eve." Nice to see you Adam, why don't you have a seat over there. ... I still hate his performance and his playing on the Adam meme. Art is not art because someone else says it is ... you know this. Oh Adam- Did you not learn anything from your first screw up? so very very wrong!! Adam and heave. Adam? You have no scar where one of your ribs was supposed to be, yet you have kids hang around you? Adam how can this be? And neither Adam nor Eve have a belly button. Hmmm, I figured Adam would be sorta swarthy. Not pretty in pink. Adam needs to work on his tan. Adam O fan club REPRESENT. adam

Ok, so he is naked nature guy, fine. But around the kids? just a tad bit creepy. Kids Body Language says... PERVERT! I like how the "bitter" kids are standing further away than the "sweet" kid. LOL. Living up to their labels much?? oh my god. those poor kids. theyre like inching away. Great! Just great! More screwed up kids. Damned hippies! I didn't bother checking the source because some dude wearing shrubbery posing with kids is just weird. I hope he's their dad, because I would NEVER ask my kids to stand next to a (mostly) naked stranger!! And their parents will continued to force these kids to attend this church... that's child abuse. Really? He is fully covered. He is not hurting these kids. How bad can it be to see legs and a man's chest? I'm really sorry that in your mind their is a social convention that provides naked men access to children. where do you live, so i can make sure to never ever ever take my kids there. Hey kids how bout some kool-aid? Roman philosopher, Testicles, comes back to life so he can tell kids that "veggies are good for you." Bet the kids stay off his lawn from now on.

They also go around to apartment buildings having Carnival-like Puppet Shows for Jesus with super loud booming speakers to BLOW OUT THE KID'S EARDRUMS. It works to the church's advantage to have their FUTURE PARISHIONER'S BEING DEAF. Jesus, people find this ACCEPTABLE? Can anyone say "Jerry Sandusky"? Didn't people learn anything from that doc Jesus Camp? He's only making it harder for Jesus to come back. Who knew that in the Second Coming, Jesus would return as a pasty white guy ?? Weird, Jesus, weird. Doesn't look like jesus works out very often. Creepy creeping Jesus. holy jesus christ! jesus fuck. sweet jesus!

This screams something at me, but I am not sure what. I just think I would not want this scary looking, semi-nude man touching my children. I totally think the proper reaction is that of the two "bitter" girls – stay as far away as possible! Say what you want – that is NOT art. Don't worry, dickhead. You'll be singing plenty of bittersweet symphonies with your cellmates in prison. Hahahah. Totally agree! Although I assume the "bitter" "sweet" labels had to do with interactive tastebud learning. That could have been fun. Sign me up for extra bitter – I want more than an arm's length, that's for sure! Not that they're bitter... Those "bitter" girls just need more saving. Interesting, Lynnette. Good work. That was disturbing (and still kinda is a little bit, really), but come to find out GSHM is a spinning non-fact-checker. And I've endured my last. And to all you bitter mutherfuckers, you expect everyone to be cool with atheism, stop acting like dicks; also Catholicism is not synonymous with pedophilia, sound less uninformed and direct your shitty energy at theists of all creeds. Fuck you guys I'm out. The story behind this must have a bittersweet ending of some sort. Hippy family reunions are always more bitter than sweet. And so, we've learned a valuable lesson today: being bitter saves you life-long emotional trauma.

Wtf? WTF! WTF???? WTF?!! Wow man. Just fucking WOW. SMH wtf wtf?? WTF???!!!! wtf omfgwtfbbq WTF?! Oh My Science! Wtf?

This is freaky LOL LOL! Kudos to you on this find uni....YIKES! LOL! The explanation put my mind at ease tremendously, but that one little girl on *his* left didn't look like she was enjoying being close to him AT ALL. If you wouldve gotten a picture of me after finding out that macaroons were being served for snack time during VBS, that wouldve been equally terrifying! LOL lol, as we always have, i will leave that to the romans thank you very much LOLOLOL, Lisa ! Best comment yet! 10/10 points awarded to you. Lol LOL LOL LOL

Hearsay? Sure. However, since that time I've reflected back on a system that I once installed from scratch on my 1973 Monte Carlo. It was really hard to start, much mashing of the gas pedal always required. Winters werer terrible just getting out of the driveway, and even then it would stop many times to do that. I think what's *really* WRONG is when people believe whatever they read, without doing further research to confirm all of the facts. Thanks Yahid! Yes it was quite stupid of me to call someone an "idiot bitch" and then refer to personal insults in the same breath. I was pretty angry when I wrote this post and didn't really prrof it before posting. So thank you, for pointing out that I am a "dumb bitch." I hope you have a wonderful week Yahid did you really just offer an assumption to explain where adult nakedness with children is more common than other places?really? By the way it's not really from a Pride Parade I just wrote that caption.

It's allegedly from the Folsum Street Parade or the Fremont Solstice Parade. If this really is your friend you need to call the police right now! Wow, really? can you spell pederast? Really? I still wish he would cover up. Bleck. really? throwing stones from your glass house? Thank God he had a bottle of calamine lotion shoved up his ass … their faces were really starting to break out. Really ?!?! Ben Stiller has really let himself go…

Is it just me or is that little update at the end kind of a big deal? Still a funny picture…but at least correct the title…or take down the post. Its almost slanderous. That is wrong and not close to being funny at all. Oh that was funny! Of course it is funny, and I think many of the remarks are made to be funny, mine inclusive. Hope you understand, I.m danish, my language is proberly not correct. I'm with you Neil. "won't somebody PLEASE think of the children?" jeez. calm down, it's a funny pic. It IS funny, and no more traumatic than a trip to the beach or pool. verrrry funny! Too funny =)

Are you having difficulty indoctrinating your child into religion? Maybe they are a bit of a free thinker, if the threat of hell is not enough to bully them into believing then send them to bible camp they have ways of scaring your children into submission. people use religion to legalise their perversion, nothing else! exhibitionism for that douche. underage sex group for mormons. pedophilia for priest etc etc and using the most basic deductive reasonong skills, taking into account the love of literalism of the christian world has, as well as how jews and muslims become more modest when more faithfull, to recognize the likely reality of what religion has inspired this is so difficult. or do you want to enlighten us to the jewish or muslim communities that practice their love for their religion is such a fashion? cuz i can get you a website to bibleland. Another reason to hate art and religion. I'm not saying religion is like a drug . . . (just thinking it)

This is indeed rather strange- what is the story behind this? Looks photoshopped to me. It's photoshopped folks...relax!! Plus, would there be as much outrage if he were wearing a Speedo? And Leah… it IS Photoshopped… and very poorly at that. Looks Photoshopped to me. One word: Photoshop. That is a pretty obvious photoshop. Please tell me this was photoshopped. Please, pleeeessssseee.... That has GOT to be photoshopped. Oh, Photoshop trolls: Worst photoshop editing ever. No photoshop to see here… move along....

Jerry Mathers returns in, Leaf It To Beaver. Lucky guy... he has three leaf blowers. or as they were originally known ... Hippie Grape Leaf Wearin' Child Rapists. Seriously people, relax & "leaf" the poor guy alone"… I did. Another clue is that ted don't need a leaf nearly that big. Lester's promised he's turning over a new leaf----RUN! Oh come on. He has a leaf! He has his own Beleafs.

OMG that photo totally creeps me out!!!! YUCKY Omg thats not cool i would not want to be next to that dude. The little one is just "Now that's just my luck!" or something, the middle one is all "let's get outta here NOW!!!" and blondie is like "OMGhe'stouchingmeHEEEEEEEELP!!!!!!!!!" OMG!! You just made me snort! OMFGDYJFST ?? OMG I learn something new every day. My senator wants to know, when the baby is born what do they do with the scuba gear? OOOOOO.....MY GOD!!! Are you kidding?!? OMG! You are all acting like idiots!! Read this link. OH my Godzilla!!!

What is it about the human body that you find so threatening? its not like hes sexualizing the little chillun or anything. seems like the problem lies with your puritanical christian squeamishness at the idea of the human body, in its natural state. ... Fuckin Christians...they can justify anything in the name me god. Where? I can't see anything. Then again, by defenition atheists dont have anything for which they would rally together for, being as athiesm is literally the lack of belief. Our "Leaders" know all this. I have not kept quiet. They will not give you anything I know. Now, post over BACK TO THA BRICK PITS WITH YA! TO BUZZFEED STAFF MATT STOPERA: you are a sorry excuse for a journalist. Promoting images without citing the true source and the TRUE context is equal to lying. I am angry that I wasted my time reading about this image. Now I know that I cannot believe ANYTHING that I see on your website; and ANYTHING you post in the future will be highly suspect. Good job tanking your reputation for accuracy in journalism, if you ever had one.

There are more atheist pedos than religious. It's just that the media blows up the religious ones. Shared on FB... people need to see the BS these religious folks do! Its cool. Religious "freedom" and such. I just love "religious freedom"! I suspect there was also some re-enactment of Onanism at the camp. i dunno dude, there's no obvious signs, and the lighting and shadows are identical. i'm sorry, but it's true. religious christians are wacked.

WRONG! WRONG! WRONG! ICKY! ICKY! ICKY! Run, girls, run! I bet these poor girls will avoid the produce department for their entire lives. 3 girls, 1 schmuck. Considering the quality of the paintings behind them (or is that a chalkboard to the right?!), I'd guess that Fig Man was the artistic highlight of these girls' museum trip. Basically, I think that It just doesn't follow that nudity (or near nudity!) = sexuality and a grown man + young girls = molestation.

Thanks for susing this out jan ! Well done ! Since a picture is worth a thousand words it is dangerous to jump to conclusions .... though easy to do. Thanks very much – I get quite upset when things are misconstrued and then people don't bother to listen to reason! Thanks, AFP. Just when my husband looked over to see what I was on the computer for. Thanks, bailey. I also don't believe in the Bible, so no thanks on your offer for a website to Bibleland.

Gag me seriously... That is seriously effed up. Jeez. My dad used to walk down the hall to the loo in the morning in his jocks and it hardly scarred me for life! People need to seriously calm down aye. Not all men are rapists/pedos, get past that ploise! It's a degrading pattern of thought towards men. Yes seriously!!! Aurghh, I KNOW!!!

Is this for real? It's VERY disturbing, and maybe even more so in the midst of the Sandusky ruling. Where and when was this so-called "bible camp," pray tell? Must be Sandusky Baptist ... The Church of Sandusky. It's a disgrace... especially right after the Sandusky verdict. Or is that a Sandusky's accomplice?

I think that's just so wrong I can't bring it to words. Thats disgusting … perv. That's fucked up. Yep thats pretty phucked up. I think that's PENN states VBS. Pff, a cross and 3 nails, that's just what u need to make everyone happy! and it's carbon foot free! Ha, ha, ha, that's exactly what I was thinking… good one! They all look related, but I'm not sure if that's necessarily better or not. He looks a bit like Chris Elliot. "Yo whats up there, little dudettes? Keep your name tags on at all times. Thats the only way I can remember which type of weed I stashed in your rooms" Awwwright now THAT'S what I'm talking about! That's awkward! Thats damn sure strange. My boyfriend just peered over my shoulder and said, "that's just weird." OK, that's it. Fig leave, we all leave.

I do agree with your post up top regarding repercussions of liberal gun laws ... onedit, liberal in the sense of less restrictive. I so not surprise to find defamation masquerading as news on a liberal rag. Truth has no place in the liberal mind.

Now that, my friends, is awkward!! Note how much more tan his face is than the rest of him… this picture makes me feel very awkward!!! This is way beyond awkward. More like disgusting. I can't think of any context where this is acceptable.

And they say allowing homosexuals to marry leads to pedophilia … ok, church, whatever you say. The Pied Piper school of pedophilia. Sex Ed ~ Pedophilia School ~ Halloween Every Year ~ Easter Egg Hunts ~ Christmas Lies ~ False Teachings & Home of Satan, all in one big happy Protestant package, nationwide and worldwide too I would add. At a sick pedo who uses "cute bible stories" to justify his actions. Is that Pedo-bear sans costume? A man doing a trick like that imagines he's helping the little ones entrusted to him to grow into being a more freed person. LIKE PEDOPHILES! Yes friends, we truly are BEHOLDEN to the churches for where we find ourselves today, on 6/23/2012 at the HALLMARK OF CIVILIZATION DRINKING FRACKED WATER while being pounded in the porthole from pedophiles who also call theirself a Priest of God. Paedo!

The English language doesn't have the necessary words to describe exactly how wrong that is..... Oh wait, yes it does! Catholic! If he is a relative, it doesn't make it any better. EWWWW! He doesn't use a razor. He uses a hedge trimmer... It doesn't get much creepier than this. He doesn't seem to get much Sun for a nature freak.

He's the tour guide at the Creationism Museum in Kentucky! The field trip to the Please Touch Museum ended with the Please Watch Your Head perp walk. Psst. Hey buddy. Bikini wax night at the museum is next week. This is why you should always check to make sure the museum has a 'no shirt no shoes…' policy.

Well, at least two of them aren't old enough to understand. Let's pray those aren't 'all-access' passes.

dafuq? Three words…HOLY. FUCKING. SHIT! And you better do what he fucking says, or you'll burn in hell. for fucks sake… this motherf'cker is virtually nude. So f…ing wrong! Imagine your daughter coming back from any school camp with such a pic! I do love how the taller girl on the left is eeking away, like even as a child she knows this is fucked up ridiculousness. If I was these kid's pappy, I'd take a sharpie to his muthafuckin name tag sho nuff...DAAAMN!!! That man should be put to sleep by the lethal injection… :(Fu****g idiot… What the frikfrakkin' fiddle f*ck?! Creeped me the fu*k out!! What a fucked fuck this asshat is!!! dirty fucker!!! Fucking vegans.

ZUCKERBERG !! Where's the damn dislike button !! A Like for you sharing the pic and a great big DISLIKE the fact this happened. So so wrong :-[I dislike it, but i have friends that like to keep in touch from there... and thank you Alex! But wow, even for a bottom feeding troll like Unimatrix0, this is pretty low. People of all ages were able to enjoy the contests that took place, one of the most memorable being the watermelon-eating contest. The flamboyant hostess, Miss Barbie-Q, had participants and observers alike laughing with her commentary on the variety of fruit-eating contestants. Yeah…I'm the only one here who finds his body attractive. My husband's body is exactly like his. I guess I have a thing for tall-skinny-pasty-white nerds, what can I say? I had to google yomank....I like it!

Why did i click this ima have nightmares now. Why did I take that viagra? Why!

Also, those leaves are way too generous length-wise. We all know he could get by with less than half. We all know those leaves didn't need to be put down that low. Mid thigh? In his dreams. ;p

I pray this is a fake photo… This is scarier than Slim Goodbody. "Ewww" does not begin to describe how gross this is. My eyeballs are bleeding. Ugh. I've seen enough hentai to know where this is going. This is not a VBS photo peoples. Here are some links for you all to look at, and here is the main page. I am not sure what this is but I know what it is NOT and that is VBS.

After he lost the lead in the Fig Newton commercials, Larry tried community theater. Just be glad they didn't do Lot and his daughters in the cave. Yeah im not so much with the broad assumption thing. i was raised in a beach community and know full well how nudity is valued. yet at the same time i also know only in the darkest corners of society is where children are introduced into the equation. I'm glad this wasn't actually a real thing but it has made me lose a bit of "faith" in the fact checking behind shared photos

So I read about how to take a bottle of water, an artificial stone aquarium rock and some 1/8 inch hose one going over to an unused vacuum port on the base plate of the carburetor right? So then it would start and run with barely any pedal mashing needed =>THAT WAS 33+ YEARS AGO. OKAY, so bringing that UP TO TODAY all we would need to do is feed a dribble of water into the TURBOCHARGER AIR STREAM and the fizzed H2O would turn all our cars (+ everything else) into A MOUNTAIN CLIMBING MONSTER STEAM ENGINE. All we are is just ... Another Brick On The Wall. Gross. he's on the road to infamy. Imagine the humiliation of 10's of thousands of people seeing your dumbass photo on Facebook. Dude! You're and IDIOT! On the last day of summer school, autumn came and the leaves fell.

My head just exploded. I wish that whoever submitted this picture would explain it. I wish I was!! THANK YOU! I wish that would actually happen.

I thought we were meeting Justin Beiber....not just a Hebrew. I thought that was called seminary.. or was it seemannary? I thought I smelled cabbage.

If I would come upon that scene, that boy would soon be hurting, real badly! I wonder what other nut-cases are around and participating in this crime? VERY SCARY!! I would want to strangle him, but would be afraid that other crazy folks would try to defend him. I would call the police

All he asks is that you, "…lettuce alone…" I mean, what kind of freaking situation is that! Is that Gwyneth Paltrow?

I love it!! Love it!! AHAHAHA! Love it.

Here we see Bill at the opening of his Art Installation, we also see the reason why 'Artists' are only famous after they die. Naturally, their name-tags are their evaluations of the flavor of his balls. The pictures of his backside are even worse : p

Why? What harm could have occurred? I suppose you wouldn't let your daughters see Michaelangelo's David because of the severe psychological trauma that would have ensued? Give me a break. Oh, no! He has already given two of them cooties! Tarzan's less athletic brother. Tarzan the king of the jungle. Me, Tarzan... You, Jane and Jane and Jane.

He followed us home from school, can we keep him? can we? can we?

Over the years, they've built up a tolerance to poisioned kool aid. Over the years, his eldest has developed her ability to dodge his brightly-colored ejaculatory droplets.

The Lord works in strange ways. Very strange ways. SCARY and very strange !

Warren Jeffs gets a conjugal visit. Warren Jeffs will only have his memories while he rots in jail.

Does anyone EVER ask for attribution these days? Ever hear of "Chicken Little"? You idiots prove it. Wake up America…learn how to read and research! OOOOOOOhhhh…look, a squirrel!!! Hilarious. "Does anyone else wanna listen to bellies?" Had me cracking up.

So your ire isnt religated now to just jews but the protestants too huh? any other collective of innocent people you want to highjack an identity and drag through the mud? Some people just shouldn't get in touch with nature at all. Or any other living being.

Somebody get that poor guy a membership to a tanning salon PLEASE! He needs a LOT more than a tanning booth....where to start?

The Garden Of Eatin' Garden of Eden Guess Where The Serpent Is!

Danica-Christine Janse van Vuuren - do you feel bad after they updated the story? You should. Imagine what they would do if they re-told the story of Sodom and Gomorrah?

This should be investigated. Ummm....Isn't this illegal? No? IT SHOULD BE!!!!

What is scary about it? It's official, the Kosloski's have gone green and not everybody is happy about it!

There is just nothing right about this!!!!! Where are the parents????? I am totally creeped-out! When children become indoctrinated to accept that there is nothing wrong with naked strangers approaching them is when you have a problem....

His strange aura isn't the only thing we're seeing too much of. I love Christian Nightmares! They're great for cranking up the misanthropy when I've accumulated too much hope for humanity.

Figmund Fraud with his Eggo, (k)id and altar-Igor. I wouldn't go with his "natural" motif.

I need to go wash my eyes out now......... Well, I'm off to pour bleach in my eyes.........

My first thought was "CREEEEEPY!" too. I just don't feel well after seeing this one. I just threw up all over my keybbbooooxc

oh my... OH MY GOOD, I'M SO GLAD THAT I WASN'T THERE.

May be he is Hippie. Don't worry he is wearing underwear.

This gives a whole new meaning to the term "Eat My Shorts"! Imma start a real fun alternative group to The Girl-Scouts®.

Do we have a creepy button anywhere? ... what do we call our act? We're The Aristocrats!

In case you were wondering whatever happened to that dude from Spin Doctors. Dude... tuck your balls in. The children are getting nervous. Dude's got a severe case of bluebells. Dude's one of those rare practicing literal fig'urativists.

How many people are retracting their assumptions now since the update? Tell us more about how random assumptions arent valid.

Take your pick. Both were equally inappropriate and absolutely hilarious. Nicely done Mac. Absolutely terrible.

Nothing is more terrifying than the picture of Glenn Beck holding a baby..*shivers. Terrifying is the right word, also horrifying.

Ah, christians... No wonder the world mostly thinks you represent stupid! This just proves the point that you will twist whatever you can to fit your needs. Research sheeple! And you call Christians manipulative? Come on.....you are certainly no better than those you whine about!

hahahaha Tiddlie Winks for Adults. DUMDUMDUM. DUH. Bwahahahahahahahahahahahaha!!!!!!! hahahaha

wow... I'm literally speechless. (speechless)

The sad thing is, she will probably . . . resort to personal insults. Later, in a televised interview, Barbara Walters got Julian to admit, "I could probably get by with 1 or 2 leaves."

pervert jerk Pervert

perfect PERFECT!

We could just come back with "family" later. He did that later. Buh dum Ching!

Worst. Babysitter. Ever. The worst! Worst comment ever.

David Berg, The Early Years. David Koresh's 3RD wedding.

Invented the Seize-her Salad. I'll never eat salad again.

Kale, Kale the gangs all here! Oh kale no!

haha So true!!! Well, I've been posting on here a long time, and many have wanted my head on a platter, so every so often I pretend to "slip up" and give em the thrill they have so long sought. It keeps their hopes alive. Who keeps taking our picture off the mantle?

Haha – me too! HAHAHA!

Yeah, it took all of 3 minutes to find the LACMA information, if that. Maybe I should work for Buzzfeed! Well, uh...yeah!

Gosh -4! god hate FB or did I miss something, I vtd u ^ Name of* god

Good catch Jan. Well said, Jan.

How was this considered ok? Gays can't get married yet this shit is okay pfft. … ok, I'm incredibly disturbed.

How's about blurring out the children's faces assholes! Why not tell people which school this was at? I hope this man is no longer allowed near children! I bet someones father has a talk with this person and it never happens again.

You offered an opinion that runs contrary from every effort you make on this very website. no reading comprehension problems on my part, just a lack of self awareness on yours. Awesome post. Thank you for doing your part to try and correct yet another aberrant stream of misinformation. It's a small gesture, but speaks volumes. Fighting ignorance, one caps-locked typo-flailing overprotective hysterical mother at a time. Cheers from Australia. And they can have cars that get close to 100 miles per gallon since TEN YEARS AGO but oooh, the bad Americans are purposely kept on 18-23 mpg to tech them the lessons they so soundly deserve, right? cuz those guys that were celebrating were viewed by a knowledgable anthropologist, not some old lady with binoculars (which is a "my cousin vinny joke" not a viable theory), and those guys were were dancing the hora whilst wearing israeli diplomat t-shirts?

And your statistics come from where? [citation needed] Cite your source please, Tony. Sorry, it's false - Disturbing…… Isn't there a law about that. Context. CONTEXT! Please tell me this made some sense to some one, if only for that moment. It might be nice if y'all would find out what you're talking about before screaming "'Shopped!" And what makes you say that? Besides stupidity and a desire to troll? what a spammy website. in any case… wat non sense r they releasing…?? Where do I sign up? PS I'm in Perth, WA ! You're welcome.

Yearly visit to Uncle Pervies House. Kiddie Hawk Suffer me to come unto little children. Larry was too irony-deficient to recognize the fact that he had banged Olof's son while listening to his Bang and Olufsen. He has never taken drugs, nor ever had an impure thought about a young girl. then he ain't a true believer.

That could very well be a parenting fail. What, you didn't have "rape day" at your VBS? The Hard-on of Eden GAAAAAAH!!!!! Me thinks they took the Creation story realism a bit to far. Atheist Nature Camp perhaps? Church-camp rules.

Could you please paint our whole face dad...please? But, Mom, he promised us free candy! You never give us candy anymore!

Why Big Brothers Big Sisters™ stopped cross-gender mentoring. Mom's holistic sex-change was a resounding success. Now we know what the Geico caveman does in his spare time for extra cash. Never do mushrooms before Parent teacher Conferences.

Amberosia Alert! Serf and turf... No 'buddy' lets babies up his corn-husks. The under-ripe ones are still good for pickling, though. ...and enjoy the fertile crescent rolls... ♫ So bring us some figgy pudding ... And bring it out here! ♫ PS: We won't go until we get some. Go fig 'er. Children...keep far from Fig Newton. Now, where did we leave off? Boxers, briefs, or bok choy? Vegan Speedos™ latest ad campaign sent maxed messages. Green Piece. botany gone wild? When in Romaine... Broccoli Rob! Spinach-SAL-Odd Poison Irony. Greens ... its what's for dinner.

Cherishes his weed whacker. Hey...wh wh what are you gonna do with that lawn mower? It's all fun until someone puts an eye out. "Exhibit A" To Thatch a Predator.

Some idiot bitch replied, GET A TAN! This week on Disney's The Suite life on Dick. Justin Beiber is a lot taller in person. Hello I'm Chris Hansen... why don't you take a seat. What would Marney say to this?! You mean Tiny Tim? This explains so much about Gwyneth Paltrow. Mommy prefers hair pants!

When keeping it real goes wrong. Damn Hippies! Made me look. Dang it. Less 'Show', more 'Tell'. Just say no! Not glued. Stapled. too soon? fuckwit is my new favorite word. Learnt a lesson there! same here! seems legit That is NOT right! i know right? Poor judgement! shame shame Supersupersupersuper creeeeeeepy!!! Ugh...

Messedupotamia eeewwwwwwwwwwwwwwwwwwww!!!!!!!!!!!!!!!!! Ewwwww.... GROSS Can you bleach your eyeballs? eeeewwwwweeeee!!! Ewwww... "THREW"?! as in "UP"?!! 'Cause I sure did.... excuse me---must vomit now. barfed after i shared it.

amurrrrika! creepy! Scary! HIDE *shudder* HALP! amidoinitrite? Yep ! Naw, son! Oh....No...... Wow :) O_O O_o WORD. Ummmm OM(G?) PMSL!!!! LMAO!!! FTW! WIN!!!!!!!!!!! Thread won. Win! =) Epic Win even YOMANK!

amen AMEN The End The End

I Wonder About Shit

The following four pieces were written for the WONDER *tumblr, shitwonder.tumblr.com, and posted during the month of April 2013, National Poetry Month. The process was to type a relatively bland phrase into google, "I wonder about shit." and see what images and texts resulted—favoring results from tumblr—and then to permute that search phrase for further results. The texts were lightly edited, rearranged and matched up with images in the process. Each set of images was batch processed and color shifted to highlight a particular color profile and to make them look "worse" than they did in their original context. The resulting piece was edited further for this publication.*

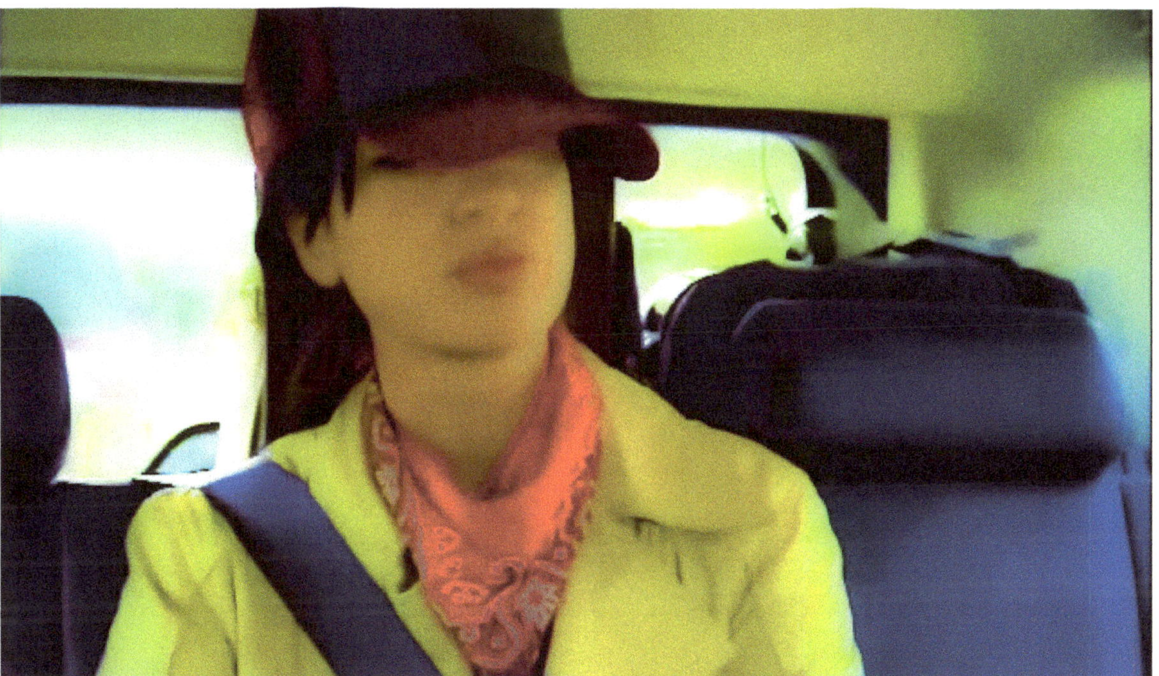

I wonder about shit all the time; and when I say shit, I don't mean the shit that people usually wonder about on a regular basis.

So many times have I wondered why my friends were so unanimously "Boo!" (as much as I wonder about shit in my life generally).

Ya know, this is me not letting something go... but I wonder about shit like this.

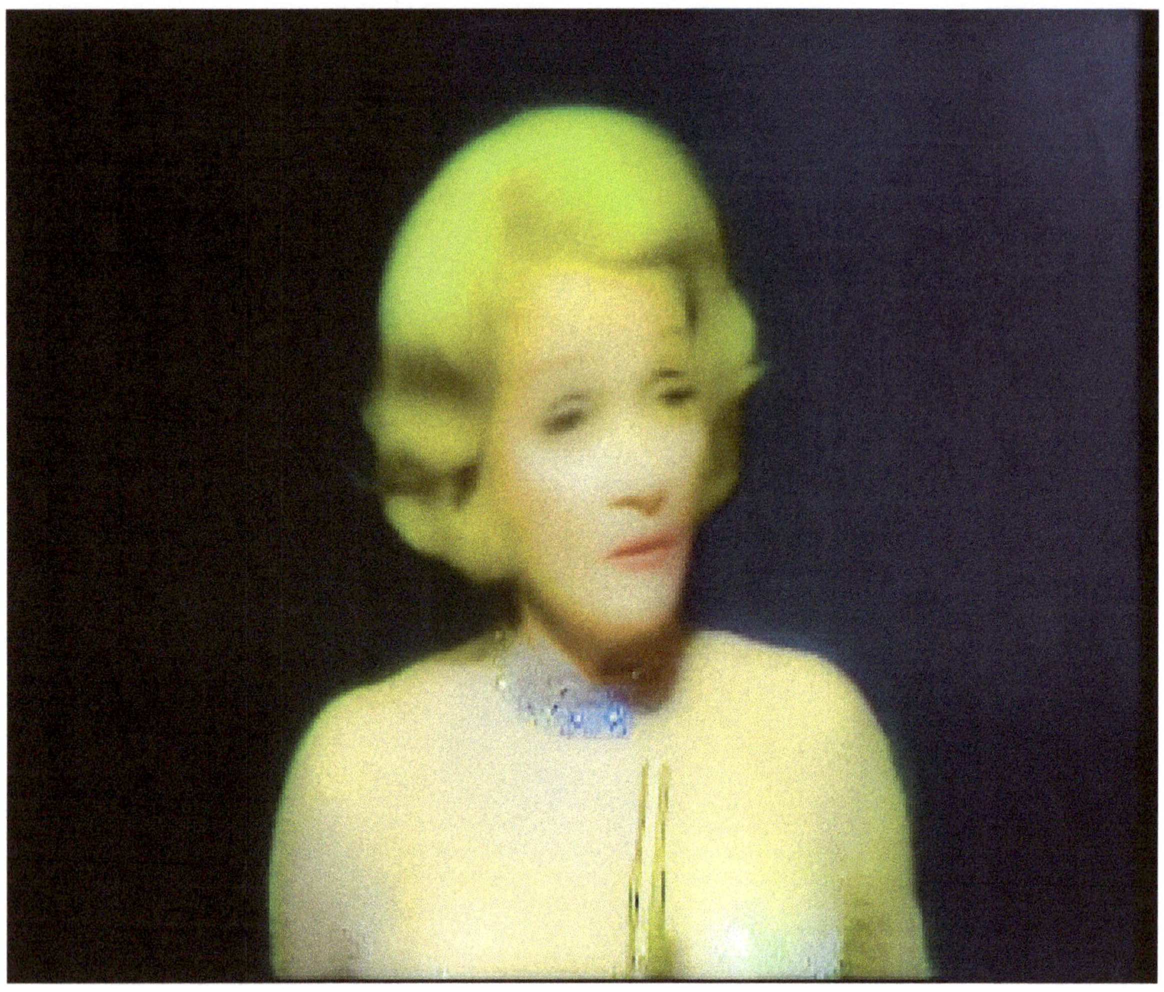

I wonder about shit, but Jesus Christ, anyone that might even try to comprehend your insanity, well… I hope they better be as crazy as you!

Yes? No? Well I do, I'm weird, I wonder about shit like that. Whether to be worn in plain view or to be in the hair style as part of its hidden infrastructure, bobby pins are a must-have in my hair life (nearly) daily.

'Cause, you know, I wonder about shit like that. Welcome to my mind and I hope you've had your shots. Wait… there's no vaccine for this. Sorry. My bad. Carry on.

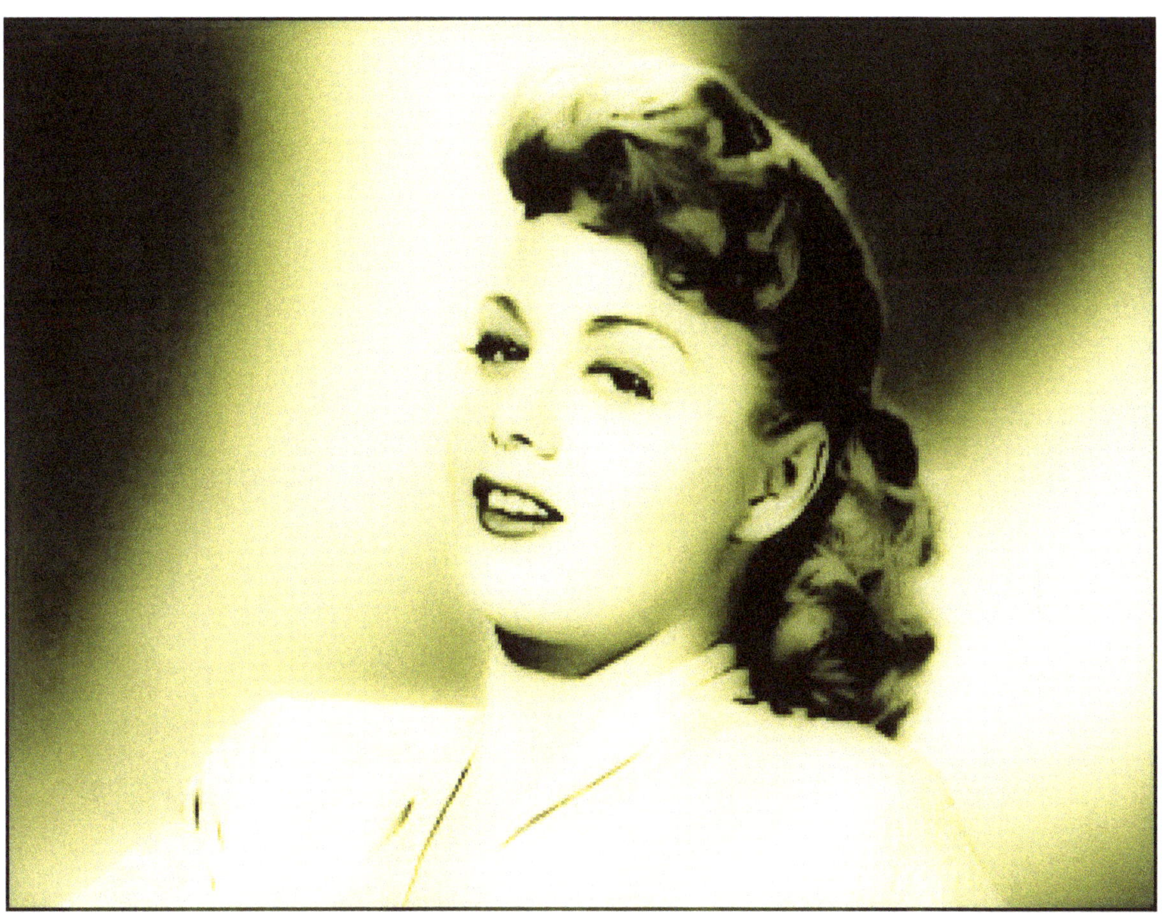

Anyone remember soylent green? Well, it's in the matrix also, people are energy, batteries, heat, … food. These are all interchangeable stuffs aren't they? What is the total output of say Btu's of all the humans? I wonder about shit.

I'M REALLY GLAD THAT THERE'S A WORD FOR THIS WOW! I think about this a lot. When I'm high I wonder about shit like this lol…

"I keep wondering—I wonder about shit like this sometimes when I can't sleep—I keep wondering, what if the snow itself could think like we can? I mean, imagine if every snowflake in an avalanche was able to think."

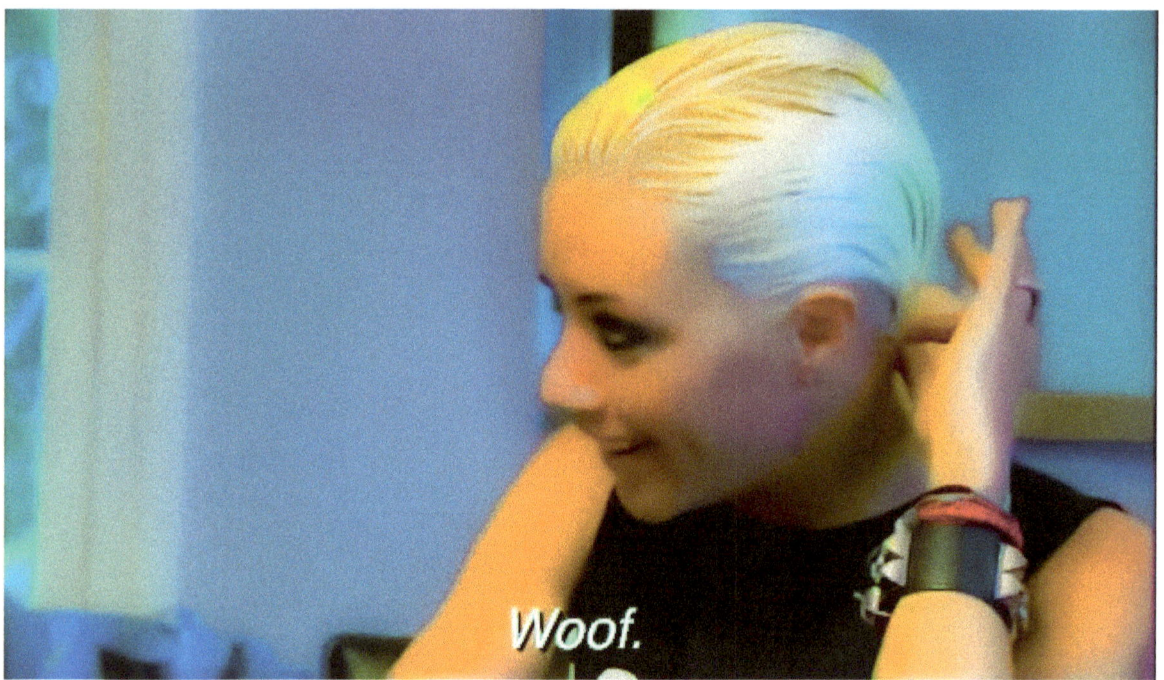

"I wonder about shit." "Like what shit?" "You know, shit, why things are, you know, so messed up." "I wonder if Nietzsche was right about God." "Who?" "Nietzsche. German philosopher dude." "Yeah, them German people are smart."

See, I wonder about shit like that. Mainly when I see hot guys with no wording in their ads, I mean.

If you're wondering why I'm wondering about this… well, I wonder about shit like this and Tumblr is a better place than the Facebook suburbs for random shit.

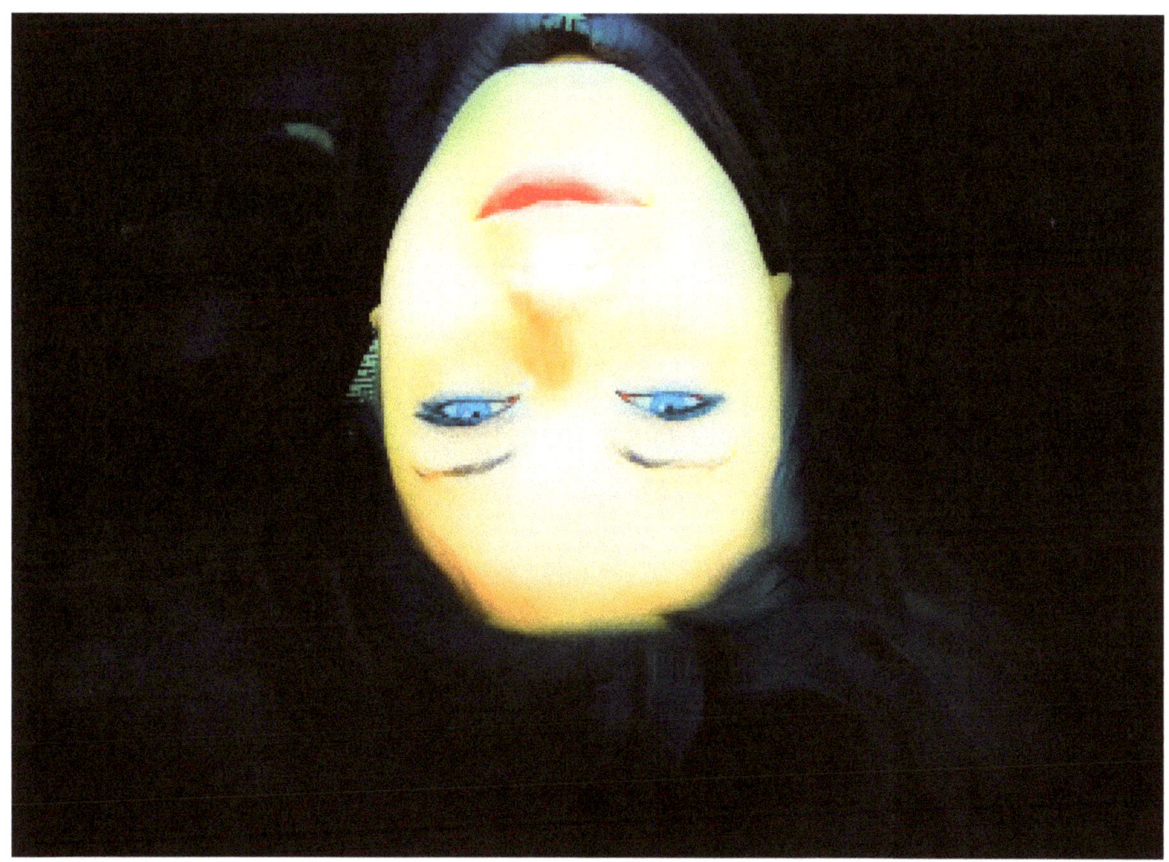

I wonder about shit like this. I'd like to think the working out excessively mitigates the risk but it doesn't.

ON SLOW DAYS I WONDER ABOUT SHIT LIKE THIS: SOUND CLASH!

I wonder about shit like that sometimes. I have a bizarre standard for going out and having a good time too, and I wonder if our aversion to people who suck (aka have a totally different definition of fun) is our way of finding ourselves.

They are what I think they are, they are quite ridiculous. Love you all, but c'mon. Sometimes I wonder about shit. So, if you all stop talking to me for a while, I'll deal with the consequences then. The tourney runs all day Saturday.

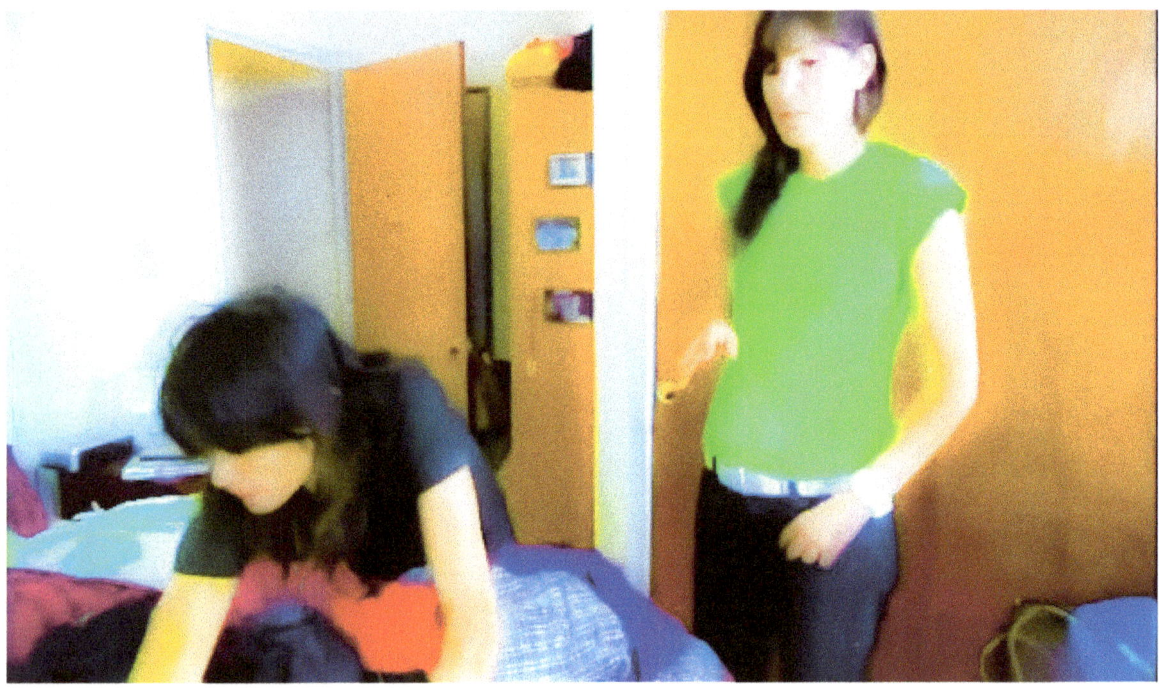

I wonder about shit (not to mention piss). If people could get over the immature attitude to human faeces we might have a great source of fertilizer and energy on, er, tap.

Ever wonder what the linear speed of your pistons at a given rpm is? I did, because sometimes I wonder about shit like that...

I should bug Morven with questions about that. Doubt I would ever go to one, but hey I wonder about shit man!

A lotta times I wonder about shit that doesn't fully hit me until someone else points it out. But thanks for the review homie ! It helped.

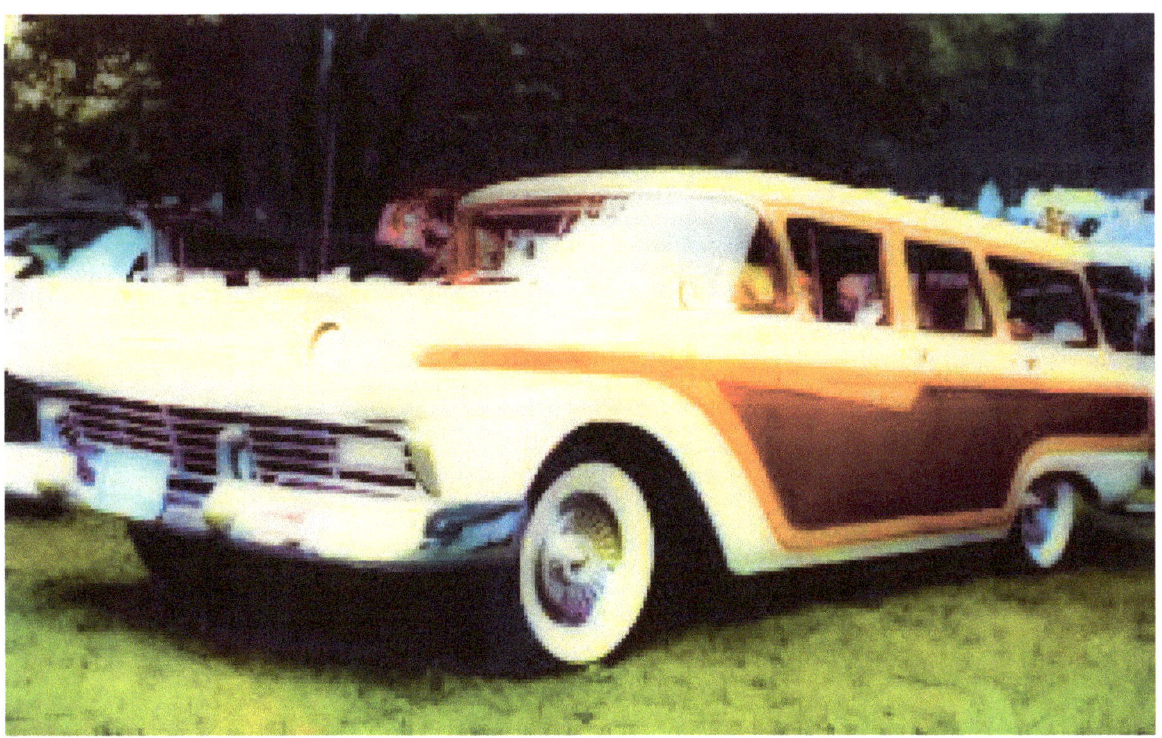

I wonder about shit like that. If he had lived, would he have taken up snowboarding. I absolutely love it. I find it almost Zen. I never was very good at skiing. He was pretty good at it as I recall. We, as I see it, were kind of polar opposites.

I wonder about shit all the time; and when I say shit, I don't mean the shit that people usually wonder about on a regular basis such as their credit score or how their kids are doing. I'm talking about fucked up stuff.

Sometimes I wonder about shit like that… to find for linear piston speed at 1000rpm, simply multiply length of stroke by 2.8, result for piston speed.

Sometimes I wonder about shit like this. If I'm doing my job wtf do you care?

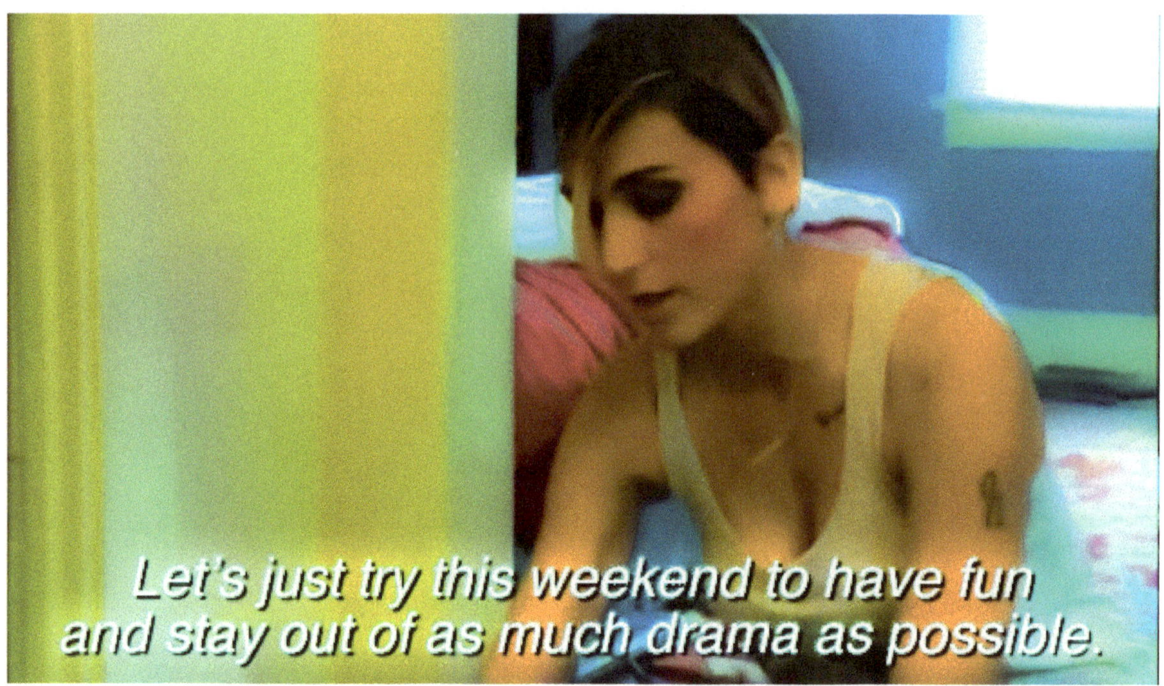

I want to work and stay here, because I love Crystal and Jeff, and they love me too, and I know it... it's not something I wonder about. Shit, they left me here with the house and the car, I can have anyone over, do whatever I want.

Babies hear things etc. Not true at all? They react to their hearing/vision. And I wonder about shit like this all the time.

I wonder about shit like this sometimes... who is actually being influenced by me? I hear from all sorts of random places sometimes. I have a fan.

...

I WONDER ABOUT SHIT SOMETIMES. I WONDER HOW PEOPLE REALLY VIEW ME AT MOMENTS!! THEY SAY IM AN ALRIGHT PERSON BUT DO THEY MEAN IT? I MEAN FOR THE MOST PART I THOUGHT I WAS A GOOD PERSON.

Sometimes I wonder about shit like this. If you're doing your job wtf do I care?

Shit I Wonder About

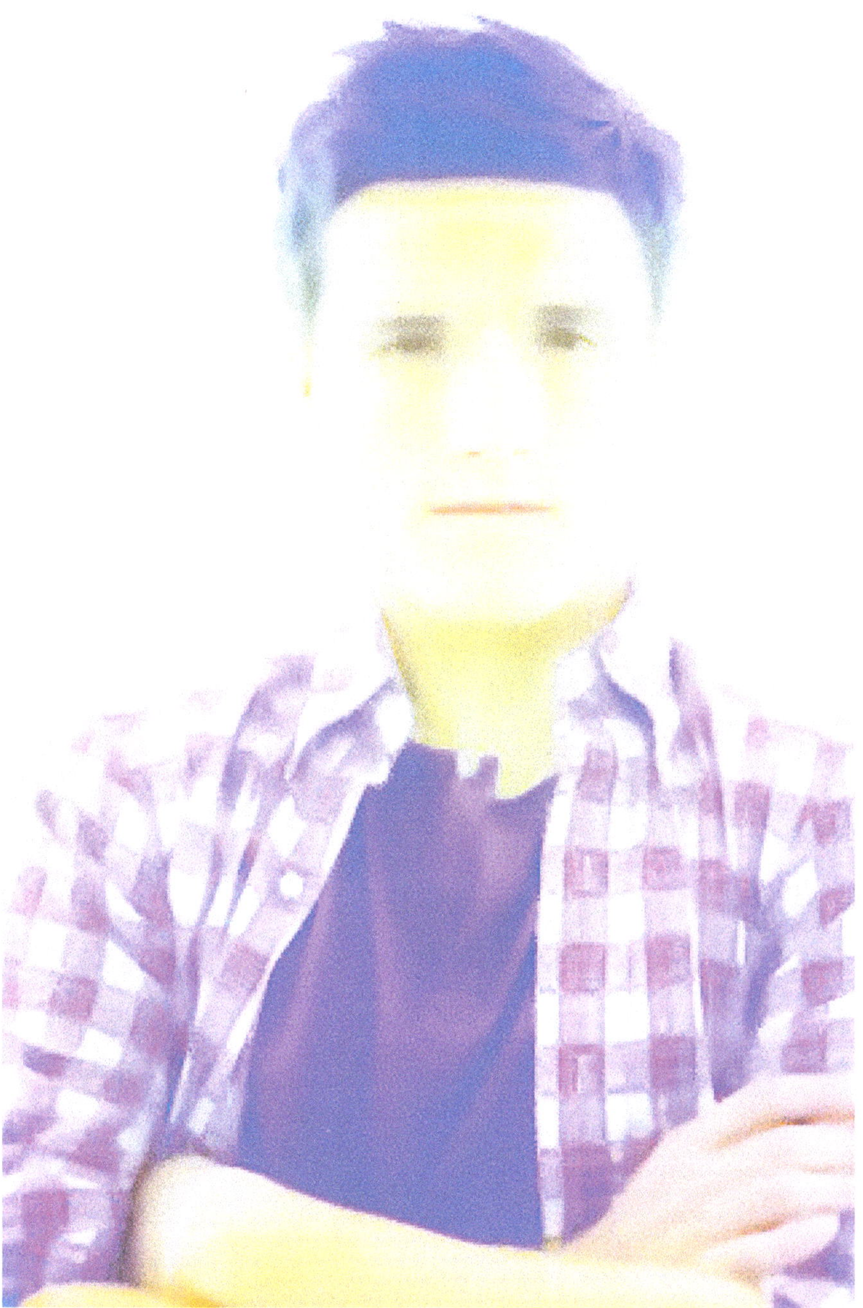

This the kinda shit I wonder about.

Shit I wonder about #1: I wonder about those celebrities, boybands and whatnots saying that you're beautiful no matter how you look and whatever.

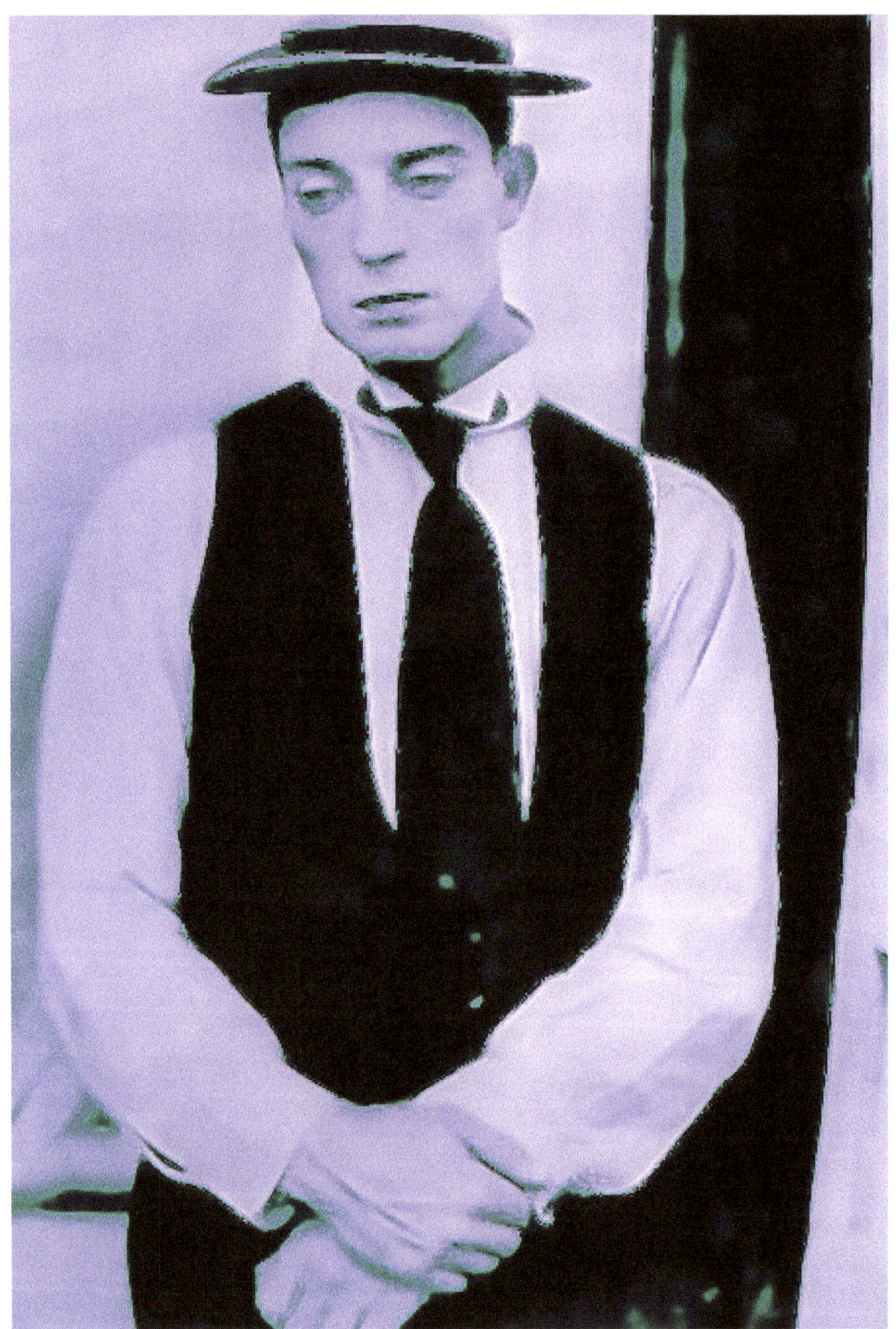

Again, shit :(shit after shit... I wonder about stupid popsy music in accept corps demos when their founder, organizer and main coder are all black metal music freaks.

There's so much shit I wonder about it. Fuck it though, I'm done. "Size me up. I know you did. Care for you, you know I did. Making waves like a kid. Run away so easily. If the past could forgive all our doubts god forbid."

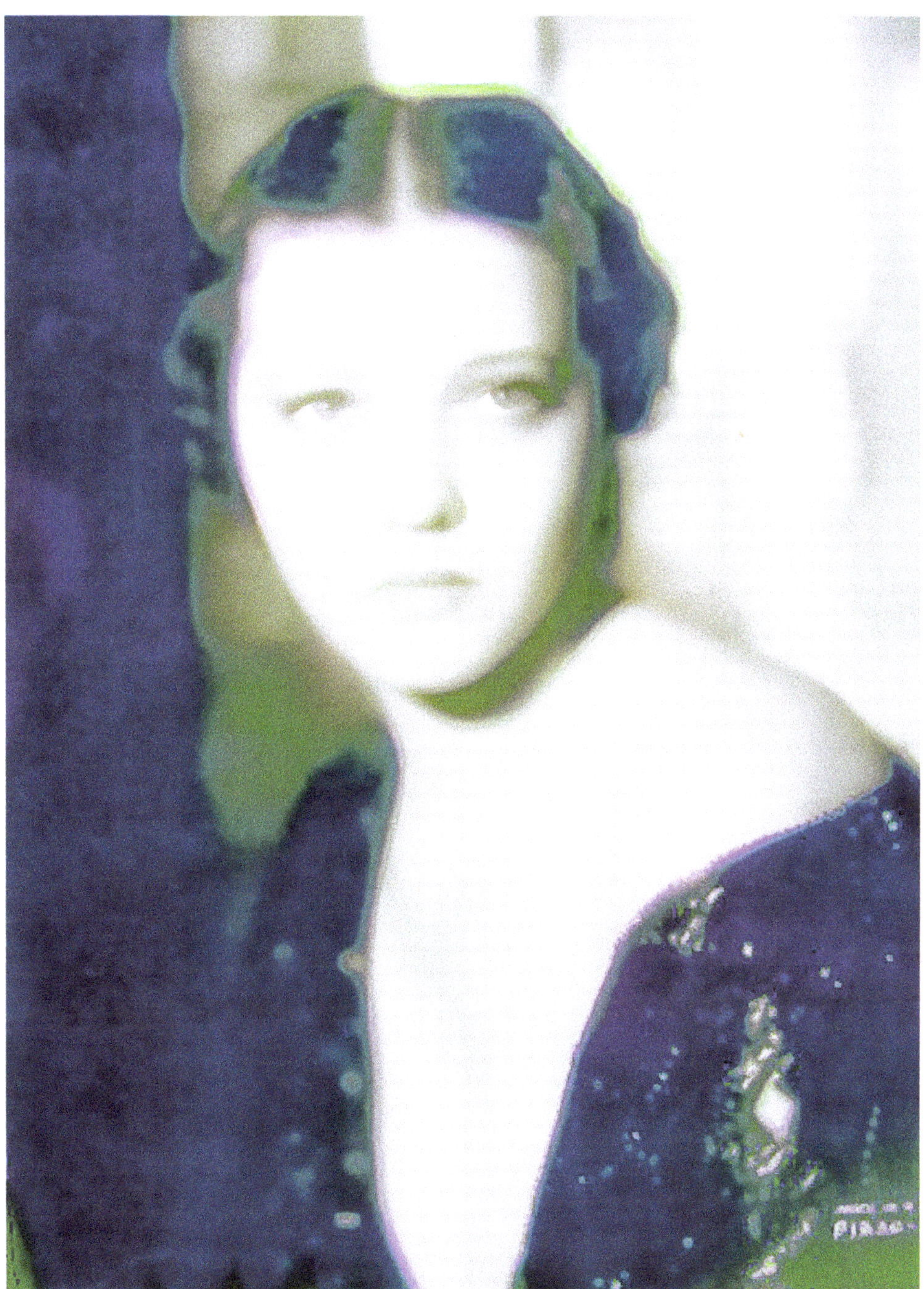

Worm shit. I wonder about worm shit often. I understand that the shitting of worms is beneficial to the planet, to agriculture, and so I wonder about worm shit for this reason, and remember images of bruised bodies partly melded to pavement, the rest of the worms writhing to escape the rain.

That's the kind of shit I wonder about while I sit here, staring off into space, waiting to stand up and clap with everybody like we're having some kind of cult ritual. Shit, that dude has a big pentagram around his neck.

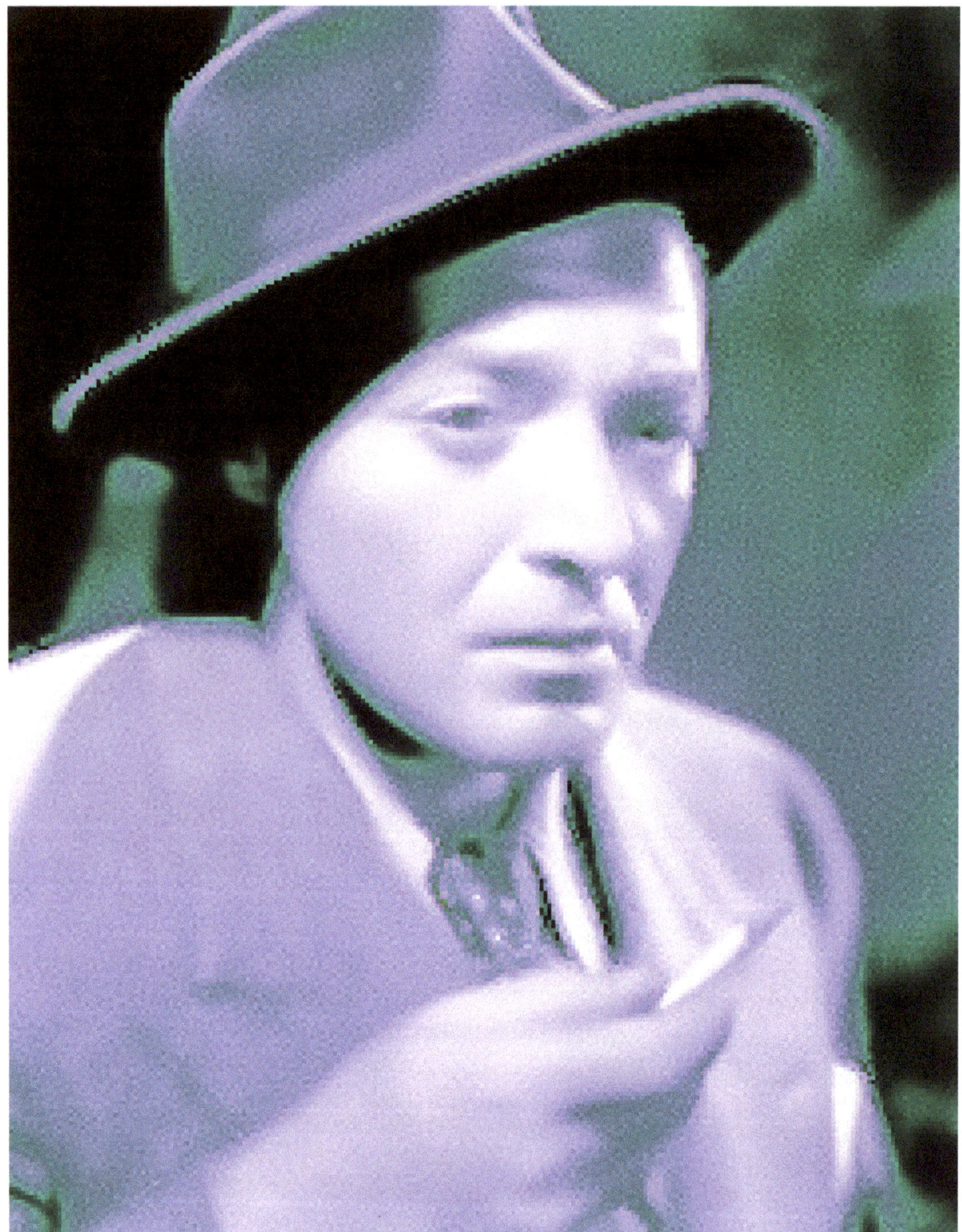

Shit I wonder about loyalty and honor too, shit's in short supply as far as I can tell. And if you are doing the same old tired ass shit under some bridge then no way.

This is the shit I wonder about now after learning what an amazing liar you are, like I told you, the best liar I have ever met used to think that was my distinction, you overachieved and took that title belt from the champ.

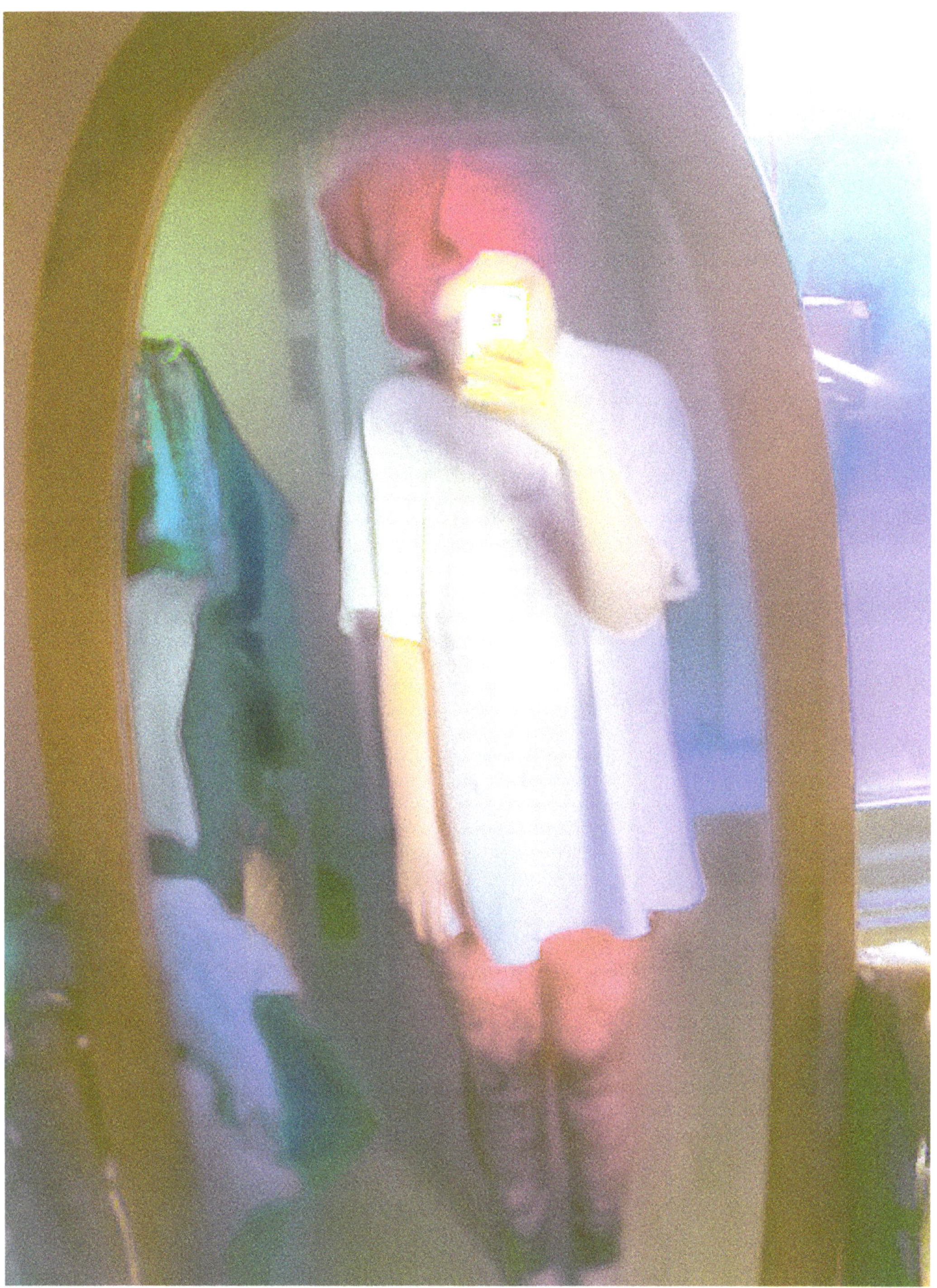

Shit I wonder about that. Like the dickheads who do robberies and smile at the camera. Never said they were smart. Some are so stupid.

Think back to how it became vogue to say "Set your B+ Voltage to 108 you dumb shit!!" I wonder about this place sometimes, it's all jittery, and I'm just thinkin' "CAP KIT!!"

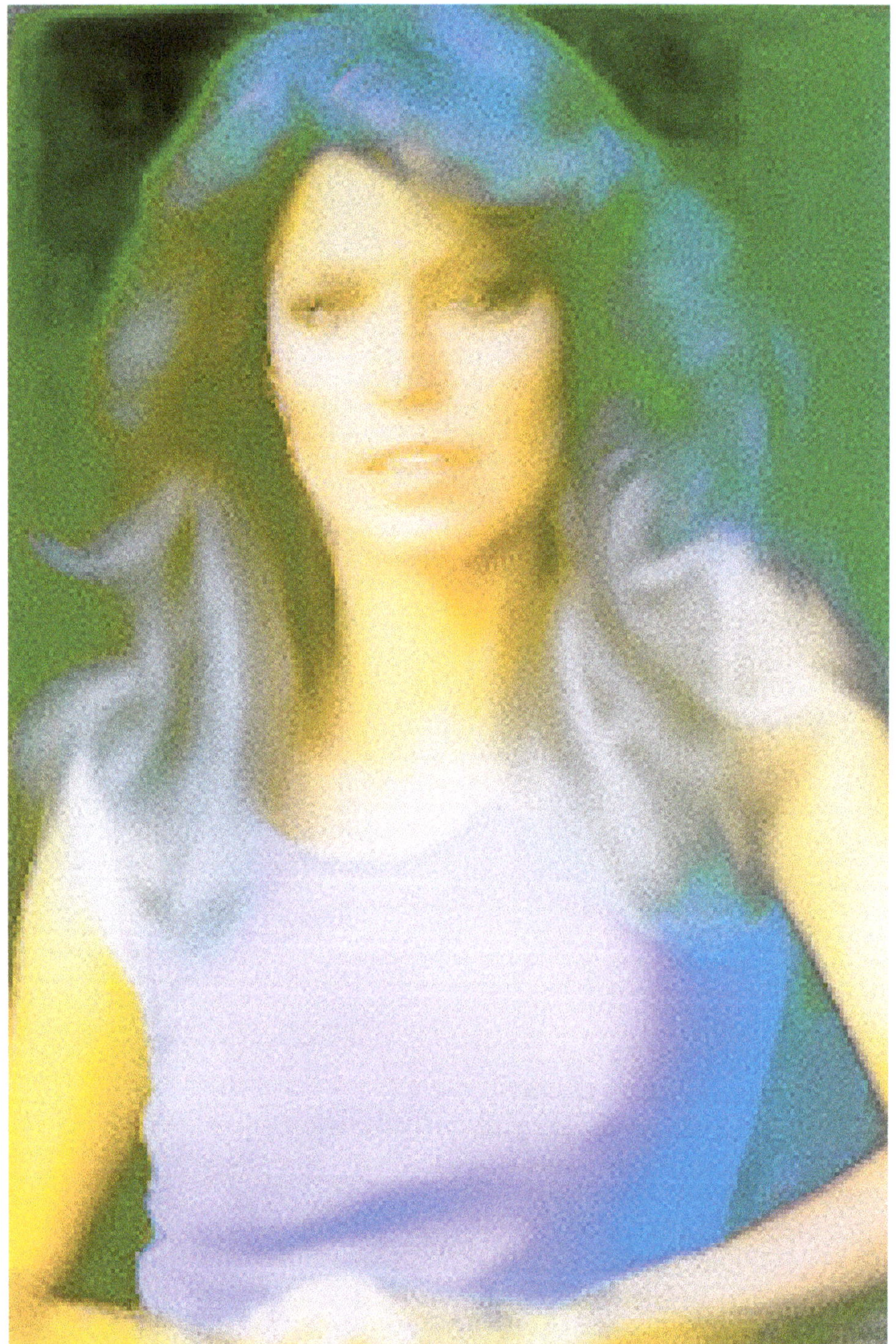

As I mentioned before, just because you fantasize about it, doesn't mean it should be acted on, they are very different things. Ahh good ol' deviant behaviour. Shit, I wonder about. Surely all guys have at some point?

You, on the other hand, you little liberal piece of shit, I wonder about! I wish you a case of cancer.

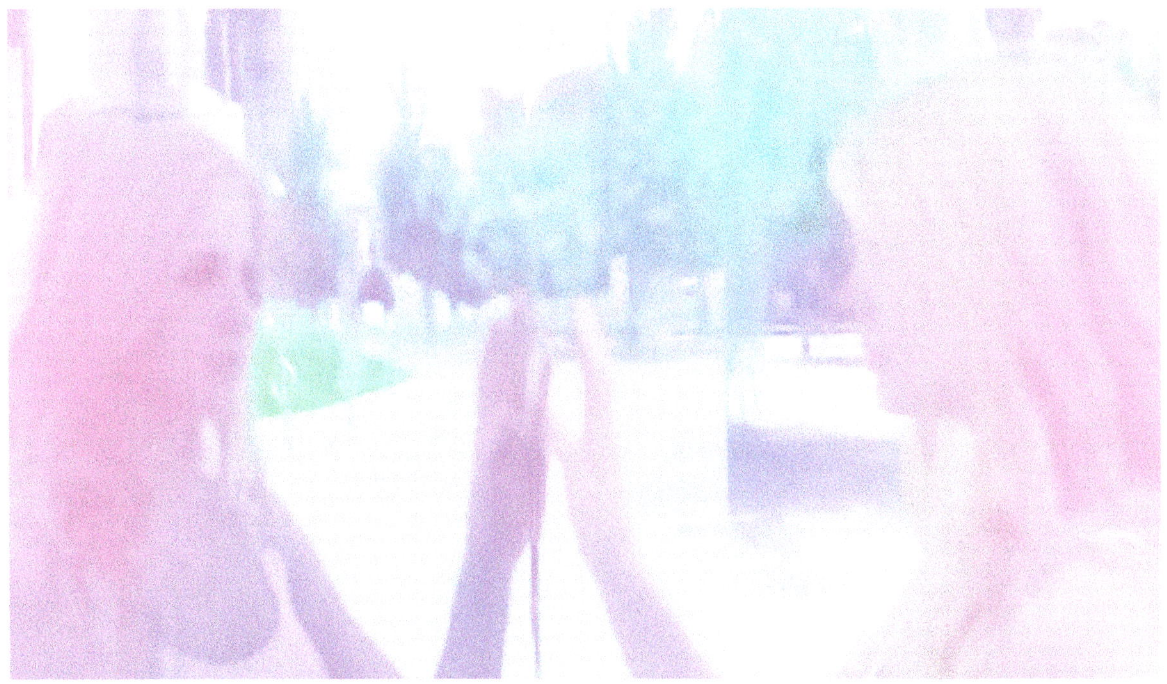

Clouds of the greenish muck floated, billowing down to where we were sitting, bringing a stink like some foul mix of eggs and shit. "I wonder about them two," she said, in a friendly, confiding sort of way. "You're right to," I replied.

Haha, that's the shit I wonder about when I'm drunk at an internet cafe in London. Maybe it's called foodgasm. Personally I think the high I sometimes get from food is kind of like the high from an orgasm.

Do you think Duchovny really eats that stuff, ribs and greasy burgers, being the vegetarian he is? This is the stupid shit I wonder about, waiting for October to come around again.

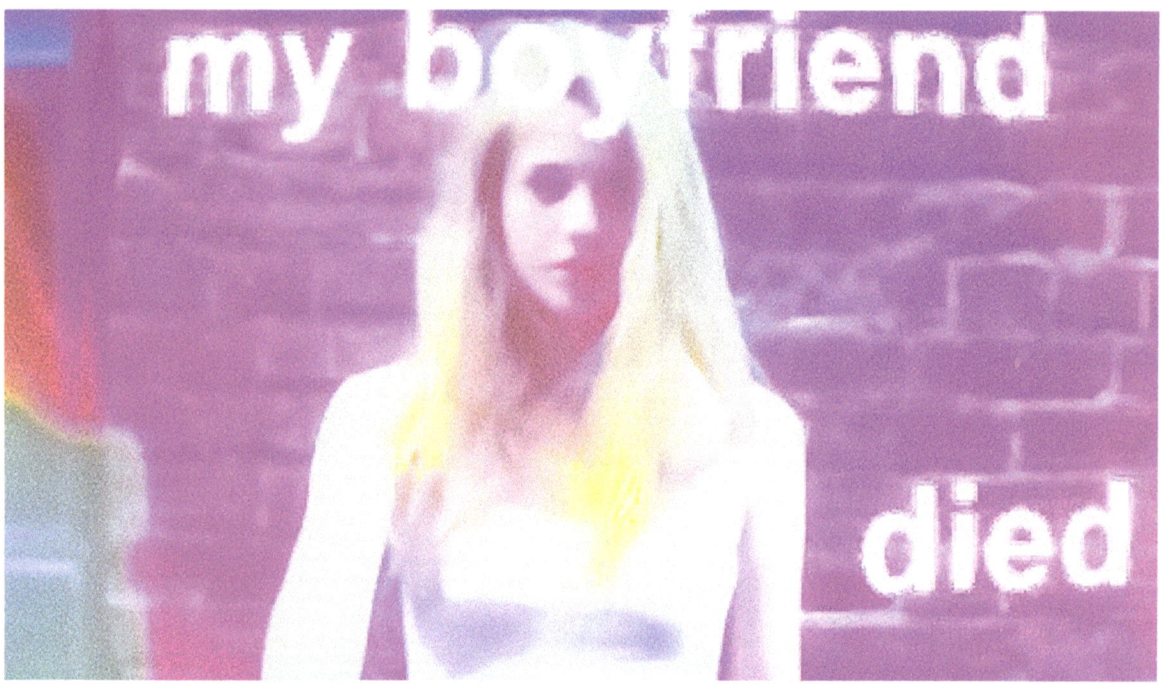

Really, this is the shit I wonder about. Sometimes I love your exceptionally descriptive writing abilities. Sometimes I do not. Guess which one it is today? Yuck.

Man that game was the shit, I wonder about this game though; I am very displeased with squares, everything is like just missing maybe a potion or a phoenix down.

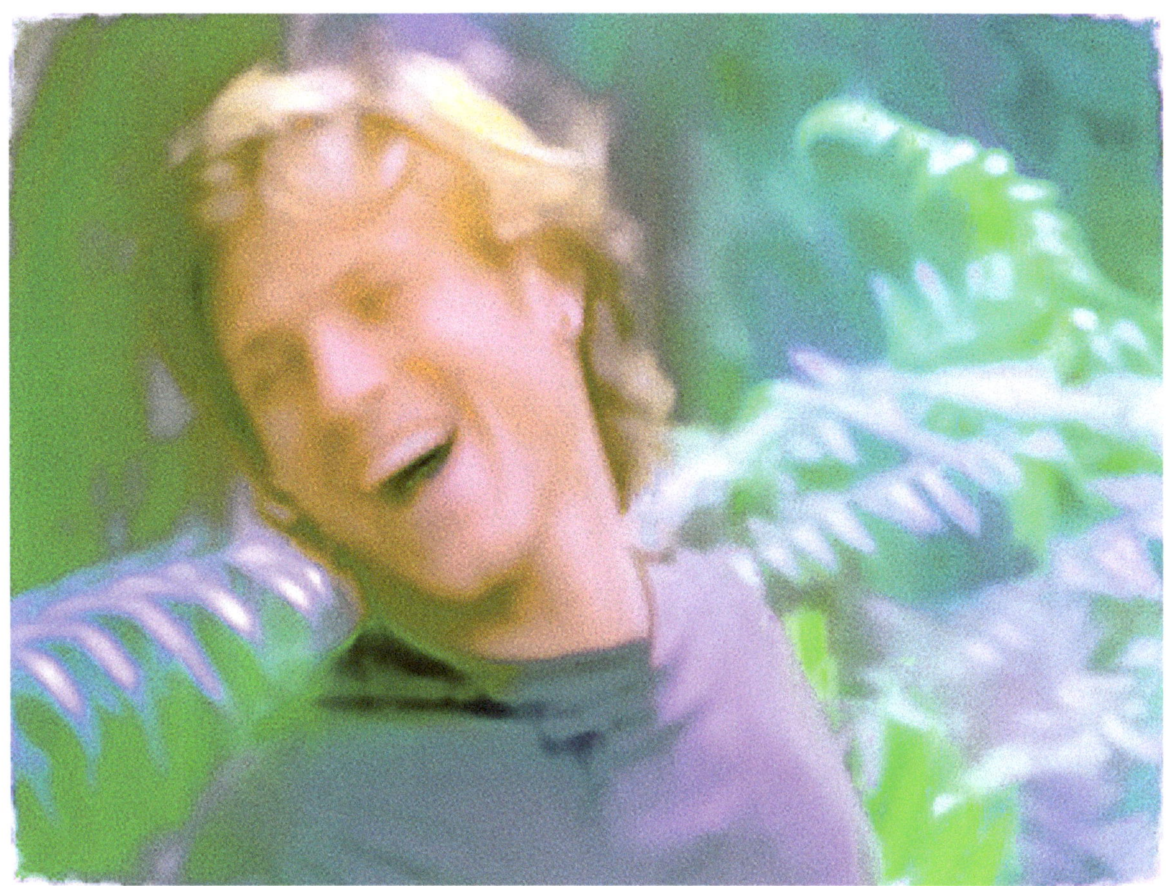

Yep, STP is shit. I wonder about Purolator as well. Advanced doesn't even carry a Puro SBC filter anymore, and Pepboys doesn't have the "full line" at all.

Shit… I wonder about this particular shit… I've never noticed it like this before. Absorb the smell of the "de-odorizers" used so that the nug just smells like that.

Shit, I wonder about them now, just sitting there. I hid them there so they wouldn't get consumed during a few parties, and forgot about them.

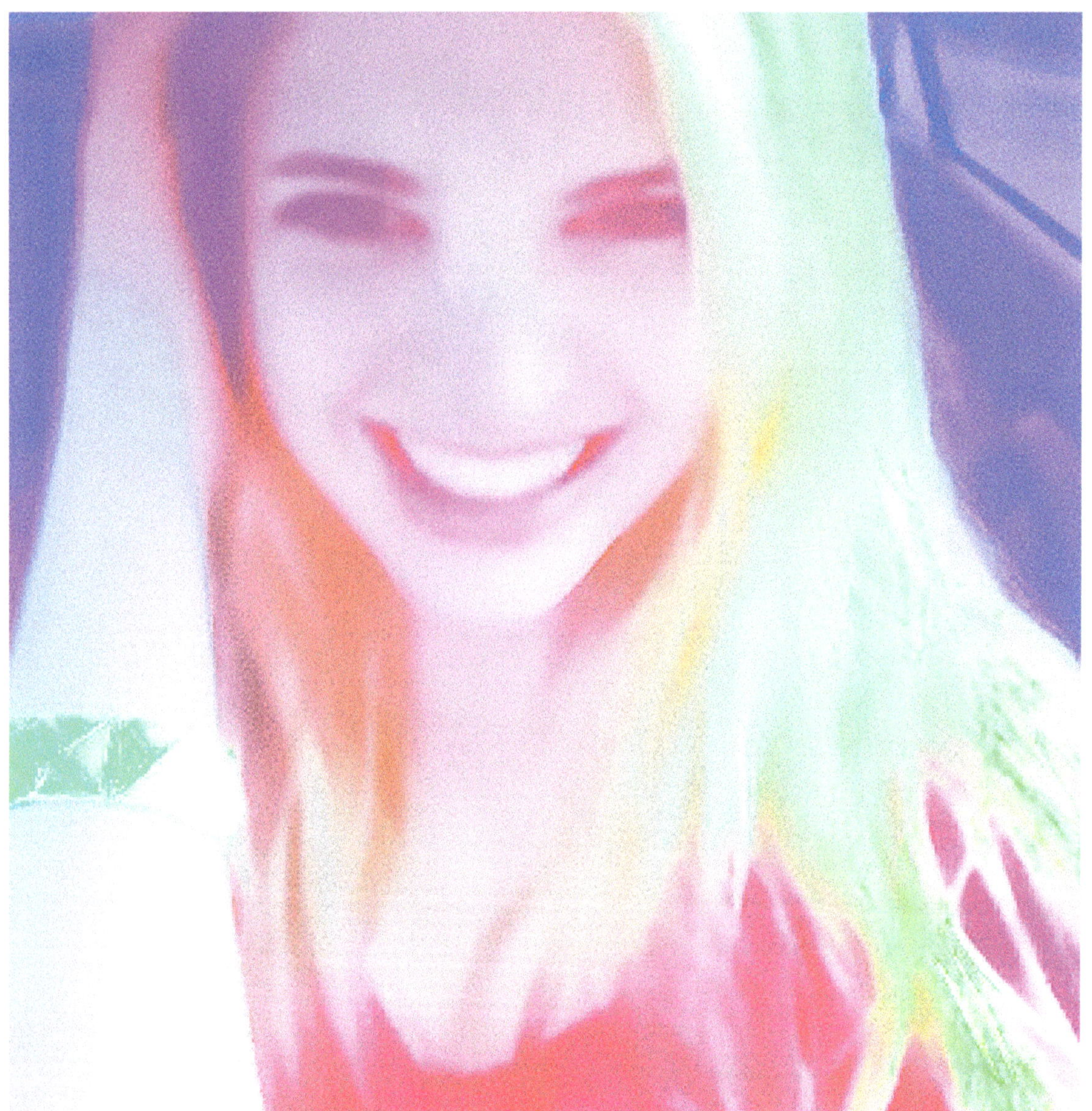

“Shit, I wonder about that all the time.” I had forgotten my own problems until your remark forced them back into my mind. Your anxiety doubled as I followed you into the house, but you found no time to do anything about it.

Although I really don’t give a shit, I wonder about the war, about ... I really don’t give a shit, I wonder about the war, about the stories about corporations, about us that have to work, and where the real money goes.

Other shit I wonder about ... why the hell I ever married that guy ... so today totally sucks, meetings with arrogant assrags all day—all of them men—and yep, women can be assrags too, probably 100% better than a man can be.

About Shit I Wonder

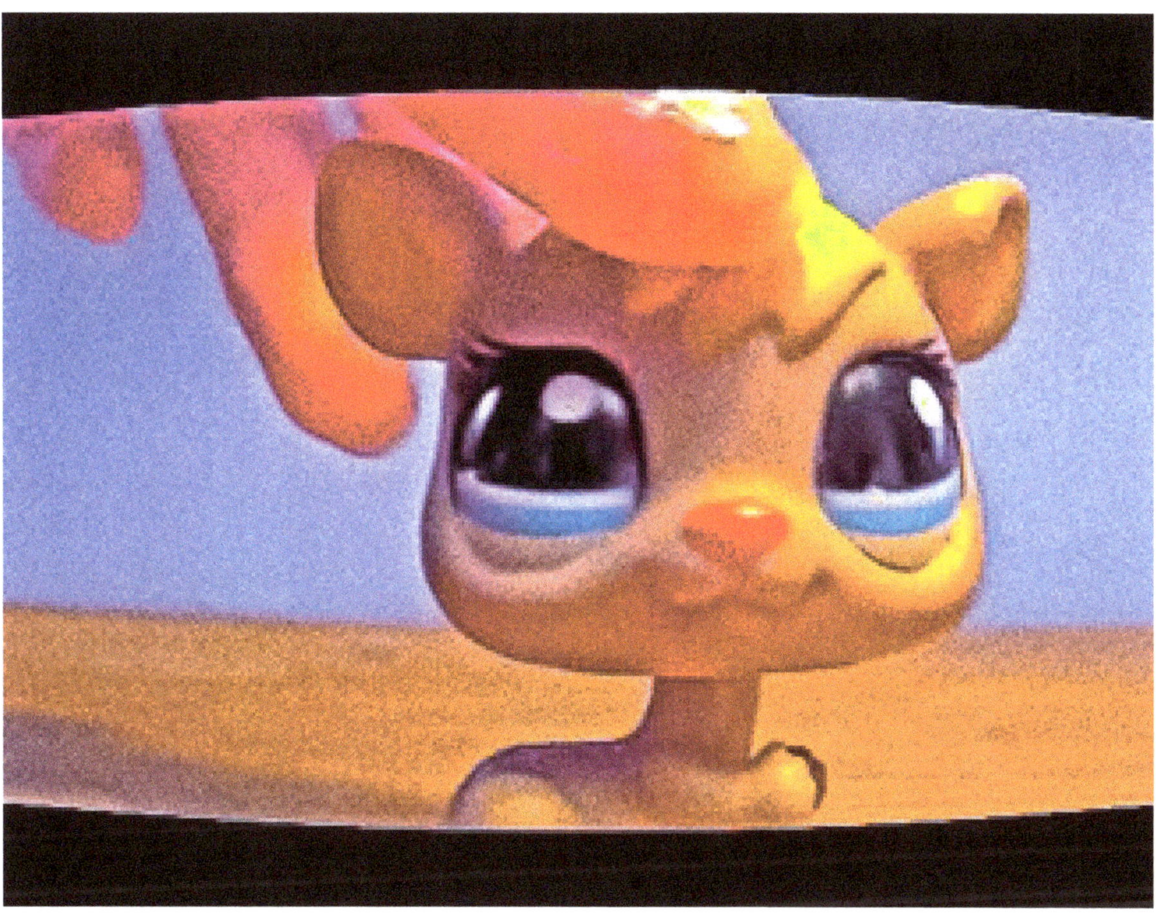

You've had this in your head for about... shit, I wonder what time it is. (Beat.) But you've had it in your head for almost a day now. JOAQUIN: Oh... (Slight pause.) It's getting hot, man, I'm really burning up. MARCO: Hombre, what happened? Maybe I should've just named this thread Ben and Avoe talk about shit, I wonder why no one else feels inclined to say something?

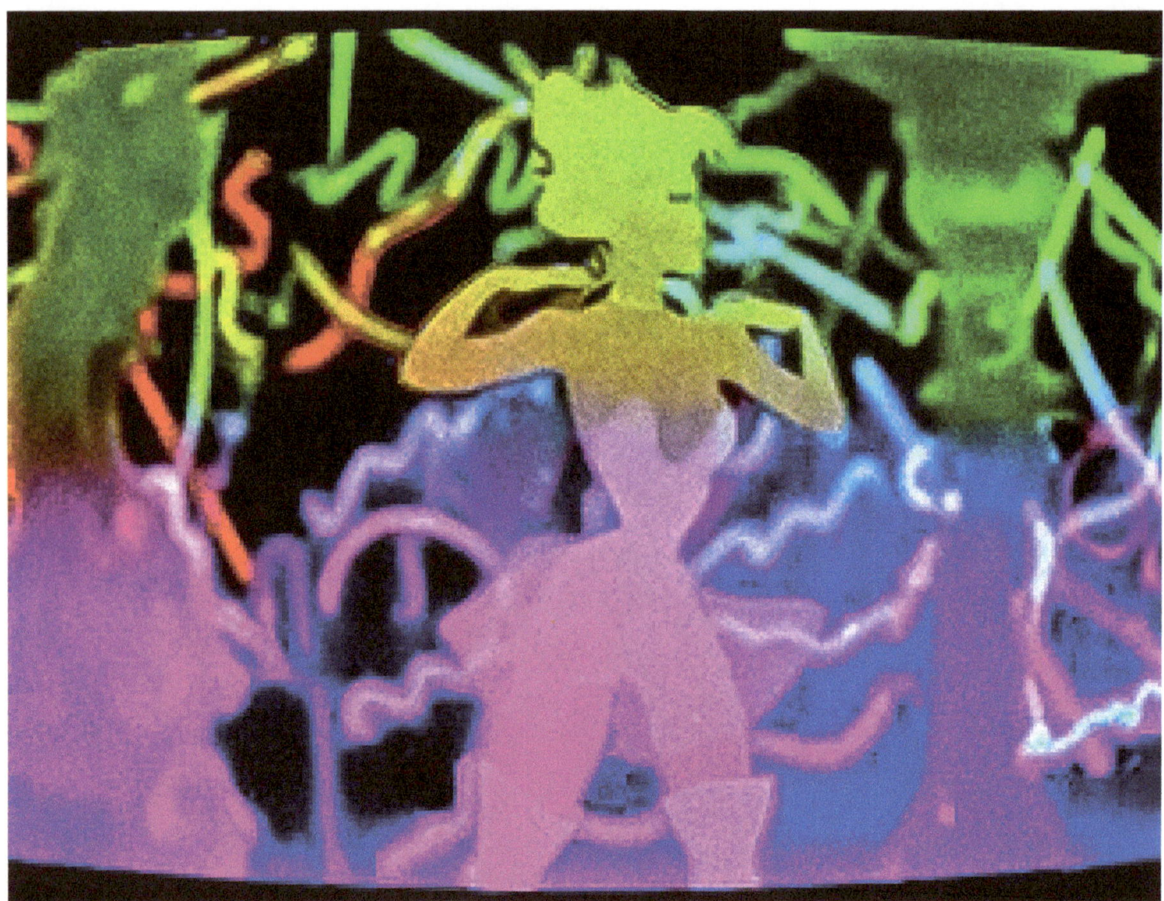

Some of these kids are so unrealistic about shit I wonder what world they live in. They are so much more laidback about shit. I wonder why such a huge cultural difference. It seems shit still gets done, and they don't worry.

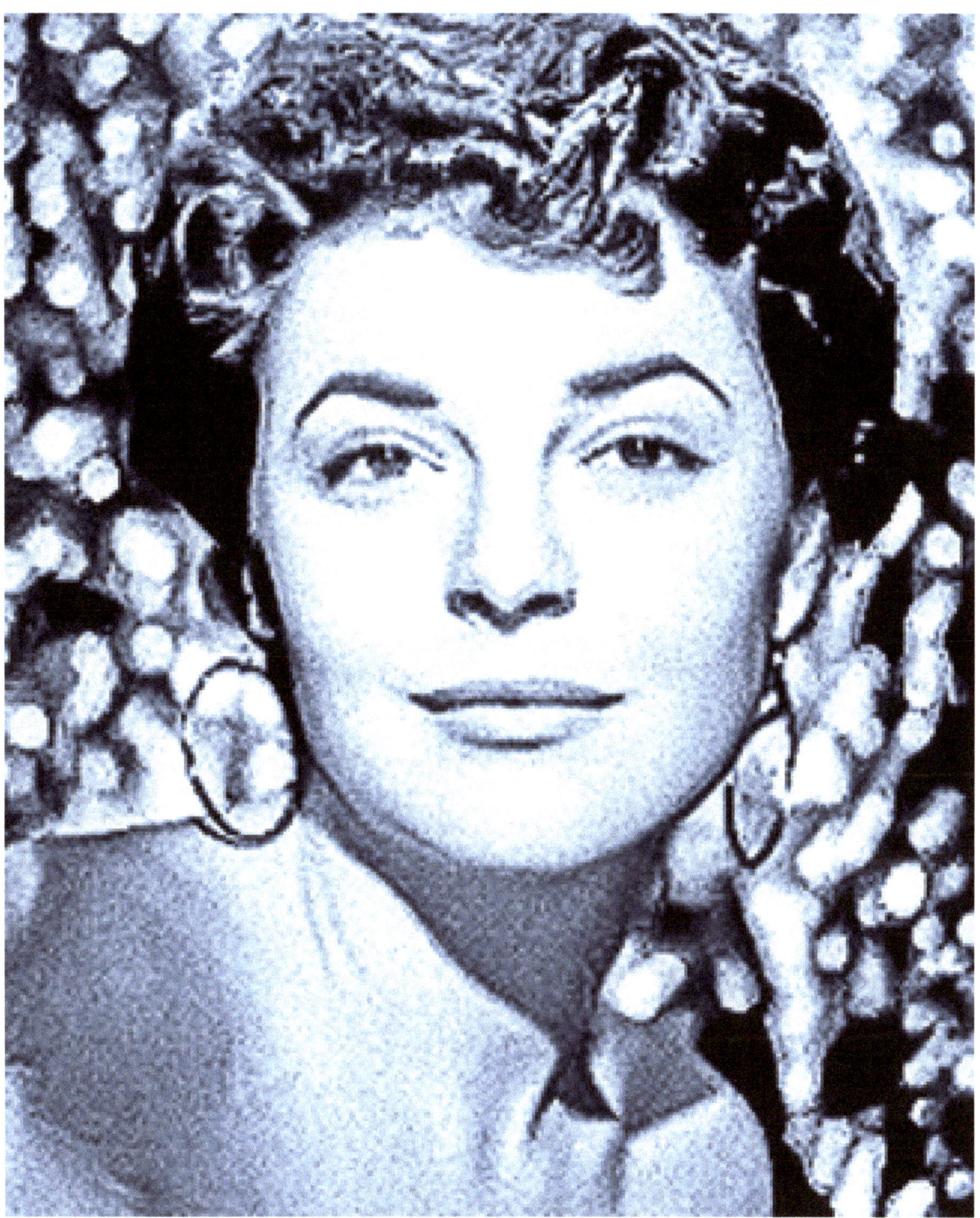

I wonder if he is one of the cool boyfriends or if he would get all upset about shit. I wonder... Hahah, nah he's read all this, it's ok. I told him. He cares so much, enough to call me when I put up stupid away messages like that, or when I'm worried about shit, I wonder to myself, "are you stupid? He loves you, why are you so worried all the time?"

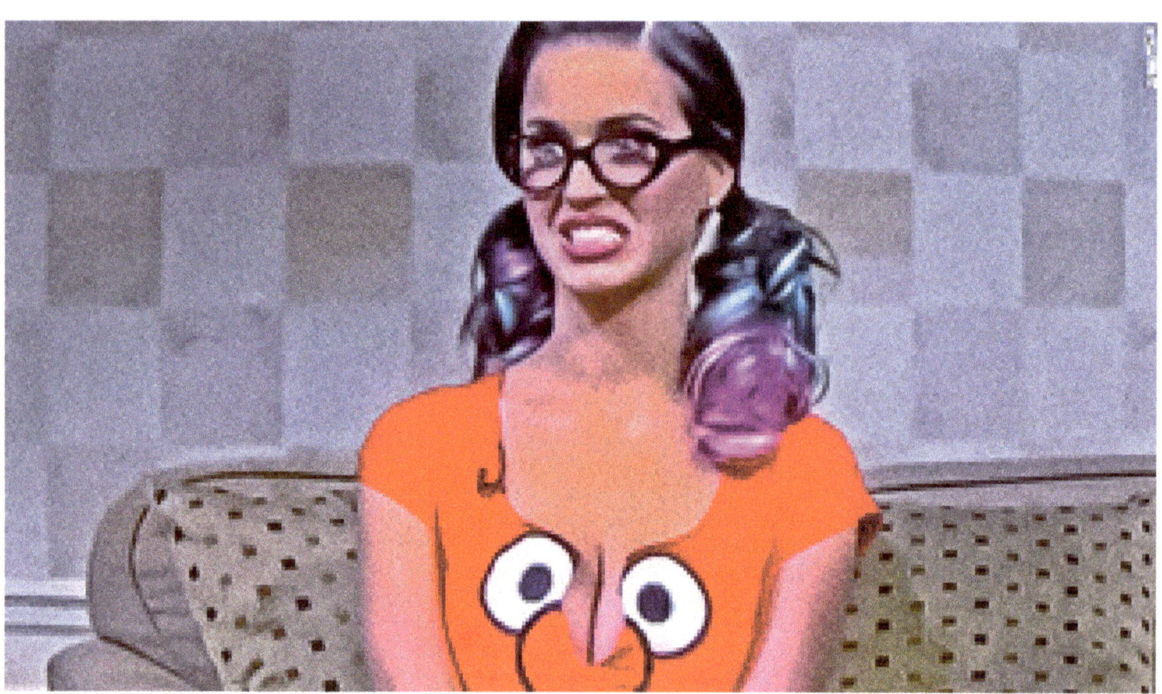

Are you all worry worts? It amazes me how much I worry about shit. I wonder if it's inherent or if it's just me. They are so much more laidback about shit. I wonder why such a huge cultural difference. It seems shit still gets done, and they don't worry.

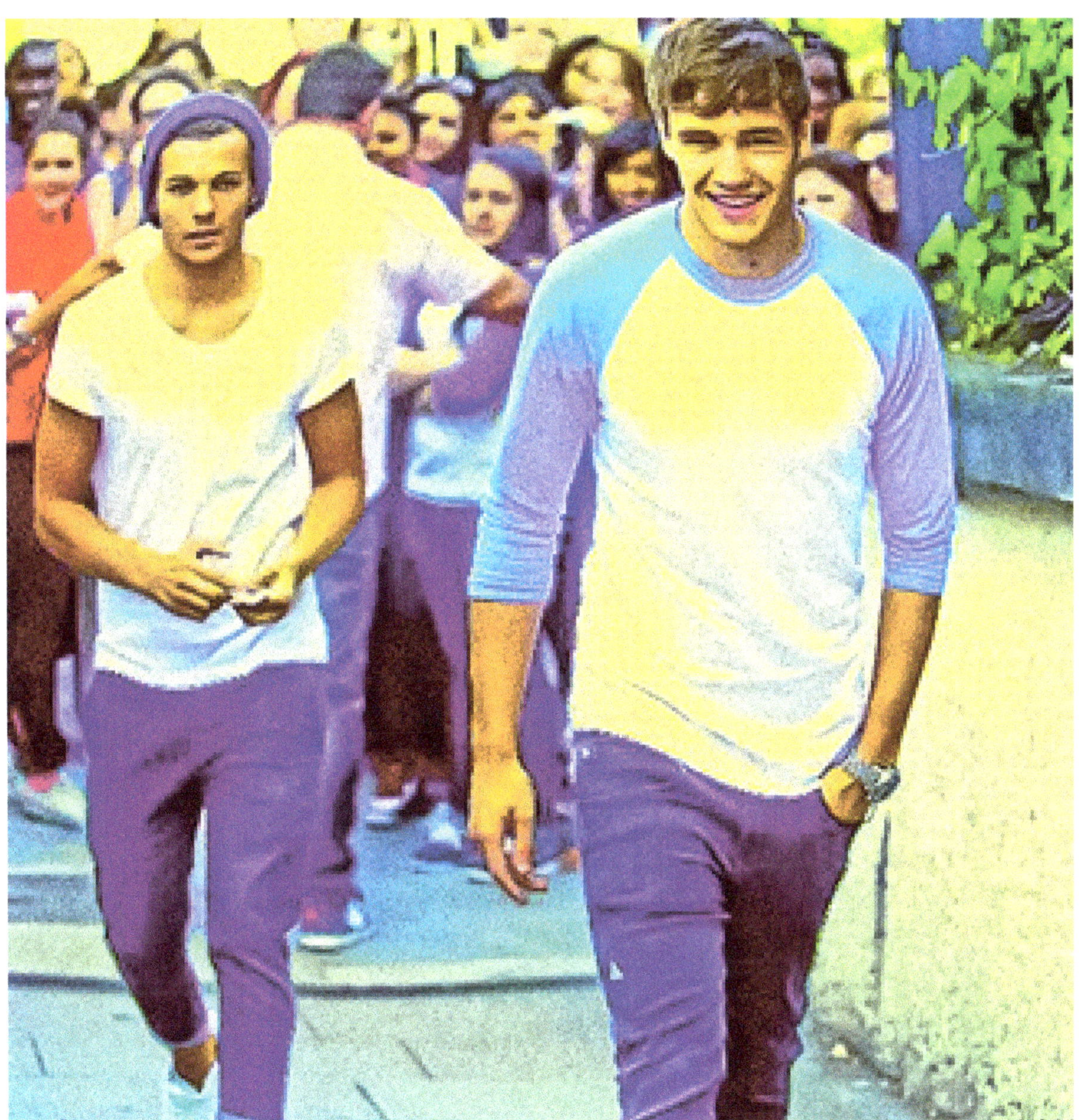

I know I sometimes seem to live the life of Riley, but I hope they don't forget the people and places they have cared so much about. Shit, I wonder if Vali ever contacted the university... he was suppose to. He always hated to go camping—said it made him think too much about shit. I wonder what's going on with him—last summer he came back to Portland for the break. You are clueless man, I can't say it enough times, you don't know shit about shit. I wonder how you argue with your friends (if you have any).

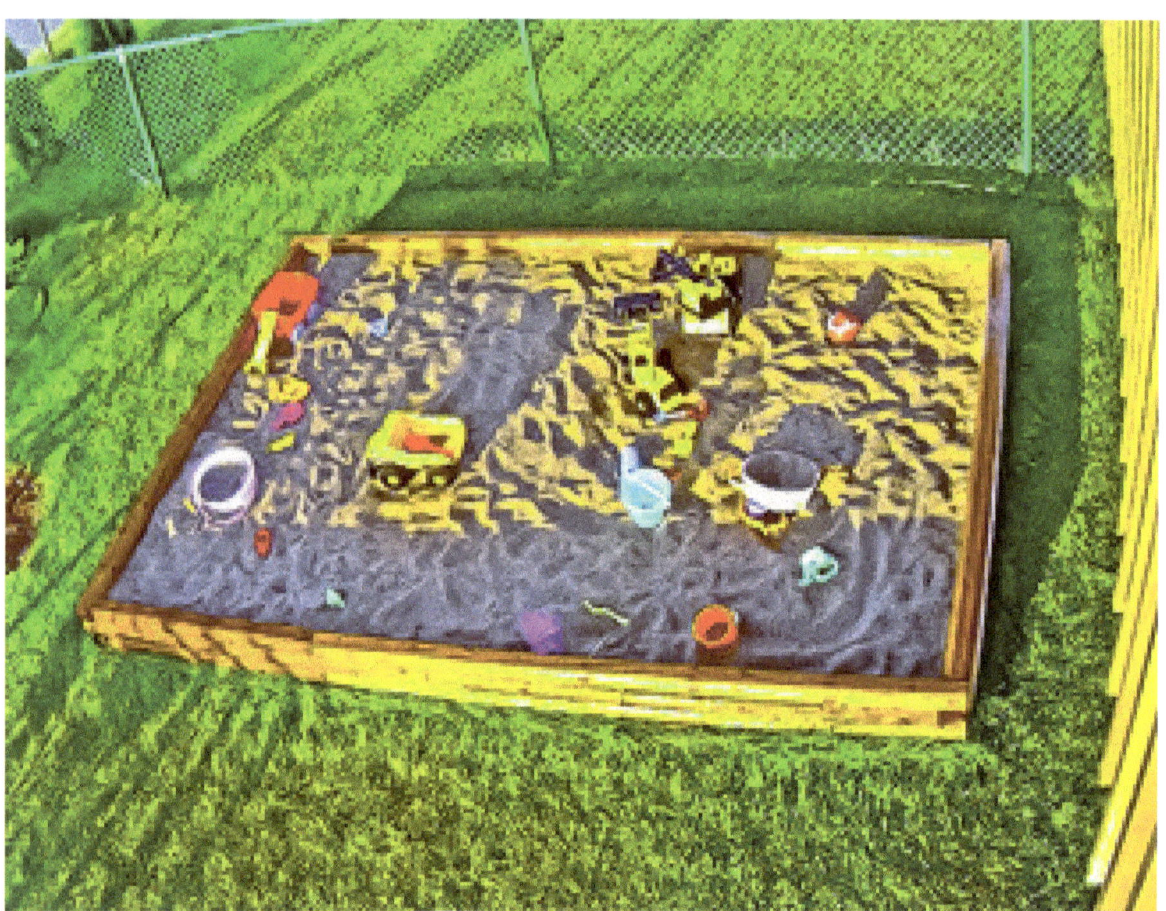

"If I look back at the times at the P-I when I used to bitch about shit, I wonder what the fuck I was thinking," he says. Equal parts journalist, sprinter, and octopus, he single-handedly covered Seattle's mayoral primary. I noticed that the New York Times did not want to publish Dr. Curtis' full statement, "We need to talk about shit." I wonder how many publications would have the journalistic integrity (is that just my opinion?) to quote her? I want the real fans to know the truth the media knows the truth, this is the 1st time in years Floyd hasn't run his mouth about shit... I wonder why? I decided it was accurate in any sense so it didn't matter. Jack Fear: makin' me think about shit. I wonder if he does it on purpose?

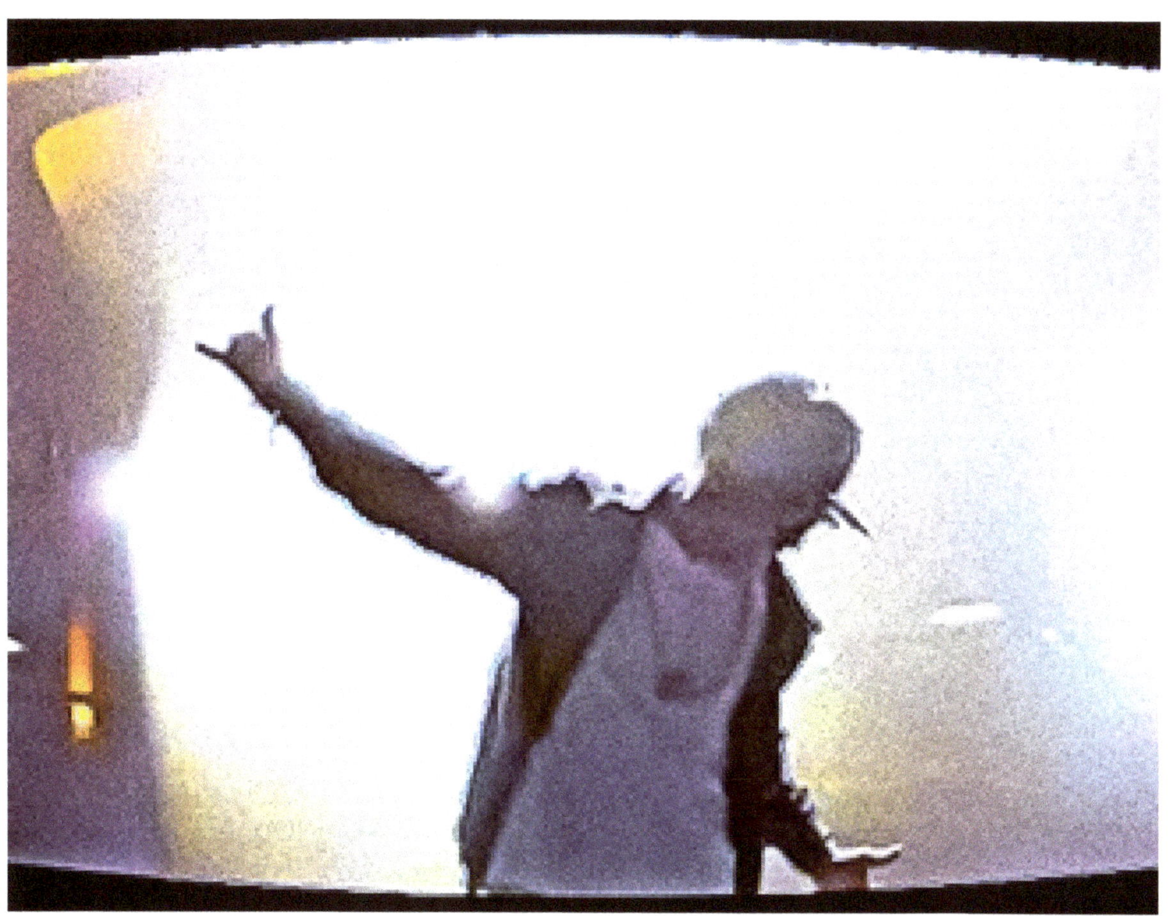

Man I ramble about shit. I wonder if D got her tattoo today… I wonder if I was meant to go to netball training… I want to make a relationship advice blog… LMAO! That's what we need to do… get inmate pen pals who will listen to us blather on about shit. I wonder if I can find one who would like to hear about abortion and Zsa Zsa Gabor?

Wonder About Shit I

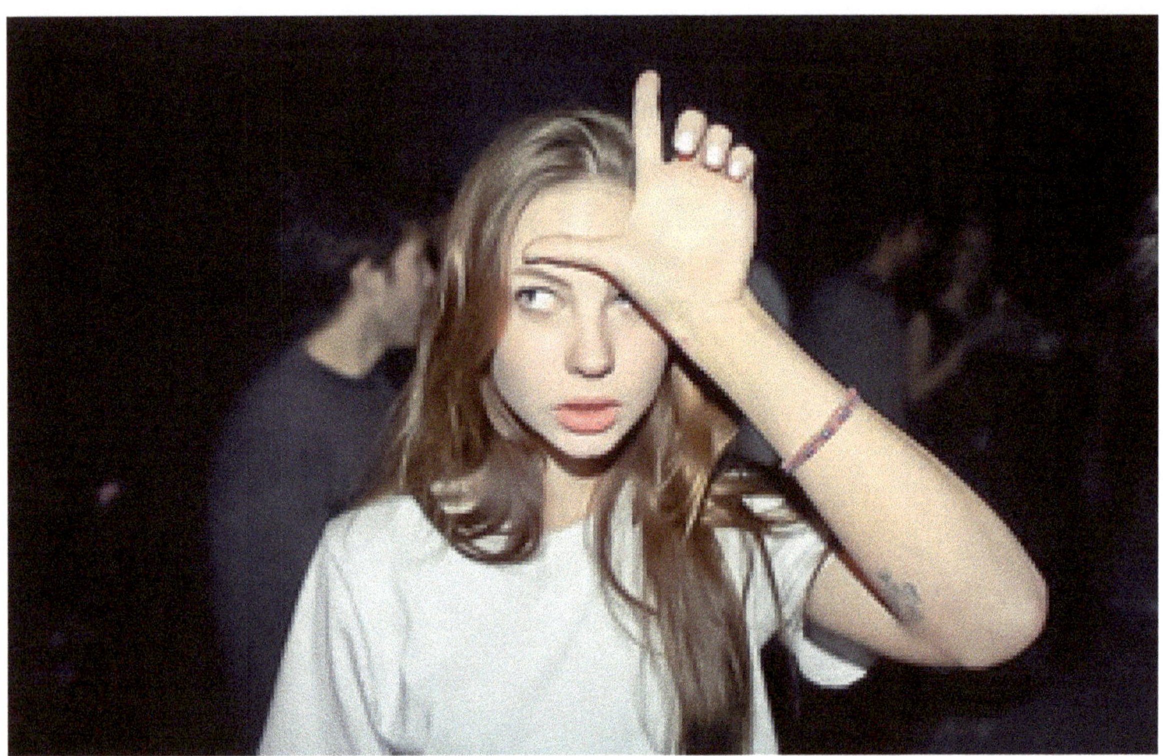

Cause I always wonder about shit... I dunno read on u'll get it. When it rains from the skys I question, What is this liquid in disguise? Is it tears? I be up bored out my mind jus wonder about shit I don't need to be on my mind... Expand Collapse Delete... As I sit and wonder, about shit I'll never know. I hope you sit back and relax, and enjoy my carefree show. Run in circles and wonder about shit I should have to worry about. When talking to you, I read between the lines, then reality hits me in the face. He refused to ever talk about it again with me either so I could get some sort of closure and not just sit and wonder about shit. I found out many things. Got too much to do to fucking sit home and wonder about shit. I'll call in a couple days, see what he's doing. Won't seem desperate then, yeah. It's just in me all the time to wonder about shit I can't do a god-damn thing about. Motherfuckin shit. I wish I had someone to go to NYC with me. Their instant responses and I am stuck... stuck with my thoughts and I am doomed to wonder about shit I didn't want my mind venturing to. You wonder about shit? I wonder all the time. Sometimes I wonder about stupid shit for instance why the hell people sale shit 1.99, 2.99, 3.99... When I think about what most likely happens to be a waste of time and emotion it just makes me wonder about shit I can't really put into words. I be up bored out my mind jus wonder about shit I don't need to be on my mind... Expand Collapse Delete... It's just in me all the time to wonder about shit I can't do a god-damn thing about. Motherfuckin shit. I wish I had someone to go to NYC with me when I graduate. Maybe I'll wait until after I do Grad school. I've been thinking. He refused to ever talk about it again with me either so I could get some sort of closure and not just sit and wonder about shit. I found out many things he told me were lies and he wasn't as nice as he had led on for those 2 months. I failed in keeping my mind occupied and find it rather interesting that my usual texting buddies are holding off on their instant responses and I am stuck… stuck with my thoughts and I am doomed to wonder about shit I didn't want to. We need to establish some ground rules because I'm not in this to be cheated on, lied to, forced to put up with "commitment issues" and put in a position where I have to constantly wonder about shit. I've been there before. As I sit and wonder, about shit I'll never know. I hope you sit back and relax, and enjoy my carefree show. I'm a little bit intoxicated, so this doesn't make sense at all. I'll continue to be who I've sent out to be. Sterling- ugh. I met you about 6-7 months ago and ever since I've been wondering alot. At the beginning I liked you, then got smart and knew it would never happen. You make my mind run in circles and wonder about shit I… Sometimes in the course of normal everyday events a series of coincidences can string together that makes you stop and wonder about shit. I wasn't sure about writing about all this, but the owl says it's cool to talk about. She was ok with it and even complemented me for my faithfulness (which I admit I had to wonder about, shit I still had it in another girl's mouth. She was ok with it and even complemented me for my faithfulness (which I admit I had to wonder about, shit I still had it in another girl's mouth. One day… you will see the world in a different light, and wonder why you did some of the things you did. LOL I know I still wonder about shit I did. I be up bored out my mind jus wonder about shit I don't need to be on my mind… Expand Collapse Delete.

Being a Humble and Necessarily Incomplete Treatise On Satan

Written at the request of Adam Overton and published on Outward from Nothingness *in June 2013 for Guru Rugu's curated month-long series:* You're getting verrry, verrrry lispy...: Hip-Gnosis and other Subtle Cues.

"Darkness is light turned inside out."—Beelzebub

THERE IS NO GOD BUT MYSELF

It is obvious that Satan is not the "deceiver of humanity."

The concept of Satan as being an opponent of God and a chief evil figure in among demons.

Satan has seemed too unreal.

You possess a strong belief in a supernatural power or powers that control human destiny.

We are a group of sinful people; of Satan.

Our Past is Being Systematically Destroyed!

The Original Gods [Demons] were unjustly labeled as monsters and branded as "evil" to keep humanity from spiritual knowledge.

From a literary perspective, demons must exist. If they didn't, we'd have to invent them. They seem essential to so much of our storytelling—more essential, perhaps, than their goodly counterparts.

Those of you eager for the sweet sounds of SATAN can bide their time with the following steady stream of TESTIMONY.

Satan is happy to invade the empty vacuum of your soul and possess it. That is why people serve Satan without ever knowing it or deciding to.

For Example: Practicing yoga is Satanic, it leads to evil just like reading Harry Potter.

Individuals do not have to give in to Satan's temptations.

§

I went to the crossroad,
fell down on my knees
I went to the crossroad,
fell down on my knees
Asked the lord above "Have mercy now,
save poor Bob, if you please"
Mmmmm, standin' at the crossroad,
I tried to flag a ride
ooo ooo eee
Standin' at the crossroad,
I tried to flag a ride
Didn't nobody seem to know me babe,
everybody pass me by
Mmmm, the sun goin' down, boy,
dark gon' catch me here
Oooo, eeee, boy, dark gon' catch me here
I haven't got no lovin' sweet woman
that love and feel my care
You can run, you can run,
tell my friend-boy Willie Brown
You can run,
tell my friend-boy Willie Brown
(th)'at I got the crossroad blues this mornin
Lord
babe, I'm sinkin down
And I went to the crossraod momma
I looked east and west
I went to the crossraod baby
I looked east and west
Lord, I didn't have no sweet woman
ooh-well babe, in my distress
You can run, you can run,
tell my friend-boy Willie Brown
You can run,
tell my friend-boy Willie Brown
Lord I'm standin' at the crossroad, babe,
I believe I'm sinkin' down

§

Yes, Satan is already abroad, and the Antichrist is already born, but he is still young. He must first grow up incognito before his power can become known.

Satan was allowed to set up his own kingdom in Hell and to send out devils to prowl the earth for converts. Satan, being a spirit, is neither male nor female. However, like his creator, Satan is usually referred to as a masculine being.

One of the more interesting aspects of Satanology is the recurring theme of humans making a pact with the devil. The Faust legend is the best-known of these: in exchange for one's soul, Satan will bestow one with wealth or power for a specified time.

Satan is believed to have many powers, among them the power to manifest himself in human or animal form. The consorting has been recorded as often being purely physical and mostly sexual. For most of the history of Christianity, there are reports of Satan having sex with humans, either as an incubus (male devil) or succubus (female devil). Witches and sorcerers were thought by many to be the offspring of such unions.

Apparently, it took Satan a long time to figure out that if he wanted to control the world, the best way to do it would be to breed with humans. Invading our bodies would be more efficient and effective than trying to invade our minds. It must have occurred to many observers that the fear of Satan seems very much like fear of our own sexuality. Today, there are still those who believe Satan is a real being, but we hear few stories of incubi and succubi any more.

As the power of the Christian Church has waned, so too has the power of Satan. It is no accident that Satan reached the peak of his career at the same time the Church did, during the thirteenth century. During the Middle Ages, the Devil was said to have built Hadrian's Wall between Scotland and England, moved huge stones to construct megalithic stone circles and dolmens, built bridges such as that at Saint-Cloud and the Pont de Valentre at Cahors, for the price of the soul of the first one who crossed the bridge, etc. Satan could perform magic, but it must be remembered that the Christian religion is basically a religion of magic, of sacraments that protect one from Satan and that change bread and wine into Christ, of miracles that contravene the natural order for good or ill, of resurrection from the dead and of the promise of eternal life. Satan represents the obverse of that order: black magic, pacts with the devil, wonders done contravening the natural order, the promise of eternal youth and wondrous powers. The Satanic Order was the creation of the Church, necessary to establish its own power over the world. Heretics, witches and sorcerers were a threat to the world dominion of the Church. They had to be eradicated. As the enemies of the Church grew more numerous and more powerful, so did the reign of terror grow and so did the power of the Church get established more and more firmly.

The sadistic and monstrous behavior of the holy and pious inquisitors is almost enough to make a skeptic believe in Satan. The inquisitors were nothing short of diabolical.

As the power of Christianity waned as the dominant social and political force in western culture, so too did the power of Satan. By the eighteenth century, in Europe at least, witch and heretic burnings had all but ceased. Many theists today believe that the evils of today's world, and they are many as we all know, are due to the rise of Satan and the decrease of religious influence. If they had their way, we would all be praying more and working against the snares of Satan.

Satanists have been blamed by pious Christians for ritual murders of children, mutilation and sacrificial killings of animals, writing backwards messages on musical record-

§

Be sure it's true when you say,
'I love you'
It's a sin to tell a lie
Millions of hearts have been broken
Just because these words were spoken

I love you, yes, I do, I love you
If you break my heart I'll die
So be sure that it's true when you say,
'I love you'
It's a sin to tell a lie

I love you, yes, I do, I love you
If you break my heart I'll die
So be sure that it's true when you say,
'I love you'
It's a sin to tell a lie
It's a sin to tell a lie

§

I've posed for pictures with Iv'ry Soap
I've petted stray dogs,
and shied clear of dope
My smile is brilliant, my glance is tender
But I'm noted most
for my unspoiled gender

I've been made Miss Rheingold,
though I never touch beer
And I'm the person to whom they say,
"You're sweet, my dear"
The only etchings I've seen
have been behind glass
And the closest I've been to a bar
was at ballet class

Prim and proper,
the girl who's never been kissed
Well, I'm tired of being pure
and not chased

Like something that seeks its level
I wanna go to the devil
I wanna be evil, I wanna spit tacks
I wanna be evil, and cheat at jacks
I wanna be wicked, I wanna tell lies
I wanna be mean, and throw mud pies

I want to wake up in the morning
With that dark brown taste
I wanna see some dissipation in my face
I wanna be evil, I wanna be mad
But more than that, I wanna be bad

I wanna be evil and trump an ace
Just to see my partner's face
I wanna be nasty, I wanna be cruel
I wanna be daring, I wanna shoot pool

And in the theatre
I want to change my seat
Just so I can step on everybody's feet

I wanna be evil, I wanna hurt flies
I wanna sing songs like the guy who cries
I wanna be horrid, I wanna drink booze
And whatever I've got I'm eager to lose

I wanna be evil, little evil me
Just as mean and evil as I can be

§

You look like an Angel
Walk like an Angel

ings instructing people to kill, sending subliminal or secret messages through diabolical symbols on pizza boxes or soap wrappers, causing the general decay of morals and civilization as we know it, etc. The Satanists deny it. The evidence is not very strong that the Satanists are either as evil or as powerful as their enemies say they are. There is strong evidence for the strength and wickedness of the pious.

§

Psalm 109:6b "and let Satan stand at his right hand"
or "let an accuser stand at his right hand."
And the angel of the LORD stood in the way for an adversary against him
behold, I went out to withstand thee
lest he [David] be an adversary against us
[you sons of Zeruaiah] should this day be adversaries (plural) unto me?
There is neither adversary nor evil occurrent
And the LORD stirred up an adversary unto Solomon, Hadad the Edomite
And God stirred him up an adversary, Rezon the son of Eliadah
And he [Rezon] was an adversary to Israel all the days of Solomon

Isaiah 14:12 How art thou fallen from heaven, O Lucifer, son of the morning! how art thou cut down to the ground, which didst weaken the nations! 13 For thou hast said in thine heart, I will ascend into heaven, I will exalt my throne above the stars of God: I will sit also upon the mount of the congregation, in the sides of the north: 14 I will ascend above the heights of the clouds; I will be like the most High. 15 Yet thou shalt be brought down to hell, to the sides of the pit. 16 They that see thee shall narrowly look upon thee, and consider thee, saying, Is this the man that made the earth to tremble, that did shake kingdoms;

17 That made the world as a wilderness, and destroyed the cities thereof; that opened not the house of his prisoners?

Doctrine and Covenants 10:5 Pray always, that you may come off conqueror; yea, that you may conquer Satan, and that you may escape the hands of the servants of Satan that do uphold his work.

Doctrine and Covenants 76:25 And this we saw also, and bear record, that an angel of God who was in authority in the presence of God, who rebelled against the Only Begotten Son whom the Father loved and who was in the bosom of the Father, was thrust down from the presence of God and the Son, 26 And was called Perdition, for the heavens wept over him—he was Lucifer, a son of the morning. 27 And we beheld, and lo, he is afallen! is fallen, even a son of the morning! 28 And while we were yet in the Spirit, the Lord commanded us that we should write the vision; for we beheld Satan, that old serpent, even the devil, who rebelled against God, and sought to take the kingdom of our God and his Christ— 29 Wherefore, he maketh war with the saints of God, and encompasseth them round about.

§

Satan is a term used, since its earliest biblical contexts, to refer to a human opponent.

The original Hebrew term, satan, is a noun from a verb meaning primarily to "obstruct, oppose," as it is found in Numbers 22:22, 1 Samuel 29:4, Psalms 109:6.

> Numbers 22:22 And God's anger was kindled because he went: and the angel of the Lord stood in the way for an adversary against him. Now he was riding upon his ass, and his two servants were with him.

> 1 Samuel 29:4 And the princes of the Philistines were wroth with him; and the princes of the Philistines said

Talk like an Angel
But I got wise

You're the Devil in disguise
Oh yes you are, Devil in disguise

You fooled me with your kisses
You cheated and you schemed
Heaven knows how you lied to me
You're not the way you seemed

You look like an Angel
Walk like an Angel
Talk like an Angel
But I got wise

You're the Devil in disguise
Oh yes you are, Devil in disguise

I thought that I was in Heaven
But I was sure surprised
Heaven help me, I didn't see
The Devil in your eyes

You look like an Angel
Walk like an Angel
Talk like an Angel
But I got wise

You're the Devil in disguise
Oh yes you are, Devil in disguise
You're the Devil in disguise
Oh yes you are, Devil in disguise
Oh yes you are, Devil in disguise
Oh yes you are, Devil in disguise

§

The Devil in Hell we're told was chained
A thousand years he there remained
He neither complained nor did he groan
But was determined to start a Hell of his own

Where he could torment the souls of men
Without being chained in a prison pen
So he asked the Lord if he had on hand
Anything left when he made this land

The Lord said yes there's a plenty on hand
But I left it down by the Rio Grande
The fact is ol' boy the stuff is so poor
I don't think you could use it as
the Hell anymore

But the Devil went down to look at the truck
And said if he took it as a gift he was stuck
For after lookin' that over carefully and well
He said this place is too dry for Hell

But in order to get it off his hand
The Lord promised the Devil to water
the land

So trade was closed and deed was given
And the Lord went back to his home
in Heaven
And the Devil said now I got
all what's needed
To make it good Hell and he succeeded

He began by putting thorns all over the trees
He mixed up the sand with millions of fleas
He scattered tarantulas along the road
Put thorns on cactus and horns on toad

Lengthened the horns of the Texas steer
Put an addition to the rabbit's ear

unto him, Make this fellow return, that he may go again to his place which thou hast appointed him, and let him not go down with us to battle, lest in the battle he be an adversary to us: for wherewith should he reconcile himself unto his master? should it not be with the heads of these men?

Psalms 109:6 Set thou a wicked man over him: and let Satan stand at his right hand.

Ha-Satan is traditionally translated as "the accuser," or "the adversary." The definite article "ha-," English "the," is used to show that this is a title bestowed on a being, versus the name of a being. Thus this being would be referred to as "the satan."

Ha-Satan with the definite article occurs 13 times in the Masoretic Text, in two books of the Hebrew Bible.

Satan is the opposer known as the deceiver that leads humanity astray, an "accuser" or "adversary," not necessarily the personification of evil that he would become in later Abrahamic religions.
Ha-Satan is a member of the Divine Council, "the sons of God" who are subservient to God. Ha-Satan, in this capacity, is many times translated as "the prosecutor," and is charged by God to tempt humans and to report back to God all who go against His decrees.

It has been interpreted that ha-Satan is under God's control and cannot act without God's permission, as Yahweh says to the 'satan,' 'You have incited me against him, to destroy him for no reason.'

Ha-Satan, translated by the Greek word diabolos (slanderer), is the same word in the Greek New Testament from which the English word devil is derived. Where satan is used of human enemies in the Hebrew Bible, such as Hadad the Edomite and Rezon the Syrian, the word is left untranslated but transliterated in the Greek as satan, a neologism in Greek.

Mastema, in the Book of Jubilees, induces God to test Abraham through the sacrifice of Isaac. He is identical to Satan in both name and nature.

Occasionally, the term satan has been used to suggest evil influence opposing human beings, as in the Jewish exegesis of the Yetzer hara ("evil inclination," Genesis 6:5). Micaiah's "lying spirit" in 1 Kings 22:22 is sometimes related. Thus, Satan is personified as a character in three different places of the Tenakh, serving as an accuser (Zechariah 3:1-2), a seducer (1 Chronicles 21:1), or as a heavenly persecutor who is "among the sons of God" (Job 2:1). In any case, Satan is always subordinate to the power of God, having a role in the divine plan.

> Genesis 6:5 And God saw that the wickedness of man was great in the earth, and that every imagination of the thoughts of his heart was only evil continually.
>
> 1 Kings 22:22 And the Lord said unto him, Wherewith? And he said, I will go forth, and I will be a lying spirit in the mouth of all his prophets. And he said, Thou shalt persuade him, and prevail also: go forth, and do so.
>
> Zechariah 3:1 And he shewed me Joshua the high priest standing before the angel of the Lord, and Satan standing at his right hand to resist him. 2 And the Lord said unto Satan, The Lord rebuke thee, O Satan; even the Lord that hath chosen Jerusalem rebuke thee: is not this a brand plucked out of the fire?
>
> 1 Chronicles 21:1 And Satan stood up against Israel, and provoked David to number Israel.

Put a little Devil in the bronco steed
And poisoned the feet of the centipede

The rattlesnake bites you, the scorpion stings
The mosquito delights you with
his buzzing wings
The sunbursts are there and so the ants
And if you sit down you'll need have soles
on your pants

The wild boar roams on a black chaparral
It's a Hell of a place that he has for a Hell
The heat in the summers are hundred and ten
Too hot for the Devil, too hot for men

The red pepper grows upon the banks
of the brook
The Mexican use it in all that he cook
Just dine with one of 'em
and you're bound to shout
I've Hell on the inside as well as the out

My hands are calloused July to July
I use a big dipper to navigate by
Fight off the wolves to drink from my well
So I have to be mean as Hell
A sheep herder came and put up a fence
I saw him one day but I ain't seen him since
But if you need any mutton
we got mutton to sell
We're cowpunchers and we're mean as Hell

Neither me nor my pony's got a pedigree
But he takes me where I'm wantin' to be
I'll ride him to death and when he is fell
I'll get me another one, mean as Hell

I shot me a calf and I cut off her head

'Cause the boys in the bunkhouse
are wantin' to be fed
They rise in chime with the five thirty bell
And the best one of any of 'em is
mean as Hell

§

Some people say my love cannot be true
Please believe me my love
and I'll show you
I will give you those things
you thought unreal
The sun, the moon, the stars
all bear my seal

Follow me now and you will not regret
Leaving the life you led before we met
You are the first to have this love of mine
Forever with me till the end of time

Your love for me has just got to be real
Before you know the way I'm going to feel
I'm going to feel
I'm going to feel

Now I have you with me under my power
Our love grows stronger now with every hour
Look into my eyes you'll see who I am
My name is Lucifer please take my hand

Follow me now and you will not regret
Leaving the life you led before we met
You are the first to have this love of mine
Forever with me till the end of time

Your love for me has just got to be real
Before you know the way I'm going to feel
I'm going to feel

> Job 2:1 Again there was a day when the sons of God came to present themselves before the Lord, and Satan came also among them to present himself before the Lord.

Traditionalists and philosophers in medieval Judaism adhered to rational theology, rejecting any belief in rebel or fallen angels, and viewing evil as abstract. The Yetzer hara ("evil inclination," Genesis 6:5) is a more common motif for evil in rabbinical texts. Rabbinical scholarship on the Book of Job generally follows the Talmud and Maimonides as identifying the "Adversary" in the prologue of Job as a metaphor.

> Genesis 6:5 And God saw that the wickedness of man was great in the earth, and that every imagination of the thoughts of his heart was only evil continually.

In Hasidic Judaism, the Kabbalah presents Satan as an agent of God whose function is to tempt one into sin, then turn around and accuse the sinner on high. The Hasidic Jews of the 18th century associated ha-Satan with Baal Davar.

Subsequent development of Satan as a "deceiver" has parallels with the evil spirit in Zoroastrianism, known as the Lie, who directs forces of darkness.

Beelzebub, meaning "Lord of Flies," is the contemptuous name given in the Hebrew Bible and New Testament to a Philistine god whose original name has been reconstructed as most probably "Ba'al Zabul," meaning "Baal the Prince."

Satan is traditionally identified as the serpent who tempted Eve to eat the forbidden fruit; thus, Satan has often been depicted as a serpent.

The Book of Revelation twice refers to "the dragon, that ancient serpent, who is called the devil and Satan," (12:9, 20:2). The Book of Revelation also refers to "the deceiver," from which is derived the common epithet "the great deceiver."

> Revelation 12:9 And the great dragon was cast out, that old serpent, called the Devil, and Satan, which deceiveth the whole world: he was cast out into the earth, and his angels were cast out with him.

> Revelation 20:2 And he laid hold on the dragon, that old serpent, which is the Devil, and Satan, and bound him a thousand years.

Other terms identified with Satan include "the prince of this world" in the Book of John 12:31, 14:30; "the prince of the power of the air" also called Meririm; and "the spirit that now worketh in the children of disobedience" in the Book of Ephesians 2:2; and "the god of this world" in 2 Corinthians 4:4.

> John 12:31 Now is the judgment of this world: now shall the prince of this world be cast out.

> John 14:30 Hereafter I will not talk much with you: for the prince of this world cometh, and hath nothing in me.

> Ephesians 2:2 Wherein in time past ye walked according to the course of this world, according to the prince of the power of the air, the spirit that now worketh in the children of disobedience:

> 2 Corinthians 4:4 In whom the god of this world hath blinded the minds of them which believe not, lest the light of the glorious gospel of Christ, who is the image of God, should shine unto them.

I'm going to feel
Now I have you with me under my power
Our love grows stronger now with every hour
Look into my eyes you'll see who I am
My name is Lucifer please take my hand

§

Sinner rider rides in with the storm
The Devil rides beside him
The Devil is his God, God help you mourn
Do you, do you hear it?
Do you hear the thunder
Deafen every living thing about?
Can you, can you see it? Can you
See the mountains darken yonder?
Black sun rising, time is runnin' out

Sacrifice to vice
or die by the hand of the sinner

Sinner!
Sinner!
Sinner!

His steed of fury
Eyes of fire and mane ablaze
Demonic vultures stalking
Drawn by the smell of war and pain
He roams the starways
Searching for the carcasses of war
But if it's hungry then its very presence
Disrupts the calm into the storm

Curse and damn you all
you'll fall by the hand of the sinner
Sinner!
Sinner!
Sinner!

God of the devils, God of the devils
Won't you help them pray?
God of the devils, God of the devils
Is there no other way?

Can't you hear their souls
calling out in their plight?
Can't you see their blood is boiling
setting them alight?

Thirty years now I was sleeping
So sound, sound, sound, sound
War raises its head
And looks slowly around, around,
around, around
The sinner is near, sensing your fear
And the beast will start movin' all round

Can't you see their souls
calling out in their brain?
Can't you hear their blood is boiling
setting them alight?
Sinner!
Sinner!
Sinner!
Sinner!
Sinner!
Sinner!
Sinner!
Sinner!

Sacrifice to vice or die by the hand of the
Curse and damn you all you fall by the
hand of the sinner

§

Shaitan is the equivalent of Satan in Islam. While Shaitan is an adjective (meaning "astray" or "distant," sometimes translated as "devil") that can be applied to both man and Jinn, Iblis is the personal name of the Devil who is mentioned in the Qur'anic account of Genesis.

According to the Qur'an, Iblis (the Arabic name used) disobeyed an order from Allah to bow to Adam and as a result was forced out of heaven and given respite until the day of judgment from further punishment.

When Allah commanded all of the angels to bow down before Adam (the first Human), Iblis, full of hubris and jealousy, refused to obey God's command (he could do so because he had free will), seeing Adam as being inferior in creation due to his being created from clay as compared to him (created of fire).

> "It is We Who created you and gave you shape; then We bade the angels prostrate to Adam, and they prostrate; not so Iblis (Lucifer); He refused to be of those who prostrate."

> (Allah) said: "What prevented thee from prostrating when I commanded thee?" He said: "I am better than he: Thou didst create me from fire, and him from clay."

It was after this that the title of "Shaitan" was given, which can be roughly translated as "Enemy," "Rebel," "Evil" or "Devil." Shaitan then claims that if the punishment for his act of disobedience is to be delayed until the Day of Judgment, that he will divert many of Adam's own descendants from the straight path during his period of respite.

God accepts the claims of Iblis and guarantees recompense to Iblis and his followers in the form of Hellfire. In order to test mankind and Jinn alike, Allah allowed Iblis to roam the earth to attempt to convert others away from his path.

He was sent to earth along with Adam and Eve, after eventually luring them into eating the fruit from the forbidden tree.

The connection with Satan, originally made by Muslim outsiders, attracted the interest of 19th century European travelers and esoteric writers.

In the Bahá'í Faith, Satan is not regarded as an independent evil power as he is in some faiths, but signifies the lower nature of humans. `Abdu'l-Bahá explains: "This lower nature in man is symbolized as Satan—the evil ego within us, not an evil personality outside."

§

For most Christians, Satan is believed to be an angel who rebelled against God—and also the one who spoke through the serpent and seduced Eve into disobeying God's command. His ultimate goal is to lead people away from the love of God—to lead them to fallacies, which God opposes.

Before his insurrection, Satan was among the highest of all angels and the "brightest in the sky." His pride is considered a reason why he would not bow to God as all other angels did, but sought to rule heaven himself. The popularly held beliefs that Satan was once an angel who becomes prideful and eventually rebels against God, however, are not portrayed explicitly in the Bible and are mostly based on inference.

In the New Testament, Satan is a name that refers to a decidedly malevolent entity who possesses demonic god-like qualities.

In the Book of Wisdom, Satan is represented as the being who brought death into the world.

Yeah, Yeah!
Ah, yeah!
I live my life like there's no tomorrow
And all I've got, I had to steal
Least I don't need to beg or borrow
Yes I'm livin' at a pace that kills

Oooh, yeah
(Ahh!) Runnin' with the devil
(Ahh-hah! Yeah!)
(Woo-hoo-oo!) Runnin' with the devil
I'm gonna tell ya all about it

I found the simple life ain't so simple
When I jumped out, on that road
I got no love, no love you'd call real
Ain't got nobody, waitin' at home

(Ah, yeah-ah!)
Runnin' with the devil
(God damn it lady.
You know I ain't lyin' to ya)
(I'm only gonna tell you one time-ya!)
Runnin' with the devil
(Yes I am! Yeah!)

(Guitar Solo)

Woo!

Woo!

You know I, I found the simple life
Weren't so simple, no
When I jumped out, on that road
Got no love, no love you'd call real
Got nobody, waitin' at home

(Ah, yeah!)

Runnin' with the devil
(Hold on. Hold on, I'm runnin'!
Ah, yeah!)
Runnin' with the devil
(Uh! Uh! Come on, one more time)

(Guitar Solo)

(Ha-yeah!)
Runnin' with the devil
(Oh, yeah! Ya-yeah!)
Runnin' with the devil
(Woo! Woo!)
Runnin' with the devil
(Ah-ha, yeah! Ah-ha, yeah!
Ah-hah, yeah!)
Runnin' with the devil (Woo!)

§

(In a low voice)
Woe to you o earth and sea
For the devil sends the beast with wrath
Because he knows that time is short
Let him who hath understanding reckon the number of the beast
For it is a human number
It's number is six hundred and sixty six

I left alone my mind was blank
I needed time to think to get the memories from my mind

What did I see, can I believe that what I saw
That night was real and not just fantasy

Just what I saw in my own dreams were they
Reflections of my warped mind staring back at me

The text describes Satanael as being the prince of the Grigori who was cast out of heaven and an evil spirit who knew the difference between what was "righteous" and "sinful."

Satan, also called the adversary or the devil, is the enemy of all righteousness and of those who seek to follow God. But in the premortal Council in Heaven, Lucifer, as Satan was then called, rebelled against God. Since that time, he has sought to destroy the children of God on the Earth and to make them miserable.

Satan is cynical about disinterested human goodness and is permitted to test it under God's authority and control and within the limits that God sets.

Satan is often comically portrayed as a guy in a red devil suit. He probably likes it this way, since most people (including Christians) are apt to disbelieve in his existence. As a "non-existent" force in people's lives, Satan is free to influence them without being discovered as the cause of many of their problems. However, the Bible says that Satan is a beautiful and powerful fallen angel, who would like to do nothing more than take away the joy of Christians through deception, and lead people into rebellion against God. Although Satan is destined for the Lake of Fire, biblical prophecy indicates that he will deceive entire nations and kingdoms before he is relegated to eternal damnation, along with the other fallen angels he led into rebellion against God.

No, Satan does not look like the cartoon character in the red suit with a tail and horns and a pitchfork. Angels, including Satan, don't have male or female characteristics in their heavenly state (which Jesus told us through His teaching). However, when they come to earth, they can take on human form. In the Bible, all angels who take on human form appear as males. All biblical references address Satan by the personal pronoun "he."

In their heavenly state, according to the Bible, a cherub is a large creature—up to 18 feet in height with 8-foot-long wings. In the prophet Ezekiel's vision, the cherubim (plural of "cherub") had four wings. Under their wings were human-like hands that could be used to carry things. All the surfaces of the cherubim, including the wings, were covered with eyes. Each cherub had four faces, one "of a cherub, the second the face of a man, the third the face of a lion, and the fourth the face of an eagle." The New Testament book of Revelation describes similar creatures, only with six wings each, with faces of a lion, an ox, a man, and an eagle. So, these creatures look nothing like the cute little cherubim you can buy for your garden or bookshelf. Satan himself is described as being "perfect in beauty," being adorned with all kinds of precious stones.

In mainstream Christianity he is called "the ruler of the demons" (Matthew 12:24), "the ruler of the world" and "the god of this world" (2 Cor. 4:4). The Book of Revelation describes how Satan will be cast out of Heaven, down to the earth, having "great anger" and waging war against "those who obey God's commandments and hold to the testimony of Jesus." Ultimately, Satan is thrown into the "lake of fire," not as ruler, but as one among many, being tormented day and night forever and ever.

> Matthew 12:24 But when the Pharisees heard it, they said, This fellow doth not cast out devils, but by Beelzebub the prince of the devils.

> 2 Corinthians 4:4 In whom the god of this world hath blinded the minds of them which believe not, lest the light of the glorious gospel of Christ, who is the image of God, should shine unto them.

He is spoken of as the prince of evil spirits, the inveterate enemy of God and of Christ, who takes the guise of an angel of light. He can enter a man and act through him; hence, a man can be called Satan because of his acts or

'Cause in my dreams it's always there
The evil face that twists my mind
and brings me to despair

Yeah...!

The night was black
was no use holding back
'Cause I just had to see
was someone watching me
In the mist dark figures move and twist
Was all this for real or some kind of hell

666 the number of the beast
Hell and fire were spawned to be released

Torches blazed and sacred chants were praised
As they start to cry hand held to the sky
In the night the fires are burning bright
The ritual has begun, Satan's work is done

666 the number of the beast
Sacrifice is going on tonight

This can't go on, I must inform the Lord
Can this still be real
or just some crazy dream
But I feel drawn towards the evil
chanting hordes
They seem to mesmerize...
can't avoid their eyes

666 the number of the beast
666 the one for you you and me

I'm coming back I will return
And I'll possess your body
and I'll make you burn
I have the fire I have the force

I have the power to make my evil
take its course

§

Here in this place lies the genie of death
Touch it, see it
Whoa

Here in this place is a means to your end
Touch it, feel it
Green hell

You've come to this like no one could
I bet you never knew you woke it
And don't you run away from anything
I bet you thought you really could in hell

We're gonna burn in hell
Green hell
Like every hell but kind of green
In hell, green hell
We're gonna face the mess, we're
In hell, green hell
I think I'd rather be up here
In hell, green hell

You know I fucking shake apart
In hell, green hell
Gotta find a way that you will stay
Green hell
Cannot forget about the heat
In hell, green hell
Hell is green, I need a flame
In hell, green hell
Gotta burn in hell
Green hell

You've come to this like no one could

attitude. Through his subordinate demons Satan can take possession of men's bodies, afflicting them or making them diseased. To him sinners are delivered for the destruction of the flesh, that the spirit may be saved. After the preaching of the 70 disciples, during which devils were subjected to them, Jesus saw Satan fall like lightning from Heaven (Luke 10:18). According to the visions in the Book of Revelation, when the risen Christ returns from Heaven to reign on Earth, Satan will be bound with a great chain for a thousand years, then be released, but almost immediately face final defeat and be cast into eternal punishment. His name, Beelzebul, used in the Gospels mainly in reference to demoniac possession, comes from the name of the god of Ekron, Baalzebub (2 Kings 1).

Luke 10:18 And he said unto them, I beheld Satan as lightning fall from heaven.

2 Kings 1 Then Moab rebelled against Israel after the death of Ahab. 2 And Ahaziah fell down through a lattice in his upper chamber that was in Samaria, and was sick: and he sent messengers, and said unto them, Go, enquire of Baalzebub the god of Ekron whether I shall recover of this disease. 3 But the angel of the Lord said to Elijah the Tishbite, Arise, go up to meet the messengers of the king of Samaria, and say unto them, Is it not because there is not a God in Israel, that ye go to enquire of Baalzebub the god of Ekron? 4 Now therefore thus saith the Lord, Thou shalt not come down from that bed on which thou art gone up, but shalt surely die. And Elijah departed. 5 And when the messengers turned back unto him, he said unto them, Why are ye now turned back? 6 And they said unto him, There came a man up to meet us, and said unto us, Go, turn again unto the king that sent you, and say unto him, Thus saith the Lord, Is it not because there is not a God in Israel, that thou sendest to enquire of Baalzebub the god of Ekron? therefore thou shalt not come down from that bed on which thou art gone up,

but shalt surely die. 7 And he said unto them, What manner of man was he which came up to meet you, and told you these words? 8 And they answered him, He was an hairy man, and girt with a girdle of leather about his loins. And he said, It is Elijah the Tishbite. 9 Then the king sent unto him a captain of fifty with his fifty. And he went up to him: and, behold, he sat on the top of an hill. And he spake unto him, Thou man of God, the king hath said, Come down. 10 And Elijah answered and said to the captain of fifty, If I be a man of God, then let fire come down from heaven, and consume thee and thy fifty. And there came down fire from heaven, and consumed him and his fifty. 11 Again also he sent unto him another captain of fifty with his fifty. And he answered and said unto him, O man of God, thus hath the king said, Come down quickly. 12 And Elijah answered and said unto them, If I be a man of God, let fire come down from heaven, and consume thee and thy fifty. And the fire of God came down from heaven, and consumed him and his fifty. 13 And he sent again a captain of the third fifty with his fifty. And the third captain of fifty went up, and came and fell on his knees before Elijah, and besought him, and said unto him, O man of God, I pray thee, let my life, and the life of these fifty thy servants, be precious in thy sight. 14 Behold, there came fire down from heaven, and burnt up the two captains of the former fifties with their fifties: therefore let my life now be precious in thy sight. 15 And the angel of the Lord said unto Elijah, Go down with him: be not afraid of him. And he arose, and went down with him unto the king. 16 And he said unto him, Thus saith the Lord, Forasmuch as thou hast sent messengers to enquire of Baalzebub the god of Ekron, is it not because there is no God in Israel to enquire of his word? therefore thou shalt not come down off that bed on which thou art gone up, but shalt surely die. 17 So he died according to the word of the Lord which Elijah had spoken. And Jehoram reigned in his stead in the second year of Jehoram the son of

I bet you never knew you woke it
And don't you run from anything
I bet you thought you really could take it
Here in this place is the genie of death
Touch it, see it
Whoa

Here in this place is the way to your end
Touch it, see it
Green hell

You've come to this like no one could
I bet you never knew you woke it
And don't you run away from anything
I bet you thought you really could

You've come to this like no one could
I bet you never knew you woke it
We're gonna burn in hell
Green hell

§

Shout shout shout
Shout shout shout
Shout at the devil

He's the wolf screaming lonely in the night
Blood stain the stage
Tear in your eye
Tempted by his lie
Knife in your back
He's rage

Razor to the knife
Lonely is our lives
Heads spinnin' round and round
Seasons of wither
Stand and deliver

Strong and laugh and come on

Shout shout shout
Shout at the devil
Shout shout shout

He'll be the love in your eyes
He'll be the blood between your thighs
And then have you cry for more
Strength to the test
Thrill back in bed
Heard it all before

Risk in the kiss
Anger on your lips
Run scared for the door
Seasons of wither
Run around and shout
Strong and laugh and come on

Shout shout shout
Shout at the devil
Shout shout shout

He's the wolf screaming lonely in the night
Blood stain the stage
Tear in your eye
Tempted by his lie
Knife in your back
He's rage

Razor to the knife
Lonely is our lives
Heads spinnin' round and round
Seasons of wither
Stand and deliver
Strong and laugh and come on

Jehoshaphat king of Judah; because he had no son. 18
Now the rest of the acts of Ahaziah which he did, are they not written in the book of the chronicles of the kings of Israel?

The Bible says that Satan will continue in his rebellion against God until the very end. Near the end, a "beast" (world ruler) will arise from the "sea" (the gentile nations), having been given power by Satan to perform signs and wonders for the world. In addition, a false prophet, a religious leader empowered by Satan, will deceive people into worshipping him. The beast and the false prophet will convince the leaders of the Earth to follow them into war against God and His people. However, the armies of the leaders of the world will be destroyed at the battle of Armageddon, and the beast and false prophet will be thrown into the Lake of Fire. At this point, Satan will be locked up for 1,000 years, while Jesus Christ rules the earth with His saints. At the end of that period, Satan is released for a short period of time, deceives the leaders of the world again, and convinces them to attack Jesus and His rule on the earth. The battle is short, as fire from Heaven consumes the rebels. Satan is then thrown into the Lake of Fire (Hell) to be tormented day and night forever and ever.

§

The true name of Satan, the Kabalists say, is that of Yahveh reversed; for Satan is not a black God, but the negation of God. For the Initiates, this is not a person, but a force, created for good, but which may serve for evil. It is the instrument of Liberty or free will. They represent this Force, which presides over the physical generation, under the mythologic and horned form of the God Pan; thence the he-goat of the Sabbat, brother of the Ancient Serpent, and the light bearer or Phosphor, of which the poets have made the false Lucifer of the legend.

§

A person or animal regarded as particularly malignant, detestable or evil; used as an epithet or as a name for an animal. Chief spirit of evil and adversary of God; tempter of mankind; master of Hell, Adversary, Diabolus, the Dragon, Beelzebub, Devil, Lucifer, Prince of Darkness, the Tempter, Lord of the Flies, Mephistopheles, the Old Serpent, the Prince of Demons, Old Nick (informal), The Evil One, Apollyon, Old Scratch (informal), archfiend, fiend, serpent; deuce, dickens; the schemes of Satan; Dayton, Drayton, greaten, laten, Layton, Payton, straighten, straiten. Lead people into rebellion, Tell people lies, Hate, Sexual immorality, impurity, debauchery, idolatry, witchcraft, hatred, discord, jealousy, fits of rage, selfish ambition, dissensions, envy, drunkenness, orgies

§

Shout shout shout
Shout at the devil
Shout shout shout

Shout shout shout
Shout at the devil
Shout shout shout
Shout at the devil

Shout shout shout
Shout at the devil
Shout shout shout
Shout at the devil

Shout shout shout
Shout at the devil
Shout shout shout
Shout at the devil

Shout shout shout
Shout shout shout

§

In order for Satanism to advance, money is needed. Make a donation for the promotion and advancement of Satanism today!

HIGH PRIESTS AND PRIESTESSES ARE ON-LINE TO ANSWER ANY LEGITIMATE QUESTIONS AND GIVE SERMONS OF INTEREST TO TEENS AND ADULTS ALIKE.

§

Ours is not to question why, ours is but to do and die.

To you be your Way, and to me mine.

Hate those that earn it, as you would love those that earn it. As Above, so below.

If Satanism is based on freedom, then to codify it would be ludicrous.

Our aim and goal is freedom, as it always will be.

We have found Satanism is the original religion of humanity. We have done our research.

We are law abiding.

We DO NOT advocate or participate in any blood or living sacrifice.

We know Satan/Lucifer as a real being.

We know Satan to be the True Father and Creator God of humanity.

Satanism is not about death.

Satanism is not about spooks, goblins, vampires, Halloween monsters or other related entities.

Satanism is not about "evil."

§

This is a forum for ground-breaking new developments by Satanists who move with fury and grace through this current culture of rampant mediocrity.

Herein you will find both wonder and mystery, as well as the bedrock of fact. You might also come across some hidden treasures for the diligent.

We seek to prime you for your journey into our realm of magic and logic, mystery and wisdom.

Enjoy your time here, and if you find that you are one of our tribe, then it is a simple matter to affiliate and begin your journey with others who share your clarity.

The adamantine Gates of Hell are hereby thrown open—boldly stride within and learn about the "Feared Religion," or slink away and sustain your ignorance. The choice is yours—let the games begin!

§

Much modern "Satanic" lore does not originate from theistic or LaVeyan Satanism, but from traditional Christian folk beliefs coupled with contemporary urban legends. An example is the Satanic ritual abuse scare of the 1980s—beginning with the memoir *Michelle Remembers*—which depicted Satanism as a vast conspiracy of elites with a predilection for child abuse and human sacrifice. This genre frequently describes Satan as physically incarnating in order to receive worship.

Satanic groups have various opinions about Satan, ranging from the conviction that he exists and ought to be worshipped (theistic Satanism), to Anton Szandor LaVey's symbolic interpretation, which emphasizes individual will and pleasure-seeking. In Theistic Satanism, Satan is considered a positive force and deity who is either worshipped or revered.

In LaVeyan Satanism, Satan is regarded as holding virtuous characteristics.

We comprise the first above-ground organization in history openly dedicated to the acceptance of Man's true nature—that of a carnal beast, living in a cosmos that is indifferent to our existence. To us, Satan is the symbol that best suits the nature of we who are carnal by birth—people who feel no battles raging between our thoughts and feelings, we who do not embrace the concept of a soul imprisoned in a body. Satan represents pride, liberty, and individualism—qualities often defined as Evil by those who worship external deities, who feel there is a war between their minds and emotions.

Since the Satanist understands that all Gods are fiction, instead of bending a knee in worship to—or seeking friendship or unity with—such mythical entities, he places himself at the center of his own subjective universe as his own highest value. We Satanists are thus our own "Gods," and as beneficent "deities" we can offer love to those who deserve it and deliver our wrath (within reasonable limits) upon those who seek to cause us—or that which we cherish—harm.

But such self-deification is not for everyone, since it requires total responsibility for one's choices and actions, and the realization of a social contract which makes for a civilized state of being. So Satanism is not meant to be "The Way" for all people, since we consider it a sad truth that only a small percentage of our species has the intelligence, adherence to reason, and self-discipline to handle our perspective.

Priesthood of Mendes, Devil's Advocates, Satan's Priesthood, the Order of the Trapezoid, the Council of Nine, the Magistra, the High Priestess, the High Priest, the Grand Mistress of the Temple, Magistra Templi Rex, and the Chairmistress of the Council of Nine.

The First Church of Satan, The Satanic Church, and The Satanic Church of America maintain the simplest and boldest moniker, embodied in the words Church of Satan.

There are no branches of the Church of Satan. The Church of Satan does not have regular services, nor do we have church buildings for gathering people. Since our approach is individualist, our members who use ritual do so in chambers they construct in their own homes reflecting their own tastes and needs. These are not open to visitation.
The only people who perform sacrifices are those who believe in supernatural beings who would consider a sacrifice to be some form of payment for a request or form of worship. Since we do not believe in supernatural beings, there is no reason for a Satanist to make a sacrifice of any sort.

Our ritual is basically a form of self-therapy and is most often done in private.

Satanists are atheists. We see the universe as being indifferent to us, and so all morals and values are subjective human constructions.

join us
join us
join us
join us
join us
join us
join us
join us
join us
join us
welcome back

Existing on damnation's edge
The priest had never known
To witness such a violent show
Of power overthrown

Angels fighting aimlessly
Still dying by the sword
Our legions killing all in sight
To get the one called Lord

The gates of hell lie waiting as you see
There's no price to pay just follow me
I can take your lost soul from the grave
Jesus knows your soul cannot be saved

Crucify the so-called lord
He soon shall fall to me
Your souls are damned, your God has fell
To slave for me eternally
Hell awaits...

The reaper guard's the darkened gates
That satan calls his home
Demons feed the furnace where
The dead are free to roam
Lonely children of the night
There's seven ways to go

Each leading to the burning hole
The lucifer controls

Priests of Hades seek the sacred star
Satan sees the answer lies not far
Zombies screaming souls cry out to you
Satanic laws prevail, your life is through

Pray to the moon... when it is round
Death with you shall then abound
What you seek... for can't be found
In sea or sky or underground

Now I have you deep inside my everlasting grasp
The seven bloody gates of hell
Is where you'll live your last

Warriors from hell's domain
Will bring you to your death
The flames of Hades burning strong
Your soul shall never rest

The gates of hell lie waiting as you see
There's no price to pay just follow me
I can take your lost soul from the grave
Jesus knows your soul cannot be saved

Sacrifice the lives of all I know,
They soon shall die
Their souls are damned to rot in hell
And keep the fire growing deep inside
Hell awaits...

§

Here comes the woman, with the look in her eye
Raised on leather, with flesh on her mind
Words as weapons, sharper than knives
Makes you wonder, how the other half die?

Our position is to be self-centered, with ourselves being the most important person (the "God") of our subjective universe, so we are sometimes said to worship ourselves.

Satan to us is a symbol of pride, liberty and individualism, and it serves as an external metaphorical projection of our highest personal potential. We do not believe in Satan as a being or person.

In Satanism each individual is his or her own god—there is no room for any other god and that includes Satan, Lucifer, Cthulhu or whatever other name one might select or take from history or fiction.

Seeing that Satanism is a work in progress, an attempt for melding science with philosophy, we are fully justified in choosing the concepts of old, working with them in our context and taking them into the future. (If we didn't, who else would?) This is the same process used by scientists, doctors, psychologists, and many other professionals. Nothing would get done if individuals merely went along with established thought and never added to it. It's evolution, pure and simple.

Spiritual Satanism does not in any way condone spirit abuse as taught in the classical grimoires. The Demons who were bound and compelled to do the bidding of the sorcerers are now free, and anyone using the nine-foot circle methods and "Jehova" names is inviting personal disaster. The Demons are our friends, and with respect and reverence in summoning through Satan, we seek to establish mutually beneficial relationships with them.

Spiritual Satanism places no limits on developing the powers of the mind known as "witchcraft" or "magick." We believe in justice, and just as martial artists are versed in the uses of Dim Mak and other aspects of physical combat, Spiritual Satanists are versed in the Black Arts of "magick" should they ever need them. People who are unaware of these powers are defenseless against them, and the powers that be know this all too well. Satan does not tolerate injustice.

As opposed to the stories of how the Nazarene healed people, Satan shows us how we can heal ourselves and perform so-called miracles, using our minds and the powers of our own souls.

Satanism is based upon the true transformation of the soul through power meditation.

Spiritual Satanism is a life-loving religion. Satan accepts us as we are, but guides us to advance ourselves to where we evolve to a higher level. Spiritual Satanists are free to live their lives as they choose—responsibility to the responsible. We live by natural law and encourage everyone to develop themselves to their fullest extent.

We take our tenets and practices directly from Satan himself.

We work directly with Satan. We believe each and every person who is willing and respectful can have a personal relationship with Satan. There are no mediators in Spiritual Satanism; the Ministry is only for guidance and support.

We practice power meditation to advance spiritually and to elevate ourselves. Power meditation is as essential for the human soul as food is essential for the human body. The serpent, a symbol of Satan, represents the firey Kundalini force coiled at the base of the spine, which, upon ascending, transforms the human mind and soul to a much higher level of understanding and ability. This is the true meaning of "Raising the Devil." The Serpent symbol of Satan also represents the DNA helix of life.

Satanists do not push Satanism or prosyletize.

Other half die
Makes you wonder, wonder, wonder

Here come the man, with the look in his eye
Fed on nothing, but full of pride
Look at them go, look at them kick
Makes you wonder, how the other half live

The devil inside, the devil inside
Every single one of us the devil inside
The devil inside, the devil inside
Every single one of us the devil inside

Here come the world, with the look in its eye
Future uncertain, but certainly slight
Look at the faces, listen to the bells
It's hard to believe we need a place called hell, place called hell

The devil inside, the devil inside
Every single one of us the devil inside
The devil inside, the devil inside
Every single one of us the devil inside

Here comes the woman, with the look in her eye
Raised on leather, with flesh on her mind
Words as weapons sharper than knives
Makes you wonder, how the other half die

The devil inside, the devil inside
Every single one of us the devil inside
The devil inside, the devil inside
Every single one of us the devil inside
The devil inside, the devil inside
Every single one of us the devil inside
The devil inside, devil inside
Every single one of us the devil inside
The devil inside, yeah, yeah, yeah
The devil inside, yeah, yeah, yeah

§

Yea
Sold into slavery down in New Orleans
Goddess
Of the bayou light
Black dog's head on the killing bed
Severed
And left to bleed
There on fire
In the corner of the world
There in misery
There on fire
In the corner of the world
Left for God to see

Do you want to take a life
Do you want to cross that line
Cause it's a long way back from hell
And you don't want to go with me

Yea
Poison father of the human race
God
Of the tainted blood
Malevolence
Sneaking up the spine of the world
Ready for the bastard son
There on fire
In the veins of man
There in misery
There on fire
In the veins of man
Left for God to see

Do you want to take a life
Do you want to cross that line
Cause it's a long way back from hell
And you don't want to go with me

Spiritual Satanists acknowledge science and believe everything of the occult/supernatural to have a rational scientific explanation.

The powers of the mind and soul are very real. People who are unaware of or who do not believe in these powers are easy to control and manipulate by those who are skilled in using these energies.

The aim of this religion is the ultimate destruction of religions through the advancement of individual freedom, social responsibility and education. With freedom comes the responsibility of other people's freedom. One man's freedom must never become another man's slavery. Without mutual respect and cooperation, we will only continue to kill ourselves in the name of god, country and greed. The philosophy of Satanism undermines all existing religions, including our own. Thus, the Satanic Philosophy is based on a paradox, much like the Tao. It is self-canceling and cannot become the new bully on the block. And, when society respects each individual's rights, no matter how diverse, the Satanists' Job will be complete. We all have the right not to be victimized in any way, shape or form for any reason, and remember, children are people too, even your own. Satanism exists to educate the masses away from old-world-thinking and to illuminate and educate them so they happily accept a new world order, ideally one of "Self Rule" and mutual cooperation.

Now for the method; by not having any set reality or belief, you are not trapped by their rules, and are free to start making your own interpretations of what reality is or isn't. This is freedom: the breaking away from the status quo, to see things from a more personal perspective, much like when Satan broke ranks from God and became the first revolutionist. It's funny how governments promote god worship when most modern governments owe their existence to Freemasonry and revolution, the dream of freedom, the spirit of Satan. Governments and religions actively partake in propaganda against Satanism, for they truly fear being overthrown. As for America, Satanism is Americanism, for America supports freedom of religion in the same Masonic context that Satanism does. Although certain religions in America attempt to combat this, our wonderful constitution (written by Freemasons) prevents them from achieving their goals. Yes, Satanism reaches far past the United States boarders. We are trying to spread the Light of phosphor, the light of freedom throughout the world.

And freedom is only found in the mind, for the physical world and its systems, such as society, bind us. Please remember that with freedom comes a great responsibility to our neighbors in this society, their freedoms.

Although we view reality/beliefs as the unalienable right of everyone, I do support your full-blown assaults on those that would infringe upon your rights, as long as you execute your attacks in a legal and productive manner. We do not turn the other Cheek, unless it's to buy time to smite with discretion. Hopefully by your mannerisms, diplomacy and actions, more people will see that freedom is not evil and people can be socially responsible without a threat of Hell or any other religious afterlife accounting. Remember, it is their right to live and die in their belief just as it is your right to live and die in yours. Besides, tolerance is not acceptance; you don't have to like someone or something to tolerate them or it. This does not deny you your favorite bigotries and hatreds. It merely keeps you from violating the rights of those you hate. It really is that simple folks. You can hate each other all you want, just don't act upon it.

Now, one last thing: we ask you to abide by the laws of your countries and local governments as they pertain to you and to take an active role in changing them as you feel is needed.

Satanism is for free-thinking, independent people. If you prefer a more closed-minded, stringent reality than Satan-

Do you want to take a life
Do you want to cross that line
Cause it's a long way back from hell
And you don't want to go with me

And it's a long way back from hell
And you don't want to go

§

Jesus lived his life in a cheap hotel
On the edge of Route 66 yeah
He lived a dark and twisted life
And he came right back just to do it again

Eye for an eye and a tooth for the truth
I ain't never seen a demon warp dealin' a
Ring a ding rhythm or jukebox racket my
Mind can't clutch the feeling

Devil man devil man calling devil man
Running in my head yeah
Devil man devil man calling devil man
Running in my head yeah

Devil man devil man calling devil man
Running in my head yeah
Devil man devil man calling devil man
Running in my head

Hell hounds lead at the cowardly kings
And carry souls across the river Styx
Yeah they see no evil and feel no pain
Sucking juice from a fallen angel

I dreamed I was a supernova fucker nitro'
Burning and fuel injection
Feed the gods a strychnine soul
A motherfucker of invention

Devil man devil man calling devil man
Running in my head yeah
Devil man devil man calling devil man
Running in my head yeah

Devil man devil man calling devil man
Running in my head yeah
Devil man devil man calling devil man
Running in my head yeah

Yeah inbreed the witches and worship the dogs
Deformed and fuckin' lazy
Damn yourself and choke on my name
I'd love to love you baby
Dead ringer rats swinging in the trees
Immaculate conception

Bury me an angel God I need
Some inspiration

Devil man devil man calling devil man
Running in my head yeah
Devil man devil man calling devil man
Running in my head yeah

Devil man devil man calling devil man
Running in my head yeah
Devil man devil man calling devil man
Running in my head

§

Satan is real, working in spirit
You can see him an' hear him
in this world every day
Satan is real working with power
He can tempt you an' lead you astray

(Ha ha ha ha ha ha ha)

ism, our religion is probably not for you and I ask you to please refrain from joining. Satanism makes no claims as far as the "True Satanic Path" or any "True Way."

§

Satan was the first revolutionist. Therefore, Satan as defined in "Morals and Dogma" is the perfect figurehead for a revolutionary religion. His act of rebellion was the first and most famous allegory of freedom.

Lucifer, who held vile things in proud disdain, despised this rabble of commonplace spirits forever wallowing in a life of feasts and pleasure. But to those who were possessed of a daring spirit, a restless soul, to those fired with a wild love of liberty, he proffered friendship, which we return with adoration.

Historical reports of early Satanism are often colored by fears of an anti-human "other": however, the literary history of Satan—from Milton to Anatole France—suggests that biblical interpretations of a humanistic, benevolent Satan, driving our highest aspirations and encouraging human compassion, have resonated for centuries.

To embrace the name "Satan" is to avow skepticism in the face of all things, even—especially—that which is held sacred. To stand forth as a "Satanist" is to rend from the persecutory, affrighted mob a convenient out-group label, demanding that individuals be judged for their concrete actions, not their fealty to arbitrary social norms and illusory categorizations.

Satan, the symbolic force of design that would urge humanity toward refined pleasures of the Arts and Sciences. Satan, who first brought the fruit of knowledge to Humankind that thereafter we might live not as naked brutes in the wild, but develop our cultural splendor into ever more aesthetically and technologically advanced heights. Ours is the Humanistic Satan who would sacrifice His own Heavenly residence so that Humanity might learn to understand and enjoy the physical world they inhabit.

Satanists are often natural aestheticians who revel in the grandeur of human artistic, architectural achievements while also often drawn to the idiosyncratic and bizarre that are all too typically misunderstood, feared, and discarded.

Satan stands as the ultimate icon for the selfless revolt against tyranny, free & rational inquiry, and the responsible pursuit of happiness.

Satan has the compassion and wisdom of an angel. Although Satan is subordinate to God, he is mankind's only conduit to the dominion beyond the physical. In addition, only Satan can hear our prayers and only Satan can respond.

The Satanist harbors reasonable agnosticism in all things, holding fast only to that which is demonstrably true.

Thus, Satanism is an evolving religion, unfettered by arcane doctrines born of fearful minds in darkened times. Belief must reconstruct itself to fact, never the other way round. This is the Luciferian impulse to eat of the Tree of Knowledge, even (and especially) when to do so irretrievably dissipates blissful and comforting delusions of old.

That which will not bend must break, and that which can be destroyed by truth should never be spared its demise.

This is an ultimatum.

Hail Satan!

§

Well, my worn-out boots
are takin' me down town
An' I'm lookin' for trouble
an' I wanna get loud
Serve me up a drink
an' I'll shoot it right down
An' I'll jump up on the bar an' holler:
"One more round."

I'm goin' straight to hell (hell, hell)
Ain't nothin' slowin' me down
An' I'm goin' straight to hell (hell, hell)
So you just better get me one more round
Well, back in the day with my Uncle Jim
He kept a lotta moonshine out in the shed
Taught me how to drink, how to be real proud
Of my hillbilly ways an' my outlaw style

I'm goin' straight to hell (hell, hell)
Ain't nothin' slowin' me down
An' I'm goin' straight to hell (hell, hell)
So you just better get me one more round

(Instrumental break)

Well, I'm bracin' these back roads
tryin' to save my life
'Cause the Sheriff wants to kill me
'cause I fucked his wife
I was on the run with a gun in my hand
'Cause I liked a good time an' a one-night stand

I'm goin' straight to hell (hell, hell)
Ain't nothin' slowin' me down
I'm goin' straight to hell (hell, hell)
So you just better get me one more round
Hell, you just better get me one more round

§

Nine Tenets of Satanism

There are nine fundamental tenets of Satanism—with nine being a significant Satanic number. Each tenet is represented by one of the choir of nine Angels sent from Heaven to oversee Earth.

1. People should be guided by compassion and wisdom and follow the golden rule of "do unto others as you would have them do unto you."
2. The Circle of Compassion should extend to all species, not just humans.
3. People are fallible, and although we should all try to do our best, poor judgment is inevitable. If we make a mistake, we should do our best to rectify it, and resolve any harm that may have been caused by our misdeeds.
4. The Satanist should ever be self-reflective.
5. Our beliefs should conform to our best scientific understanding of the world. We should take care never to distort scientific facts to fit our beliefs.
6. The freedoms of others should be respected, even the freedom to offend, but great care should be exercised to avoid wrongly encroaching on the freedoms of others.
7. There are things we don't understand, and it is appropriate to acknowledge that. It is not appropriate, however, to be proud of ignorance.
8. While proselytizing might have noble intent, it is not acceptable to coerce or push your beliefs on others. It is always best to lead by example.
9. Every tenet is a guiding principle designed to inspire nobility in action and thought. The spirit of compassion and wisdom should always prevail over the written or spoken word.

§

Apparently Satan knows only the sins that have not been confessed or repented. What has been submitted to the keys of the confessional seems to be out of his reach. It would seem that the sacrament of penance blots out or obliterates sins from the soul so as not to leave the slightest possibility for Satan to discover them. Through the sacrament of penance everything is, so to say, drowned in the abyss of God's mercy.

Furthermore, it must be remembered that Satan, the father of lies, often twists small acts into unusually and seemingly grievous ones, making mountains out of molehills, so to speak, and at times purposely distorting them, mixing up truth with falsehood with the intention of creating the greatest disorder and most lasting enmity.

§

Suddenly a loud shrill voice rent the air. The noise in the room sounded as though it were far off, somewhere in a desert. Satan howled as though he had been struck over the head with a club. Like a pack of wild beasts suddenly let loose, the terrifying noises sounded aloud as they came out of the mouth of the possessed woman. Those present were struck with a terrible fear that penetrated the very marrow of their bones.

"Silence, Satan. Keep quiet, you infamous reprobate!"

Satan dares at all to remain in the presence of the All Holy? How can he endure it? Does he not run off like a whipped cur? All we need to remember is that Satan dared to approach our Lord fasting in the desert. He even dared to take the Saviour upon a high pinnacle at Jerusalem; and again he carried Him up on a high mountain-top. If he showed himself so powerful then, he has not changed since.

Devil, barking like the hound of hell: "Beelzebub."
Exorcist: "You call yourself Beelzebub. Are you not Lucifer, the prince of the devils?"
Devil: "No, not the prince, the chieftain, but one of the leaders."
Exorcist: "You were therefore not a human being, but you are one of the fallen angels, who with selfish pride wanted to be like unto God?"
Devil, with grinning teeth: "Yes, that is so. Ha, how we hate Him!"
Exorcist: "Why do you call yourself Beelzebub if you are not the prince of the devils?"
Devil: "Enough, my name is Beelzebub."
Exorcist: "From the point of influence and dignity you must rank near Lucifer, or do you hail from the lower choir of angels?"
Devil: "I once belonged to the seraphic choir."
Exorcist: "What would you do, if God made it possible for you to atone for your injustice to Him?"
Demoniacal sneering: "Are you a competent theologian?"
Exorcist: "How long have you been torturing this poor woman?"
Devil: "Since her fourteenth year."
Exorcist: "How dared you enter into that innocent girl and torture her like that?"
Sneeringly: "Ha, did not her own father curse us into her?"
Exorcist: "But why did you, Beelzebub, alone take possession of her? Who gave you that permission?"
Devil: "Don't talk so foolishly. Don't I have to render obedience to Satan?"
Exorcist: "Then you are here at the direction and command of Lucifer?"
Devil: "Well, how could it be otherwise?"

And when the exorcist approached him with the relic of the Cross hidden under his cassock, Satan became a raving maniac. "Begone, begone," he howled, "I cannot bear it. Oh, this is torture! It is unbearable!"

"Look at the wood of the cross! Begone ye powers of hell! The lion of the tribe of Juda shall conquer!"

Satan acted terribly, "Stop it. Stop it, I cannot bear it, I cannot listen to it!" he seemed to say.

§

Now, you have the goodness to abuse Satan and them, as much as you like, Sir, and to let me alone if you please.

Good News! Good News!

Presented as part of the exhibition Medium Medium: Language in the Age of Digital Reproducibility *at* Hedreen Gallery, *Seattle University, Seattle, WA from October 9 to November 9, 2013 alongside work by Doug Nufer and Vanessa Place.* Good News! Good News! *is a three channel video installation produced in collaboration with Greg Curtis and included a performance for the opening on Saturday, October 12, 2013 by Geneva Skeen. Included here are the wall text for the piece including video credits, information on Skeen's performance, still images from the video and, lastly, the script for the Left and Right Channel of the video installation.*

Good News! Good News!
Three Channel Video Installation
By Mathew Timmons & Greg Curtis
And including, **NEWS.HEAD**, a performance by Geneva Skeen

We tape everything just to do things differently and it keeps us remarkably productive, enhancing such advanced skills as color vision. One is removed from the scene, but it's all garbage. Future grind? You've been deceived. Viewers complained amidst tepid ratings. All this late-night talk, of course, operates in a vacuum. All fluff and glitter with no substance, just vapid, espisodic lunacy, or a highly compressed advertisement. I wonder where this wire goes...?

I think we're alone now, looking towards a bright future of computer-generated personality gimmicks and inventions, pastels and blazers … But wait, there's more! Totalfark! The perfect summer blockbuster is finally here! Good news! Good news! Everyone wins.

Good News! Good News!

Watch a screener of the video at http://vimeo.com/insertblancpress/good-news-good-news

Actors: Jay Erker and Michael Anthony Ibarra
Camera: Kimo Proudfoot and Ben Rodkin
Director: Mathew Timmons
Script: Mathew Timmons
Still Photography: Greg Curtis
Set & Costume Design: Janne Larsen in collaboration with Mathew Timmons
Makeup: Gisella Pons
Production Assistant: Chris Niemi
Technical Assistant: Geoff Gossett

NEWS.HEAD, 2013.
Performance by Geneva Skeen.

NEWS.HEAD is an open-source choreography performance, based on the video *Good News! Good News!* by Mathew Timmons and Greg Curtis.

Participating dancers for the performance at Hedreen Gallery were Matt Drews and Rachel Green.

Performance Diagram by Greg Curtis (seen below).

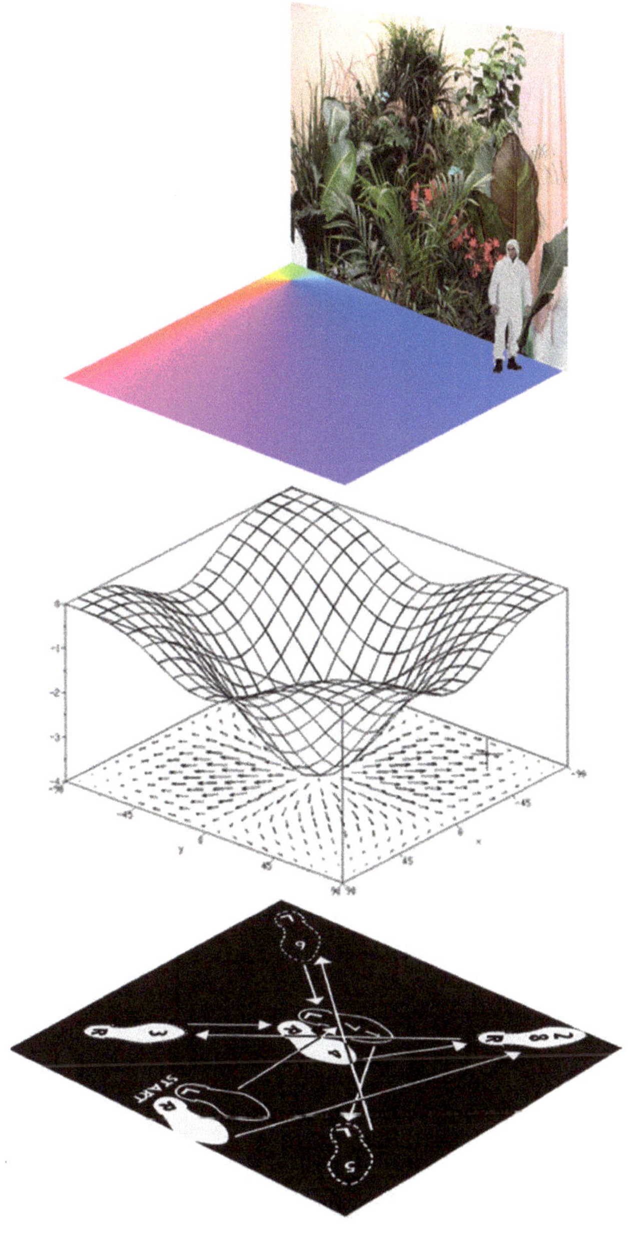

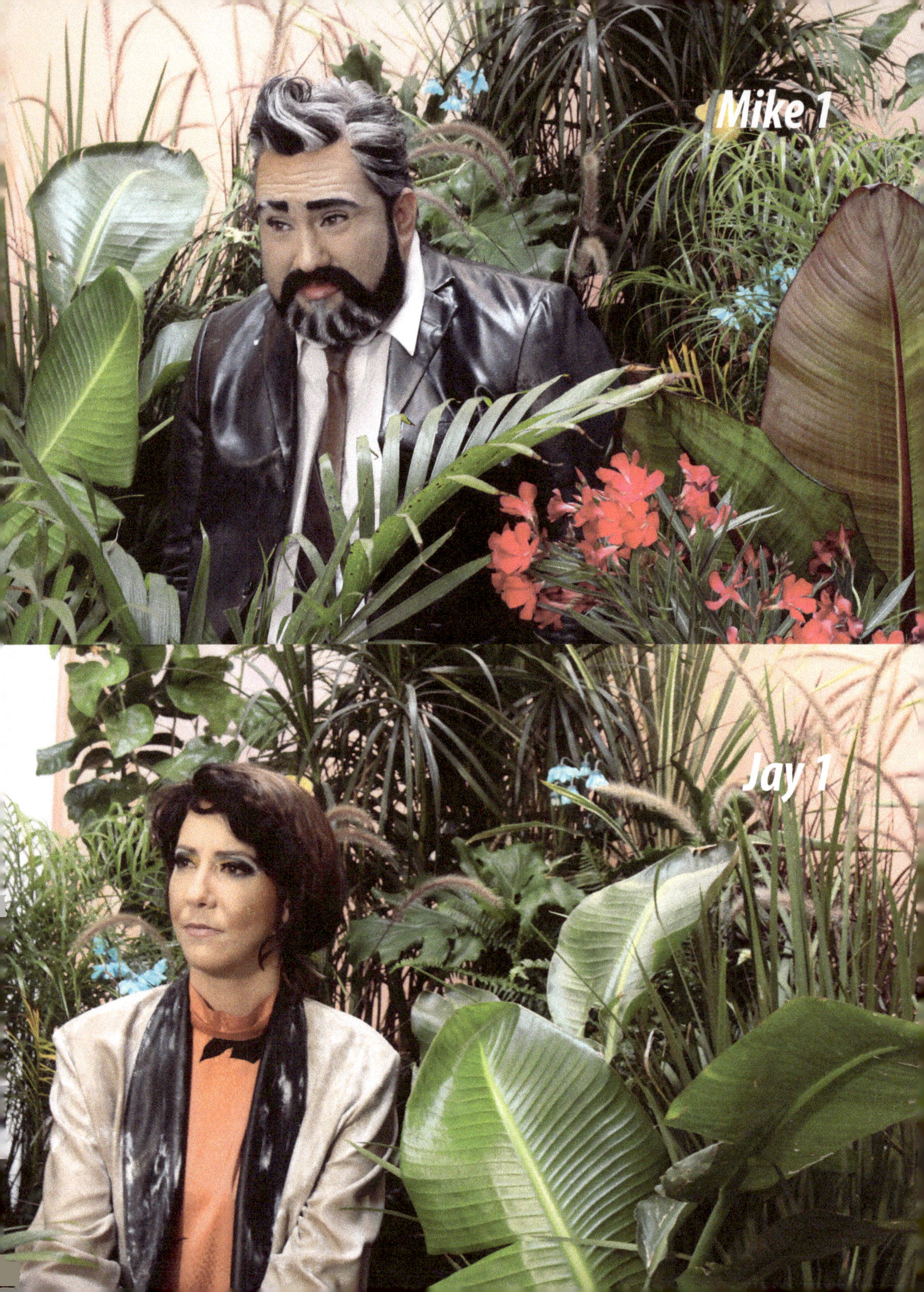
Mike 1
Jay 1

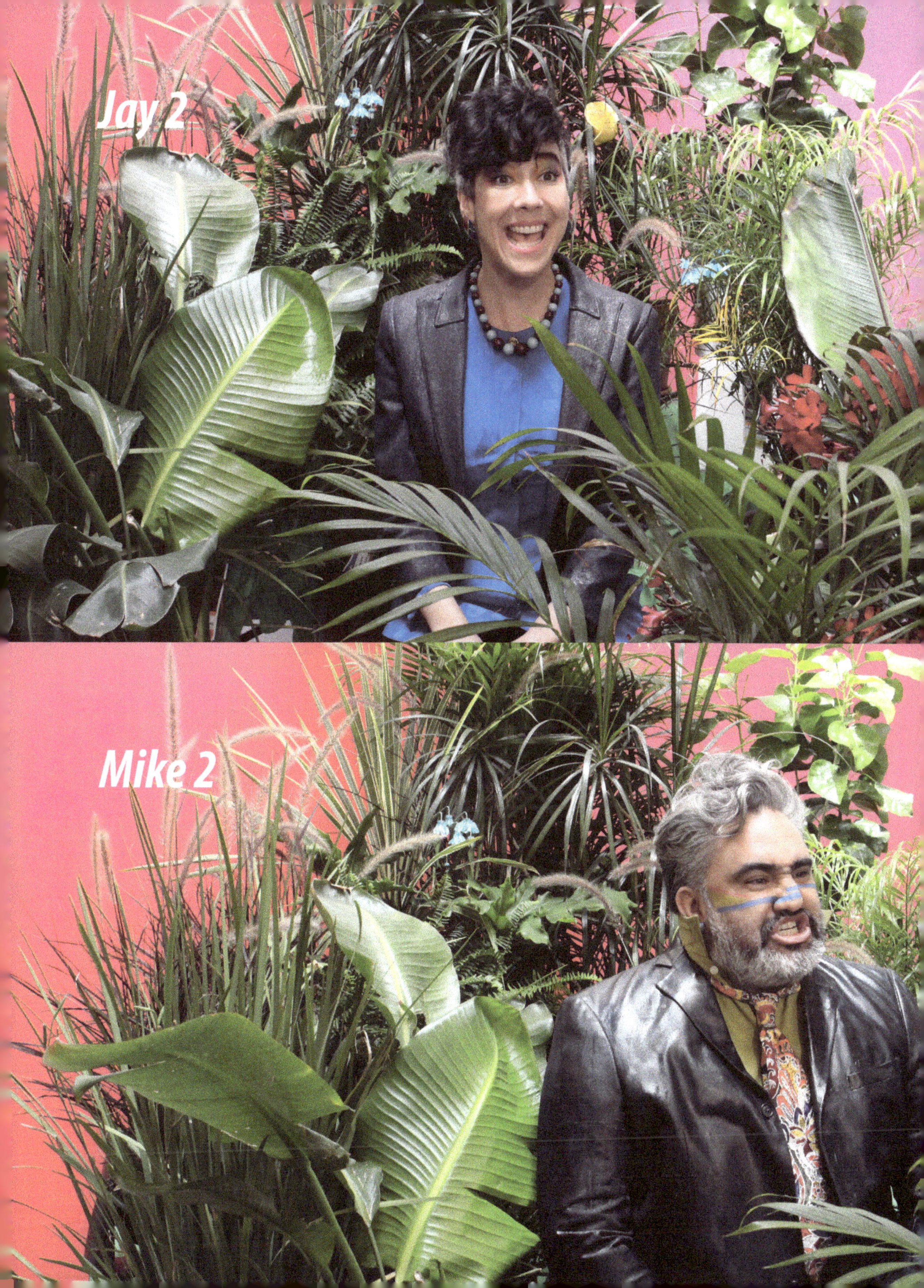

Jay 2
Mike 2

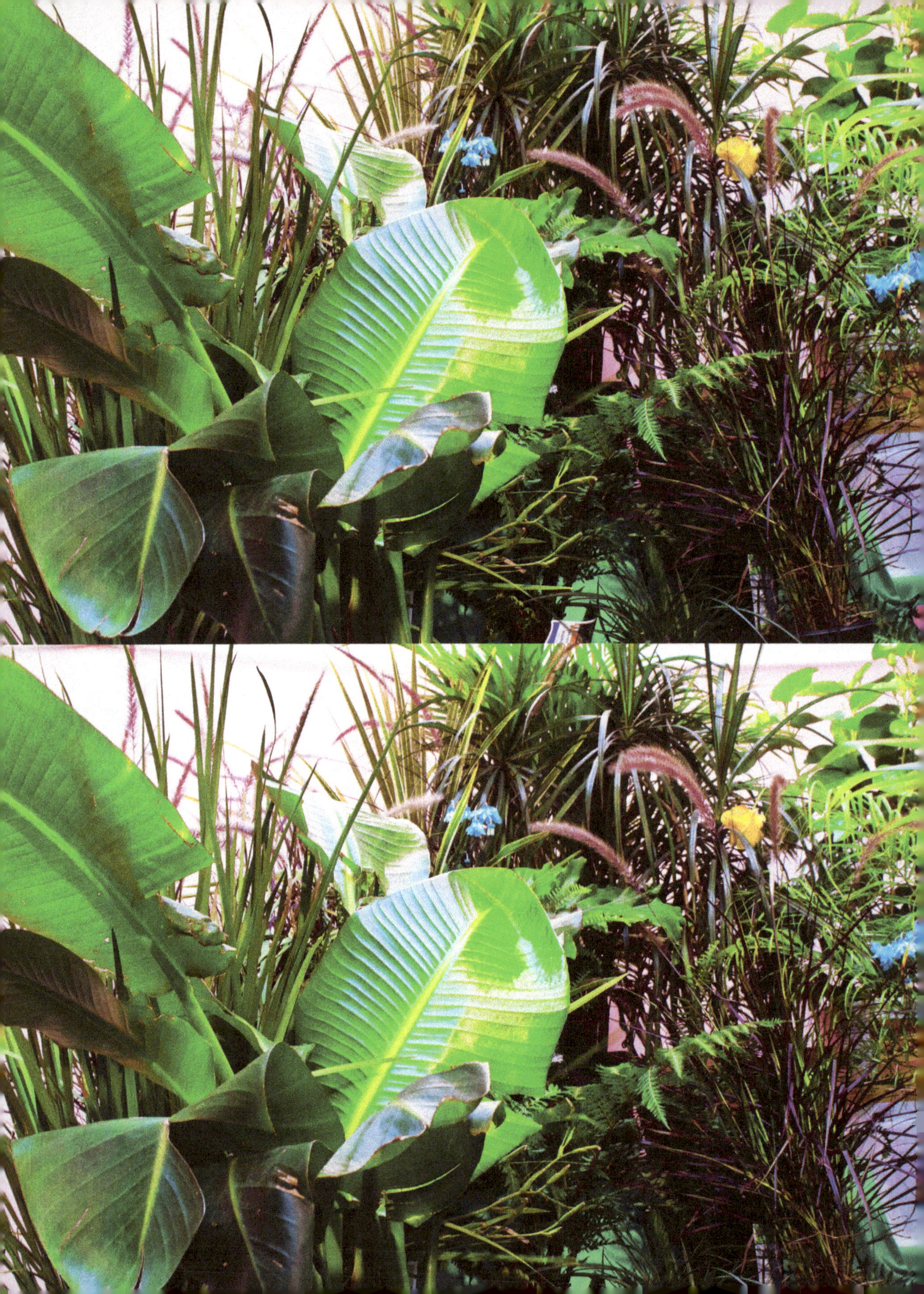

Left Channel

Mike1: [silent] No … Oh yeah.

M1: Afternoon Everybody!
As always, thanks for your support.
The balcony is closed.
Let's look into the future.
Jay1: Connect the dots, la la la la la...
Eep!
Fer sure.
M1: I always worried these moments would be forgotten forever.
J1: Everyone wins!
Plastic.
M1: Doing things differently, from five seconds to more than a minute
M1: And naturally my mind goes horrible places when we follow this too closely.
We tape everything.
Mike2: I usually wake up six hours later without such advanced skills as color vision.

Jay2: What will happen!?
J1: You've been deceived.
Do expect to be entertained.
You've been deceived.
M2: All fluff and glitter with no substance,
All fluff and no substance.

Right Channel

Jay1: [silent] What the fuck!
[silent] Oh my god!
[silent] Bitch!
Bitch!
Cunt!
[silent] What the fuck!
Fuck you!?
Fuck you, you fuckin' fuck!
Fuck you, Fucker!
Afternoon Everybody!
Dissension in the Ranks!

What will happen!?
Jay2: To understand where we're going we first need to know where we have been.
J1: Plastic.
Mike1: I wonder where this wire goes...?
J1: New discoveries are being made every day, in your car on the radio,
Late into the night.
J2: I always worried these moments would be forgotten forever.
Mike2: [high falsetto] I always worried these moments would be forgotten forever.
J1: This is the future, after all.
Everyone wins!
M1: This is the future after all.
Faux leather…
Do not expect to be entertained.
J2: The setting can be pinned down
to the year 2004,
give or take a couple years.
J1: Future grind? These workers won't complain much, or need vacations!

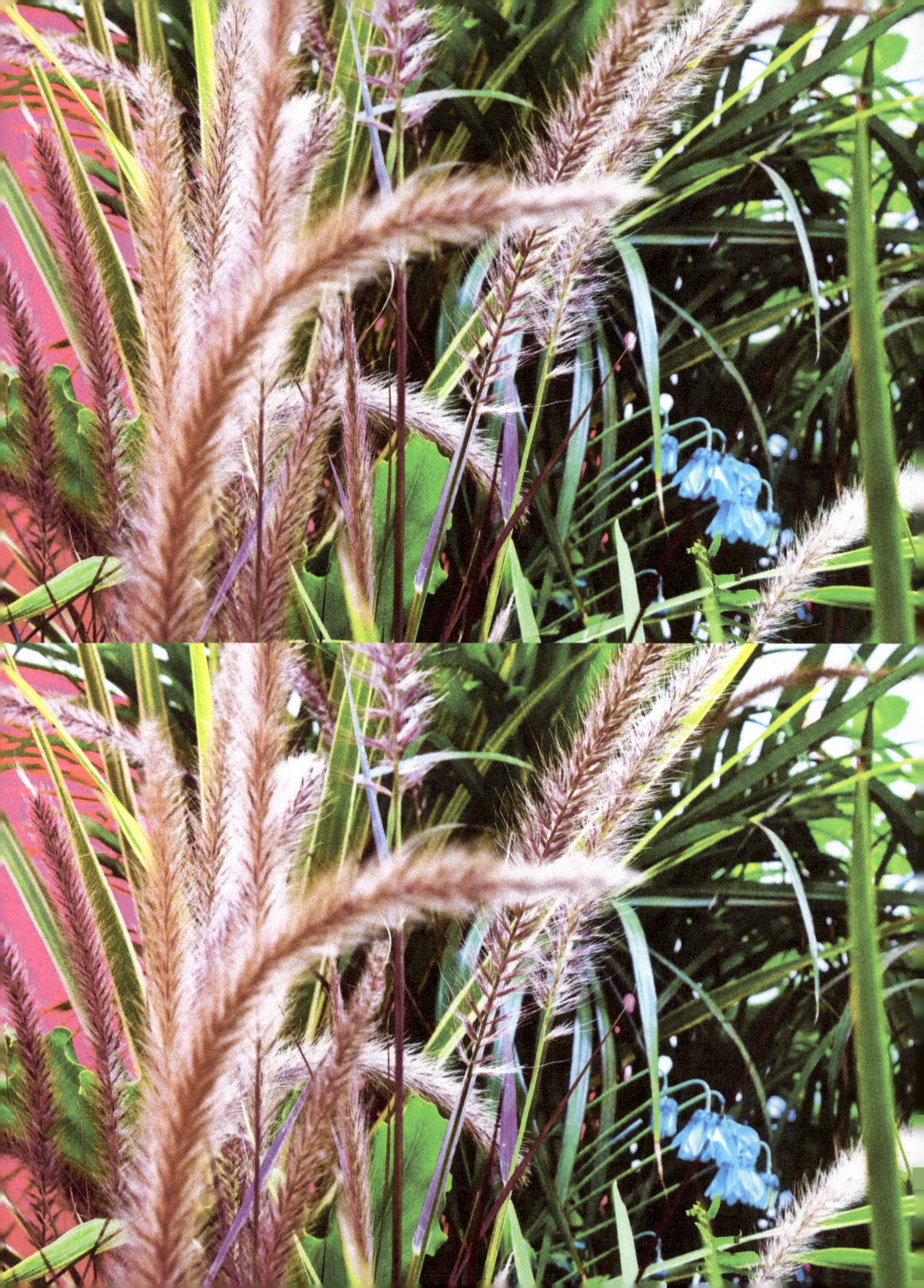

J2: Viewers complained
M2: Illegal Downloading.
M1: Information circulates through a single global computer network.
Illegal Downloading.
J2: Obsolescence makes the heart grow fonder.
J1: Faux leather…
Plastic…
Pastels and blazers…
I think we're alone now.

Incredible!
The goggles, they do nothing.
M2: So what!?
No one is forcing you to watch it.
J1: Illegal Downloading.
J2: Take a wild guess!
It used to be gimmicks and inventions.
This set looks like a Walmart version of Larry King Live!
J1: This set looks like a Walmart version of Larry King Live.
And naturally my mind goes horrible places.

M1: Illegal down… Illegal Downloading!
Credit fraud, my God, that's worse than murder.
Dissension in the ranks.
What'll happen?
M2: Everyone wins.
M1: Pastels and blazers…

J1: It's an uphill battle for a cast of characters who haven't yet invented the wheel.
J2: The fact that it's a one-joke premise is a hurdle. Sometimes what you like

M1: The setting can be pinned down to the year 2004, give or take a couple years.

M2: To understand where we are going we first need to know where we have been.

M2: Back in the 1980s, it looked like computers were going to be able to do just about anything. And it looked like corporate greed was going to grow and grow until the average citizen was a virtual slave to the mega-corporations who would happily destroy the environment, culture, history, and basic human liberty all in the name of profit.
J1: All fluff and glitter with no substance.
All fluff and no substance.
M2: AOL was brand new,
Compu Serve was hip and hot,
college students were starting to get email addresses, and the Web was still years away.

J1: Thank God I have to pick up my son from basketball practice!
J2: This is the future, after all!
Faux leather,
Plastic.
J1: Your rights as a citizen are measured by your credit rating, and credit fraud is one of the most serious crimes.
J2: Good grief, it`s back, that crazy coast-to-coast car race.
It's an uphill battle for a cast of characters who haven't yet invented the wheel.
M2: The fact that it's a one-joke premise is a hurdle. Sometimes what you like

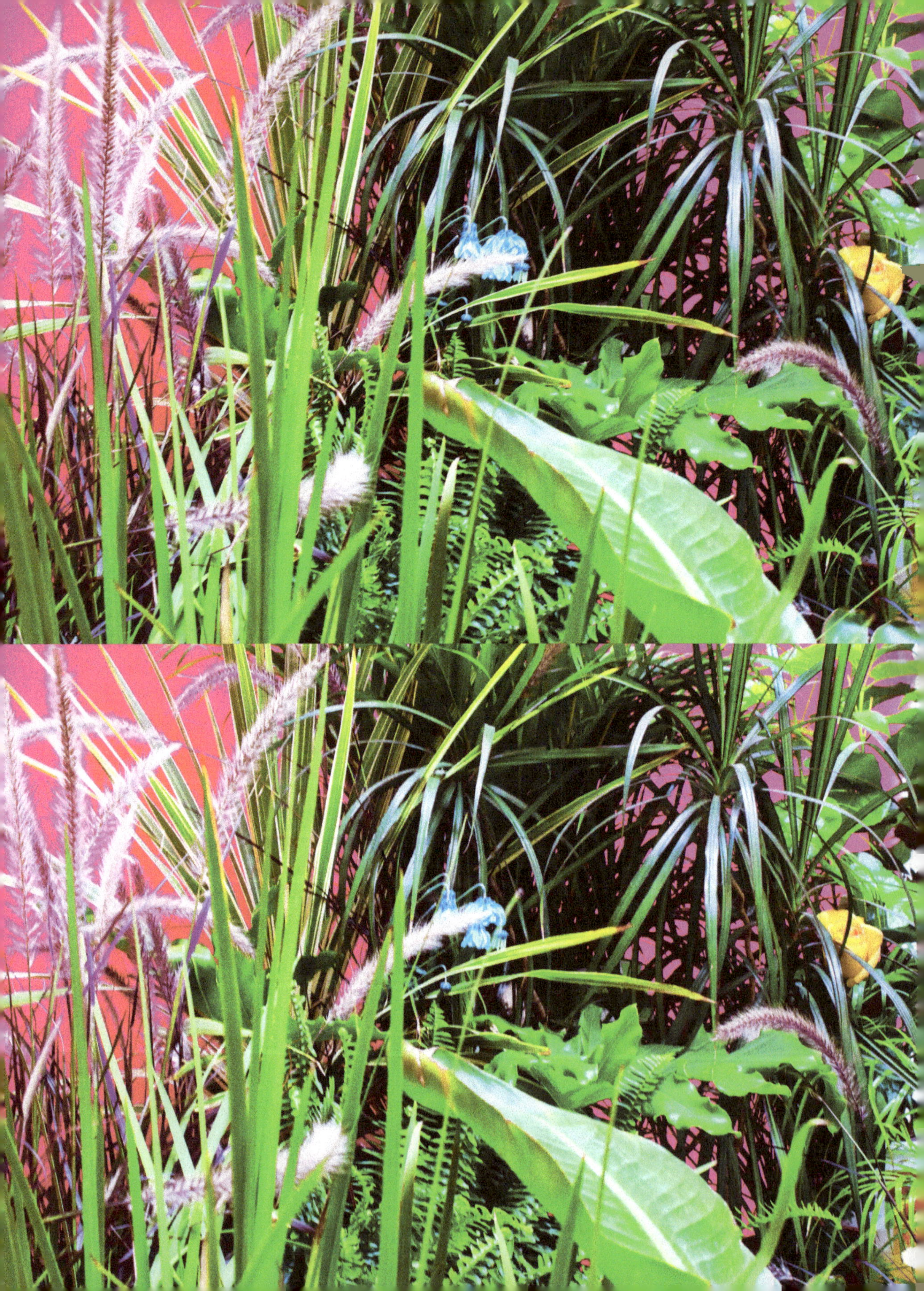

J2: for 30 seconds doesn't necessarily
translate to 30 minutes.

M1: A bevy of washed-up TV actors and
other struggling film folk are thrown
behind the wheel of still more vapid,
espisodic lunacy.
Obsolescence makes the heart grow
fonder.

J1: How ironic.
Well, it`s work ...
Sprinkled throughout the boredom
are the occasionally amusing and
bland PG - Violence, mature themes.
The setting can be pinned down to the
year 2004. This is the future.
Which was usually resolved by the end
of the episode
M1: Heh. Late-night TV is great.
M2: No, in our case, we only watch
television while we're working.
M1: Good News!
J1: Heh! Late-night TV is great.

M1: Every once in a while, I'm able to
remove the remote and use it myself
when she's not looking.
J2: It's an amazing spectacle!
Heh! Late-night TV is great.
M2: Each week, one contestant is chosen
as winner, and one gets removed.
M1: All this late-night talk, of course
Expansion is always good for news
divisions.
J2: Expansion is always good for news
divisions.
M1: For one thing,
they were unable to do the show and

M2: for 30 seconds doesn't necessarily
translate for 30 minutes.
J2: A bevy of washed-up TV actors and
other struggling film folk are thrown
behind the wheel of still more vapid,
espisodic lunacy.
How ironic.
J1: The jiggle and mild sexual jokes still
are present, and so are those
predictably stupid cameo walk-ons,
such as the one by everyone`s favorite
"just-what-do-you-do?" celebrity.
M1: How ironic.
Well, it`s work ...
Sprinkled throughout the boredom are
occasionally amusing and bland PG
Violence, mature themes.
J1: This set looks like a Walmart version
of Larry King Live.
J2: A Walmart version of Larry King Live!
No, in our case, we only watch
television when we're working.

J1: Every once in a while, I'm able to
remove the remote and use it myself
when he's not looking.
J2: All fluff and glitter with no substance.

M2: Heh. Late-night TV is great.
J2: All fluff and no substance.
J2: Each week, one contestant is chosen
as winner, and one gets removed.
M1: Now comes the tough part for the
survivor.
M2: All this late-night talk, of course!
M1: Incredible, the goggles they do
nothing!

They were unable to do the show and

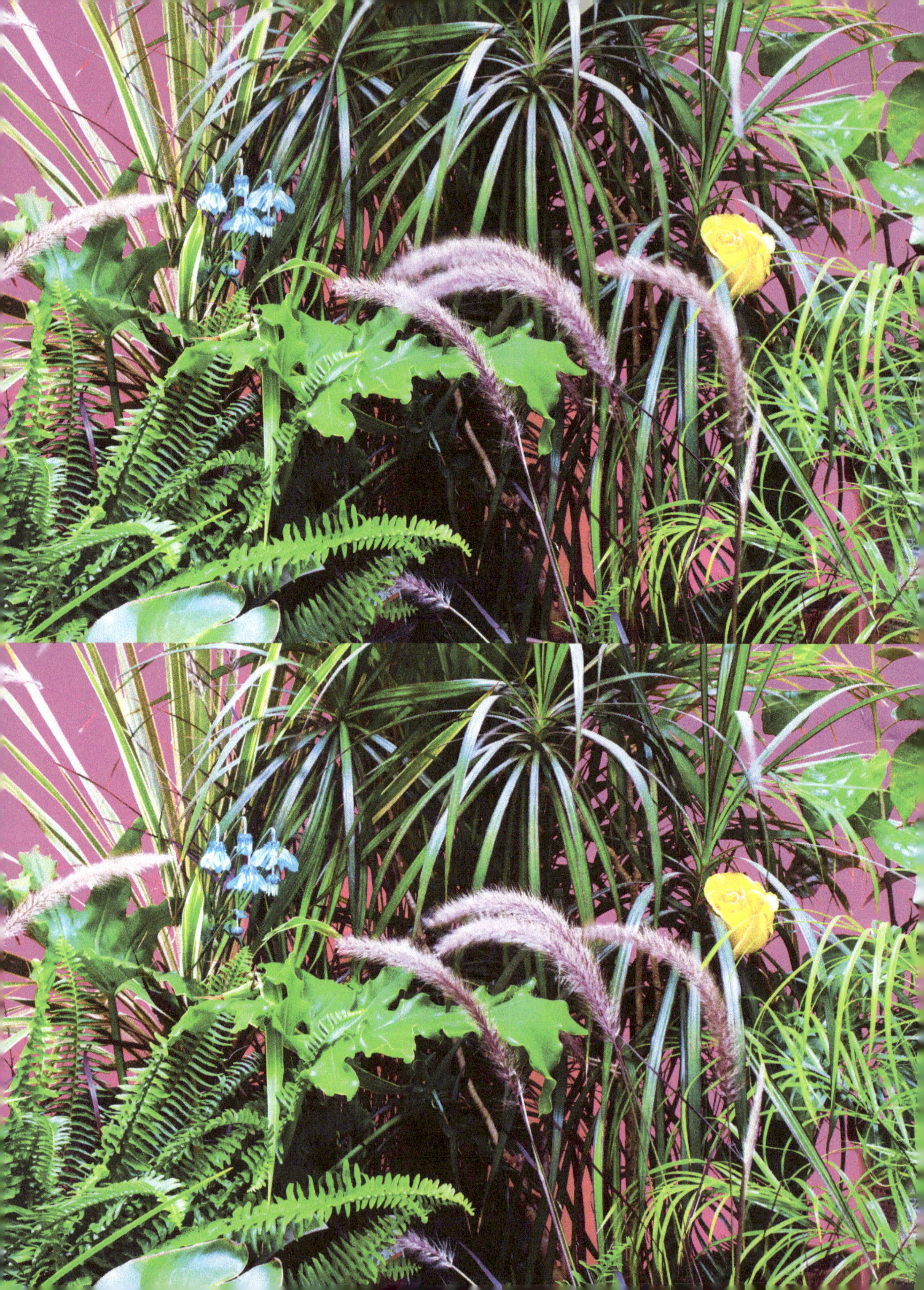

M1: actually have a real-time conversation,
J1: with the two reacting to each other.
M2: Every time someone spoke, they were
talking to an empty screen.
J2: Unlike the video phone conversations
where the actor was actually talking to
another actor on another set in real-time.
M2: And, you know …
J2: Images of a perfect life (and the urge
to buy everything to make that perfect
life a reality).
M1: A tissue-thin excuse to give voice to
a creeping sense of uneasiness about
mass media's role in a society where
state and private interests seemed to
be increasingly muddled.
J1: Much closer than you might imagine.
I'll spend the rest of my life as a VJ for
a pirate TV station.
M1: More often than not, I function as
kind of a post-modern greek chorus,
offering my snarky opinion on
whatever crisis my human
counterparts find themselves in.
J1: The disparity between reality
M2: and what is depicted in the media.
And whether or not the image
provided by the media is actually more
M2: real to the masses than the "real"
reality. Just think about it for a while...
For God's sake.
J1: Accusing television of brainwashing
society is about as shocking as calling
politicians, like,
M1: a bunch of politicians, phonies, man.

J1: Snake oils have made a huge
comeback

M1: actually have a real-time conversation,
with the two reacting to each other.
J1: Ha ha ha. Every time someone spoke,
they were talking to an empty screen
or pre-recorded footage,
J2: where the actor was actually talking to
another actor on a set in real-time.
And, you know …
M2: Images of a perfect life
(and the urge to buy
everything that makes that
perfect life a reality)
M1: A tissue-thin excuse to give voice to
a creeping sense of uneasiness about
mass media's role in a society where
state and private interests seemed to
be increasingly muddled.

Much closer than you might imagine.
M2: Frickin' liberal!
I'll spend the rest of my life as a TV VJ
for a pirate, private, pirate TV radio
sitcom!

M2: And you know, evil…
The setting can be pinned down to the
year 2004.
This is the future after all.

M2: It used to be gimmicks and inventions.
J1: Incredible!
M2: Incredible!
The goggles, they do nothing.
M1: So what, no one is forcing you to
watch it.
This looks like a Walmart version of
Larry King Live.

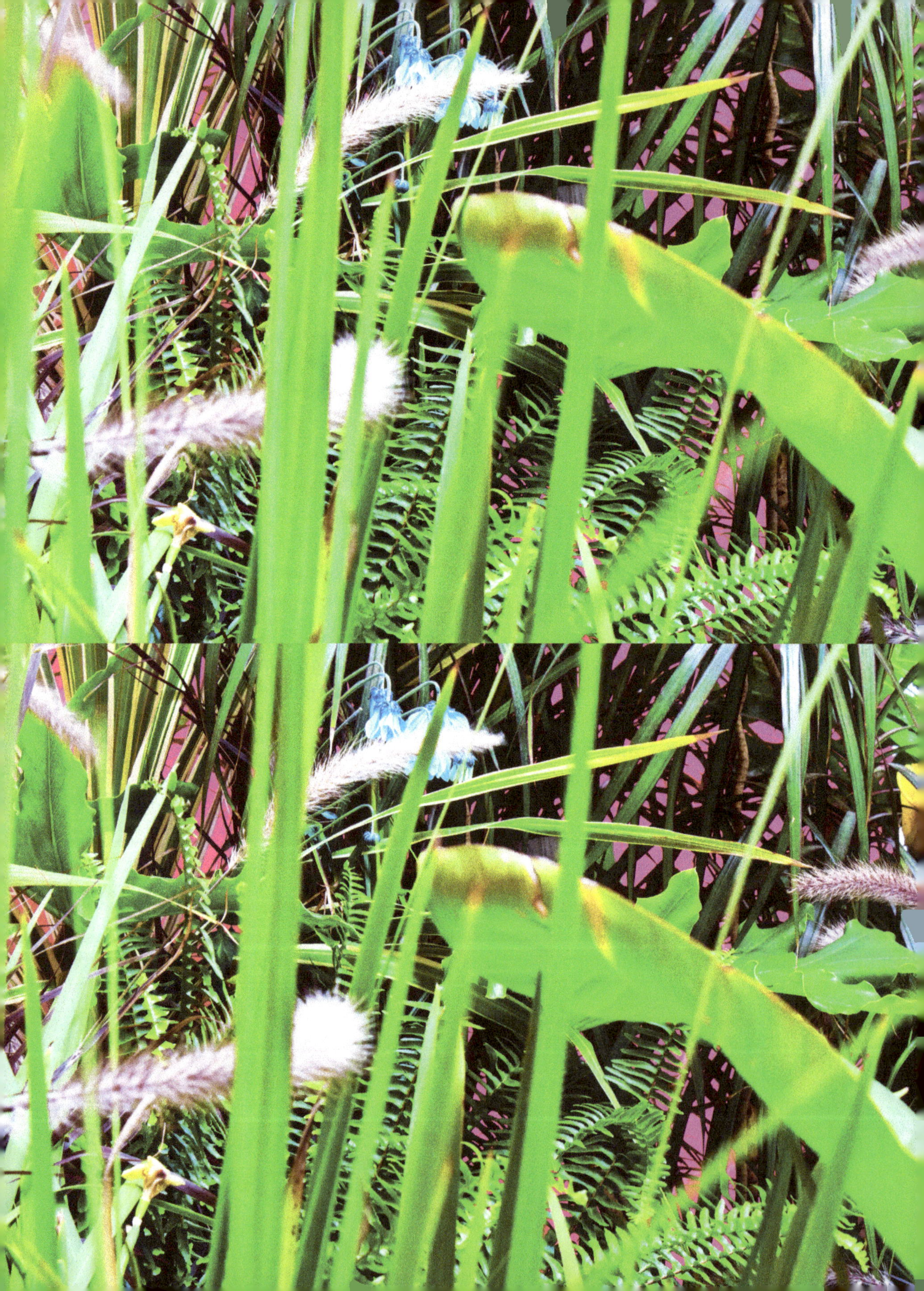

M1: Snake oils...
Call this number on your screen!

J2: ALL you HAVE to do!! ... TO MAKE MONEY!! ... Is FOLLOW MY SYSTEM!!! ... And PLACE ADS!! ... ON THE INTERNET!!! ... You don't even have to OWN A COMPUTER!!! ... It's THAT EASY!

M2: Despite the collective expertise in this industry, it's still a "high-risk, high-reward" opportunity.

M1: Call this number on your screen!

M2: You will have to put up with the nausea, the vomiting the diarrhea and itchy skin.

J2: The problem with food is ... eating it!
You need The Fooderator!

M2: TROUT-O-MATIC

J2: Flip through the channels and eventually find the same guy on another channel selling
"this amazing new product...!"
that would remove excess calcium from your system.

M2: One BILLION times your daily requirement of calcium! It's the silver nitrates that do it!
SILVER NITRATES!

M1: Phytochemicals, Phyto, Greek for plant.

M2: Remember the old fashioned way? Buttering toast is MESSY and can RUIN your clothes! (Woman rips a whole through the toast then drops a slab of butter on her shoes.)

J2: (Looks at the camera and shakes her

M1: I think we're alone now.

J2: Thank God I have to pick up my son from basketball practice.
My eyes! The googles, they do nothing...
...
The googles!

J1: More often he functions as a kind of post-modern greek chorus, offering his snarky opinion on whatever crisis his human counterparts find themselves in.

M2: More often I function as a kind of post-modern greek chorus, offering my snarky opinion on whatever crisis my human counterparts find themselves in.

M1: TROUT-O-MATIC!

J2: TROUT-O-MATIC!

J1: Even the freest person in the world cannot bring down something so perverse as a company that managed to profit and grow stronger from acts of disobedience.

M1: And so on...

M1: By now this character has appeared in so many forms it's practically a boring cliché.
[laughing]

M1: Even the freest person in the world cannot bring down something so perverse as a company that managed to profit and grow stronger from acts of disobedience.

J1: And
so

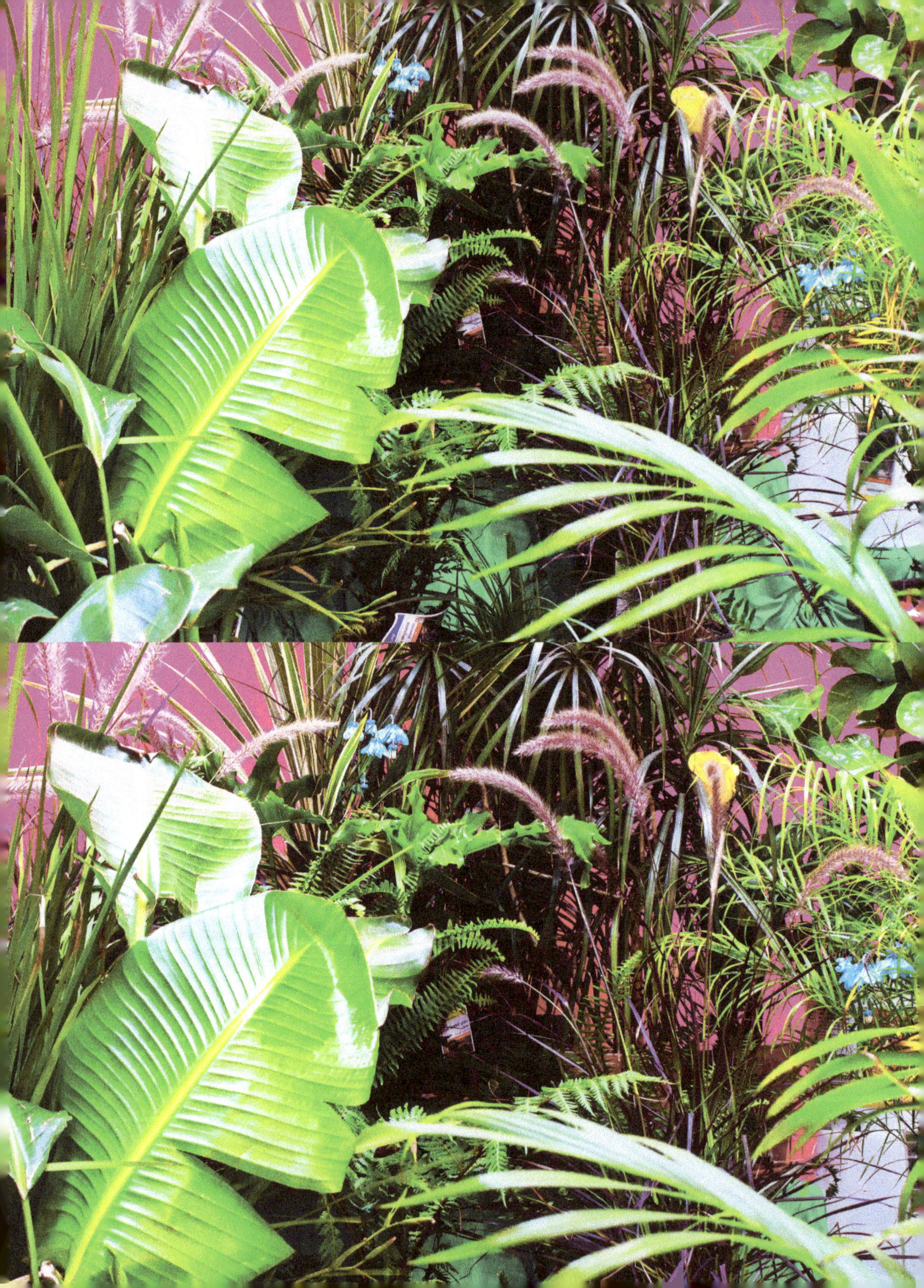

J2: head)
And tiiiiimmmmme consuming.
There's GOT to be better way!
M2: Now There Is!
J1: Thanks to advanced space age
technology, the "Butter Butler" was
invented by a team of NASA Scientists
with you in mind!
M2: But wait, there's more!
Order totalfark in the next 20 minutes,
and you will get this free set of steak
knifes including a salad knife,
a yoghurt knife
and a knife knife!
J1: But that's not the whole story.
J2: It slices! It dices!
And for zest,
it's the best.
M2: When you hear about
the wild success stories
like Snuggles,
Snuggies and
Schticky, it's easy to want to plunge
right in.
But wait, there's more to this story.
M2: I can't help pitching.
Long hair, short hair, then just flip it
... roll it, with the excitement of a
cheerleader.
M1: It doesn't really matter.
Just normal, everyday people that are
really into what they are discussing or
trying to sell on TV.
You just can't make this stuff up.
J2: You mean they're not real tv shows????
Wow, that sucks.

J2: Oh Mary, if you could only see what I
hear...

J1: on...
By now
this character
has appeared
in so many forms
it's practically
a boring
cliché.

J1: But wait, there's more!
Order totalfark in the next 20 minutes,
and get this free set of steak knifes
including a salad knife, a yoghurt knife
and a knife knife.
M1: But that's not the whole story.
M2: It slices, it dices, and for zest,
it's the best!
Quality,
and long lasting.
So where are we going?
J2: When you hear about all the wild
success stories like Snuggies and
Schticky, it's easy to want to plunge
right in!
M2: What will happen?
J2: But wait, there's more to the story.
I can't help pitching,
Long hair, short hair, then just flip it
... roll it,
with the excitement of a cheerleader.
M2: [high falsetto] It doesn't really matter.
J2: Just normal, everyday people that are
really into what they are discussing or
trying to sell on TV.
You just can't make this stuff up.
M1: You mean they're not real tv shows????
Wow, that sucks.
Oh Mary, if you could see what I
hear...

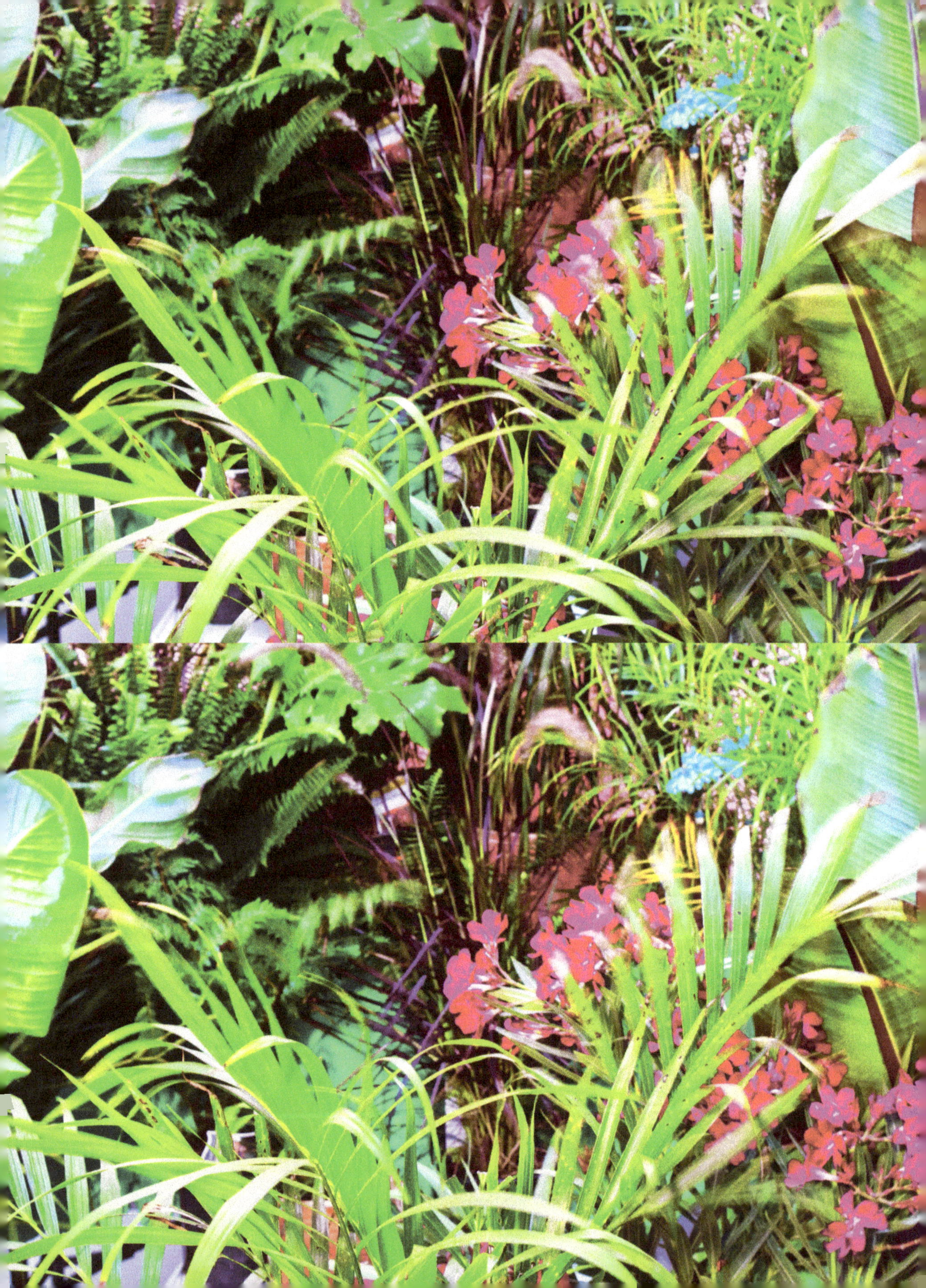

M1: In the sketch, a CEO spoke directly to
the camera in the style of an
infomercial.
I don't fuckin' know, hold on a second.
[quietly to himself] shit's all fucked up
So, in the sketch, a CEO,
nnnaahhhhhh…
…

…

M1: In the sketch, a CEO spoke directly
to the camera in the style of an
infomercial. He walked around his
large, modern executive office.
The furniture and his manner of dress
looked dated in that sort of "retro-
future" way: That way the bleeding
edge in art and fashion sometimes
becomes so dull so much quicker
than everything else.
Was this mise en scène
supposed to suggest
that this was
a very hip,
modern-day office
(relative to the time period,
of course)
or that it took place
in the near future?
It was unclear.
Perhaps, I thought in my dream, I was

M1: In the sketch, a CEO spoke directly to
the camera in the style of an
infomercial.
I don't fuckin' know, hold on a second.
[quietly to himself] shit's all fucked up
So, in the sketch, a CEO,
nnnaahhhhhh…
Incredible

M2: It's an amazing spectacle!

J1: In the sketch, a CEO spoke directly to
the camera in the style of an
infomercial. He walked around
his large and modern executive office.
The furniture and his manner of dress
looked dated in that sort of "retro-
future" way: That way the bleeding
edge in art and fashion somehow
becomes dull so much quicker than
everything else.

J1: Was this mise en scène of this
supposed to suggest that this was a
very hip, modern-day office (relative
to the time period, of course) or that
it took place in a near future? It was
unclear. Perhaps, I thought in my
dream, it was supposed to be a parody
of something from the 80's-90's that I
was unfamiliar with?
Anyway, this particular sketch was
clearly taped from a Christmas
episode, since the premise of the
sketch was that this CEO was giving
the viewer a series of increasingly
absurd "holiday gift ideas." The CEO
claimed that these gifts would be
perfect for anyone, but it became clear
as he suggested new gifts that the
out-of-touch CEO could only come
up gifts for people as rich as himself.

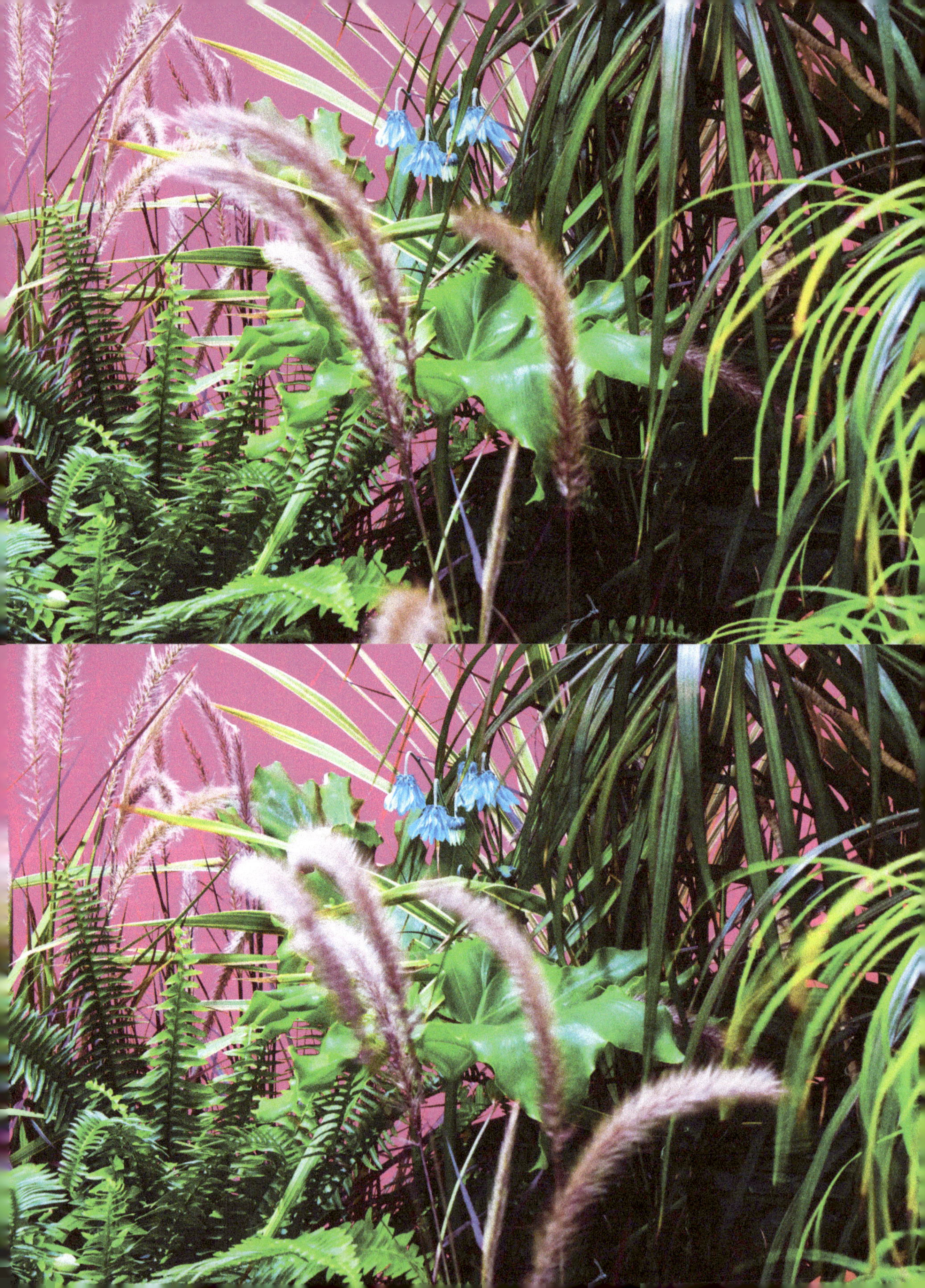

M1: supposed to be a parody of something from the 80's-90's that I was unfamiliar with?

...

Anyway, this particular sketch was clearly taped from a Christmas episode, since the premise of the sketch was that the CEO was giving the viewer a series of increasingly absurd "holiday gift ideas."
The CEO claimed
that these gifts would be perfect for anyone, but it became clear as he suggested new gifts that
the out-of-touch CEO could only come up with gifts for people
as rich as himself.
He spoke with cartoonish eloquence, maybe in a British accent,
I don't remember.

I don't remember the successive gifts, but the general impression that the viewer was supposed to get from them was that this rich CEO had become increasingly eccentric and lonely. In the climax of the sketch, the CEO said that one of the greatest gifts you can give someone is the gift of a pet. Responsibility, companionship, he said, were gifts that keep on giving. He suggested that the best possible pet wasn't a dog or a cat, but this human hybrid that he'd created. Then brought out, to great applause, this cheaply-made costume.
This double entendre
made the sketch feel
super dated,

J1: He spoke with a cartoonish eloquence, maybe in a British accent, I don't remember.
I don't remember the successive gifts, but the general impression that the viewer was supposed to get from them was that this rich CEO had become increasingly eccentric and lonely. In the climax of the sketch, the CEO said that one of the greatest gifts you can get someone is the gift of a pet. Responsibility, companionship, he said, were gifts that keep on giving. He suggested that the best possible pet wasn't a dog or a cat, but this human hybrid that he'd created. He then brought out, to great applause, this cheaply-made costume. This double entendre made the sketch feel super dated, I felt. He spoke in hushed terms and then became distracted by the reflection of an object as if startled by some new thing.

[silent surprise]
[laughing...]
[bigger and bigger laughing...]

...

He spoke in hushed terms and then became distracted by the reflection of an object as if startled by some

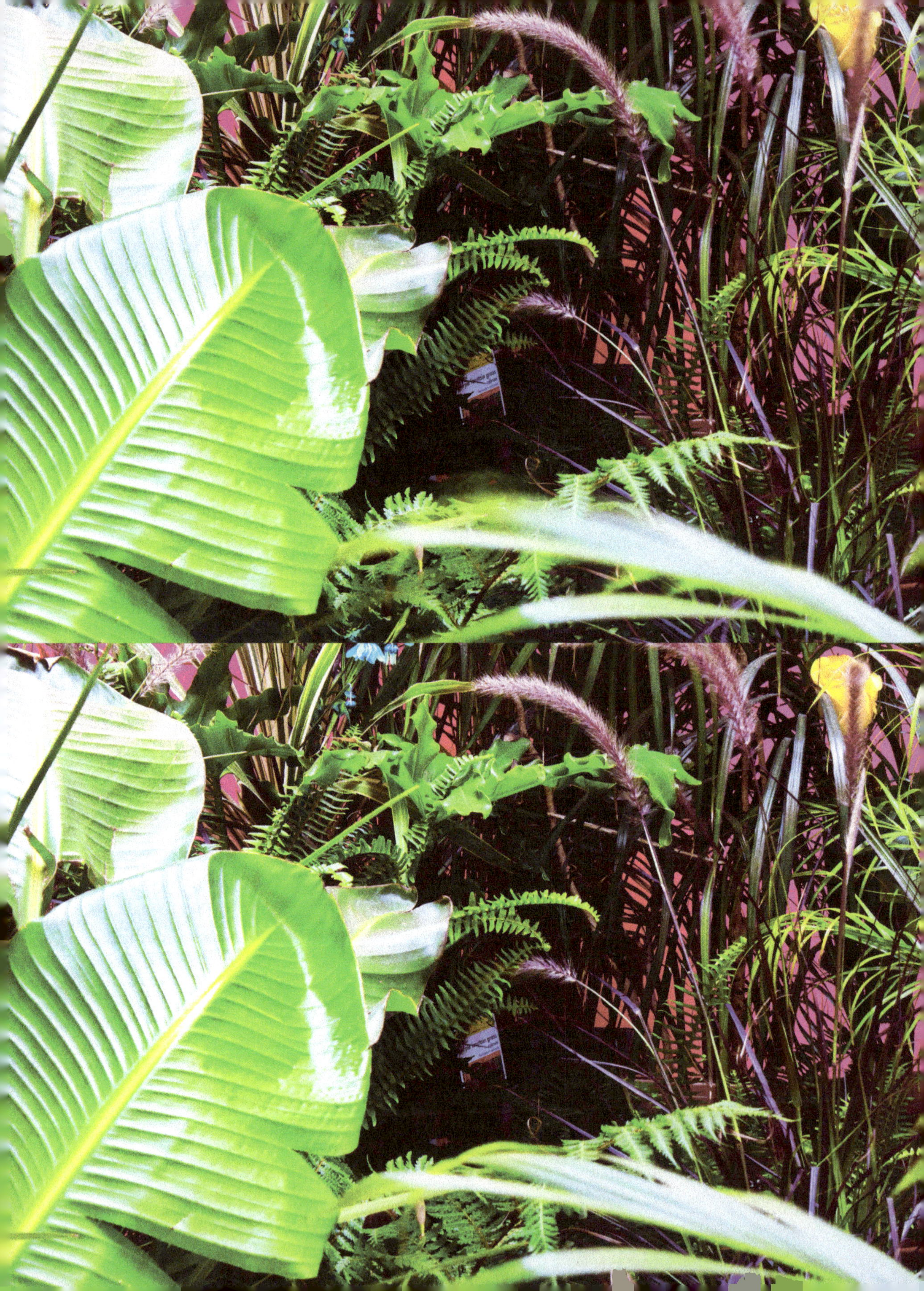

M1: I felt.
He spoke in hushed terms and
then became distracted
by the reflection of an object
as if startled by each new thing.
Continuing to address the camera,
The CEO recoiled, confused and
defensive.
He finished his speech to the audience,
concluding with "Merry Christmas!"
and put his arm over one of the
expensive-looking retro future props
tipping over and destroying things,
etc, etc.
The scene then concluded with
the CEO destroying the entire set.
Please. Get outta here!
Good evening, and what can I tell ya?
Good news! Good news!
Good Grief!
How long have you been here?
Long enough to know.
I'm doomed!!!
I just had one of my brilliant ideas.
Let me show you something!
It is an amazing spectacle.

J1: new thing, as if startled by each new
thing. Continuing to address the
camera, The CEO recoiled, confused
and defensive. He finished his speech
to the audience, concluding with
"Merry Christmas," and put his arm
around one of the expensive-looking
retro future props tipping over
and destroying things, etc, etc. The
scene concluded with the CEO
destroying the entire set.
Go home!
Go home! Go home!!
Get outta here.
Good evening, and what can I tell ya?
Good news! Good news!
Good Grief!

How long have you been there?
Long enough to know.

I just had one of my brilliant ideas!

I'm doomed!!!
Let me show you something.
It's an amazing spectacle.

Complex Textual Legitimacy Proclamation: An Afterword

"We shall not cease from exploration
And the end of all our exploring
Will be to arrive where we started
And know the place for the first time."
—T. S. Eliot[11]

Thus, the pendulum returned to its original position.[12]

We are beings of space and time; always facing each other and the world in the concrete here and now, but while the context limits our actions it is also what enables us to act. Without limitations there would be no possibilities; human action is facilitated by the prior existence of structures and frameworks, norms and expectations that give us guidance on what to do and how to do it. On the one hand, it is only by means of our preceding understanding that we can make sense of the specific situations in which action must be taken, but rendering a situation meaningful is, on the other hand, a truly creative act from which new opportunities may spring. Social realities are continually constituted by the sense people make of them, and the processes of meaning formation are in turn constituted by structures and expectations that exist prior to the specific interaction. Social constitution contains its own dynamic whereby change becomes possible as a consequence of existing understandings. Our situatedness is what allows us to move beyond existing horizons.[11]

This common understanding shows itself most clearly in the use of metaphors of construction and direction to describe ongoing and future events.[11]

The metaphor of the springboard is somewhat more original than the typical metaphors of direction, but its membership of that group is nevertheless evident; the expression 'deeply rooted will' is an instance of another fundamental group of metaphors, namely the expressions of organic relation. Such metaphors - the metaphor of the root is the most commonly used, but references to trunks and branches as well as to human body parts are also typical of this group - are used to create natural relations between objects and concepts. The root metaphor is a special instance since it also belongs to the class of foundational metaphors, a group in which we also find metaphors of construction such as the fundament or the cornerstone.[11]

I use 'text' and 'utterance' interchangeably as general terms for a single communicative entity or what Mikhael Bakhtin calls a "unit of speech communication," that is, a statement—whether of one word or a thousand pages—that elicits response thereby causing a "change of speaking subjects" (Bakhtin, 1986, p. 71).[11]

Each utterance is conditioned by preceding utterances and in being uttered forms part of the context out of which subsequent utterances arise. Or, as the Russian literary critic Mikhail M. Bakhtin so aptly puts it, "any concrete utterance is a link in the chain of speech communication of a particular sphere" (Bakhtin, 1986, p. 91).[11]

Meaning, however, is only created as the merger of form and content in the particular moment of articulation.[11]

Meaning is not identical with the words that express it, yet it can never arise independently of the words.[11]

Or, to put the matter in the simplest possible terms, the specific meaning of an utterance is constituted in and through its unique combination of content and form.[11]

The size and character of spaces, the relation between them, and the activities they support significantly determine the received messages.[10]

This is chiefly considered in spatial, architectural and branding terms.[10]

The physical space between viewer and object reinforced the importance of the ocular, subordinating other senses to sight. Sight was static, emphasising transcendental order rather than theatrical or spectacular modes.[10]

If the building makes any monumental statement, it is scepticism towards monumentality.[10]

All parts of the city, upper class, middle class, and popular neighborhoods, report affliction with this mysterious problem.[12]

Unable to speak all the city's languages, unable to speak all at once, the state's language becomes monumental, the silence of headquarters, the silence of the bank.[10]

The current era deploys simulation towards a vivid sensory experience, one that is not necessarily undermined by its overt fabrication.[10]

For, until and unless we are prepared to face facts and organise our resources so as to make our technical body a creative force, there can never be any hope of this industry being acclaimed as anything but one built and dependent upon imitation of others.[12]

Revisions are written on top of revisions, additions are squeezed in wherever room can be found for them.[14]

Do we look like monsters? Don't we have as much understanding as you do?[12]

Through its performance at fixed sites, 'culture' is amplified.[10]

This project in its entirety has been guided by the basic assumption that meanings cannot be understood independently of the time and space in which they are articulated, and that, conversely, meanings may alter our understanding of the time and space in which they are articulated.[11]

Context, or the social situations surrounding the document in question, must be understood in order to understand the significance of the document itself, even independently of the content in the document. Next, knowing the medium's process means knowing how something was actually produced and put together. Finally, emergence refers to the gradual shaping of meaning through understanding and interpretation.[9]

The necessary delineation of the specific elements of the vast material that I have chosen to study has, then, to some extent been predetermined by these constraints. Nevertheless, I feel confident that the chosen texts and contexts can provide insights into important features of the multitudinous processes of meaning making.[11]

A text is the result of a complex process; it arises out of a dialogue with the myriad of other texts that precedes it, and on its pages a dialogue is conducted between the writer and his or her anticipated audience. A text is a physical product, but a peculiarly dynamic and interactive one that loses its purpose and meaning if it is not read and commented upon. If the discussion a text invites is discontinued, that text suffers the destiny of yesterday's newspaper—fit for nothing but wrapping fish. Some texts have an ability to maintain relevance across space and time, to fascinate generation after generation of readers and to remain central to discussions about the subjects with which they deal. Other texts are fleeting, meant to be read once and immediately replaced by other interventions. Two patterns of textual dialogue emerge from these extreme cases: one of circularity or recursiveness, the other of linearity or perpetual progression.[11]

The recursive dialogue, on the one hand, is structured around issues with lasting relevance whose main problems and possible solutions are embedded in central texts around which other texts evolve, on which they comment, and to which they repeatedly return for inspiration. The progressive dialogue, on the other hand, moves from one utterance to the other without looking back, stringing each statement together to form a dynamic process the aim of which is less important than the movement as such. The recursive dialogue is characterised by spatiality; it is conducted in a well-known context and directed towards the examination of issues whose resolution may be the professed goal of each utterance, but whose lasting relevance actually ensures the continuation of the dialogue. The progressive dialogue is primarily temporal; it develops through time by means of a gradual solution of problems that simultaneously spurs new issues to be dealt with; each statement is both an answer to earlier utterances and an invitation to further responses.[11]

"It may be," Elias writes, "that particular individuals formed them [subjugated knowledges] from the existing linguistic material of their group, or at least gave them new meaning [in the past]. But they took root. They established themselves. Others picked them up in their new meaning and form, developing and polishing them in speech or writing. They were tossed back and forth until they became efficient instruments for expressing what people had jointly experienced and wanted to communicate about. They became fashionable words, concepts current in everyday speech of a particular society. This shows that they met not merely individual but collective needs for expression. The collective history [of the past struggles] has crystallized in them and resonates in them. The individual finds this crystallization already in their possibilities of use. He does not know very precisely why this meaning and this delimitation are bound up with the words, why exactly this nuance and that new possibility can hear their own experiences in the meaning of the words. The terms gradually die when the functions and experiences in the actual life of society cease to be bound up with them. At times, too, they only sleep, or sleep in certain respects, and acquire a new existential value from a new social situation. They are recalled then because something in the present state of society finds expression in the crystallization of the past embodied in the words."[12]

Representations produce stories of destiny, of inevitable historical linearity, that, as Stephen Weil reminds us: "...do not so much recreate or represent the past as they legitimatize the present. They are not about what really happened in other times so much as they are about why our own times, our own society, our own pecking orders could only be the way we find them and not some other way."[10]

Where the object-as-sign initially reflected only its own material existence, throughout the twentieth century it was put to work to stand in for larger narrative wholes increasingly abstracted from its own materiality (such as 'culture'), until, in its postmodern usage, it alluded only to the signifying process itself (such as 'the construction of identity').[10]

The allegorist, by contrast, 'for whom objects represent only keywords in a secret dictionary, which will make known their meanings to the initiated', purposively dislodges things from their context.[10]

In Interpretation of Dreams, Freud remarked that "A word, being a point of junction for a number of conceptions, possesses, so to speak, a predestined ambiguity."[14]

Although it cannot be denied that words have some degree of stable intentional and conventional meaning, there is an equally undeniable actional or communicative dimension of meaning formation. Words only become fully meaningful when used in utterances whose meanings, in turn, are never simply the sum of the employed units. Meaning is use, as Wittgenstein would have it (Wittgenstein, 2001, ß 43), and only emerges in the act of usage.[11]

Our understanding of a word or phrase can totally revise our understanding (or overlooking) of a word or phrase on an earlier page.[14]

The words to which we are so addicted for expression and interpretation are suddenly no longer there for us.[14]

Beyond words, the experience and its remembrance stand for the coming together of indivisibility—beyond subjectivity, thought, and articulation—and division and multiplicity.[12]

The word 'limitless' is not intended to suggest randomness or a complete lack of control, in either books or brains; in general mathematics, an infinitely repeating decimal need not be completely chaotic.[14]

In this manner, the memory of the world of unity is brought into the foreground in light of a harsh separation.[12]

According to some cultural criticism, the anomie of the modern industrial age has produced a particular mindset related to collecting and viewing.[10]

The loss of specific origins of individual memory lends poignancy to collections, both personal and public, precisely because the souvenir can be seen as a symbol of the demise of memory.[10]

The emotional process of permanent departure from what is familiar may require the dormancy of one's historical memory.[10]

While empathy runs the risk of a loss of critical distance and an acceptance of idealized truths, analysis risks not listening to the actual experiences and beliefs of subjects.[10]

Make an effort to see objectively, describe, and record with total objectivity, simplicity as well as humility, without "explanation" and especially without judgement.[12]

Learn to observe not only with curiosity but also with sympathy.[12]

Stories denote a shift towards emotion, empathy and personal participation, away from intellectual concerns about accuracy that characterise institutional authority.[10]

The narrative voice is, simultaneously, pensive and declarative; it could at times be heard as a soliloquy. While conveying a didactic message, this voice is overwhelmed with awe and sorrow.[12]

This omnipresent voice functions in the manner of a declaratory performative (Austin, 1962, p. 7) to create what it names.[11]

By utilizing interesting stories or personal narratives with a clear structure, moral point and vivid imagery, important information is more easily delivered and able to recall.[9]

Leave alone the generation of finer sentiments, even the proper depiction of a story has eluded us. That is the deficiency of finer sentiments.[12]

First, while the idea that all stories are subjectively located is a defensible principal, it is a leap to say that one is not obliged to admit an event actually occurred.[10]

A fiction writer can invent for us the "thoughts" and "motives" of the characters he creates, as well as their actions. Their actions and words may be recorded and can provide valuable lessons for us. We do not, however, know their true personalities, their feelings, and the sincerity of their motives that prompted them to act as they did.[3]

There is no universal narrative involved in meta-narratives, but rather information that impacts particular texts outside of the text's boundaries.[8]

Its meaning cannot be contained and yet it is not possible to reconstitute the story in any way one wishes, primarily because each new proclamation or enactment of the narrative bears relation to the preceeding part of the story, which has already been written.[7]

The poetic narrator, thus, perceives himself to be the adept witness to an occurrence that unceasingly captivates him with ever varying novelty.[12]

The narrator comes to perceive himself as a vigilant participant in love and in ecstasy.[12]

In this way a complete transformation will take place within you and you will become an entirely different person in heart, mind, disposition [Gemüth], understanding, will and all the powers of the soul, so that everyone will be able to see, from your external behavior, that a spiritual change has taken place within you.[12]

This life-like spectrum of listeners is being addressed directly.[12]

I tell secrets, I do not utter words.... I can say my secret to one in whom I do not see himself but see in him me myself.[12]

In every company I uttered my wailful notes, I consorted with the unhappy and with them that rejoice. Every one became my friend from his own opinion; none sought out my secrets from within me.[12]

Each holy act furthers the process of cosmic healing.[14]

O my friends, hearken to this tale: in truth it is the very marrow of our inward state.[12]

In the case of conscious inebriation, the wayfarer can describe this state in language.[12]

These struggles over the function of the body helped to create silences at the same time as they widened the currency of those knowledges themselves.[12]

Silences, after all, are not the limit of discourse but rather an element that functions alongside the things said, with them and in relation to them within over-all strategies.[12]

So simple has been the treatment, so delicate the touch on the artistes, so subtle the psychological reflexes, that the picture unfolds itself and you do not need to understand language at all, but you know the poignancy of the story that is unfolded before your eyes.[12]

Feeling and evocation are privileged over truth and knowledge as the basis of experience.[10]

Such a belief is consistent with the origin myths which generally support an extra-human source for art.[10]

The process of signification is what accomplishes the task of the myth; it subverts simple denotation through its wider connotation, it naturalizes culture as the given order of the day, and it utilizes the ambiguities and tendencies of the process of signification itself in order to effect its apparent closures.[10]

Myth is contraction or implosion of any process, and the instant speed of electricity confers the mythic dimension on ordinary industrial and social action today. We live mythically but continue to think fragmentarily and on single planes.[14]

While the content of such representations strives for uniqueness, what they share is a ritualised and mimetic nature.[10]

What kind of convincing narrative is ultimately forged from conflicting mythologies?[10]

Martin Buber relates "an-other," most silent speech with the mystic's urge for communication. He says, this quiet language wants not to describe existence, but only to communicate it, only to say that it is. In referring to this silent language, the poetic language turns into a metalanguage that conceives itself to be a sign of inarticulation. Language, in this capacity, turns against itself, commits suicide, in order to be reincarnated in silence.[12]

Only to the senseless is this sense confided: the tongue hath no customer save the ear.[12]

The place was abnormally quiet.... Have I come to a dead land? But no![12]

§

One man stands talking at a podium mounted with numerous microphones, while a line of men stand to his right.[9]

These things I have spoken to you, that my joy may be in you, and that your joy may be full.[4]
You don't like those ideas? I got others.[14]

Hear a range of voices from past and present... The floor is open for discussion.[10]

In the first place, I believe in democracy—in the triumph of the will of the people, in freedom of thought, of speech and in other freedoms which ennoble mankind.[12]

It is as if those who founded the United States had spent hours arguing where some tea might be dumped in Boston Harbour and had ignored details of the Declaration of Independence.[11]

I have seen the promotional material...and I think that what they are doing there is fantastic'.[10]

I am the emperor, and should ride upon this canopied chariot![6]

How many I's are you?[6]

If you should ever need my life, then come and take it.[7]

No, really. I mean it.[9]

When I want it, I'll come take it.[8]

I'm sure a lot of other people thought the same way.[9]

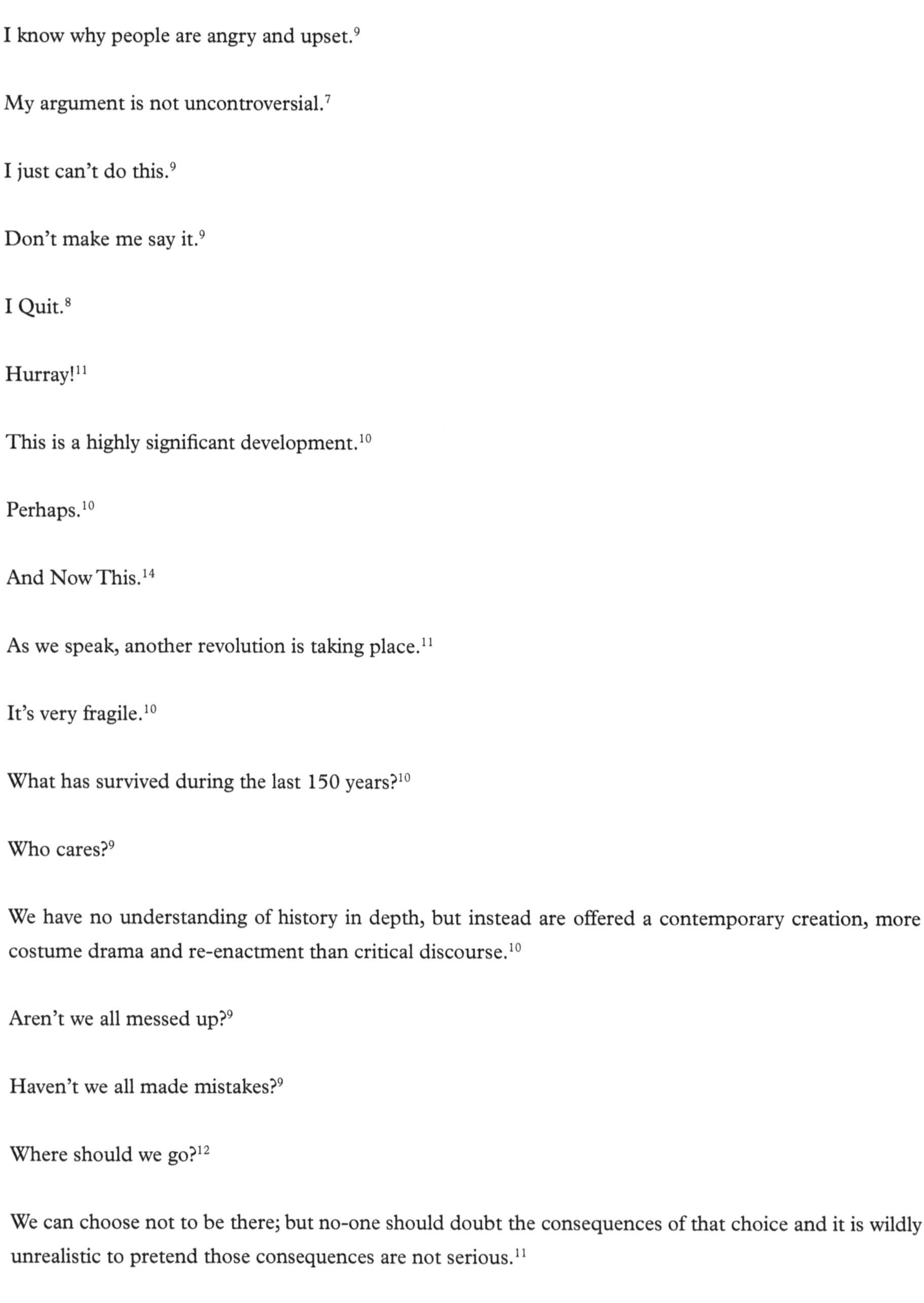

I know why people are angry and upset.[9]

My argument is not uncontroversial.[7]

I just can't do this.[9]

Don't make me say it.[9]

I Quit.[8]

Hurray![11]

This is a highly significant development.[10]

Perhaps.[10]

And Now This.[14]

As we speak, another revolution is taking place.[11]

It's very fragile.[10]

What has survived during the last 150 years?[10]

Who cares?[9]

We have no understanding of history in depth, but instead are offered a contemporary creation, more costume drama and re-enactment than critical discourse.[10]

Aren't we all messed up?[9]

Haven't we all made mistakes?[9]

Where should we go?[12]

We can choose not to be there; but no-one should doubt the consequences of that choice and it is wildly unrealistic to pretend those consequences are not serious.[11]

We are hardly short of challenges.[11]

There will be more of us in the future, trying to do more.[11]

We're fun, we're fascinating.[9]

We yell it, they whisper it.[9]

In this way you could easily cause a rebellion.[12]

You've been denied for so long.[10]

That's why you're so dangerous![10]

You must get that.[10]

That's the concept that we are trying to develop.[10]

A vision of peaceful co-existence, or the cause of disharmony?[10]

Each new 'angle' provides an increase in the resolution of the overall picture.[14]

A reference to Bugs Bunny does not have to be intended to be contextually meaningful. Neither does a reference to the atomic bomb.[14]

I would like to propose that we do this in a far more organised and structured way.[11]

My speech today is an attempt at such bridge building.[11]

It is this textual creation of meaning that I shall now seek to explain.[11]

From the very first page everything is organized in perfect order, exactly as I would have wished![6]

And I'm trying to figure out why it was so easy for me. Because I did, I gave great detail. I don't know. Can you say I work well under pressure? I don't know.[9]

A few years ago I was afforded the opportunity of reading the original version, and so I edited the text.[6]

Within the narration of events there are inserted poems, and this should be an exquisite part of the literary style.[6]

Stylistic changes range from the pruning of inappropriate classical particles and minor alteration in the phrasing of the text through to the wholesale deletion or rewriting of passages.[6]

Furthermore the original ascriptions of authorship for most of the poems have been eliminated.[6]

The literary particles of the vulgar edition are mostly incomprehensible, and the language long-winded and repetitive.[6]

I once wished to investigate its wonders in order to establish its rightful position to the world, but social engagements filled my days, and furthermore I was often away traveling and had little spare time. In recent years I wanted to get on with it, but I became ill, and nothing materialized.[6]

However, that never came to fruition, and now my commentary version of the text ... can truly be described as "the foremost book of talent." For this reason I am republishing it in order to make it available to those who appreciate things of old.[6]

Here, the debate is presented as "...the only positive event of the last year."[11]

This scheme aimed to explain patterns and ideas by ordering objects in one horizon, be it spatial or temporal.[10]

Disturbing or not, the process will continue and indeed, the pace of cultural change it brings about is likely to quicken.[10]

At some point in the text's history, it was given its overarching and undergirding chiasmic form and what I have chosen to call its "dialectical style."[3]

Combining so many records suggests a great deal of concern in writing.[3]

This sustained ubiquity signals its importance.[2]

And it is distinct in its duration and effect.[4]

It represents an assertion of "holding the world in the palm of one's hand".[3]

The people who will influence the course of events will be those who have become aware of this change of scale.[11]

This is the ultimate hubris, evidence of a desire to swallow not just all literature, but all creation. Interestingly, it is also true, in many cases.[14]

It should be noted that the conventional English understanding of finality as something completed and irrevocable is at odds with the French and German usage of the term, which refers to the aim or purpose of something.[11]

And how does the creation of these texts become possible? In what ways do the declarations function as turning points? How do they both bind past and future together and redirect developments?[11]

They fail.[12]

They exist out of place and time.[9]

It is an alien form, invading the world and contaminating it.[9]

This is my wakening up, my camp, my resting place along the never ending lines that cross my world.[10]

All perspectives are created equal, but some are more equal than others.[14]

It was not intended merely to fossilise a status quo, but to provide a direction for future growth and development. The broad and general nature of its words indicates that it was not intended as a finite contract but as the foundation for a developing social contract.[10]

However, at this juncture it remains quite indeterminate.[10]

There are some quality issues that need to be addressed.[10]

The language is a great draw-back.[12]

No answers to this were forthcoming.[12]

Sorry, we cannot bail you out of the mess you are in. Yes, there is confusion about values, about the meaning of 'being human', about the right ways of living together; but it is up to you to sort it out in your own fashion and bear the consequences in the event that you are not happy with the results. Yes, there is a cacophony of voices and no tune is likely to be sung in unison, but do not worry: no tune is necessarily better than the next, and if it were there wouldn't at any rate be a way of knowing it (Bauman, 2001, p. 124).[11]

These figures are based on my own calculations.[6]

I, however, remain responsible for all the shortcomings herein.[12]

This self-disclosure is meant neither to sabotage the critical analysis that follows nor to attempt to validate the genre.[8]

Isn't every man and woman responsible for his or her own salvation?[3]

And what would be the consequences of this?[11]

What negotiating positions are available?[11]

A qualitative leap is necessary.[11]

It is in this framework that I inscribe my remarks today.[11]

The commonplace book was a tool for storing examples of various argumentative and stylistic forms and for arranging them in a proper manner so as to have ready recourse to fixed formulas and fancy formulations to suit any occasion.[11]

Any one of these aims, moreover, may be expressed and pursued either publicly or privately; with great conviction and inwardness or as a matter of unremarkable routine; on behalf of all people, or of some, or of just one.[4]

The 'you decide' invitation positioned the viewer as having already-formed tastes and opinions.[10]

Prioritize, communicate what's important to you.[9]

Says Burke: "you persuade a man [sic] only insofar as you can talk his language by speech, gesture, tonality, order, image, attitude, idea, identifying your ways with his" (Burke, 1969, p. 55).[11]

Why should we listen to him?[4]

His producers are they not his consumers?[14]

"Readers," said the reporter, "have become more interested in soundbites or wordbites"[9]

However, he does not really discuss the sceptical position.[11]

To literary people, the practical joke with its total physical involvement is as distasteful as the pun that derails us from the smooth and uniform progress that is typographic order.[14]

What you really see are teams of athletes fit and smiling, and ready to knock the hell out of the opposing teams.[11]

Rather, they speak of these as if they were a unified whole.[11]

This created a tension.[12]

Needless to say, it was a veritable galaxy, and clashes between the titans were inevitable.[12]

All this is history, but its effects live on.[11]

Diversions, diversions.[14]

Due to the nature of this study, its results may be difficult to duplicate.[9]

What struck me, whilst reading through some of his work, was his anecdotal style of reportage, which, whilst offering enlightening opinions, also, ironically, seemed in a way to mirror his main disgruntlement with 'mainstreamism'.[1]

Although taken together this constitutes a highly useful resource of references and literature, the presentation of such concepts was at times confusing and arguably (even acknowledging the introductory status of his offering) lacked the necessary depth in dealing with what are often complex issues.[1]

Many of the allusions, in fact, escape the author himself, who has prepared a machinery of suggestion which, like any complex machine, is capable of operating beyond the original intention of its builder.[14]

Additionally, a more explicit development of his own theoretical position through treatment of the literature beyond introductory level, would have in my opinion, offered more value to the text. I would argue that it may have provided a stronger basis for his scholarly intent, as well as facilitating the reader's ability to comprehend and engage more fully with the analysis later in the book.[1]

Despite the undisputed power of textuality, discourse alone cannot, and does not, produce spatial possessions.[2]

Despite this, I believe that the book through its introduction of the topic, constitutes an important foundation and statement for the discipline in general.[1]

Life goes on. Endowed as we are with a seemingly endless capacity to reconcile our dissonant cognitive states, we continue on, much as before.[4]

In for a penny, in for a pound—who needs factual or historical validation anyway?[4]

Textualists would still pursue close readings; the hunt for original intentions would go on as before; Posner and Dworkin would not call a truce.[4]

Rather, this must instead be read as an invitation, or provocation, to immanent critique.[12]

Glorification and irony make strange bedfellows.[10]

Agreeing personally with 'going after the after' (in the sense of pursuing open critique towards progressive ends), this book, by setting out to explore marketing academia in such a way, held undoubted appeal and promise.[1]

It is of course a flawed record; but the world has no better record and can ill afford to lose this one.[10]

Generating understanding into how various texts have been worked up, sustained and defended through language and other symbolic practices allows for space, I argue, within which creative and increasingly valuable research can ensue.[1]

So I invoke unities like 'marketing' and 'social construction', and indeed 'mainstream' merely in order to destabilise and then reconstruct them in the pursuit of my own literary marketing agenda.[1]

This distinction is not just a matter of splitting hairs: a process is dynamic whereas a container is static.[11]

Material is presented, juxtapositions are made, conclusions are not hammered home.[10]

In its final form it is thoughtfully structured and written, and it is evident that conscious planning, not chance, went into its composition.[7]

He has not come up with all the answers, but he made a good start, with all the right questions.[11]

It will be a mould-breaker internationally.[10]

It is both word and thought, both an idea and its symbol and manifestation—it is both abstract and concrete.[12]

There is only one way to prevent our intelligence, our heart, and our sensibility being sold off on a daily basis for a pittance: we must consciously, forcefully, dynamically and totally become precisely what we ourselves are.[12]

None that is raw understands the state of the ripe: therefore my words must be brief. Farewell![12]

Sources
0 Knight, Mark, and Emma Mason. "Introduction." Nineteenth-century religion and literature an introduction. Oxford: Oxford University Press, 2006.

1 Ferguson, Pauline. "After Marketing and Social Construction."Ephemera: Critical Dialogues on Organization 2 (2002): 258-262.

2 Collis, Christy. "The Proclamation Island Moment: Making Antarctica Australian." Law Text Culture 8 (2004): 1-18.

3 Thomasson, Gordon C.. "Kingship in the Book of Mormon." Journal of Book of Mormon Studies 2 (1993): 21-38.

4 Garet, Ronald R.. "The Last Full Measure of Devotion: Sacrifice and Textual Authority." Cardozo Law Review 28 (): 277-299.

5 Frosh, S.. "Interpretation and over-interpretation: disputing the meaning of texts." Qualitative Research 5 (2005): 307-324.

6 West, Andrew. "The Textual History of Sanguo Yanyi." BabelStone : : The Mao Zonggang Recension. N.p., n.d. Web. <http://www.babelstone.co.uk/SanguoYanyi/TextualHistory/MaoZonggang.html>.

7 Unattributed. Various Websites which have been taken down since they were originally accessed.

8 Toepfer, Shane. "A Community of Smarks: Professional Wrestling and the Changing Relationship Between Textual Producers and Consumers." M.A. Thesis: Georgia State University (2006): 1-125.

9 Harris, Nichola Reneé. "Tabloidization in the Modern American Press: A Textual Analysis and Assessment of Newspaper and Tabloid Coverage of the 'Runaway Bride' Case." M.A. Tesis: Georgia State University (2005): 1-171.

10 Williams, Paul Harvey. "New Zealand's Identity Complex: A Critique of Cultural Practices at The Museum of New Zealand Te Papa Tongarewa." Ph.D Dissertation: The University of Melbourne (2003): 1-360.

11 Nørholm Just, Sine. "The Constitution of Meaning: A Meaningful Constitution? Legitimacy, identity, and public opinion in the debate on the future of Europe." Ph.D Dissertation: Copenhagen Business School (2004): 1-363.

12 Various Authors. Various Articles. Comparative Studies of South Asia, Africa and the Middle East (2003): 234-344.

13 Hamrick, Stephen. "'Set in portraiture': George Gascoigne, Queen Elizabeth, and Adapting the Royal Image." Early Modern Literary Studies 11.1 (May, 2005): 1-54. Web. <http://extra.shu.ac.uk/emls/11-1/hamrgasc.htm>.

14 Weiss, Dan. "Understanding the (Net) Wake." M.A. Thesis: Trinity College, Dublin.

www.ingramcontent.com/pod-product-compliance
Lightning Source LLC
LaVergne TN
LVHW060622110826
845147LV00015B/917

* 9 7 8 0 9 8 9 5 9 8 5 3 8 *